BRISTOL

C.1500

NOT TO SCALE

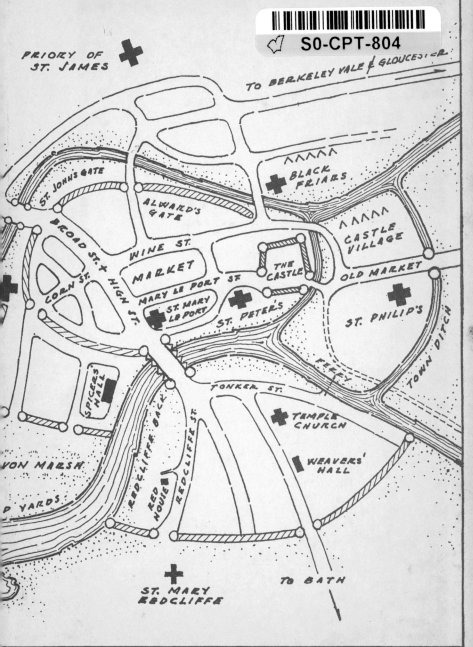

PRIORY OF ST. JAMES

TO BERKELEY VALE & GLOUCESTER

BLACK FRIARS

ST. JOHNS GATE

ALWARD'S GATE

CASTLE VILLAGE

BROAD ST.

WINE ST.

THE CASTLE

OLD MARKET

CORN ST.

HIGH ST.

MARKET

MARY LE PORT ST.

ST. MARY LE PORT

ST. PETER'S

ST. PHILIP'S

TOWN DITCH

SPICERS' HALL

FERRY

TONKER ST.

REDCLIFFE BACK

RED HOUSE

REDCLIFFE ST.

TEMPLE CHURCH

WEAVERS' HALL

VON MARSH

P YARDS

ST. MARY REDCLIFFE

TO BATH

Map of London may be found inside back cover

WARM WIND, WEST WIND

Myrtle + Jimmie
Lawson

Western wind when wilt thou blow

The small rain down can rain?

WARM WIND, WEST WIND

ANNE IRWIN MATTHEW

CROWN PUBLISHERS Inc., New York

TO MY HUSBAND

WARM WIND, WEST WIND

I

Cotswold that great king of shepherds
To whom Sarum's plain gives place tho' famous for her flocks.
Yet scarcely doth she tithe our Cotswold's wealthy locks.

DRAYTON

Most dear Cousin I am right glad ye be welcome to this land and namely
to this town which I, Brennus, King, builded of old with her walls and
called it Bristowe.

*(From the pageant for Henry VII's
reception at Bristol in 1486)*

It was so early, on an April morning, that market carts were not yet at the gates of Bristol and ships along Quayside and the Back dozed breast to mud like flocks of river ducks. Rushlight in a few windows yellowed them against a white mist which was lifting in the east above the square Norman tower of St. Peter's and the dark mass of the castle with the sky silver gilt behind.

Bristol would soon be up, bustling about the business of England's second largest port in this spring of 1507. But for the moment a girl in a red cloak had the streets to herself as she crossed town from Mary le Port, near the Back where the Bridge spanned the Avon, to St. John's Gate in the north wall.

Outside the gate, with St. John's Church above it candlelit for Prime, the Frome flowed sluggishly from Castle Moat westward past Quayside, to join the Avon on their way to the Channel. It was beginning to rise with the tide which would soon turn the six miles down river into the town's busy seaway. Across Frome Bridge, a road climbed northward through the ring of religious houses to the downs above Severn, and a lightly-rising wind was driving the mist from it.

The girl paused to look anxiously along it. She was slight and young and moved gracefully; when she pushed back the hood of her cloak the wind ruffled fair hair of no distinctive shade about a face that was more noticeably eager and sensitive than pretty. It changed near enough to beauty as she ran forward to meet a tall figure coming out of the mist.

"Tony! Oh Tony, I've been missing you so just now," she cried.

"I've been missing you for months!" Anthony Jestyn said indignantly. "Come along to Brandon Hill, Crede—didn't you get my message straight?"

"Whoever you sent to throw gravel at my window in the middle of the night," she said with equal spirit, "told me to go there. I happened to stop here on the way. When did you get back, Tony? Were you at Peter's last night? Why didn't you come home to us?"

"A dozen questions at once, as usual!" Anthony laughed. "There's a lot to tell, Cre, and we can't talk here. Come on to our old place."

[3]

They turned off the road into a lane which ran westward behind the White Friars' garden wall to Brandon Hill. The hill, crowned with trees, looked down upon river meadows where Frome joined Avon, and as children they had played all over it, defending their castle keep or embarking on fabulous voyages with the passing ships.

They had grown up together, for Sir Peter Jestyn, in his tumble-down manor near Severn, had been glad to send his young brother into the comfortable household of a cousin in the shipping trade, which was making merchants richer than gentlemen these days, and Philip Canynges, with only a motherless daughter to inherit four good ships, had offered inducements. None of these had been enough to hold Anthony when the lessons and playtime he shared with Crede turned into dull hours in the counting house; last summer he had run away to Cornwall, where Jestyn cousins lived more excitingly, and Crede, who had never ceased to miss him, had never missed him so sharply as just before this unexpected return.

Near the hill top an overgrown path brought them to a rock they had considered their own discovery and had called the east bastion when they played at sieges.

"It's just the same!" Anthony kissed her suddenly and kept his arms around her.

"Let me look at you!" She stepped back and stood happily admiring him. "What a giant you have grown, Anthony Jestyn!"

No one in the world could be handsomer than Tony. He looked more than a year older and had already outgrown a tall boy's awkwardness, but his eyes danced with their old mischief as he struck a pose for her, his long green traveling cloak thrown open, one hand at his dagger belt. He wore a sword as well, a fashion just reaching England from the Continent, and his green velvet jerkin which suited his dark hair and eyes was of the new short style, called a doublet, with trunk hose. The little flat cap stuck on one side of his head had a jewelled buckle. Altogether Crede had never seen a more modish young gentleman than her old playmate had turned into.

"Are your cousins so grand, Tony?" There was dismay in her voice.

"It's like the stories we used to make up, Cre. Remember how we used to choose one of the ships that passed here—to sail away and make our fortune? It's coming true! I've had a share in two ventures that turned out well, and my cousin has promised me a ship of my own soon."

"Oh, Tony, I thought you had come home to stay! Father always meant you to have a ship some time if you liked that better than the counting house."

"Did you think I wanted to go plodding round with a trading ship?

Jestyns aren't traders, Cre. My cousin holds privateer's papers with the royal seal, to take ships of the enemy and seize their cargoes."

"But we aren't fighting anyone just now, not even France. And King Henry won't get us into wars. He knows they spoil trade."

"Well, treaties are the Welshman's business," Tony said carelessly. "But his arm can't reach as far as Cornwall to take back commissions every time he makes a deal to please a lot of niggling shopkeepers and sheep farmers. He hasn't tamed Cornwall much."

Crede sighed. King Henry the Seventh, whom she admired loyally because her father did, was a tiresome bone of contention between her and Tony, and a difficult hero to defend against the more colorful ones of his choosing. But this time Tony wasted no more words on him.

"My cousin lives as old families used to live in England," he said. "Every ship in the harbor below the castle is his, the villagers are all in his service, and half the gentry and clergy of the neighborhood have a share with him. Crede, it is better than St. James's Fair when a ship comes home—feasting and dancing in the Great Hall, and finer silks and jewels worn, I'll wager, than at our penny-pinching court."

Piracy, Crede's father called it, and maintained that the wild hawks in Cornwall preyed upon English ships as readily as they did upon foreigns. Yet there had always been privateers, and when war came every country was glad to use them. Henry Tudor was determinedly building up a royal navy, but no king could afford enough trained men and ships of his own to defend England in war.

"There is a secret tunnel from the harbor, Crede, and you should see the treasure stored there. It is the best way left for a gentleman to mend his fortune—half the captains have names as old as mine."

He spread his cloak on a ledge of the rock and drew her down beside him while he talked eagerly, painting quick, bright pictures as he always could, making her see the old stone house on its rocky headland, with its hidden treasure inside and its wild winged brood riding the inlet below—as he used to make her see Robin Hood's greenwood or King Arthur's Camelot. It was like slipping back into one of their old adventures here, and she was listening as she used to listen then.

"Cre, I came back for you!" He pulled her close. "All these months I've wanted you there with me. You must love me, Cre—you must!"

Of course she loved Tony. There was no one like him, and she had missed him dreadfully. But his arms around her were not the boy's arms that had sometimes held her carelessly in romping games. This Tony who kissed her until she was breathless had suddenly become strange. Yet strangeness had always been in him, in all the familiar things they did, part of the charm, part of this new enchantment.

"Cre, we'll be married today! Father Andrew would marry us—"

[5]

No other word could have recalled Crede so quickly. She twisted free and leaned against the rock to steady herself.

"I am to marry Walter Thorne."

"I wouldn't believe Giles!" He seized her arm in a grip that hurt. "Young Giles took a notion to run off from the farm to me lately and brought a tale I couldn't—who the devil is Thorne?" His black brows flew together. "By all the saints, Crede—I'd never even kissed you to count, yet the first stranger that came sneaking around—I'll kill him!"

"Walter Thorne didn't come sneaking around!"

In their childhood quarrels, which had been lively ones, Crede had always held her own nicely. But now her mind was recalled to anxieties that Anthony's return had surprised from it, and her anger wilted. She said dolefully, "I've never even seen him. Oh, Tony, I'm so miserable. Stop lowering over me and I'll tell you about it."

With one of his quick changes of mood Anthony drew her back beside him and, folding his arm around her, said, "Now tell me about your Walter."

"He's not mine!" Crede sighed and relaxed a little, and the bothersome matter of Walter Thorne became less threatening with Anthony to confide in. He seemed friendly and sensible again, and his arm was comforting. "He is the dutiful son of Master Gilbert Thorne of London—"

"And you aren't feeling so dutiful!" Anthony burst out, laughing. "You should see your face, Cre! Well, I needn't kill him yet. Must we bother about him any more?"

"His father is Father's oldest friend," Crede said slowly. "He was a poor cousin of the Thornes here, as Father was of the Canynges, and each of them earned ships and a good trade for himself. Walter Thorne has been trained for his father's business. And I am all that Father has to work for and all he has to leave his work to—he talked to me about it."

"There is no betrothal yet?" Anthony put the question sharply. Headstrong though he was, he knew that a formal betrothal, even by proxy, was almost as unbreakable as marriage.

"Father is giving me time to think about it. He could never make himself beat or starve me into it, even if it seemed his duty, but—he wants to make what he has earned safe for me—as he grows older. And he has never before asked me to do anything for him."

Crede was sixteen and Anthony eighteen, both of them old enough to know that this was the way marriages were made. It was only so fond and indulgent a father as Philip Canynges who would have discussed the matter with his daughter. But Anthony looked relieved.

"If all this is just beginning—"

"I think it began last winter when Father was in London. Master Thorne is strongly for it and Walter seems not to mind. It was understood that they would visit Bristol in the spring when one of their ships came this way and yesterday our *Brigid* passed a Thorne ship near the Channel."

"I am here now." Anthony's face brightened as it used to when an adventure took some turn that swept them into reckless behavior.

"Perhaps it carries only letters," she said without much hope. Apprehension pressed upon her again, and she was sure now that the ship carried Walter Thorne.

He was a fine young man, her father had said, steady and trustworthy. Some day all the Thorne ships would be his, for the younger son was going into the law, and Gilbert Thorne and Philip Canynges foresaw all that each of them had worked to build joined together for the generations after them. It was in this way that families strengthened themselves. Apparently it seemed a good enough way to Walter Thorne.

What it was that Crede wanted more than this she scarcely knew. Most of their solidly respectable neighbors would have said without hesitation that she had been spoiled by her father. He could have married again and raised sons to secure his fortune if he had made himself forget the young wife who had left him only a baby daughter. He had let Crede follow at his heels from the time she could walk, while he went from his counting house to Quayside and among other merchants; he had given her a playmate from the wild Jestyn side of the connection; he allowed his elderly and eccentric cousin Alward Lusted to fill her head with things of no possible use such as Latin verse and geometry when she should have been learning housewifery from Mistress Mona O'Colum who made a home for them.

But whenever Crede had watched the ships rounding Brandon Hill toward the sea that was opening so suddenly wider and farther, or plunged with Cousin Allie into the spring flood of the New Learning, it had seemed to her that to be growing up while these wonders broke upon the world held some special promise—something more than to be a link in the generations.

This breathless promise had been in all her adventures with Anthony. But it had waited, temptingly yet unalarmingly. Surrounded by her father's devotion and Mona's care she had been like a child who pauses inside a fairy ring to make a wish, knowing that whatever she chose would only add something new and interesting to what she already had.

Then, suddenly, she was grown up, and things had rushed upon her to change her whole life and limit all her choices.

"We needn't care what this Thorne tub is bringing." Anthony tightened his arm around her. "Crede, you little goose, it's well I got back! Come home with me now."

"We'll go right away." Crede jumped up, her spirits rising too.

[7]

It was only at first that Tony had seemed changed. She had forgotten that he could always carry her along with his wildest romancing and that much of it was teasing. For all his praise of Cornwall he had come back, and they had found their old alliance unbroken. In the warmth of that familiar companionship, the rest of her world was slipping reassuringly back into place.

"Father will be glad you are home again, Tony. You know he always meant, if you didn't like his trade, to help you to something else. He will soon see how well you can do and will know that we don't need these Thornes."

"Did you think I had crawled back for his favors? Oh, Cre, don't look like that—don't let us quarrel." Anthony caught her roughly and held her breathlessly close again. "Come with me to Peter's now. His old chaplain will marry us without sticking about betrothals and things, and tomorrow we'll be toward Cornwall."

Only his arms spoke to her for a moment. His words more slowly reached her mind, disappointing her and then, as she understood them more fully, rousing swift anger.

"I didn't think you meant it before, Anthony. To run away, without a word! You haven't even meant to ask Father for me!"

"What good would it do? He is set against me even if he weren't set now on this fat burgher. Crede, this is our only way. The ship will just wait tonight and—"

"You must have felt sure," Crede said in a flat voice, "that I should be in great haste to play Father such a trick. You said that it was Walter Thorne who came sneaking around—like a coward—"

Anthony dropped his arms, his face stormy.

"By God, Crede, if anyone else—"

"It is true!"

Yet surely it was not true. Tony would show her that she had mistaken him, that he could not have forgotten all her father's kindness, or think so meanly of her.

But Anthony brushed past her and strode down the path.

She stood as he had left her, still expecting him to turn back. While they had been talking, the morning had cleared: Bristol was in bright sunshine below. From this high spot its double-battlemented walls and the tangle of rivers and streets, gables and spires and shipmasts, with the castle towering behind, seemed held in a fold of the downs. The downs rolled past the Norman ramparts, crowded the garden walls of the convents which the church had ringed round Bristol, and spread out toward the Channel. They were patterned with stone outcroppings, yellowing gorse, and the light spring green of the beeches. Here and there a straggle of cottages dotted them, a church spire, the tapestry-like fields of a manor

[8]

farm, or ridges which covered ruined breastworks so old that it was for-gotten now whether they had been raised against invading Celt or Ro-man or Northman. Yet the downs were scarcely marked by these things. They seemed still frontier land, still waiting. As always they lifted Crede out of herself.

Anthony did not return. But this must be only one more of the quarrels their quick tongues got them into. Nothing had ever stood between them for long. When his temper cooled he would remember happier things which had drawn him home, and he would come to the house. Needing time to compose herself, Crede took the path that led toward St. Brendan's Chapel.

One of her earliest recollections was of coming here with Mona who counted this shrine to the Celtic saint part of the Ireland she had left behind for love of her cousin, Crede's Irish mother. They had come often, to light a candle here together, for that older Crede who had been Mona's foster child too and remained, in the stories by which Mona kept her memory green, so young and gay and beautiful that she became a sort of fairy playmate in Crede's imagination, never of the generation of par-ents.

She would go in to light a candle now, but she paused for a moment outside, watching the first of this tide's ships rounding the hill toward Quayside. The chapel overlooked the bend of the river and where it turned into Giant's Gorge on its way to Avonmouth had looked down on countless passing ships, while seamen made their prayer to the seafaring saint who, ages ago, had sailed into the Western Ocean to find the Is-lands of the Blest.

All the westward-moving tribes that peopled Britain had felt the salt of the west wind in their faces and dreamed of a still farther west. The Blessed Isles of Irish saints, the Tir-nan-Og of Druid bards, Prince Madoc's New Wales, the Norseman's Vineland, had all lain somewhere across the Sea of Darkness; and west, toward that ocean, was the true aspect of Brandon Hill. Ships which the river tides carried past St. Bren-dan's Chapel into Bristol had come from the saint's own Ireland, from Portugal and Spain in the continent's outstretching west, from Iceland, and now, sometimes, from farther westward still.

Crede could just remember, when she was six, ten years ago, standing here with Tony—all the church bells ringing—while the *Matthew* came upriver with John Cabot and sixteen men of Bristol who had found the western land.

It was far north of the islands that Christopher Columbus had found five years before them—the tropical coast he had reached after them and believed to be part of Ind. Northerners had always thought it was there. Each generation of seamen in their west ports had its tale of some ship, storm-driven from the Iceland route, which had caught a glimpse of a strange coast. For, from the time when England and Ireland were part of Canute's Empire of the North, Bristol's trade had reached as far as Iceland; and in Iceland stories were remembered of the Vikings' wide sea empire at the turn of the tenth century when their longships had sailed on to Vineland. After that, while the growing kingdoms of Europe were busy with their own turbulent affairs, the Sea of Darkness had seemed to close beyond Iceland and its call had not been felt again until the fifteenth century was nearing its end. Then Portuguese seamen ventured farther and farther south, to find a way around Africa to the spice trade of the East. Christopher Columbus, after going from king to king with his plan of sailing westward to Ind, got ships from Spain. Bristol merchants sent out, each year, a ship to search the sea's northern part, and one at least of these had seen the far shore before John Cabot set King Henry's royal standard on it and won his reward.

It did not seem to be full of gold like Spain's new-found lands, and no one had come upon towns there to trade with; it might be only an obstacle in a seaway for England to the rich trade of the East. No one really knew. Bristol still sent ships to find out, for each year of this new sixteenth century brought new marvels and the English had no mind to be left out of them.

But one of the ships making port this morning might have brought these troublesome Thornes from London. Crede was recalled to the tangle of her own affairs and the need for prayer and meditation.

As she turned to enter the chapel, another who had stopped there for his morning devotions came out. He was a young man of a few years more than twenty, richly dressed in orange tawny, with a clever, strong-featured face and wide-set eyes which were bold and curious. She returned his greeting without enthusiasm, for Sebastien Cabot was apt to loiter and talk endlessly, and just now she was not in the mood.

"Have you been watching for Warde's ship?" he said. "I heard too that it was seen in the Channel before dark last night."

"They are only three weeks gone," Crede cried. "They can't have—!"

"Of course they haven't got near Amerike," young Cabot said scornfully. "They will have run into trouble and turned back like half that sail under the new patent. If they would take the pilot that found the true course first of all—"

It was the old admiral, his father, who had done that. Since his death, however, Sebastien talked as if a voyage on which he had been taken as a boy of fifteen had been his own. He had spoken of the new land just now by the name his father had proposed in honor of his friend Master Richard Amerike, sheriff of Bristol and steward of the king's customs in its port, who had faithfully paid him King Henry's pension out of them so long as he lived, though royal memories were apt to be short about such things. Some thought Sebastien would have liked to set his own name on the western coast that had been called by so many different ones in legend. Crede, who used to run away with Anthony into the foreign quarter south of the Bridge to listen to Sebastien's stories about that first voyage, knew how his own share in it had grown in the telling.

Nevertheless, she had always felt a force beneath Sebastien's boasting which was restless to find its true channel. It pressed with urgent greediness toward some vague but stirring promise of a world waiting for this moment and this generation, wide and wonderful beyond imagination. She had often been willing to soothe his vanity for a brief, unsettling, glimpse of that prospect.

But now she said only, "Father will be disappointed. He had put something in that venture."

"Well, we shall soon hear another tale of blundering."

There was satisfaction as well as bitterness in Sebastien's voice. Bristol merchants had tired of his pretensions, and the association which now held the king's charter "to discover and settle regions of the earth previously unknown to Christians and to trade there for five years without customs dues" always sailed without him in their attempts to find some use or profit in Amerike.

He had been obliged to content himself with an allowance from King Henry "for diligent service about our port of Bristol." Some of his elders and betters thought that it was too diligent, and he said now, "I want to get the story first. My information was that they would need to anchor in King's Road and I have a horse waiting below to take me down to Avonmouth."

He hurried off impatiently, leaving Crede to her own preoccupations.

TWO

The Canynges were not what Anthony meant by an old family, yet for a long time there had been Canynges in Bristol and they had built their share of the town's prosperity. Generations ago they had been weavers of coarse cloth in Tonker Street, south of the Bridge; then William Canynges the Elder had turned to the shipping trade, and William the Younger had made his name in it the greatest of all his generation in England. King Edward the Fourth had been his friend and had made trade treaties to suit him. Bristol had made him mayor again and again and had sent him to several parliaments, whenever in the confusion of the Wars of the Roses somebody remembered to call one. He had rebuilt St. Mary Redcliffe, below the Bridge, to give Bristol the handsomest parish church in all the nation; and, for himself, he had built the finest house in town, the Red House. He had kept ten ships at sea and nine hundred men sailing or building and repairing them. He had richly endowed the college of Black Cannons at Westbury on the downs and, finally, giving up his worldly occupations, he had entered it as a priest and died there—a dozen years before Henry Tudor won the crown on Bosworth Field and began to build the new England that was becoming a power in trade.

Philip Canynges had grown up in the great William's shadow when it no longer had material benefits to confer upon poor cousins. He, too, had chosen the shipping trade, and he had made his own modest success in it, with two ships now in the Dublin trade and two that traded with Spain and Portugal and sometimes poked their noses into the Mediterranean.

When he had become rich enough for a good house, he had not enlarged the rooms above his storage vaults on Quayside as many prosperous merchants did, looking down from the North Wall on their ships; nor had he angled for a lease on one of the tall houses on the Bridge which had storehouses in the piers and overlooked the Avon and were in great demand. He built new for himself as William had done, finding space even to lay out a garden in Mary le Port Street.

The house stood near the corner of High Street down which the main traffic of Bristol jostled toward the Bridge, and its garden ran back to a lane near the market. It faced St. Mary le Port Church and a close-built row of houses on the south side of the street behind which river barges plied the upper Avon. Beside the older houses of the narrow street it still looked new, with the new generosity of window glass and chimneys, although it had been built nearly twenty years ago for his bride, Crede Kildare of Dublin. The best Cotswold stone and slate had gone into it with oak brought across Severn from Dene Forest, for it was meant to house Canynges for generations—sons and their sons whose ships would sail from Quayside. Two stout doors with Philip Canynges' sign of the golden gorse flower above them opened into the street—one from the hall and one from the counting house—and a lane ran at the side to the kitchen gardens and stable yard.

Crede came in by this back way to the kitchen where Mona had her granddaughter, Kate, and the new maid, Sadie Orr, waiting upon her while she made a pasty. Both girls looked hot and flustered, but Mona, her red-gray hair neatly parted beneath a white linen coif and the sleeves of her plum-colored gown folded back tidily, was unhurried as always.

[12]

Her hands moved deftly among a collection of spices and saucepans and wooden bowls on the long table.

"Master Thorne of London is here and will dine with us," she said, her eyes, which were a very bright brown, fastening upon Crede's face.

Crede put her hand against the table and drew a deep breath.

Mona's skin was like cream and still unwrinkled; emotion had never been permitted to pucker it untidily and did not now; only her eyes softened.

"Sit down by the hearth, Crede, and warm yourself; you look pinched. You, Sadie, fill a bowl of broth from the kettle, and don't slop it. Kate, get some bread—the fresh manchet."

Then she did both things herself before either girl could move and stood over Crede as if prepared to feed her.

"Your father is asking for you, but you'll not go into them fasting after traipsing out before Christians were awake. And was it St. Brendan's you went to?" she added softly.

Crede nodded. Trying to deceive Mona, who knew by instinct everything which concerned her household, was never of the least use. She drank the strongly spiced broth while she was warmed outside by the fire which crackled up the wide chimney and hissed when fat dropped from a joint of mutton turning on the spit.

"It was but a passing moment's homesickness might take your mother there—and her no older when she came here than you are now," Mona said.

She presented her long straight back to Crede and turned the spit carefully.

The kitchen was a big square room with stone walls and hearth and floor, and thick oak rafters. A wide cupboard held pewter and woodenware, while cooking pots and implements hung from hooks by the fireplace. Everything shone, for no corner of the house escaped Mona's crusades against dirt and clutter. One window and the door opened upon the lane, the other overlooked the kitchen garden, and Kate and Sadie had taken advantage of this lull in the pasty making to lean out of it.

Kate was shorter and rounder than her grandmother, her hair was a plain carrot, and her good-natured face a blurred reproduction of Mona's finely-modeled features. She had married a seaman from a Canynges ship last summer and was going to have a baby soon, and now she leaned on the low window ledge to rest her swollen ankles.

Sadie Orr leaned far out to smell the damp earth of the borders which Will, the man of all work, was planting, and let waves of homesickness roll over her. She had come from a farm on the Cotswold edge; she was just thirteen, as firmly round and brightly colored as one of her father's cider apples and, in Mona's opinion, as unteachable.

[13]

Crede finished her broth, hid the bread behind the bowl, and stood up. "They are in the green parlor," Mona said. "It is only the old one came." She followed Crede across the kitchen, tidying her dress as if she were a child, then gave her a little push into the passage that led to the front of the house.

Opposite the steps going up to the dais of the main hall, a doorway through the paneling led to the little parlor which had been built on as an afterthought in the angle behind the counting-house wing. The parlor was at garden level so that you entered it by a gallery, on whose rush-covered floor Crede's footsteps made no sound. She stood there, unnoticed by her father or their guest, gathering her courage to go down.

The railing against which she leaned was carved so deeply in a pattern of trailing vines that although it was solid enough it looked unsubstantial, an illusion heightened by the strange color of the wood. Dye got from the clothworkers of the Cotswolds had been rubbed into it until it was tinged with the faint green of budding trees; the paneling of the room below was the same shade and, at any season—even when the garden outside its long windows was leafless—the light in the green parlor might have filtered down through a summer tree.

Most people thought the room queer in an otherwise handsome house. There were no rich colors and massively carved pieces in it, no tapestries even. Plain curtains of a soft blue could be drawn across the windows for warmth, and the low couches were covered in grayish yellow homespun, but except for some silken cushions and the jewel-like sheen of a few pieces of Venice glass there was little evidence here of Philip Canynges' prosperity.

As Crede took a step down from the gallery the two men in the room looked up and then came forward, Master Thorne holding the ruby cup from Venice and her father the amber one. Beside Philip Canynges' lithe, dark slimness the larger man seemed to have slackened and faded. He looked too old to be Philip's school friend. His face was a little flushed, his blue eyes a little vague, and, as he bowed, Crede suspected that the ruby glass held Bristol milk and that he had forgotten its strength.

She braced herself for a kiss which reeked of the drink, and said, "I bid you welcome, Master Thorne," with the smile which Mona had taught her must greet a guest of the house whatever the state of her own feelings.

"Why, it is her mother's smile, Phil, and her voice that was as golden as—" Master Thorne's eyes had strayed from Crede to The Portrait.

Crede knew that she had inherited little of her mother's golden beauty except her voice, but this need not matter to any sensible person, Mona said, so long as she behaved well. She might count herself fortunate, Mona said, that she was passable enough not to spoil a pretty gown and

[14]

that her father loved her for herself. She turned her own eyes toward the portrait for the assurance it always gave her of something perfect and changeless.

The portrait hung beside a long window as if that other Crede had just stepped through it from the garden, bringing with her all the brightness it could ever hold. It was all gold—bright sunlit hair and sun-warmed skin and shadowed amber eyes above a gown the shade of old parchment with the sweeping lines of slender height; at her feet was a bush of the wild gorse which gilded the downs and which Philip Canynges in his youth had chosen for his seal and sign. The painter who painted so oddly with only one color had not bothered to fill his picture with the usual careful details of dress and ornament. The eye caught only lines of graceful movement—arrested but for a moment it seemed—and the life of the face. Because a foreign vagabond who had learned some magic from the painters of Italy had paid with his brush for passage in a Canynges ship, this loveliness could still live.

Crede's attention was recalled by her father's voice.

"Gilbert brings us heavy news," he said gravely. Cormac, the big Irish hound who was asleep by the chair his master had left, stirred as always when Philip spoke. "There was sweating sickness again in London last winter, and Walter was taken by it."

Crede sat down so suddenly that Cormac jumped. With a slower movement she got to her feet again, her hands spread toward Gilbert Thorne in an impulsive gesture that might have seemed to beg forgiveness, as she cried, "Oh, Master Thorne, I do grieve for you."

Her father's eyes were sharply upon her, but Master Thorne's remained vague.

He took both her hands and said unsteadily, "My dear, we shall like one another. There are—things to explain—"

"Not while you are still tired from your journey, Gil," Philip Canynges said easily, and he stepped as easily between Crede and his friend, his hand on Master Thorne's arm. "You will want to rest before dinner, for Mona is putting her best foot foremost, I promise you."

"Robin can't go on being such a fool," Master Thorne said. "I—Oh yes, Phil, perhaps I should. I have slept poorly at sea and my head—I fear that my head is not altogether steady."

He attempted a bow which confirmed this, and Crede, watching them go up the stairs, thought with thankfulness, "How different they are!"

She had never seen her father even momentarily confused by misfortune or wine or anything else. Whatever happened, you knew that he would be equal to it, his sympathy wide enough for the clumsiest blunders, ready to set them right, yet somehow slightly withdrawn, slightly amused.

He can even afford to laugh at the years, she thought with a sudden lift of her heart. Last night he had talked of growing old, and Master Thorne did, indeed, look dreadfully old—he sagged and the fine cloth of his wine-colored suit could not hide it. But there was only a touch of white in Philip Canynges' dark hair and not a slack line anywhere about him.

Feeling that the day, although not far advanced, already made a moment's rest grateful, Crede was glad to be left alone in the parlor. She sat on one of the soft, low couches which gave the room a foreign air and provided a great deal of comfort. Cormac, who had unaccountably chosen not to follow his master, settled his weight on her feet.

Whenever she and her father were away from home, it was this little room they thought of most often. It had pleased a younger Philip Canynges to build his bride a lady's bower—like the house built for Crede of the Yellow Hair in an old tale of that long-lost Ireland of the High Kings—"Its color like the color of limes, within it couches and green rushes, within it silks and blue draperies, within it red, golden, and crystal cups"—but it had become his own favorite spot and his daughter's. His best loved books were apt to be left here, and Crede's lute and embroidery frame. And whether the curtains closed it in to firelight and candles or opened upon the garden outside, it was a restful spot.

For Crede, the portrait had always been the visible form of the fairy playmate of Mona's stories. Lately the girl in it had seemed sometimes younger than herself, but as she turned her eyes toward it now this was no longer so, and for a swift breath the lovely face seemed to share her newest, most intimate speculations. The passing of the illusion was like the sharp closing of a door. For an instant it shut from her even the painting's own familiar life and charm; for the first time she perceived that it might not always be comfort to Philip.

Her father stepped down so quietly from the gallery that Crede did not notice him until his hand was on her shoulder. He could move like a cat, having a cat's fine balance, and Cormac, who had been sleeping more soundly than he cared to admit, sat up and looked reproachful.

"I did not know how hard I had pushed you, Crede, until I saw your face at the news."

"Father!"

"If you were glad for a minute, the fault is more mine than yours," Philip said quickly. He sat down beside her and took both her hands. "I would never have forced you, kitten—how could you think so? I mean you to help me choose for you whatever will make you happiest—but we will talk of that later. I came back to ask you to make allowances for Gilbert."

"Of course, Father." After all, a man who had overdrunk was not so unusual.

"He is not at all himself." Philip paused as if he still felt explanation necessary and was finding it difficult to make. "While this blow still has him shaken, he needs humoring. You see, he had set all his hopes on Walter. It is almost a sick fancy with him now that Robin must be made over to fit them."

"Robin? Oh, the other son—the one Master Thorne says is a fool." Philip laughed. "It would surprise Gilbert to be taken literally. Robin has the brains of the family, I think. And while he chose to turn them to things his father has no interest in, Gilbert was proud enough of him to pay for a year abroad and Oxford—so long as he had Walter at home. Robin seems to have crossed him this morning, but otherwise Gilbert can't deny that the boy has behaved very handsomely. He showed great promise at Oxford and expected to enter one of the Inns of Court, but he came home at once to take Walter's place with his father and is already useful in the counting house, Gilbert says. On this voyage which they are making to several ports he has set himself to learn the practical side of their business. I hope Gilbert will realize how lucky he is."

Crede felt a stab of jealousy. This son of Master Thorne's had been instantly ready to give him the utmost devotion while she, who had so generous a father, had been unable to hide from him how thankful she was to escape doing what he had needed of her.

"It struck me last winter," Philip said thoughtfully, "that young Robin could master whatever he chose, but that his choices might not be for everyone's understanding. I am not sure that Gilbert has used him fairly in this case. However," there was a hint of amusement in his voice now, "Robin is apparently ready to be his father's match on one point. Gilbert had to come calling alone this morning."

Crede stared at him for a moment, and then the color rushed to her face.

"Father, he couldn't! He couldn't come still with his odious bargain, just bringing along another son!"

"We must try to deal delicately with Gilbert, Crede, for I am worried about him. And he doesn't think it odious. Greater families than ours carry through alliances which seem advisable to them, in spite of such mischance." But Philip's smile reassured her. "My own ideas are simpler, dear, and I have already made you a promise. There is nothing I want so much as your happiness and security, but I want your choices to be free ones."

It seemed that everyone was suddenly anxious to settle the rest of her life, not only Philip—even Tony. She had felt beset all through this long tiring morning, and a tear rolled down her cheek now.

"Crede!" Philip's voice held a sharpness his daughter had never heard in it before. "You are not thinking of that young scoundrel in Cornwall?"

She had never told Philip half truths, and she could not speak of Anthony now as if she had not just seen him. Yet what could she say about that meeting which would be fair or honest in the present miserable confusion of her feelings? To her relief Mona appeared on the gallery with the briskness of some determined purpose in her bearing. But Philip's hand tightened on Crede's, and he made her face him.

"I don't know what I am thinking, Father," she said, and this was true at least. "Everybody is pushing me at something different lately, when I was so happy just as we are."

"Crede," Mona said, "your bath water is hot, and there is just time before dinner."

Philip's face lightened. He loosed Crede's hand and laughed as if the worn old joke of Mona and her baths could make him suddenly lighthearted.

It was his own mild vanity of book learning that had armed Mona for this part of her domestic tyranny. Quoting him, Mona had been able to inform a younger, still rebellious Crede that the Romans had bathed their whole bodies regularly and were so far from being weakened by it that they had conquered the world. Their own ancestors in ruder times had ventured into tubs swung from draughty rafters and, if window glass and chimneys made folk so tender-skinned nowadays that they relied upon scents and pomanders, they would at least not do so in Mona's clean house.

Every morning's cooking fire heated a caldron which Will carried grumblingly to someone's bedroom, and each member of the household in turn, including the shrinking Sadie, suffered a weekly ordeal by water. This was Crede's day. She rose meekly and went upstairs.

THREE

Not many girls had a room all of their own. Crede's, which opened off Mona's, was large enough to hold a chest at the foot of her bed and a table for her books and workbox; a bow window above the lane looked out between housetops as far as the Castle, with a faint haze behind that was the western tip of the Cotswolds. It was pleasantly warm this morning for, although sun was streaming in, a fire burned cheerfully—Mona's indulgence to temper the rigors of bathing. Crouched in the steaming, mint-scented water, Crede scrubbed herself vigorously with a fragrant herb and almond ball and began to feel much refreshed.

A good deal could happen to improve any situation, she thought, before the sun went down on it. Anthony was here in Bristol. Perhaps he was already in a more reasonable frame of mind. Perhaps he was on his way to the house.

When she had rubbed her cheeks with a lotion which Mona said would put color in them in time and had combed her hair which had enough curl in it to tangle persistently, she thought that she might, to do honor to her father's London guest and Mona's dinner preparations, take her new gown from the chest.

It had been her father's birthday gift from the best mantle maker in Bristol, the first gown she and Mona had not made at home, and it was a gown to raise anyone's spirits. Yards of costly blue velvet billowed about her, clasped with a silver girdle, and opening down the front and the long, loose sleeves upon an underdress of paler-blue silk embroidered with pink gillyflowers. It gave her a feeling of the utmost poise and elegance.

From the hall below, Philip Canynges watched her descend the wide front stairs in her small, red, heelless shoes and some turn of her head brought a fleeting memory. It was just so, coming down the stairs of her father's house in Dublin, that he had first seen Crede's mother, and it was still the clearest picture he had of her because, ever after, what his eyes had seen was only part of what she had become to him. She had been no more than Crede's age then, and he who was twice it and had spent his youth laboriously building a shipping trade had thought he could not have spent it better, since it allowed him to speak to her father of a partnership.

But surely his wife had seemed older at sixteen. Their daughter looked like a child dressed up in a too handsome gown. The heavy richness of the velvet seemed only to emphasize Crede's immaturity; it was not only her slightness but something too incautious in her quick movements, in the play of expression which gave her face its charm but made it so transparent . . . something uncertain, yet trusting and expectant, which seemed begging life to use her with no conception at all how hard the terms might be. He had so long ago fallen into the habit of sharing thoughts and interests with her amusing childish earnestness, and then with a swiftly growing mind which leaped to meet his, that this sudden apprehension of youth wakening to its own separateness, untried and unarmed, startled him and caught roughly at his heart.

She looked past him and past the table whose setting Mona was carefully inspecting, across the hall where Gilbert Thorne sat staring into the fire, then questioningly down its length.

Her father came forward to offer his arm in deference to her elegance and said, in an undertone, "You have still only one London guest to entertain. Robin has not come, and I think we may take it that he means not to call—at the cost," Philip's lips twitched, "of some discourtesy."

Crede had forgotten about Robin Thorne, and she had not the least care of his manners. It was not with any thought of seeing him that her eyes had searched the hall.

The door from the counting house opened, and Adam Bell came through it, pausing by the table to greet Mona. Crede forgot her disappointment for a moment. Her face brightened with pleasure for she had missed seeing Adam yesterday and the voyage he had brought the *Brigid* home from had been a long one.

Philip Canynges' best friend and the master of his newest, fastest ship was a big-boned north countryman in the prime of life, with fair hair and skin salt-tanned to the color of red sandstone and the general appearance of having been carved carelessly but handsomely out of it. His straight, blunt nose was so uncommonly sharp to smell shifting gusts of trade or the down-wind of a pirate that along Bristol's waterfront his share of the *Brigid*'s luck was reckoned ample to set him up with his own line and a burgher's dignities any time he chose.

Yet he did not look any more like a successful townsman than he did like the master of a crack ship. Despite years at sea he walked with a countryman's long stride and the air of one accustomed to planting his feet on his own acres. In the doublet and hose of plain gray cloth, which he wore as usual without brooches or a chain, he might have come this moment instead of a dozen years ago from his Yorkshire dales. Any temptation he had ever felt to buy gewgaws in foreign ports was for Crede; he held one hand behind his back now as he joined them and bent to kiss her from a height which dwarfed Philip's. Straightening up, he surveyed her magnificence with a twinkle in eyes of that blue which seems to have taken on the color of distance.

"Bless me, Crede, you've grown up since I left port, and into a fine lady! I could doubt you had ever rummaged through my pockets!"

"Don't you tease me, Adam!" Crede cried. "What is behind your back?"

He drew his hand forward and opened it to reveal a tiny, artfully-fashioned bird. Its feathers were of gold and silver most delicately overlaid and, setting it on Crede's wrist, he showed her that the wings and head could be moved.

Crede made the wings spread as if for flight and exclaimed, "Oh, Adam! I have never seen anything lovelier!"

"Nor such goldsmith's work!" Philip bent forward curiously. "See how gold is laid on silver! It is a trick that would puzzle the smiths of Florence. Where did you find it, Adam?"

"In Lisbon. But it had flown farther, and with it a story too long to tell fasting. My mouth has been watering through weeks of ship's fare for one of Mistress Mona's pasties." Adam looked hopefully toward the table.

And then from the end of the hall which Crede had ceased to watch came the slam of the street door. Anthony burst in upon them, pausing by the screen as much on guard as if he had forced entrance.

His bearing was an open defiance, Crede thought, and caught her breath. Then she saw that he was ill at ease, bracing himself to hide it, and she made a quick movement toward him. But Philip was swifter. Although he had stiffened with surprise, he stepped forward instantly to welcome a guest, however unexpected.

"Anthony! We thought you still in Cornwall. Come in, Cousin!"

Anthony strode forward then and took Crede's hand without kissing her. Adam Bell who had not moved a foot or offered any greeting was now the first to speak and, of long custom, spoke his mind as freely in Philip's house as on the deck of the *Brigid*.

"Have you quit that devil's brood in Cornwall?"

Anthony turned deliberately from him to Philip. "I came back to ask for Crede, sir."

The resentment of their quarrel was wiped from Crede's mind, and even the discomfort of this public test Anthony had chosen. She could remember only that she had called him a coward and might have known that he would be stung into doing something spectacular—without pausing to consider that it would ruin everything. For now, as if they had traded convictions, she could see how hopelessly he was outmatched.

"Why?" Philip asked quietly.

"Because we love one another," Anthony cried. "We grew up loving one another."

Philip seemed to find no need to look toward Crede and gave his attention still courteously to his young cousin.

"It is a common error to think rather too soon that we have finished growing up," he said, as if it were only the philosophy of this which interested him, and that mildly. But then his voice took on crispness. "A few months ago nothing here could hold you. Yet the things you found it beneath your interest to learn are Crede's inheritance. Have you learned in Cornwall how to take my place when need be?"

Anthony flushed scarlet. "Jestyns aren't bred for trade."

"By the mass, no!" Adam's color turned a shade deeper than sun and wind had made it. "Common pirates your fine Cornwall cousins are, and I'll see them pegged in chains at Thames tide yet."

Anthony's hand flew toward his belt, but Adam contemptuously made no move. "If you are in with them, my lad, I'd count my ship's boy a likelier gentleman to draw steel with. But I don't brawl with boys. You'll hear the truth when I choose, as he does."

"This is my affair, Adam." Philip had not raised his voice, but his hand had been quick to seize Anthony's arm, with a grip which others had found surprising. "I can't think you came here to roister, Anthony. Perhaps you have already discovered the truth of what Adam says, and if you have come home the wiser for it, let us talk sensibly."

His eyes which searched the boy's handsome, angry face were not unfriendly. "Your mother was my favorite cousin, Tony. If you had come to me before you left us I would have helped you to anything honest you liked better than my trade. You can please me by counting on my interest still."

It was going to be all right, after all. Crede's hands unclenched. She had never known her father to be ungenerous, and she could trust his sensitiveness to understand Anthony as she did—the uneasy pride which pricked him to be most arrogant when he was already repenting a mistake. They both knew he had been drawn home to them from Cornwall. It was only because he was Anthony Jestyn that he had to come so flamboyantly, talking of mad schemes this morning to dazzle her with what had failed to hold him.

"Stay and dine with us now, and we will talk later," Philip said, his hand still on Anthony's arm. "But you must not talk such nonsense to Crede as you have just now, Tony. There will be no playing upon a childish companionship which I have come to believe was my mistake. In London and other ports I have friends and, somewhere, away from here, you can prove, if you choose, that I have rated you too low. I think that is fair." For the first time, Philip looked toward his daughter.

For a moment Crede had thought that they could step comfortably back into their old ways but now, remembering some things about this morning, she knew that they could not and that her father had seen the only way in which matters might still be mended.

"I don't need your friends!" Anthony shook himself free of Philip's hand. "I have my cousin's commission, and his was from a king—is that so shameful? Crede was ready to go with me to Cornwall if only we go openly—ask her!"

"No! No, I'm not." In the turmoil of her thoughts it was strange that she could answer so quickly. "You were fair, Father."

Anthony swung toward her, and the darkening of his face so clearly recalled it in a schoolboy tantrum that for a moment Crede forgot that this painful scene was not one to end in ear boxing but was the sort of crisis which altered lives. His manner changed again as he bent with his new elegance to make her a low bow.

"Your pardon for coming on a fool's errand," he said, and without

[22]

speaking to anyone else he strode down the hall and out the front door.

Suddenly Crede felt at outs with them all—Anthony, Adam Bell, even Philip. She had always been part of the pleasant life around her without needing to see herself separately, but now she felt separate, with a privacy they had all roughly invaded.

Philip tucked her hand in his arm and pressing it against him led her toward their guest who seemed to have given no heed to what was happening behind him and now turned from frowning at the fire. Mona crossed the dais, composed and unhurried, and struck the gong.

It was the signal for an instant irruption from the counting house. The three apprentices, Niles Hathaway, Bob Sturmys, and Ned Leach, precipitated themselves into the hall, their arms locked, their heads close together in some private retreat of their engrossing thirteen-year-old world. Nodding absently to the family they proceeded to the lower end of the table.

Sadie carried around the finger bowls and warmed, lavender-scented towels, while Will came in with a large platter and stood by the sideboard. Mona was maintaining the magnificence of Bristol against London and meant to have dinner served in state, though it was their usual custom to have Will and Sadie hustle the dishes onto the table and then sit down with the rest while Kate left the kitchen untended.

Crede took her place on the dais between her father and their guest, with Adam Bell and Mona on Philip's other hand. At each of these upper places, separated from the others by the massive silver nef holding salt and spices, Mona had set a fork, novelties brought to her from Italy by Adam Bell, who knew by some instinct how to win an approval he valued highly. It was curious, Crede had observed, that Mona, all of whose essential beliefs were rooted deep in tradition, flew to each new refinement of personal habits as if it satisfied some inner conviction. Philip Canynges, whose mind was capable of much bolder innovations of thought, found most of these interferences with his settled habits irritating. He pushed his fork aside as he stood up to ask the blessing which brought Master Thorne's eyes upon him, for the simple English words were Philip's own and this had a taint of Lollardry.

When she had broken the fresh, crusty loaf and put part of it in the alms basket, Crede, with Mona's eye upon her, resignedly picked up her fork, hoping that it would not drop something greasy over her new gown. Will's platter held a carp stewed in wine, and this was followed by a succession of meats and fowl in spiced sauces or rich pastry, the joint garnished with herbs and greens, and a sallet. Sallets were an old fashion, lately revived, which Philip Canynges considered sensible and wholesome. It pleased him that his garden should serve the table for more than pottages and garnishing, and with his backing Mona could rob Will's

[23]

beds shamelessly ahead of season. Even so it must have cost her a battle to cut the tiny lettuce leaves just appearing from seeds that a Canynges ship had got abroad. They were rather flavorless but added a touch of pale, exotic green to pickled barberries, cress and violets, and were said to soothe and sweeten tempers.

Mona prided herself on the excellence of their table, but she seldom crowded it so ostentatiously. There were two such courses before the banquet, which was a marzipan subtlety in the shape of the *Brigid* on a sea of green jelly. And since, in Philip Canynges' house, everything served above the salt went all down the board, the hum of apprentice wit and gossip at its lower end grew slower and drowsier. The three boys were entitled by guild law to an hour for dinner and an hour in the afternoon to sleep in their loft above the counting house, but today one dispensation would blend into the other.

On the dais, Philip and Adam Bell did most of the talking. Mona was too anxiously concerned with the service, for Will's gnarled hands, so deft with sick animals or young plants, became unaccountably clumsy indoors, while Sadie was a positive menace. Gilbert Thorne was still moody and, Crede thought, still a little tipsy, and her own thoughts wandered so restlessly that it was an ordeal to sit through the long courses.

Her father noticed her abstraction after a while and said, "Where is your silver bird, Crede? And what is the story you promised about it, Adam?"

"If the story is true," Adam said, "your bird has flown across the world, Crede."

Adam's storytelling manner, which was unlike his usual bluntness of speech, recalled that he had grown up in the rich ballad country of the north border; this was his old trick of beginning his tales with a marvel.

"In Lisbon, I drank Malmsey with a battered old pilot of the *Tagus* who had kept the trinket as a charm for years but cares more now to have the price of wineskins. His speech was so mixed with Breton, Basque, and English that I'd not hazard what in Christendom his mother first taught him, but he claims to have sailed years ago with Henry the Navigator's seamen, when the Portuguese were feeling their way down Africa. Twenty odd years ago, my ancient said, he was in the ship of a Frenchman from Dieppe named Cousins. The ship was blown out of the Africa course and carried day upon day over empty ocean. After the gale had eased they were half a world westward, but land was there— and men in it who wore fine, thin cloth, and had cloaks woven by some curious art of feathers, and ornaments of such craftsmanship as Crede's bird."

Mona nodded approval. There had been too much dull talk of the

Brigid's trade. Lacking a minstrel, and unfortunately she had been unable to find one at short notice, the proper accompaniment of good food was storytelling. Adam was in his best form now.

"When they had beat their long way homeward, my ancient left the ship at Madeira, where no one listened to his tale except the Genoese map maker, Columbus, who had settled there. As we know, Columbus later reached land southwestward, yet I cannot think that anyone has found the coast this bird came from. It could not have been wrought by such simple natives as I have seen herded from Spanish ships. Although my ancient saw no great cities, I think they may have reached Ind or Cathay by a western passage—and that Spain has not."

All of them were giving Adam their attention, surprised yet ready to believe. Portugal had found a seaway east around Africa to Ind, and this ship might have blundered upon the western way which men were beginning to doubt Columbus had found. Nothing was too amazing for this modern age, in which marvel after marvel was proved to be true. Swift ships were bringing the far ends of the old world's land and river routes together and discovering a whole new world beyond them. The New Learning was uncovering a world of equal wonders. It was partly the old learning of the Mediterranean, forgotten in the west since the fall of Rome but preserved by the Roman Empire of the East and brought back in the middle of the last century by scholars fleeing from the Turkish conquest of Constantinople. It mixed with the new discoveries and inventions of the West in a heady brew—and the most revolutionary invention of all, the printing press, spread it as swiftly as if all time and space had come suddenly together.

Mona crossed herself. "Holy St. Brendan! Most like the decent men they saw came from the saint's New Ireland."

"I think that Columbus may have touched another part of Amerike and that it is great enough to contain men of different sorts and still seem empty," Philip said, his eyes brightening. "Remember, John Cabot sailed far down its coast and found no end of it. For my part, I had rather know what it holds than find a passage through it to Ind or Cathay."

The breathless questions of a widening world had carried Crede away from her own perplexities and had even aroused Master Thorne.

"A deal of nonsense is talked of new lands and new routes," he said briskly. "Your head must be hard enough, Phil, to see that Englishmen need not go scouring the seas for them, when King Henry has smoothed the way of our trade so marvelously in the old routes. With our concessions in the ports of Spain and Portugal we can do well enough without battering out our own ships on the ocean. And since the Intercursus with Flanders we are better off in the north ports than the Hanse League itself."

"True enough," Adam Bell replied. "We have got the first king with sense enough to put trade first, and the general need of English wool gives him an argument he knows how to use. Our Merchant Venturers are envied everywhere."

"And hated," Philip added. "Why need we growl over stale bones, when a whole new world may lie westward, and we have never been more than the western fringe of this one?"

"Not London!" Gilbert Thorne leaned across Crede. "London is nearer center of a world of ocean routes than Antwerp is—yet Antwerp is getting rich from them without needing to hunt any herself. A Thames tide is rising which could float a small venture far, Philip, and together we should be a sturdier craft."

"Perhaps." Philip Canynges' voice had regained its usual lightness. "Perhaps no man's special ambitions are a footrule for the new world. What more had you to tell us about Lisbon, Adam? By the way, Gilbert, your cousin Robert tells me he has been debating whether to keep young Robert there with the Portuguese syndicate or send him to Spain."

Adam began a description (dry and competent as his descriptions became when they were concerned with trade) of the concession in Lisbon within which the Merchant Adventurers of England were building guildhalls and warehouses with privileges so unmatched as to earn them the resentment of other traders and of Portugal's own merchants.

But King Manuel of Portugal sustained their pretensions. Not long ago, when Portugal was an inconsiderable kingdom whose commerce suffered from Venetian control of the Mediterranean, England had revived a trade treaty with her. England had also been ready to deal with Florence while that city struggled to break the Venetian monopoly of the spice trade—based upon control of the ancient overland routes to the East—and had won valuable concessions in the port of Pisa. And King Ferdinand of Spain, while he was fighting and intriguing to make a kingdom out of scattered provinces just freed from the Moors, had found a newcomer on England's throne who sensed that the western island and the western peninsula had interests in common. These various alliances had no sooner been made than Portugal discovered the seaway to Ind, and Spain discovered the southwestern islands, and the age-old balance of European trade began to shift toward these western upstarts among the powers. Though England's only discovery had been an awkward mass of land in the northwest Atlantic which appeared to be a hindrance rather than a help to ocean routes, it must have seemed to those who watched Henry Tudor pursue his advantages in European diplomacy that blind chance had favored him.

They sat on talking at the head of the table after the others left; but as the conversation passed from new worlds to details of trade it no longer held Crede's attention. Half unconsciously she was waiting for this day, which had been so crowded and demanding from its beginning, to take some other sharp turn and somehow resolve itself. Now, light through the hall windows showed how little was left of the afternoon, and her restlessness increased. Surely they had been sitting here for hours.

Master Thorne was leaning toward her, speaking.

"I have watched you listening patiently to a prose of old men's talk, child, but I am sure we are dull company for you. Robin must come with me tomorrow."

This tiresome old man was pressing something more upon her, but she scarcely heard him or could think of tomorrow while today was rushing past, changing everything, sending Tony back to Cornwall. She could sit still no longer.

Unthinkable as Mona's training should have made it for her to leave the table and her father's guests, Crede was on her feet now. The alms basket stood at her elbow and, clutching it as a shred of excuse, she ran down the steps of the dais and across the hall toward the front door.

"Crede!" Philip called.

Surprisingly, Mona answered him. "She will but take the basket round the corner to the good sisters. Leave her go."

FOUR

As the door closed behind her, Crede came to a sudden stop. The impulse which had driven her out furnished no direction; and wherever she was going she ought to have her street cloak and pattens. But she was unwilling to go back now.

While she stood uncertain, the afternoon which had clouded over brightened again. The sun broke through to warm the cobbles of Mary le Port Street and blend the scents of fish and tar and brackish Avon water from the river below with a farmyard tang from the nearby borough market. High Street bustled past the corner on its way to the Bridge and spilled out a pair of blue-smocked apprentices trundling a barrow and a straggling group who stared about them like strangers, their faces swarthy and black-bearded under red seamen's caps. They turned into St. Mary's Churchyard and from their gait it could be seen they had visited the taverns before thinking of their prayers. Crede drew back into the doorway until they had found the church porch.

[27]

Behind them a tall figure in green had turned quickly into one of the alleys which led toward the river. But there must be more than one jauntily worn green cloak in Bristol!

She turned her back on High Street and walked toward the Castle, the alms basket hanging forgotten on her arm. She had not known when she came out where she wanted to go, but she was taking the way to Cousin Allie's.

Mary le Port Street led east toward the dry moat of the Castle, whose mound rose on a narrow isthmus between Frome and Avon. Its keep, the largest in England, had towered imposingly over Bristol since the time when William the Conqueror had set Norman overlords in strategic places; but of late so little had been done to repair it that, when King Henry visited the town and made its citizens' luxury and magnificence the occasion for a royal homily and fine, he had shrunk from using its tumble-down apartments even as a lesson in simple living and had lodged with the White Friars. The street ended close by St. Edith's well and the Swan tavern, and this was not a good district for loitering even in daylight. The dignified old house of the Nortons stood below the castle by St. Peter's Church, but the present Thomas Norton was said to practice sorcery within it, and beyond it mean buildings straggled toward the river.

Crede picked her way through a muddy lane very different from the clean, cobbled streets of Bristol which had been recently repaved and were what Bristol citizens chose to remember when sniffing disdainfully in towns not blessed with their own lavish water supply and underground drains. She had come this way often enough, and lanes like this one, noisome with wretchedness and slatternly living, were part of the life of all towns, a life which was lived so much on the streets that one grew accustomed to its intimate detail.

But today she was strung to heightened awareness of what had been familiar and taken for granted. A group of ragged children were grubbing with a half-starved dog in a midden; in the stare of eyes turned toward her, the dog's no more wary than the rest, she felt the costly velvet she was holding out of the muck a weight in her hands and the alms basket on her arm a shameful burden. A helplessness to make the shape of things conform to her old happier picture of them had been growing all day, and now it engulfed her. She set the alms basket on the ground and fled in cowardice from the horrid scramble which followed.

Across a narrow strip of river meadow below Castle Mound, trees framed the Early English tower of St. Philip's Church. Castle village and market lay north of it, with open mead across the town ditch beyond, and near the churchyard were a few neat cottages with gardens. Cousin Allie lived alone in what was still called William Botoner's house, although twenty-odd years had passed since that curious-minded scholar and physician had ended his days there brewing simples from its garden and recording in clerkly Latin every stone and turn of Bristol.

Crede knocked several times without getting an answer, and felt sharp disappointment that admitted to herself what her errand was. It was here that she and Anthony had come daily to be initiated by Cousin Allie into the mysteries of grammar, rhetoric and logic, arithmetic, geometry, astronomy, and music, as well as certain bypaths of his own in the New Learning which he had added to the time-honored high road of the trivium and quadrivium. For in Philip Canynges' odd conception of a daughter's education it had amused him that Crede could easily outdo Anthony in Latin grammar and geometry, even that she should try to match him in archery and singlestick. It was only when the children were nearly grown that he had begun to discourage the number of things they did together. If Anthony had paused anywhere today before shaking the dust of Bristol from his elegant Cordova boots, he might have come to see his old tutor.

When the thought that Anthony might still be in Bristol had driven her out restlessly, she had not stopped to think what good it could do to see him again. She had made the only choice she could this morning. Yet the chance sight of a green cloak turning out of Mary le Port Street had held for an instant more reality than anything that had been said. And just now, passing St. Philip's, she had seen a movement of green in the porch . . . as if she must see Anthony in every green sleeve. She told herself that if only she could wish him Godspeed before he left, if only she could put something of their friendship between them and an angry parting, she could learn to think of him away in Cornwall more sensibly.

The door opened and Cousin Allie regarded her sleepily, leaning upon a cane.

"Bless us, Crede, I must have dozed off when you left. What brings you back?"

It was yesterday, after their lesson, that Crede had left him, but Cousin Allie could lose more than a day in pursuit of one of his ideas and had probably been lost in his latest discovery of Greek until sleep overcame him at his desk.

This meant that no one else had been here today to recall him to time and the world.

He stood in the doorway, blinking a little, and made the transition. "I believe it is tomorrow already," he confessed guiltily. "Come in, my dear."

The principal room of the house had a pleasant sort of orderliness even when awash with books and papers, as it was now; it had served two scholars and had the air of suiting its purpose and of being used and loved for that purpose. It was small enough so that a man at his desk with his books around him need feel no empty space but could move directly to farther distances; and it was large enough to contain his needs: a shelf for his books, a worktable by a window, and a hearth to comfort his bones in the cramps of scholarship. Crede, who had tidied the worktable yesterday, could see that its present confusion was all Greek. Greek had come lately to Oxford, and Cousin Allie had loyally followed his university into an enchanting confusion. These overflowing papers were part of his new system of the Greek language and philosophy.

A log smoldered in the fireplace, and Cousin Allie who loved warmth led Crede to the settle beside it, replenished the fire, and then stood so close to the hearth that he had to keep turning on his cane like a plump pigeon on a spit. In spite of an absent-mindedness about meals, Master Alward Lusted had the well-nourished look of a man who finds the sustenance he needs. He was small and neat with bright dark eyes, a light pink complexion which extended over most of his head, and a Roman profile. He had come of a Kentish family connected with the Canynges. He had taken minor orders but had forgotten about them long ago in the excitements of the New Learning and, since he had put his small inheritance into one of Philip Canynges' luckiest ventures while serving him as a clerk, he was now able to give full time to his discoveries. Not all of these were in books, for Cousin Allie held to the new opinion that many features of the universe not described by Aristotle merited scholarly attention. Like his late friend William Botoner he was interested in the antiquities of his own district, he listened attentively to every new tale brought home from the western voyages, and for anything called an Experiment he would risk his life or his reputation.

He was one of the few in Bristol who ventured into Master Thomas Norton's house, for he maintained that the diabolical smells and explosions which came from it were brewed in no witch's caldron but in search of knowledge which would benefit the human race. His cane and bandaged foot where the marks of a recent discovery of his own.

Adam Bell, who should have known better, had touched off this one by repeating gossip from Florence that the painter Leonardo, who was apparently very like Cousin Allie, believed the myth of Daedalus might be no myth at all. After careful experiment had convinced Cousin Allie of the soundness of this, he had tested a flying device of his own from the roof and, but for the providential softness of a dunghill in which he was combining a new mixture of enrichments for his garden, his neck as well as his ankle might have been broken. Those who loved him prayed that his new system of Greek, which seemed less dangerous, would distract his attention for a while from Adam's further disclosures

[30]

that this Leonardo believed boats could be made to sail under water and that if you bottled up steam and managed not to be blown to pieces or scalded in the process you could drive a mill with it.

Crede loved him dearly. She was his godchild and, besides the affinity of one eagerly curious mind for another, they shared a deep personal affection. When Crede was near, Cousin Allie had a much firmer grip on the present moment and could be surprisingly observant.

"How grand you are, child!" He paused in a revolution and seemed to give her new gown his full attention and admiration. "But something is bothering you," he said, "and I think you didn't come for a lesson. My dear, have you just come away to think, or will it help you to tell me the trouble?"

Crede told him some of it. Some belonged too closely to Anthony and some was a confusion of feeling which was too intimately her own, even if she could have found words for it. It took her quite a while to sort things out. Cousin Allie lowered himself onto the settle and faced the fire as often as he faced her, but when she came to an end his bright dark eyes were on her and she suspected that gaps in the story had presented no great difficulty to him.

"I'm sorry for that boy," he said.

She took it for granted that he meant Anthony but he added tartly, "Gilbert Thorne was always a fool—not the less so that he knows one thing very well and how to use everyone else for it."

Crede might have known that Cousin Allie's first concern would be for a scholar plucked from Oxford. But she had expected that he could give his attention to his own godchild's worries, and she felt cheated of his sympathy.

"Robin Thorne must be uncommonly poor spirited to be forced into his brother's shoes if he doesn't want them," she said crossly. "I'll thank them to leave me out of it."

"Apparently Robin means to." Cousin Allie chuckled. "He seems to have spirit enough to boggle at one condition."

Crede flushed and then laughed. Cousin Allie could always make her see her own conceit. For the first time she had a thought to spare for Robin Thorne as a person, with problems of his own.

"I suppose he is fond of his father," she admitted. "Master Thorne looks quite ill, and of course he is dreadfully old. All his life he has worked for something, and now he has only Robin to carry it on for him," she added thoughtfully.

"It is a constant amazement to me," Cousin Allie said, "what tough old curmudgeons the young can think too fragile to be crossed." He broke off and smiled at her. "I don't think that you came here worried about Gilbert Thorne, or afraid your father will be overruled by him—

and even in your young eyes Philip cannot seem aged or decrepit! It is Anthony who has upset you."

Cousin Allie stopped smiling and glowered into the fire. There was no sympathy in his voice for his former pupil as there had been for the stranger from Oxford, although Anthony's career also seemed to be taking a wrong turning. But then Anthony had never shown any eagerness to be an ornament of the New Learning.

"Anthony has not come here, and I don't expect he will," he said finally, disconcerting Crede by reading more of her mind than she had been prepared for. "If you could see him again, Crede, he would not have changed, and there is nothing more to be said. Some things," Cousin Allie got up and turned agitatedly upon his stick, "there is no solution for."

It was the negation of his own philosophy, and he looked at her with dismay. Nevertheless, he had helped her this afternoon. Cousin Allie could generally help her to put her thoughts into better order, as if he were helping her with logic or geometry; that in itself seemed a promise of something more constructive. Although the things about which Cousin Allie could be energetic had little to do with personal affairs, the close pressure of these was apt to lighten in his special atmosphere.

For a moment his face had lost its rosy serenity, but it cleared as he glanced from Crede to the rich confusion of his desk.

"My dear, would you like to know a beautiful principle I have just found in Greek syntax?"

Crede laughed and felt better for it. "I should like to know first whether you remembered to have your dinner and what is for supper," she said and went into the kitchen.

There was no sign that he had thought of either meal, and the fire had not been kindled. However, she found plenty of bread and cheese and carried back with her a pottage she had brought him yesterday, which she set to warm on the hob.

"I must have forgotten," Cousin Allie admitted, and he ate with good appetite, between mouthfuls explaining special refinements of expression made possible to the fortunate Greeks by the aorist tense of their verbs. He needed little encouragement to turn it into a lesson which could go on happily for as long as Crede chose, and she lingered after supper because in spite of everything she still hoped for a knock at the door.

They sat enclosed by a circle of firelight, but finally she noticed the gathering shadows of the room. When she said hastily that she must go, Cousin Allie hobbled to the door with her and peered out.

"It is coming on to rain, I think. Run straight home, child, and don't loiter."

More time had passed than even she had realized, and the darkening of the overcast sky was night closing in early. In a moment Cousin Allie's attention might untangle itself from Greek tenses to perceive this, and he would insist upon limping painfully home with her. Crede picked up her skirts and ran as if she were the young tomboy his absence of mind had returned her to.

She felt still a child's confident freedom of Bristol, but she had never before been out alone after nightfall, and as she hurried across the meadow its graying seemed swifter than her own movement. Trees became heavy dark shadows behind which only the low mist by the river held a milky, suspended light.

She saw first the horse standing by a thick clump of beeches and then the tall, masked figure which moved to block her way, dark and shapeless in a long, hooded, traveling cloak. Now she ran in panic, her wretched finery hampering her legs, and felt the figure gaining on her. Her voice froze in her throat, then freed itself as her eyes picked out in the band of light behind the trees a single wayfarer on the river path.

While she screamed, she tried to swerve in the direction of the river, but her pursuer was closing in, and cut her off. She dodged and was forced nearer the waiting horse. Risking a glance over her shoulder she could see a running figure by the river. It came crashing recklessly through the bushes, and the light glinted on a green cloak before it plunged into the darker shadows of the trees.

"Help!" she screamed again, and then put all her breath into running.

The others were saving theirs too. She kept on, twisting and evading as best she could, until a heavy hand seized her shoulder, and she stumbled and fell. But the newcomer was upon them, and Crede's assailant leaped back to protect himself. When she scrambled up, her rescuer had got between them, and both swords were out.

The only brightness now left in the failing light under the trees flashed in their blades. Neither swordsman had given the other time to throw off his hooded cape, and to their dusky formlessness the silence that hoarded breath for swift movement added strangeness. Yet Crede, when screaming for help, had seen it coming in a green cloak and now, unreasoning, she felt herself behind Anthony. She remained there, caught back instinctively from the panic of flight, meaning to help if she could.

In a moment she discovered something strange about this sword play. Englishmen who followed the new fashion of wearing swords at their belts used them as broadswords and battle-axes were used against armor—in the downward, slashing blow they practiced at singlestick. The farther sword followed this training, but the nearer one teased and evaded and thrust the point forward, quick and snake-like. It was a flimsier weapon too—the narrow blade had only quickness in it, and a dancing quickness behind it.

Did they teach this trick in Cornwall? It seemed a trumpery defence against the broadsword whose deadly downward cut could cleave a skull. The swift thrust and parry always recovered, yet what waited to break past it was slow moving death that maintained its guard, as taught in singlestick, for the solid stance from which a crushing blow could be delivered. The light, darting point found no opening in that guard and surely it must be the dancer who tired first.

Yet it was the other whose rhythm began to change, who was teased to quickness. He overreached in one stroke, faltered an instant in recovery—and only that instant was needed. The quick point reached the unguarded shoulder; the sword, half raised in a desperate parry, flew from the hand that held it and fell almost upon Crede. With an involuntary cry she jumped aside, then bent to seize it, and her champion turned his head.

"Guard!" she screamed. It was like Tony to be so careless!

But her assailant had not seized the moment to use his dagger. He had taken advantage of it to reach his horse.

"He might have stabbed you!" Crede cried. "Surely you knew I could look out for—"

A shout startled them. A lantern lighted the horse with its rider now up and swung wildly out of the way as it was almost run down. Then its beam found Crede.

"What's toward, Mistress?"

The light moved nearer, blinding her eyes which had accustomed themselves to near darkness. She tried to move back into the trees, suddenly remembering her dishevelled state, but now the light was full on her and a voice (which, alas! she knew) exclaimed in a horrified tone, "Mistress Canynges!"

"The Watch!" said Crede at the same moment and with no less dismay.

Now her mishap would be known all over town. She looked behind her for Anthony but could not see him in the darkness under the trees, which seemed blacker than ever from the patch of light in which she stood, and he did not come forward. In the past he had sometimes trusted her to provide the quickest and least sensational version of an adventure. Behind its lantern the Watch was scarcely visible, but its voice rose.

"Mistress Crede, have you no sense, to cross Philip's field alone in the dark with such lanes as there are hereabout? I'm still hunting some fly-by-night that was screaming her head off a while back, and the Fiend himself near rode me down."

This was better than she had feared. But the Watch kept the lantern turned upon her.

"Was it you screaming, Mistress Crede?"

"Timothy Polkhorn, do be sensible!" said Crede with a composure which pleased and surprised her. "I am returning from my cousin's, Master Alward Lusted's by St. Philip's, and I should have been home in a minute."

There was not a word of untruth in this, she noticed with increased pleasure, for an admonition to Timothy Polkhorn to be sensible was so apt that it need bother no one's conscience at confession.

"The old fool!" said the Watch explosively. "Letting you out in pitch dark is a deal sillier than jumping off his roof! I'm taking you home now, Mistress Crede, whoever screams in this town meanwhile."

There was no help for it. Anthony off under the trees could scarcely be added now to her elegant simplification of events. Crede cast a look into the darkness behind her and meekly followed the lantern. But she walked lightheartedly. Anthony had stayed in Bristol past the time, surely, when he should have set off to join his ship, and it must be that he found old ties too strong for breaking. Thanks to Timothy Polkhorn they had not had time for a word together, but that could wait until tomorrow.

She began a cheerful conversation with her escort, remembering to ask whether he had as important a part in this year's guild plays, already rehearsing for Whitsun week, as last year when he had been such a splendid Satan.

Timothy Polkhorn, journeyman to Master Babcock of the Tanner's Guild and serving his turn on the Watch, decided that he must have been mistaken in his first impression. He had thought at first that she looked disordered, but no doubt she had been running hard to get home, frightened to be out so late. It was risky, he told her, and she must not take such a chance again on any account, and she agreed with him at once and begged his pardon very prettily for the inconvenience she was causing him now.

It was no trouble at all, he assured her and congratulated himself that it was not some gabbling member of the Watch who had come upon her and might have seen an escapade in mere innocent thoughtlessness. She was a nice little thing, he had always thought and had been sufficiently warned now. As he left her at the door he hoped that she might be able to slip into the house without getting a scolding.

Before Crede could put her hand to the latch, she saw Mona's head at the window with the firelight behind it, and then Mona flung the door open and swept her inside. Her hands on Crede's were shaking.

"Crede, where have you been!"

Never before had Crede heard Mona's voice unsteady.

"I went to Godfather's," she began, remembering guiltily that she had not once considered how long the time might seem at home.

"I never thought of that!" Mona sat down heavily on the settle. "I might have known . . . Holy St. Brigid be praised! And may the Good Lord forgive me for what I'd been thinking!"

It bore witness to some extremity of agitation that Mona's need reached even beyond St. Brigid and the saints of her Irish pantheon.

"I went to the Sisters when it got late. The men had gone off calling on old friends of Master Thorne's before we thought of worrying, and Will couldn't find them. Crede, I was near out of my wits."

"I didn't mean to be out so late," Crede cried remorsefully. "I just forgot the time at Cousin Allie's, and then—" but, clearly, Mona must be spared the story of the highwayman until she was herself again. "Timothy Polkhorn was on the Watch and lighted me home."

"I'll not scold you, Crede. You have been bothered enough today, and if I had got my hand on— The night damp on you too, with no cloak! And mud, child!"

"I stumbled and fell," Crede said quickly. "I'm sorry it is my best gown."

"It will clean. Move up to the fire now, *mo mhornin,* and warm yourself while I make a tisane against the rheum."

Surrounded by remediable evils to be dealt with, Mona recovered quickly and got briskly to her feet. In no time at all she was back from the kitchen with a mug which she set on the hob and another which she insisted must be drained at once to the last drop, bitter though it was with catmint, camomile, and mallow. Then Crede was fed brawn and honey cakes and ordered to bed.

"I'll bring the hot posset up," Mona said. "There's dill and parsley in it to send you straight asleep, and thyme for pleasant dreams."

"I don't need it, Mona *acushla.*" Warmed by the fire, Crede was yawning drowsily.

Mona hustled her upstairs and tucked her into bed. Then she retired to her own room; and having, contrary to the habit of years, stepped out of her clothes without shaking and folding them carefully, she drank the hot posset herself.

Up under the gables, Kate, who since dinner had suffered from one of her queasy spells and from the premonition that she would never get through childbirth in spite of the piece of church-bell rope which Mona had got to tie around her waist, had been given a posset, too. With Sadie coaxed into her bed for company, she had finally fallen asleep.

Will, who had just had a word with Mona in the kitchen, climbed up to his lair above the stable to lie with his gnarled joints cushioned deep in straw, one ear always open for any unusual movement from Bess and Knight and Crede's fat, pensioned pony, Matilda, in their stalls below.

In their loft over the counting room, Ned, Niles, and Bob were cosily eating bread and cheese under their bed covers, for they could always pocket ample provision from Mona's bountiful table against night hunger.

Philip Canynges, who would not be told of Mona's panic now, turned home from Adam Bell's apartment over the warehouse on Quayside with his shadow, Cormac, at his heels, just as candle bell rang for lights out on the ships.

Curfew rang from St. Nicholas by the bridge and outside on Mary le Port Street Timothy Polkhorn passed on his round calling, "Beware your lock, your fire, and your light. And God give you good night."

FIVE

Sun was streaming onto the bed when Mona pulled the curtains back with a rattle meant to waken her. Crede floated to the top of soft miles of sleep.

"I let you sleep in." Mona looked fresh and brisk. "Sup this brewis now, and don't be hiding the bread as you did yesterday, and then get dressed for Kate is not fit to go to market. You can take Sadie to help carry things."

It was fun to go to market, though generally that was Kate's privilege. But this morning Kate's feet were so swollen that she had to sit on a stool in the buttery to churn. Her naturally plump body was growing so heavy that Mona dourly predicted twins, a low sort of thing in her estimation.

"I ought to go," Kate said fretfully. "You don't know the best stalls, Crede."

"I'll manage." Crede ran out the door with Kate's instructions following her and Sadie, though still tongue-tied, plainly thought it a holiday as she skipped along. Crede hummed, "It is full merry in the fair forest," under her breath, her clacking pattens beating their own tune in the lively morning racket of the streets. Anywhere in the street she might meet Anthony. Certainly he would come some time today in a mood to meet her father's friendly fairness, or why else had he lingered last night in Bristol?

The market, sprawling untidily over the quarter just north of Mary

[37]

le Port Street, sucked them into its jostling clamor. All around about it apprentices from nearby shops bawled for trade, boys from Cooks Row near the Bridge peddled eel pies and hot pease puddings, brewers of simples cried their wares, a ballad monger waved the latest sheets at a penny a yard.

Farther along, a one-legged vagabond had set up a wooden Turk's head to be shied at for a farthing. This popular pastime had, as usual, drawn a noisy group to cheer each hit with an enthusiasm which the Church had so far failed to arouse for more effective measures against a desperate threat to Christendom. A militant Mohammedan dictatorship had spread over Asia and Africa and nearly half of Europe, engulfing the ancient Christian Empire of the East, conquering one Christian nation after another, until now the advancing crescent of this mysterious total power stretched from Greece to Poland. Never had the Church preached a crusade with more urgent reason. King Henry's pious mother had vowed that she would go as a washerwoman in the Christian army; but this was as impractical as most of the talk of crusades nowadays, when kings and commons were so busy with other things. While the new discoveries and the New Learning widened their horizon and brought such a revolution of thought and economy as there had not been since Rome was overturned, each kingdom of the west was striving for its own place in the sun and each man for his own chances. They had time only to glance uneasily behind them where the Mediterranean, for ages the bright center of the world, was closing at their backs.

Near the Turk's head, a Pardoner had established himself. But though he offered scrolls with symbols and seals of the Church upon them as talismans against sin, and relics whose virtues he described in a singsong made impressive with tags of Latin, he was collecting fewer pence than his neighbor, and some of his listeners muttered that Christ had scourged from the temple those who would make it a den of thieves. In Bristol, chapter and verse could be fitted to all sorts of mutterings, for copies of Wycliffe's English Bible had been circulated secretly for a hundred years, and Lollardry, England's special contribution to heresies, had merely been driven underground by sporadic burnings. No one was likely to be burned for baiting a Pardoner, however; most loyal Churchmen deplored such barnacle growths, and Crede passed this scene of common occurrence without a second glance.

When they had crossed this idle fringe into the market itself, Sadie's step slowed. With a rapt expression, she drew deep breaths of the scent of sun-warmed straw and feathers, the sour-sweet smell of farm beasts, the earthy savor of fresh-pulled roots and herbs, while her round, shining cheeks grew even redder. She still had nothing to say, however. On any other morning Crede would have been drawn toward livelier company.

[38]

One of the charms of marketing was its social side, but today she did not want to be hemmed in by any of the leisurely groups refreshing themselves with saffron buns and neighborhood news, in case Tony should come seeking her here. She greeted friends as briefly as good manners allowed and passed on with Sadie in tow.

They bought on Mona's orders and Kate's fussy directions which sent them from stall to stall until the basket grew so heavy that they had to set it down. Another overloaded basket came to rest beside it, and Crede had no more than passed the time of day with a neighbor from their own street when she discovered that Sadie was gone.

"That child," she said, "has been sniffing the air like a hound pup for some reason, ever since we got here. And she is so new to town that a pup would do better in a crowd. I'll have to go after her."

Laboring under the basket's weight, she found Sadie at last—rooted motionless before a stall where rabbits were displayed, all but one hanging stiff and long. The exception was very young, a small furry ball in a rushwork cage, as still as the rest except for bright living eyes and twitching nose.

"Sadie, you should not wander off!" Crede began, easing her arms of their burden.

Suddenly Sadie's shoulders shook. Her round face crumpled in an explosion of tears and sobs.

"It will be eaten! Father gave me a baby coney and it was never going to be eaten. This one will be! Oh, don't let them kill it! Don't let them!"

"It shan't be eaten!" Sadie had touched a tender spot in Crede's own experience of the facts of life and they were instantly brought together. Dismissing an apprehension of domestic complications, Crede bargained for the coney. "It is your very own now, Sadie."

Sadie clutched the hamper to her bosom and speech, unlocked at last, came in a torrent. "There were always coneys and chickens in our house, and the farm animals were under the house at night. You could hear them move, and my own coney slept with me. It smells like home here."

She reached a finger through the rushwork to touch the coney's ears and her tear-streaked face turned trustfully to Crede.

Crede's misgivings took form now as a clear vision of Mona's lavender-scented beds. Would it be better to ask someone to keep the coney while she prepared delicately for its reception at home, on some possible compromise with Sadie's hopes? Her eyes, searching the crowd, lit upon Sebastien Cabot.

"Sebastien!" she called hopefully.

He turned and strode toward them, magnificent as always and burdened only by a penny yard of ballads. Surrounded by an overflowing basket with a large dead capon sprawling on its top, a live coney, and

[39]

a tear-streaked child, Crede felt disreputable. He regarded them with some amusement.

"Good morrow, Crede."

"Are you going home soon, Sebastien?"

Sebastien frowned as his attention returned from its indulgent recognition of her to the importance of his own affairs. "I have just time to get to a meeting at Spicer's Hall, Crede. I was right yesterday about Warde's ship. Ignorance and stupid mismanagement—they set a course like a blind duck in a storm. I talked to the seamen at Avonmouth and got a story I want to put straight to our Company of Adventurers into new-found lands!"

Crede's interest showed in her face. Ventures westward always touched her imagination, and she really did believe in Sebastien. Sebastien felt a preference for her on this account, and it brought his mind back to her for a moment.

"By the way, Crede, have you seen Tony Jestyn lately? He was at Avonmouth this morning."

Crede caught her breath, and Sebastien's bright eyes which missed nothing fastened upon her.

"Was it you sent him off looking like thunder? I misdoubt your cousin is in bad company, Crede. Early this morning a boat with young Anthony glowering in the stern was putting out to a ship in the channel. If it is a Jestyn ship out of Cornwall, as I suspect, they are no better than pirates and had the devil's own boldness to come there."

"You—saw the ship sail—with Tony?"

"It picked up the boat and came about very handily. All sails spread down-channel in no time—they're good seamen. Better," Sebastien added bitterly, "than some we send toward Amerike. I must get on to the Hall."

Crede stood suspended from the crowd, suspended even from the puzzle of Sebastien's news, realizing only that Tony had gone. It was the outcome which through most of yesterday she had seen as final. Cousin Allie's opinion had only confirmed her own that events led in a straight road to it. Still she had hoped that last night might have changed their course.

Sadie plucked at her arm. Where they stood was not the busiest part of the market; they were in a backwater of the crowd where an indifferent juggler amused a few loitering apprentices, and a handful of laborers cried their own talents by a hiring post. These were a shiftless remnant of Bristol's unenfranchised population, whose only status came through employment by members of the corporation of guilds, and they happened for one reason or another to be without a master before the regular spring hiring fair in May. What must it be like to stand there, outside the community of neighbors, shouting? Once again a familiar part of the

[40]

life she had always known struck through Crede's preoccupation with sharp strangeness, touching her own disillusion.

"I think it is frightened," Sadie said. "Can we go home now, Mistress Crede?"

"We'll go now." Crede recalled herself determinedly to the problem of the coney. "Will can make your bunny a hutch in the stable, and I'll speak to Mona."

With the basket straining her arms and the cage held tenderly against Sadie's breast, they jostled their way out of the market. In their own lane Sadie exchanged burdens reluctantly.

"Take the market basket in by the kitchen, Sadie, and tell Mistress Mona I have another errand to do."

Will was nowhere about the stable. Old Matilda neighed softly, and Bess naughtily stamped her feet demanding a gallop, while Knight looked hopefully past Crede for Philip. Buttercup, an unfriendly animal though a bountiful milker, merely switched her tail irritably. Crede was afraid to leave the cage within reach of Ginger and Spitfire, the stable cats, so she carried it up to Will's loft and, thrusting in a handful of oats, closed the door upon it.

She felt too restless to go into the house at once. The lane turned back of the stable and wandered behind the gardens of Mary le Port Street with here and there a thatched workman's cottage and here and there a pigsty, before it joined other back lanes. Crede followed these, only occasionally crossing busier streets.

If Tony had not meant to see her again, why had he stayed so long in Bristol yesterday? If, as she had come to think last night, he had not been far from her when she crossed town to Cousin Allie's and had waited for a suitable moment to mend their quarrel, why had he gone away without a word or message for her after saving her life?

Had mere chance brought him near St. Philip's? Had he come to her aid only as he would have done for any stranger and left with his anger unchanged? The fancy that he had been keeping near her must have been no more than glimpses of another tall young man wearing a green cloak, while Anthony was on her mind.

Crede stopped dead in the lane. What more than this had she seen in the near dark of Philip's Field? She had caught a glint of light on a green cloak as her rescuer appeared, and unreasoning instinct had made him Tony. She had clung to that with no more evidence of face or voice than she had of the identity of that other cloaked and hooded figure.

If she had deceived herself then, Crede was even less able now to untangle impressions of confusion and fright and darkness. It might have been some passing stranger who came when a woman screamed for help

[41]

and stepped aside as soon as she was safe with the Watch. Whatever the truth was, it had changed nothing. Some things, even Cousin Allie thought, could not be altered—though they might be alleviated with Greek verbs.

She had crossed Broad Street without noticing, and the lanes led her on to Quayside whose wharves stretched down the Frome toward the Avon with a narrow strip alongside where warehouses clustered against Bristol's north wall.

The space between the line of ships and the line of buildings was as teeming and clamorous as the market, yet it did not so hem her in. Its stir beckoned outward and swept Crede along in the stream of sound and movement that flowed beside the ships. The rhythm of loading and unloading . . . the rumble of barrows and geehoes on the cobbles (for Bristol was so undermined with storage vaults that heavier carts were forbidden on its streets). The scents of spice and wool and leather . . . a blare of song and laughter from a riverside tavern . . . the flat treble of water lapping the hulls, and the brackish smell of the tide . . . the sharp bright note of a foreign face and dress. It was here that Cousin Allie's "knowledge of the world" lessons came alive. Quayside lay open to the whole world—a world in which there was nothing men might not discover, nothing they might not invent. The quarrelsome, ambitious men of the west might lose it all to the total power of the Turk, or with gunpowder now in their reckless hands they might blow it up, but surely it had never before held such dazzling promise.

From the deck of a cog a boy leaped to the quay and landed, light as a cat, at Crede's feet. He had a round freckled face beneath a seaman's red cap, and by his youth she decided he must be a ship's boy, surely on his first voyage. Making her a bow that Anthony could not have bettered—some sprig of a ruined house run off to sea, perhaps—he whispered, "I have a pretty piece of lace in my pocket, Mistress, from Italy."

Lace was one of the latest inventions among the new arts springing so miraculously into being, especially in Italy, and so far Crede had only heard of it. She shook her head regretfully. Half the seamen smuggled under the port's nose, but Philip Canynges' daughter could not buy from them. Turning aside regretfully she almost bumped into Will's nephew, one of the *Brigid*'s crew.

Just going off shore watch, he told her, and she saw him pass the taverns, hurrying home to Billeswick Village. Tom Cousins was a good steady lad, and would spend his time ashore tending his garden and teaching the newest baby to walk.

A sense of being under observation herself drew Crede's eyes to a ship which lay beside the young smuggler's. She saw a three-masted carvel, fresh with yellow paint above the black hull, with a gilded pelican for figurehead, but she could see no sign of life aboard except the back of a man disappearing into the aftercastle. Moving on where Tom Cousins had told her the *Brigid* lay waiting to clear customs, she found her between an Oporto wine hulk and Philip's Dublin ketch. The *Brigid*'s deck was still unencumbered by porters as she waited proudly to discharge the cargo with which she had outsailed rivals and pirates and storms. She had been given Crede's own second name and launched on her saint's day. She was a beauty, Crede thought lovingly—a brig, more than three beams long, with the lower, slimmer lines and taller masts which gave speed, and, even at the end of a long voyage, clean kept. Crede knew most of her crew, but not the man on watch who was the only one about and, after admiring her for a while, she turned back the way she had come. She had wandered here in mere discontent, but Quayside was putting its old spell upon her. She began to walk more briskly and to look about her with interest.

As she passed the yellow carvel again, a seaman loitering alone on its deck called softly, "Mistress Canynges!"

He was only a long step from her, and she could look directly into his face. It was nowhere in her memory, and yet it was uncommon enough not to be forgotten.

"Mistress Canynges, when you passed here before, I heard your name. It is a good name in Bristol, and I thought a stranger might make bold to ask advice."

He was extremely odd looking. A black patch covered one eye and half the cheek, and what could be seen of his skin between a tangle of black hair which straggled below a red woollen cap and fell untidily over a swath of green neckcloth looked too dark to be English. Yet he was speaking English as if born to it—and born above the rough seaman's smock he wore. Crede's curiosity was aroused, and under its stimulus she was as apt to be lost to other considerations as Cousin Allie. The swarthy, mutilated face did not seem sinister to her; for some reason its singular ugliness disturbed her no more than the horns and tail attached to Timothy Polkhorn in miracle plays.

"I have a few rare things from abroad, Mistress—"

She might have expected it. Crede laughed and turned to walk on.

"I saw you refuse the young lad, but I'm not smuggling," he said quickly. Then, while Crede waited, he hesitated until she thought that he had given up his purpose, whatever it was, and she felt oddly let down. "I—hoped you might be so kind as to advise me how such things can be traded honestly here," he said finally.

An innocent surely, or else he had never before needed to consider the rules of trade.

"I am afraid"—Crede found herself apologizing as if any sensible person could have hoped otherwise—"that foreigns may sell here only according to strict rules after port dues have been assessed. All overseas trade, even among Bristol freemen, is supervised by the Merchant Venturers Company who have leased the port dues. It is not likely that you could get a license to sell separately from your shipmaster's cargo but, if you could, your goods would have to be approved and valued in Spicer's Hall on The Back, before anyone could buy them. And my father is not one of the Company."

"The things I brought from Antwerp can scarcely be valued by the bale or cask."

Antwerp! He had wares from that fabulous market, center of all the new trade. Even Portugal and Spain, fortunate possessors of the new sea routes east and west, measured the value of their goods from the docks and banking houses of the great port on the Scheldt, as once caravan and river routes to the Mediterranean had been measured from Venice. Yet Bristol ships had traded for ages, except coastwise, westward; and for most of them this new hub of commerce was still off course.

"If I might show you some, Mistress Canynges—"

Crede decided she could indulge her curiosity safely for she was within hailing distance of dozens along Quayside whom she knew. Picking up her skirts she jumped to the deck with the ease of long practice and looked about her. The rigging was as spruce as the paintwork, and the deck was notably clean—a tidy ship, however queer its watchman. He set up a keg for her beside the forecastle with something of an air and then, bending his height awkwardly in its low entrance, disappeared inside. His likeness to Timothy Polkhorn's easing his bulk through the stage trap door into hell made Crede smile, and she waited for him to pop out again with an anticipation of pleasure as in the moment of expectation before a play.

He was back at once with a bundle tied loosely in a kerchief and, squatting on the deck, he unrolled it at her feet like a peddler's pack. It was a queer assortment for a sailor's trading: parchment scrolls, a small book bound in leather, and he held up a necklace which trickled through his fingers like drops of new honey.

"From the rude north beyond the Baltic, Mistress, but see how finely wrought."

His voice had become a peddler's singsong. Crede looked at him curiously, but her mood was not to question, only to enjoy the diversion. She took the necklace from him and found it as light as sunshine and as warm as if his hand touched hers.

"Fairy gold without weight—and amber is a name that sings like a seashell," she said. "The names of costlier gems end sharp cut—except, of course, the loveliest of all."

[44]

"Which seem to you the loveliest of all, Mistress?"

"Pearls," Crede said without hesitation. "And the sea gives us those too."

"You know then that the sea casts this up. There is an old tale that it holds within it the souls of heathen tree nymphs, drowned in the Flood. The Greeks called it electron and found a mystery in it—look!" He pulled a thread from his disreputable sleeve and laid it across Crede's hands as he took the bauble from her. Then he rubbed it hard on his sleeve and when he let it swing against her hand the thread leaped to meet it.

Such mysteries were more apt to be part of the New Learning than of witchcraft, Cousin Allie had assured her. Crede did not cross herself but cried eagerly, "How did you do it?"

"You don't think the devil is in it, Mistress Canynges? Neither do I. But to know what strange life is there I would give—nothing I have to give," he ended flatly. He dropped the necklace and picked up the next thing his hand touched.

"The Gospels in Greek, printed from an older manuscript than the Latin by Aldus Manutius of Venice who got it from a scholar escaped out of Constantinople." He had returned to his peddler's glibness. "But I have other wares to interest a lady more."

"Why shouldn't women care about the New Learning?" Crede said tartly. "The King's own mother studies Greek."

Reaching for the book she opened it upon the beautiful, puzzling letters. When she looked up at length the man was watching her, but whether his one eye expressed respect or amusement was hard to say, for it was the blank, black patch one noticed most. She flushed suddenly. "It was silly of me to pretend. Cousin Allie's Greek is—mostly his own invention, I suppose."

She closed the little book whose cover had been tooled with patient, loving craftsmanship and accepted the square of parchment he unrolled. A needlework pattern, she thought at first, and then she knew that these forms could never be caught in silks. The sheet was covered with sketches of butterflies, so quick and fluid that they seemed alive, as if some mysterious essence of butterfly hovered there. She could not take her eyes from them.

"Don't you like it, Mistress?"

"It's—magic."

"Yet the artist must have been disappointed in it. Leonardo of Florence threw it away, and a pupil picked it up to sell. Do you know of him?"

"Leonardo of Florence?" Crede laughed and broke the spell. "Chiefly that he cost my cousin a broken leg with talk of men flying. A friend who has sailed to those parts says that he has Florence bewitched even for a town that honors painters above other artisans, and people of all sorts line up outside his shop to look at a new picture. But he must turn his mind to a number of things besides."

"To everything, I think. Music, and building, and machines—there are rumors that he has said the sun does not move around the earth and that Creation, because of signs in the rocks, must have taken longer than six days. It is to be hoped the Church loves his paintings too much to give ear to the things he says. I saw one of his paintings on the wall of a monastery in Milan, and there can be nothing on earth—" He broke off abruptly and said, "Now here is a pretty thing, Mistress."

Was he a runaway monk, perhaps, Crede wondered; certainly he had not always been a common seaman. Cousin Allie would be interested to hear about the rocks, and searching for signs in them seemed safer than some of Leonardo's other ideas. But whatever the painter's crotchets might be, it was this carelessly discarded sketch which fascinated her most, and she put it down with reluctance to examine the next offering.

This was a small painting of the Madonna, so glowing with life that Crede, who was used to a conventional stiffness in religious pictures, caught her breath with pleasure. Even in the curve of the sleeve there was love; the warm, human roundness of the arm said that life on this earth was good, and the painter had lovingly and reverently put this into it and been content.

"The other—Leonardo—saw more of mystery even in butterflies," she said slowly. "But how beautiful this is! Is it from Florence, too?"

"From some town in Italy, I think, though it is not marked, and I got it in Antwerp where South and North and East and West all crowd to market now. Antwerp would take your breath away, Mistress, even if you have seen Thames Side at London. It is the center of the seaways."

"Perhaps the real center lies farther west." Crede looked jealously along Bristol's thronging river. "Perhaps Amerike which the Cabots and Master Thorne found no end of in many days of sailing is greater than Spain's new-found islands off Ind, and Bristol has always traded westward. We have always thought that there was a great new land far west, not part of Ind or Cathay, but a new world. My father—"

How had she been carried along from an idle moment's diversion into turning her mind out as she might to Philip or Cousin Allie? With mention of her father she had been recalled to herself and to Mistress Canynges' kindly purpose toward a chance-met oddity.

"We are forgetting your wares," she said in a business-like manner. "I don't know how you could trade in them here yourself, and my father does not deal in such things. But Master Bell has an arrangement to bring in light goods of various sorts for his own profit, and he may be able to tell you how to present them at Spicer's Hall. If you wish, say that

I sent you and ask anywhere along Quayside for Master Adam Bell of the *Brigid*."

She was rising to go but felt her skirts pinned firmly to the deck. As she looked behind her a large black cat uncurled itself, stretched gracefully, and stepped unhurriedly off. Crede had never before seen such a cat, with long silky fur and a tail as bushy as a fox's brush. It sat down on the deck and regarded her with equal interest and more composure, its incredible tail curled neatly about its toes and its amber eyes unblinking. Then it came forward with an air of gracious condescension and rubbed lightly against her ankles.

"Tasia has made one of her choices, Mistress Canynges. The unchosen can't get near her."

Crede stroked the soft fur. "Tasia? What an odd, pretty name."

"She joined the ship once at Antwerp with a foreign of wandering bent, an Easterner of some sort, who left it later."

"Prmph?" Tasia said and bounded away from them to disappear below deck.

"She has remembered her kittens and wants to show them off. May I bring them?"

Crede forgot that she had been in the act of leaving. She knelt on the deck between two fat balls of fluff, one black, one silver, which Tasia captured alternately and washed with anxious scoldings. The black one bit its parent's ear and escaped behind a coil of rope, squealing triumph.

"They are growing up. She is to keep one, but a home must be found for the other."

"Which one?" Crede scarcely dared ask. The one that was soft gray with faint dark stripes marking its tiny face as gaily as a pansy's had anchored its needle-like claws in her skirt and fixed its slate blue eyes on hers with complete assurance, as it gravely considered the climb upwards. She picked it up, and it settled contentedly against her.

"Which one would you keep?"

"I'd keep— Oh, I want this one myself! What would you—what would your shipmaster take for it?"

"They are Tasia's. She could not possibly sell a child, could you, Tasia? But I'm allowed to help her establish it in life, and she has already approved of you, Mistress Canynges. If you'd like to keep it you will be doing a favor."

He was carelessly but with an odd air of authority choosing to put it that way, although the favor would be to her, for he must see how much she wanted to keep this furry atom now burrowing confidingly into her shoulder. Yet, however much his speech and manner seemed above his station, Mistress Canynges could afford to pay for a whim what would seem riches to a deck hand. She prefered to pay lavishly and feel herself the generous one. Why then should she hesitate to thrust a coin into his hand? But she could not do it. This questioning of the natural order of things which troubled her lately made it seem that only the horridest purse pride could choose to set the terms.

"I will be good to it," she said and bent to stroke Tasia. "And—I thank you very much."

The last Crede saw before Quayside swept her along in its bustle was a large, swarthy seaman holding a large, elegant, black cat. Tasia was bearing this departure of her kitten with an air of complete equanimity. An odd pair! To lose sight of them and to be caught back into the familiar rhythm of Quayside was like coming home from some outlandish parts.

But the kitten was tucked warmly inside Crede's cloak. What Mona will say I daren't imagine, she thought, reminded guiltily of the coney in the stable. What had possessed her to add a Noah's ark to the present tangle of her own affairs? A coney to set the world right for Sadie and a kitten for me, she thought—an echo of her father's wry humor which, for all their likenesses, she had not expected to share.

The kitten, disturbed by the press about them, turned into a thorny little burr. Crede had to pluck it from her shoulder, squirming with such agility that she almost dropped it. If it got free here it might be lost or trampled. Clutching it desperately she ran toward her father's warehouse.

The warehouse overlooked Quayside near the *Brigid*'s mooring and had been Philip Canynges' first house. Now the ground floor over the storage vaults was used as a workshop for craftsmen who kept the ships repaired while the hall, giving entrance to the solar above it which was Adam Bell's home ashore, had become an informal sort of meeting place for Philip's Quayside associates. It seemed full of people now, and Crede hurried past its open door into the workshop, relaxing her hold on the kitten which promptly tore through a pile of shavings and swarmed up Hugh Warden's leg. She knew all the men here, and all of them stopped work with pleased interest except old Tim Arden. Tim always sulked for days after the *Brigid* came home and drove the men under him mercilessly because every scratch on the ship which was his pride threw him into a temper; he would have liked to keep the *Brigid* always in the shipyards on the Marsh, Adam said, polishing and petting her. He nodded crossly to Crede and went on smoothing a plank while Hugh captured the kitten and held it up for inspection.

"A little champion, Mistress Crede," he said, sucking a bitten finger.

"Can you find me a basket to carry it home in, Hugh?"

"Find a basket, young Jock, and a piece of sailcloth to tie over it." Hugh held his captive in his great hands, examining it curiously. "Wooliest one I've ever seen. It'll puzzle Mistress O'Colum to keep the fleas out of that!"

A slow smile spread across his broad face. Mona's passionate feud with vermin, smells, and dirt complicated the lives, human and animal, within her reach but was wholly diverting to those just safely outside it.

Crede stroked the kitten gently, and it quieted, choosing her again with a confidence which rude events had only momentarily shaken. Through all its trials it had not cried. When it was put into a basket it heaved the cloth stormily for a moment, then subsided as Crede laid her hand over it. She could feel the tense little body relax and curl trustingly under her fingers, and felt herself sharing some of its reassurance. With the basket on her arm she stepped out into Quayside and face to face with her father.

She had not seen him since her unmannerly escape from dinner yesterday, but he made no reference to it though his smile was the teasing one which sent his left eyebrow up comically.

"We might walk home together if you will wait five minutes," he said. "Come into the hall with me. There is a sort of meeting I have to look in on."

SIX

The men in the hall were well known to Crede—a few shipmasters of superior dignity and substance like Adam Bell, and the rest prosperous merchants among whom Master Robert Thorne, cousin of the London Thornes, stood first. From the discussion in progress it appeared that most of them had come here from the meeting at Spicer's Hall, a smaller group of the more adventurous overseas traders. Several of them had an interest in this last voyage westward and were disturbed by its ill success. Of course they were nettled by Sebastien Cabot's criticisms.

Master Thorne, standing a little apart by the window with the light falling across his broad shoulders, moved them impatiently.

"Sebastien crows overloud for a young cock and is hard to get on with," he said, "but he should have been listened to more patiently. We need someone to remind us of the greatness of the venture. What matter that pounds damage has been done a ship and that there will be other losses, if we lose not, by sitting back, what we have gained already? We know the land is there. For ages we guessed it, and now more than one of us has seen it. And some of us know that it is greater than all the old tales

[49]

of it." He paused, looking out the window as if his eyes saw beyond Quayside and confirmed his words.

"When Hugh Elliot and I first glimpsed its coastline," he said thoughtfully, "some sense of untouched vastness so frightened the crew that we were forced to turn back, as you know. Later when we sailed coastwise with John Cabot from our first northern landfall into the warm south, we proved that it is no mere island we hold King Henry's patent for, unless it is a bigger island than England. Our ships which have sailed since and found Amerike too bleak should have searched farther along it. Perhaps we may discover a passage around it to the East that will bring us a trade as rich as Spain and Portugal have found. Perhaps we may find in Amerike itself so much good land that every landless man whose acre has been swallowed in sheep runs may plough his own field again. Though I am a trader I would risk something to find that too. I am ready to put up a fourth part of what we need for another voyage."

Someone began to speak of costs, but Crede's fancy had soared with Robert Thorne's. If only I could go! she thought—and she saw her father's face. He too would like to sail westward, without caring whether there's a profit in it, she thought in a flash of love and understanding. He would like some venture to call to him now for its own sake and find him free to follow.

She had supposed that only the young felt so, restless before the promise of the world, its chances beckoning to them. Then she remembered that her father's youth had been far different from her own. While she, who had grown up in the security of his success, could imagine a world spread wide for choice before her, her father had never been free. If I were settled in marriage, she thought, with someone he trusts to carry on what he has worked to build for me—or if I were a son and could be learning, myself, to give him some freedom now—

Master Elliot and Master Assehurst, in whose names the latest patent was held, both said they were ready to back another voyage this year, and Master Thomas said he would risk something again if enough others went into it, and Sheriff Richard Amerike offered to subscribe ten pounds.

"An exact reckoning," Philip Canynges said in Crede's ear. "That was the first reward Richard paid out of King Henry's customs when John Cabot found the new land. He will risk the same from his own purse now in memory of his friend John who named the new land for him. What should other stay-at-homes risk, I wonder, for an island which Robert says is greater than all England?"

There was an unusual note of mockery in her father's voice, and Crede thought that it was not directed against good-natured Richard Amerike.

Philip turned suddenly and spoke to the room. "I should like the *Brigid* to sail westward once."

It brought all their eyes upon him. Nothing in Bristol could outsail the *Brigid,* and no ship they might send to search the long coast of Amerike could cover more miles or pick her way more nimbly in strange waters; but no man had cared yet to send the pride of his fleet to be battered on that voyage. Crede glanced across the hall toward Adam Bell, who stood stiff with anger for a moment and then broke into speech.

"Are you mad, Philip? What trade route will you find better than those the *Brigid* sails—or ship to sail those better?"

"You have no wish to go, Adam?"

"I have not." Adam's face reddened, but not because anyone might dare to question Adam Bell's seamanship or courage. "And no wish to have someone else mishandle the *Brigid.* No one else has ever sailed her, and no one else, saving yourself, Philip, has a right to."

"That's fair, Adam, and you have a right to say it." There was no resentment in Philip's voice, and he smiled across the room toward his friend. "If I do not offer the *Brigid,*" he said slowly, "I will put what would be an equal risk in the venture when we draw up our plans."

But they were far enough from that yet. So soon after a disappointment, the discussion kept turning to losses and risks and the lack, so far, of any gains. Some were leaving.

"We may as well go home too," Philip said. "They will get no farther this morning."

Out on Quayside, he reached to take Crede's basket. "Have you been carrying your marketing all around town, child?"

"Let me keep it." The kitten was still remarkably quiet. "Father, a seaman alongside here had to find a home for a kitten, and I took it. It's not to be a kitchen cat! I want to keep it with me even at night—but you know what Mona is, and there is the coney to upset her, besides."

Philip laughed. "Mona has ideas no one else ever heard of. Why shouldn't you have cats and dogs in your room and your bed if you want to? But a coney—did you say a coney too?"

"The coney is for Sadie. It's the one thing her heart was set on."

"If all that Sadie lacks is a coney, let us get her a dozen," Philip said airily.

But Mona would not be won over so easily, Crede knew. She had a more important matter on her mind just now, however. Before she could speak of it they were hailed from behind and her cousin, Stephen Chalkraft, caught up with them.

"I left my horse in your stable, Philip," he said. "Good morrow, Crede."

Stephen always stayed for dinner when he rode in from the country, and he walked along with them now as a matter of course, while they made their way to the center of town. Bristol's four main streets, each running from a gate and a church, met at the High Cross in a carfax made imposing by the handsome cross, three fine churches, the Moot Bell, and the Tolzey Courthouse. It was crowded, as usual at this time of day.

Stephen bowed to a number of those who greeted them, for he was becoming well known in Bristol. His was a figure to notice among townsmen; although he dressed with the sober richness of a prosperous burgher far beyond his years, his huge frame still seemed made for heavy work and moved with the patient slowness of generations behind the plow. But in Stephen the light blue Chalkraft eye was quickened by more than a peasant's shrewdness. Crede found him tiresome, for he could talk about nothing except his own success.

This had been considerable. His father had farmed as Chalkrafts had done for generations, clinging to his small freehold at the Cotswold edge and selling the fleeces from his few sheep to agents of the Staple who led their pack horses through the hills collecting the best wool in Christendom. The Merchants of the Staple had been content to sell it from their headquarters in Calais to the looms of the Continent, and for ages the symbol of England's wealth had been the woolsack. Now it was the cloth bale, with English cloth bringing top prices abroad. Agents of the cloth merchants scoured the hills now, collecting fleeces, carrying them to cottage spinners, cottage weavers, and to the fulling and dyeing villages along the streams that ran down to Severn. A dozen new profits with part of all of them in the hands of these great merchant capitalists (a new word for a new development) brought wealth and power to England but disturbed the old order of town and countryside.

The new wealth of the great clothiers was going into bigger workshops, most of whose apprentices would not rise past journeymen to set up for themselves as masters and freemen of their guild. Capital was going into bigger sheep farms and managing to enclose the grazing commons upon which small farmers had always depended. It seemed that fewer men could hope now to work for themselves, and the shift of those uprooted was toward the towns whose growth alarmed their corporations. In hovels outside their walls, masterless men lived precariously or took to beggary and worse on the roads, crying out that a man was of less account now than a sheep.

But Stephen had seen a better chance than this for himself in the changing order. He had begun to wash and card and spin his fleeces on his own farm, a weaver's cottage appeared on it, the magic of capital began growing in his hand to increase his land and his flock, to build more cottages. Today Chalkraft of Dalewood Farm, which he was beginning to call Dalewood Manor, could talk on equal terms with most Bristol merchants, and was talking with Philip now of cloth markets and the rising price of everything.

"I settled for a fulling mill this morning, Philip. Now all the profits will stay on Dalewood, from fodder to fleece, and fleece to finished cloth."

"Soon you will be buying ships to carry it abroad and ruining us on Quayside, Stephen."

"No," Stephen said slowly, "I'll leave ships to you. But we might do well together, Philip. We might think that over."

They had reached Mary le Port Street, and Crede separated from them, hurrying down the lane toward the stable; for the coney, which she had left far too long unexplained, was now uppermost in her thoughts. Will was puttering about the stableyard and greeted her with a slow wink of one pale eye which wrought a startling transformation in the stubborn, weather-hardened mask of his face.

"Sadie's had a word with me," he said. "She said that you're into this with her and wants me to see to it without bothering Mistress Mona."

Sadie had found not only the power of speech but a resource and daring almost incredible.

"That child do be kept down too much," Will said. "But one corner that Mistress Mona don't get to with her besom and dust clout is my stable and my bit of a place over it. The coney is up there now with a leaf or so of my own greens, till I build her a hutch and a run."

"I knew we could depend on you, Will."

"Why did you have to pick a she?" Will said grumpily. "Trouble in dozens, that is."

But unless Will could foresee trouble he was seldom interested. Crede heaved a sigh of relief and hurried into the kitchen. She could hear the voices of Mona and Kate in the stillroom and knew she should have been back long ago to help with the morning's work. For the last two days she had behaved quite irresponsibly. Instead of calling to them, however, she filled a bowl from the cream pan in the buttery and ran upstairs to her own room. She set the basket on the sunny window seat and unfastened the cover.

The kitten was such a baby still that, given a little closed place of its own, it had curled up and slept off its alarms. It blinked in the sunlight, stretched itself, and stepped cautiously out of the basket. Testing the window seat and finding it reassuringly solid, it risked its weight upon it and then climbed onto Crede's lap, its first favorable impression of her persisting. She dipped her fingers into the cream and let the kitten lick them first, then discover the bowl. It lapped daintily and then cleansed itself with ritualistic fervor; though so tiny and so young it had tradition behind it. This made its trust more flattering, its weakness more touching. Crede left it still washing up in the sun and latched the door behind her.

There was nothing to do, Mona said, for there was a good dinner from yesterday's leavings, fine enough even for Master Stephen Chalkraft of Dalewood Manor, so Crede had best go into the hall and help her father listen to him.

But Stephen was less talkative than usual. When dinner came he ate through its courses with the inattention to fine cookery which annoyed Mona, but his knife was not, as usual, drawing plans of new additions to Dalewood on her good linen cloth. It was Philip who found subjects of conversation, gathering them here and there from the variety of things which interested him casually and burying them deftly when they died. If he had anything more serious on his mind that was buried too. Stephen left immediately after the meal.

"I have plenty to see to at home before dark," he said. "And what we talked of, Philip, will bear sleeping on. No bones broken either way."

"What ever ails Stephen?" Crede asked when the door had closed upon him.

"Nothing more than the chances of trade, I hope." Philip wiped his fingers carefully and got up from the table. "A good trader knows his own worth and when not to press it."

"I have just remembered there was a message from Master Thorne," Mona said blandly, as if her memory ever mislaid anything. "Master Thorne and Master Robin Thorne are calling this afternoon. But Crede and I ought to be at St. Mary's helping with plans for the church ale."

This popular social event was not in the immediate future and Crede had heard nothing about it yet. "I don't really need to go this afternoon," she said honestly.

Mona regarded her thoughtfully. When Crede got up to help Sadie clear the table, she waved her aside and said, "Go up and rest and tidy yourself, child. All you've done for two days is traipse about the town, and you look no credit to your father's house." Then, instead of waiting to see that Sadie cleared properly and broke nothing, she turned toward the stairs herself.

She still chose, sometimes, to supervise Crede's dressing and see that her hair was brushed properly. In any case, her introduction to the kitten could not have been long postponed. When Crede opened the door there was a small flurry in the fireplace and it emerged covered with ashes.

"Holy St. Brigid!" Mona crossed herself. "What has come down the chimney?"

Crede picked the kitten up and dusted it off, and it settled comfortably in her arms.

"I got it from a sailor on Quayside, Mona, and I want it for my own, not for a kitchen cat."

[54]

"A kitten, is it?" Mona approached cautiously. "It's like no Christian cat's. Some of those ships come from queer parts."

"Isn't it pretty?" Crede stroked the long silvery fur, and the kitten studied Mona gravely, retaining its touching composure. It began to purr.

"Um—" Mona said. She appreciated poise. "I dare say you should have a pet if you want it. You can get some cream from the buttery and feed it here," she added surprisingly. "It's too young to get on with Ginger and Spitfire."

Still more surprisingly she took it into her own hands and examined it with interest. Fortunately the kitten behaved extremely well and did not bite her as it had done to Hugh. But when restored to Crede it settled back with open satisfaction, rasping its little pink tongue across her hand. Its choice had been made this morning.

"You will have to comb her regularly," Mona said. "I'll make a mixture for fleas too—all that fur."

Crede burst out laughing. Yet Mona's forbearance had been equal to all that fur and more than anything else this seemed the measure of her recent indulgences. She set the kitten down on her bed and kissed Mona.

"Get your things off now," Mona said, "and wash your face and comb your hair if you mean to see visitors."

She rummaged in the chest and took out a gown which she had helped Crede to make of a soft blue wool. It was rather plain, but Mona liked it particularly.

"You draggled your new dress badly yesterday. Besides it is too fine," she said, and spreading the blue wool on the chest went into her own room.

Crede dressed between playing with the kitten which was making mountains and valleys of the mysterious softness of the bed and romping among them in a joyful frenzy. Soon Mona came to say that the guests had arrived and helped to tie the points of the gown, hurrying her and seeming, if such a thing could ever be said of Mona, almost fussy.

Mona doesn't need to fear I shall forget my manners again, Crede thought. Since yesterday she had taken stock of many things and felt immeasurably older. Today nothing could surprise her into the childish rudeness of running from Master Thorne, and she was rather curious to see his son whose manners with regard to calling or not calling seemed unpredictable, to say the least.

There was no one in the hall, and Crede went on to the green parlor. Coming down from its gallery while their guests waited below with her father gave her time to satisfy any curiosity she had felt about the new one.

What did Father see in him? she thought—for Robin Thorne, apart from his height, looked entirely commonplace. He was as big as Anthony, but the comparison which this suggested was not in his favor, for he had not grown up to his height with Anthony's grace, and he looked all bones still although he must be a year or two older. To make comparison still less fortunate, he was wearing green, which became Tony so well but which bleached his light coloring.

He made her a good enough bow and Master Thorne, looking steadier and more cheerful than yesterday, kissed her and said, "I hope you are not going to run away today, my dear," laughing as if they were on teasing terms.

By recalling her bad manners he was making her feel like an awkward child, when she particularly wanted to be composed and gracious. But, taking a desperate grip on Mona's teaching, she said, "I was sorry to—have to leave yesterday, sir. Father and I have been looking forward to a longer visit today."

She met her father's eyes approvingly on her and then, remembering that they were all still standing, sat down rather abruptly.

The men picked up their drinks, and Philip brought Crede a cup of mild hippocras. Master Thorne raised his cup.

"To Canynges and Thornes—an old friendship! But upon my word, Philip, it makes me feel ancient to have our young ones grown up and drinking it with us."

"Well, I don't feel ancient," Philip said easily. "And yet, I can remember back to early days in the Wars of the Roses! I can just remember young Edward of York, the year he seized the crown, visiting Cousin William at the Red House. Cousin William was mayor that year and had raised the town for York. But it seems only yesterday, Gilbert, that you and I were playing on Quayside and slipping away from the Black Canon's school to hang around the shipyards by the Marsh."

"Boasting that we'd own a ship some day. We have each done better than that, and now—"

"Do you remember," Philip said, "the time we made off with a skiff from the shipyard and were nearly drowned on the Ledges? We scrambled ashore at Ghyson Rock like wet rats and spent the night in Giant's Cave with the mad old hermit of St. Vincent. And when we got home we found there had been a grand fire in Bristol, and we had missed it."

Master Thorne nodded. "That was the night the Kalendars' Library and half the town records burned," he said, "and we got a penny between us for finding scraps in the ashes. When Robert Ricart was made town clerk he sorted everything out to begin the new Kalendar—and kept it for half a lifetime, and now is dead."

He leaned back against the settle savoring his wine appreciatively.

"Do you remember, Gilbert, the day a Welsh ship poked its mast

[56]

through the Bridge into the cellar of Master Carson's shop, and his pig fell into the Avon? We all swam after it—"

It was unlike Philip, with his lively interest in present events, to look back garrulously upon his life. Crede had only the vaguest idea of his boyhood. But he seemed to want to keep the conversation in the past, a past as long forgotten as the Wars of the Roses, so remote from this modern age and their immediate problems that Crede lost her self-consciousness and listened and watched with detachment.

Robin Thorne was watching his father intently. When Master Thorne relaxed further and, looking surprisingly younger, said, chuckling, "Do you remember, Phil?" his son smiled as if something had pleased him greatly.

Robin Thorne did not look in need of Cousin Allie's compassion. Nothing in the firm lines of mouth and chin suggested that he pitied himself for giving up his precious law; and though he must have been dragged here today by his horrid old father after refusing to come yesterday he did not seem at all on the defensive. Crede's attention fastened curiously upon him for a moment while she tried, with an open-mindedness Cousin Allie could have approved, to discover what her father had admired in him. At first sight he had seemed to her awkwardly overgrown with Tony's fine carriage still to learn; but his face was well composed—Tony's was easier read. Perhaps he isn't just pushed around, she thought. Perhaps he chooses whatever he does. But she could not come to any conclusion about him except that he made up his mind to his own satisfaction and that he seemed honestly fond of his father, was anxious about him, and thankful now to see him enjoy something.

By rambling on at such a rate her father had managed to take the old man's mind off his troubles and obsessions. Master Thorne was doing the talking now, in a lively manner.

"Do you remember, Phil, when William Botoner would pay us ha'-penny to hold his line while he measured all round Bristol? In those days ha'penny spent at a cookhouse would fill even a boy's stomach. It won't buy much now," he added as if he wanted to know where to lay the blame for this, "what with wool fourteen shillings a tod and wheat over two shillings a bushel and going up still along with everything else. Well, we both have more ha'pence fortunately. We took the right chances, you and I. Now, when I choose, I can afford a small chance without worrying. I have a mind to try shipping Cotswold cloth, Phil."

"I thought you were already shipping it."

"Some, of course. But we pay the clothiers their London price for it. If we could make a small connection of our own between farms and villages hereabouts, we might do better."

"You might," Philip said, giving it his consideration. "I get some from

[57]

a cousin near Dursley and a friend in Stroud, but the most we ship comes from clothiers in Bristol. In the Cotswold market towns you find agents of the big clothiers everywhere—yet some chances must slip through their fingers when all is growing so fast."

He spoke then of a ride he had taken lately from Chipping Sodbury to Stroud and made his picture of the outspreading sheep runs, the busy Stroudwater cloth villages, and the prosperous market towns with their handsome new stone houses and guildhalls, the picture of a changing world.

"I may let Robin come back to look over the ground when our summer trade has slackened," Master Thorne said thoughtfully, "since the idea was his and took him hard this morning. He is learning my business so fast," he added complacently, "that already he has plans of his own to better it. Well, it will all be his, some day. We may have to be ready sooner than we think, Philip, to trust younger hands than our own—we both have to face that."

"You and I aren't tottering yet, Gilbert," Philip replied with a smile.

"Father's sea legs are much steadier than mine, anyhow," Robin Thorne said quickly. "When we sail for Dublin tomorrow—"

Crede looked up in sudden relief and was disconcerted to find him watching her. Their glances met for an instant, long enough for her to discover that his eyes were an unusually deep blue and held some amusement within them which he seemed offering to share.

"Tomorrow morning," he said. "I could wish myself safe home now. Father sails too fast in the teeth of any wind for a new hand."

"What nonsense, Robin! I've never seen anyone take to a ship's ways more naturally than you've done on this voyage. And as for hurrying us, it was you, this morning—"

But his son had now managed to draw his attention to the hour-glass, and he got to his feet reluctantly, explaining that Cousin Robert Thorne expected them for supper.

Their farewells were made rather hastily then. And this also, Crede noticed, was the younger Thorne's doing. While her father took their guests to the door she was left with a confusing mixture of impressions. Philip returned and sat down on the couch beside her.

"Well," he said, his eyes twinkling, "Robin seems to have spared me the trouble of handling Gilbert."

He had indeed. Neither his father nor common politeness had brought Master Robin Thorne calling yesterday. Today he had chosen to satisfy his curiosity and then to get out of Bristol on the first tide. And I believe, Crede thought, remembering a hint of secret amusement, that he made it his concern to assure me of that. Perhaps he thought that her father was enough like his own to need managing.

"I don't think we had to be so gentle with him," she said crossly. "I think he is horrid."

"I warned you that Gilbert isn't like himself, dear. Perhaps he has always thought too much about his own success and so cares too much about handing it on, but he is not a harsh man even now. After all, he gives Robin some rope."

Fortunately they need not concern themselves any longer with the whims of either Thorne, and if Crede felt slightly ruffled still it was merely because she had found the younger one's manners even more objectionable than his father's. She was much relieved that he had said nothing about calling on them again whenever the schemes he had in mind about Cotswold cloth brought him back this way.

"Master Thorne isn't a bit like you," she said. "Nobody in the world has a father like mine."

"You are more trouble lately than I counted on." Philip laughed and put his arm around her, and she settled comfortably against it. "What do you think Stephen was working around to this morning?"

"Some new profit, of course. I thought that he wanted to make a bargain with you to go shares in something."

"He did. And Stephen likes to bind a bargain. Do you want to be mistress of Dalewood Manor?"

"Father!" Crede sat up straight.

"Didn't I say you are a worry to me?"

"It's not me, it's your old ships! I suppose they are the latest improvement Stephen has thought of adding to Dalewood."

Stephen was not alone in thinking that those ships would work in well with his own business, she decided. Robin Thorne must have come here today to see whether they were worth the price. Tony was the only one who had never cared about them.

"I hoped that your heart would not be set on Stephen." Philip's left eyebrow curved upward. "Shall we burn the ships and have no more of these troubles?"

"Father, I'd like to learn to be some use to you. If I could learn to help you like a son, everybody would not think you needed one so badly."

"But I don't." Philip tightened his arm around her. "I wouldn't change you for ten sons, Kitten."

"I think I could be nearly as good as one," Crede said earnestly. She had been considering what she wanted to say since morning and got it out quickly now. "You know I have always been around Quayside and the counting house with you, and Cousin Allie says that I am quite good at figures. Father, I could learn fast—I truly could—and be a help to you. You wouldn't have to work so hard."

"You haven't let Gilbert frighten you into thinking your tough old parent is feeble?"

"No! You aren't like him, Father—you are young! But you have been so tied down always. I want you to have more freedom—for things you would like to do. And I want to work with you."

Philip's face softened. Even in their closest moments Crede had never seen it without the slight detachment which seemed part of him, and when he spoke his voice had lost its accustomed lightness.

"If you want to learn my trade, dear, I shall be prouder to teach you than I have ever been of anything. We'll begin tomorrow."

Crede leaned back happily against his shoulder, and her mind began to busy itself with tomorrow. She meant to make him really proud of how quickly she could learn. And Philip seemed content to sit without talking, looking into the fire. Their comfortable silences together, when the thoughts of each could go on from a word spoken without needing to explain all its meaning, were the best things they shared.

She could learn quickly, she knew. From the time she could walk she had been at Philip's heels in the warehouse and workshop and counting room, hearing talk of markets and goods, of prices and costs and dues and what gave a fair profit. She knew a great deal about her father's business already, and working with him would be so pleasant for them both that she wondered why they had not thought of it sooner. In a short time he would be able to trust her for long enough to make a voyage westward if he chose, something he must have felt himself too closely tied here to do, something she could give him.

Watching the log whiten and sparks crawl over it like columns of slow-moving ants, she thought that life seemed to have settled down very reassuringly after all the violent pulling this way and that, the last two days. Even the parting with Anthony seemed less final than it had seemed in yesterday's sharp alternatives or in the shock of finding him gone this morning. Anthony, somewhere on the sea toward Cornwall, was no farther away than he had been before when old ties pulled him homeward, and nothing had been set between them that time could not change.

Crede was half asleep with her head on Philip's shoulder when Mona called them to supper. She roused herself to eat it with an appetite which won even Mona's approval; and, still sleepy after it, went early to bed, carrying a selection of dainties from the table for the kitten.

The kitten had come to the end of a tiring day, too, and had endured the final trial of a bath and brushing at Mona's hands. Smelling of lavender and soft as a ball of thistledown, it curled warmly against Crede's shoulder as they sank deep in feathers and the bed curtains closed them together in a small safe world. It fell instantly asleep, but Crede's descent was slower.

Through pleasant, uncounted moments she slipped, as easily as she had slipped into the soft feathers, past the sharp landmarks of thought and over the boundary between wishing and dreaming, to drift safely on a tide deeper than reason with the sureness of a benevolent direction.

The kitten stirred and burrowed into her shoulder. I'll call her Fand, she said to herself, not bothering to wonder why the name had come to her and seemed just right. But as she drifted on toward sleep the sound of waves was in her ears, plashing on some wide, sunny shore. In Mona's folklore, Queen Fand ruled far westward in Tir-nan-Og, the Island of Youth. "The distant isle, round which sea horses glisten." Was that Tir-nan-Og, or was it Moy Mell, the Celtic paradise? No matter. "Lovely land, throughout the world's age, on which uncounted flowerets fall . . . Treasures of every worth are in the gentle land . . . Golden chariots on the sea plain rise with the tide to the sun."

II

The answer to this I lette to divynis
But well I woot that in this world gret pyne is.

CHAUCER

After a day of heavy fog this was a fair June morning, with the tide flowing out of Bristol Channel and a fresh down-channel wind. The *Brigid* ran before it, wild for the open sea. Crede, standing on the headland by the Avon's mouth, watched her until she was only a spread of taut sail between blue sky and widened Severn and seemed already ocean borne.

"Come away, Crede!"

Adam Bell put his hand on her arm, and Crede looked away with stinging eyes, then looked seaward again.

The *Brigid* had waited in Hung Road for this favoring wind, and through yesterday's bad weather Crede had been restless with the thought that she might be no farther from home than Bristol's outer anchorage. Finally, Adam Bell had brought her and Cousin Allie down river in his skiff. He had not wanted to come. It had been sufficiently trying, he thought, to say good-by once at Quayside and watch his trim, high-strung *Brigid* nose down-river for the roughest voyage of her life . . . without her master, and with Philip setting off—at his age—to chase after new islands. Philip had not sailed his own ships in a dozen years and had forgotten what it was like to sail even as far as Spain or Gotland—winds failing, or storms blowing you off course, days of crowded quarters, food going bad, stench and grumbling and sickness, perhaps mutiny, perhaps pirates—but at least a known course and the hope of a Christian port at its end.

Yet Philip had gone off to Amerike as if he had no care on his mind once Crede had shown herself equal to managing the counting house, with Adam chained ashore by his own promise to help her. She was a clever little monkey and must have been picking up their trade all her life, to learn so quickly in the few weeks since she had made up her mind to this folly of Philip's. She had seemed to want him to go.

She had waved good-by from Quayside without a tear. Yesterday when Adam, against his better judgment, had brought her here, she had behaved well again. The four of them—for Master Lusted who distrusted all boats had surprisingly insisted upon taking the trip down river too—

[65]

had supped in Philip's cabin, making a celebration of it, with Philip pressing Crede to notice the abundance of his provisions and that the whole crew could live like lords at sea. Afterwards, before Crede and Master Lusted went to lodgings ashore, they had sat together on the afterdeck while some of the crew below sang to the music of a mandore. This morning Crede's voice had been as clear as any in the Hymn to the Virgin as the *Brigid* cast her moorings. But then she had wanted to come out here to watch them down channel, and there had been no getting her away since. As she stood straining her eyes after the ship she looked as forlorn now as a frightened child.

"Your cousin is waiting in the boat," Adam said, "and just sitting there is enough to make the old gentleman seasick."

"We can't go home till the tide turns."

"Well, then, we'll have some dinner. I know a good inn. Come and rescue Master Lusted."

The *Brigid* with all she held seemed no larger now than a wide-winged gull. Crede looked once more down channel and then turned away.

They had left Adam's boat by the mouth of a pill, but now it was stuck in mud that was covered with tidal refuse. Cousin Allie was climbing out onto the marshy bank with a cat's distaste for such footing.

"Your boat is settling in, Adam," he said indignantly. "That cockle is no safer in mud than in water, and I think there is a quicksand here will suck her down." He brushed crossly at his spattered shoes and hose.

"She is safe enough," Adam said. "We can leave her here till the tide is back over pilot's rock and have some dinner meanwhile. I know a better inn than these riverside ones, a little along the road toward Westbury. A walk will do us good."

He doubted the wisdom of this by the time they reached the inn, for Crede looked white and tired. But the Golden Bough was worth coming to. Its latticed windows bulged comfortably as if pushed out by the good cheer within, and two doors stood hospitably open upon a tidy stable-yard at the side. Music and a savory smell of roast meat came from the open door of the ordinary, while the entrance which they took led into a small sunny parlor with clean rushes on its floor and its benches gaily painted. Crede sank down on one of them. No one was in this room, but Adam put his head through a door which connected it with the ordinary and shouted, "Mistress Tomaris!"

Their hostess came bustling in. "Bless me, 'tis Master Bell! It's as good as sun after fog to see you, sir."

She had a warm, pleasant voice which matched her brown eyes and rosy plumpness, and her russet gown, her white sleeves and cap, were as clean as the room.

"I've brought Mistress Canynges and her cousin who need your best

[66]

dinner, Tomaris. What have you got for us? Mistress Lloyd's goodman sailed with me years ago, Crede."

"Aye, the dear lad, rest his soul," Mistress Lloyd said cheerfully. "It's happiness you bring to this house, Mistress Canynges. We have got a joint and brewis and hare pie for the ordinary, but if you will wait a shake, Master Bell, there can be a bird and a sallet too—and will you have it here, and maybe Jock to play and sing to you?"

"We'd like it here, please," Crede said, "and anything you have ready, Mistress Lloyd, will do."

"'Twill be the best we have, I promise you, and you'll have the room to yourselves except for two foreigns from the south, a lady and her son who stopped the night. Would Mistress Canynges take a cup of my own perry now?" she added, her eyes on Crede's face.

"As quick as you can bring it, Tomaris," Adam said, "and some of that famous ale of yours for Master Lusted and me."

"Jock will be here in a twinkling."

Mistress Lloyd hurried off and in a moment Jock came in with their drinks. He was a small leathery man who worked as well as sang, apparently, and he laid two tables deftly with clean white cloths. Crede sipped her pear cordial and felt its warmth gratefully. She had not slept last night.

The foreigns came in together. The lady was tiny, with very beautiful white hair only partly covered by her hennin and a figure as slim and straight as Crede's own. The young man was slight and not very tall, and something about him made Crede think suddenly of her father—his build and litheness, perhaps, and a way of moving that was quick and yet seemed quiet because it was so effortless. The elusive likeness roused her to a moment's attention as they said good day courteously and crossed to the farther table. They were English, undoubtedly, the peculiarity of their accent was no more than that of the London Thornes, but to Bristol anyone not bred in the nearest parishes was a foreign.

They excused Jock from singing, but the dinner when he brought it was as good as Adam had promised, and Crede, with the perry warm inside her, was managing to eat some of it when they were interrupted.

Someone of consequence had arrived in the yard. There was a bustle outside with shouts directed to the ostler's care of the horses, and then the newcomer strode into the parlor. It was Stephen Chalkraft!

"Why, Crede! Oh, of course, the *Brigid* was sailing. I suppose they got off this morning, a pity—!"

"What brings you here, Stephen?" Adam interrupted brusquely.

"I always use the Golden Bough if I ride this way. They have passably good food and a clean stable," Stephen said with the air of one who knows the best. "Today I am meeting—Ah, there they are!" He crossed

[67]

the room to the foreigns. "You will be Cousin Alison Perry, Mistress?"

But then these must be the Perrys from London who were Crede's cousins too. It was no wonder that the young man, Edgar—no, Edwin—looked a little like Philip. Crede had never before seen these cousins, but Alison Perry's name was well known to her because of an old story. There was a time in her childhood when the story had frightened her so at night that Mona had been very angry with Cousin Allie for thinking that she was old enough to hear it, but there was nothing disturbing in the appearance of this composed elderly lady. Cousin Allie had got to his feet and was hurrying across the room.

"Alison! I should have known!"

Mistress Perry had risen, smiling. "Stephen! You are more like your father than like Cousin Jane. But he was younger than you are when I saw him last. Dear me!" She turned, still smiling, to Cousin Allie. "I think I should have known you, Alward, had I expected to see you here. But indeed how could you have known me again when I was only sixteen the last time we met?"

She had been sixteen in the story. Now she was smiling, her face marvelously fresh in spite of the lines in it, laying that ghost of Crede's childhood. Crede and Adam were drawn into the group then, and while Stephen was served his dinner Mistress Perry wanted news of her Cousin Philip, and Edwin Perry wanted to hear more about the Bristol ventures westward.

"London is slow to see what they may mean," he said. "But we have two friends there, Thomas More and his brother-in-law John Rastell, who say that King Henry may win as much by encouraging them as he got from the Spanish marriage."

His questions showed more knowledge than was usual away from Quayside; and as he spoke his gray eyes, quickened by thought and imagination beyond the present moment and his own concerns in it, reminded Crede again of her father.

The conversation became the mixture of odd bits of news that is usual when members of a scattered family meet. It appeared that Mistress Perry still owned a strip of land which had been in her grandmother's family and had a cottage on it. She supposed it might be in ruins now, but she hoped they could make it habitable. For "Win" had come up from Oxford and was just recovered by a miracle from sweating sickness, and they had thought that while he got his strength back and planned what he should do next they could live more quietly here than in her cousin's busy household—Lisbet, you know, in London. So they had written Cousin Stephen to ask about the place which was near his own, and he had been kind beyond all need, arranging to have word sent him when their ship reached Avonmouth and to meet them here.

Adam's glance toward Stephen held some speculation, but Crede's attention was centered upon the newcomers. Win Perry had attracted it first, but she had been almost as instantly drawn to his mother. It was Alison Perry's voice she listened for, and it held a charm as hard to define as the impression of something youthful and engaging behind the lines of her face and the quietness of her manner. She was disappointed when Stephen began to hurry the departure. While the Perrys went for their wraps he stood twirling his riding gloves, moving impatiently from one foot to the other.

"Why didn't you tell us they were coming, Stephen?"

"I haven't seen you lately, Crede."

"I had forgotten about that bit of land," Cousin Allie said. "Alison can not have a great deal more in the world than that and the little her mother left her. Nor Win—his father's goods were confiscate too, of course. Is the cottage livable?"

"Barely," Stephen said. "I'll have them to stay at Dalewood."

Stephen was really putting himself out, and Crede was ashamed that she had always found it hard to credit him with generosity.

"We should like to have them too," she said eagerly.

She had felt an attraction beyond this happy chance of cousinship, and she would have liked to take them home with her now to the emptiness of the house.

"They want to see their bit of property first," Stephen said quickly. "It's not much, you know. Even the land is not much good. But I may offer them something for it. I think I should do that."

"I believe they spoke of it as touching Dalewood," Adam said.

"Why, yes, it does," Stephen said carelessly. "It is on the poorest side, but Dalewood is big enough now to take it off their hands without straining me."

"I have wanted for some time to see the improvements at Dalewood," Adam said—and if this was the case he had concealed it well, for he had never shown more than the barest civility when Stephen prosed on about them. "We must ride out soon. You'd like that, wouldn't you, Crede?"

"I may have news for you then." Stephen smiled complacently. "Well, I suppose I have it now; it is pretty well settled. Dalewood is to have a mistress."

"Stephen! Who is it?"

"Do you remember Bessie Annet, Crede? You and she used to play together when Philip brought you to Dalewood. Mistress Annet of Brookdale Manor," Stephen said smugly.

Brookdale had always been the largest holding in the Dale, and Bessie Annet was an only child.

"A good match," Adam said. "Brookdale touches Dalewood also, I remember."

"When is the wedding, Stephen? You'll invite us, won't you? Will it be this summer? There is no time so nice for a wedding in the country."

"Why, so I said." Stephen looked less smug. "And Bessie could be settled into Dalewood before the harvest. But the fact is, she has a notion for us to ride off straightaway after it on a pilgrimage—some vow she has made—and how we can leave the place before autumn for days of junketing about the country with a pack of idlers is a puzzle."

Stephen frowned at his boots, and Crede almost laughed. Unless Bessie had changed greatly she was not likely to be committed to many unnecessary religious devotions, but pilgrimages were gay holidays. It would be really funny if Bessie should lead Stephen a dance.

Win Perry returned then with Jock and their bags, and his mother appeared wrapped in a gray cloak, and there was only time, in Stephen's continued haste, for hurried good-bys. They waved from the inn yard as the Dalewood party rode off, and then Adam said, "The tide will be well over the Ledges now. We had best get away ourselves."

The dinner and the company had so restored Cousin Allie that he resumed the perils of river transport almost lightheartedly. But he lost confidence in Adam's seamanship before they had passed the Ledges and Breakfaucet Rock to enter the Bristol Mile, and by the time they got his feet on land he had turned a very queer color. Fortunately they were almost at their own door then, for instead of turning along the Frome to Quayside Adam had gone on up Avon to The Back, where river boats and barges and lighter coastwise craft moored near Bristol Bridge. The handsome stone bridge with its row of tall houses was in the center of town, only a step from Mary le Port Street.

Mona was watching for them. She had been waiting overlong, she thought. This delay had added to her anxiety for Crede and whenever she thought of Philip monstrous fears grew out of the jumble of legend and superstition which served as her geography of foreign parts. Her state of mind was now a general crossness.

"Well?"

"Everything well," Adam said cheerfully. "They went out on the morning tide."

"And it is hours since the tide came in again! Sit down, all of you, and I'll bring supper right away. Inn food since yesterday," Mona said with a sniff, "and inn beds."

Fand and Cormac came bounding down the stairs. They, too, had felt the disturbance in the house and the loneliness in it today but now, with their family restored to them, past fears could cast no shadow. Cormac paused at the foot of the stairs and looked from one to another. Then his tail drooped, and he crossed to Philip's chair and lay beside it.

Fand leaped lightly onto Crede's lap, kneaded it into a comfortable hollow and rounded herself contentedly in it. She had grown into a beautiful creature with long, silvery fur and golden eyes, and she would soon be as large as the full-grown stable cats. With them she maintained an armed neutrality, but she and Cormac had formed an odd friendship. Cormac had let her take outrageous liberties while she was still so small that an ill-advised gulp of his might have swallowed her, and as she grew larger she could coax him to forget his dignity in giddy romps. Crede was certain they talked to each other, whatever their differences of dialect. Now, Fand stirred restlessly on her knee, then left that coveted position to curl between Cormac's listlessly outstretched front paws.

EIGHT

Crede sat at her father's end of the long table in the counting room, while Ned, Niles, and Bob copied cargo lists. It was one of those warm late October days that feel like summer.

If they all yawn at exactly the same minute again, I shall scream, she thought. Cormac, feeling her restlessness, looked up, hopeful of a walk, then settled back at her feet with a gusty sigh. The apprentices echoed it, squirmed on their stools, yawned in unison, and bent their heads over their ledgers again, their pens moving at a snail's pace.

The unanimity with which they did everything had long ceased to amuse Crede, remarkable though it seemed that three boys could so exactly match even their stupidities. Only three years older than they were, she found their childishness an irritation which she had not forseen last spring when she worked beside them under her father's supervision. Then, concerned with her own performance and a desire to prove that she and Adam Bell could give Philip a few months of freedom, she had taken no time to consider what it would be like without him. Now the hours of tedious detail were not lightened by his presence and his effortless control of them. And there were unexpected difficulties too.

Yet she and Adam had done pretty well, she thought, with grateful recognition of Adam's support and competence. He lived in his rooms on Quayside, supervising the work at the wharf and warehouse and workshop and dropping in every day to help Crede at the counting house.

She had mastered the routine quickly because she was good at figures; except when the boys irritated her she delighted in the pull of threads from this room to the bustle of Quayside and the far ports and markets beyond. With the *Brigid* away they still had three vessels working. The bark *Swallow* kept on the Peninsular route, and John Burns, her master, was making swift and profitable trips, taking out cloth and corn and tin and lead and bringing back spices and wine and oil and Madeira sugar, Spanish fruit, saffron, ivory, and silk brought by Portuguese ships from the East, cochineal to dye cloth the famous Bristol red, and woad from Toulouse for Coventry blue. The cog *Brennus* and the ketch *Belinus*—named for the figures on St. John's Gate of the two claimed by Bristol among the numerous sons of King Priam of Troy who had set out to found English cities—plied back and forth to Ireland, carrying over coarse Welsh cloth and Portuguese wine and returning with hides and pelts and fish. With the good weather which had favored them into autumn, Crede was proud of the account which they could give Philip.

And he might be home very soon to hear it. She prayed daily that the weather was favoring him also. The *Brigid* had been gone four months and she had tentatively set that time in her mind for the cruising, remembering that John Cabot in a slower ship had taken only from May until August to find and return from the new land.

They had carefully avoided making too close estimates of time when Philip left, and she and Adam avoided mention of it now. She would not begin to worry before the winter storms set in. Even then she would not worry, she told herself, for the *Brigid* might be harboring in Amerike until spring. But anniversaries which marked the passing of summer and then of autumn disturbed her. On Lammas Day when the parishes beat their bounds and Bristol held a gay festival of setting the Watch, summer had entered its last month. With St. James's fair it had ended. By Michaelmas autumn was settled in, and you could not close your eyes to the date with the winter hiring fair set up in the market. The Moot Bell clanged as the new mayor received the king's sword and was led through the streets by the town minstrels and all the guilds to St. Michael's Church, to pray for the inspiration of the Holy Ghost in the task of keeping Bristol orderly for another year. Now Michaelmas was past too and its goose eaten.

But she must not let herself begin to expect the *Brigid* every day. She brought her mind back to immediate problems.

There were several to consider. All three ships were in port at the moment and this seemed bad management and had Tim Arden driving his men like mad. The *Brennus* was ready to load, but the *Belinus*, which should have been away before her, had been delayed by the illness of her elderly shipmaster who now wanted to settle down with his married daughter in Portbury. Philip would have known who should replace him. Surely, however, the *Brennus* and *Swallow* could take on cargo tomorrow. There had been a delay about that, too, and a problem which both Crede and Adam would have been glad to defer until Philip's return. This morning Adam had gone to Spicer's Hall in an attempt to hasten the inspection of their goods, and Crede was waiting for him now.

The Merchant Venturers Company who used Spicer's Hall on The Back and were now the most important merchant guild in Bristol had first become prominent as a loose association of cloth exporters and had received a charter two generations ago from Mayor William Canynges. As the cloth trade grew, their power and influence had grown with it. King Henry favored them greatly, for in such ports as Bristol and London he found the Merchant Venturers the best organized means of expanding English trade, with ambitions as bold as his own; he had helped them by all his brilliant network of treaties and had granted them a new charter increasing their privileges at home and giving their depots abroad governance of all English trade in those ports. Though it had been an old established liberty of freemen of Bristol to buy and sell any goods they chose, subject to guild standards, the Merchant Venturers now had nearly a monopoly of the overseas trade here in all commodities, and their control of it had tightened since they received a lease on the port dues. There were still a few young men, such as Philip had been, struggling to get a foothold, and there were still a few shipping merchants such as he was now who had not joined the Company, but their position was becoming more difficult.

Adam came in by the street door, a frown between his eyes. "There's a fine lot of swelled heads in Spicer's Hall, Crede!" He flung himself down in the chair beside her, and his frown deepened.

"They are still haggling over our samples. They've been given the right, of course, to say whether goods meet Bristol standards, but you know ours do. It is as plain as my nose that they are badgering us to pay the membership fee."

"How would it count from anyone but Father?"

"I picked up a hint that you could join, Crede. I think that is their idea. They have never pushed Philip so hard—he is not an easy man to push—yet they would like to count us in. From their point of view we set a bad example. I don't think Philip ever meant to hold out to the point of damaging himself. He just preferred to go on as he always had done, and most of the Company have known him for years and did not press the matter. But there has been a movement to tighten up lately; some of them would like to make it a seven-year apprenticeship for full membership as in the regular guilds, and if it ever comes to that we'd do better to get in before it. I don't know what to do. And I wish," Adam said, scowling, "that I had nothing to worry about except sailing the

[73]

Brigid. If I had some of those fat burghers on my deck they would not be telling me how to run Philip's business."

It was the first complaint Adam had made of his role ashore.

"We have always had to obey most of their regulations, anyhow," Crede said, chewing her pen thoughtfully. "And Adam, Father is well liked and has friends in the Company, so if they are pushing us now perhaps they know that it is time he got in. I am going to do it," she said suddenly. "You're sure we can?"

"Sure enough." Adam looked at her a moment in silence. "Crede, if Philip doesn't realize that you have done amazingly well here, I'll tell him. By the saints, you make up your mind as fast as he does, and you don't cry over burned cakes either."

Crede flushed with pleasure. Adam seldom praised, and his approval was worth having. The *Brigid's* master was a personage to Niles and Ned and Bob too; now, as whenever he entered the room, they had ceased to yawn and were bent over their work with conspicuous diligence.

"Oh, Adam—about the *Belinus.* Why shouldn't Clem be her new master?"

"Clem Hathaway, Kate's husband? He's in the *Swallow's* crew, due to sail with her."

"You could fill his place there. You know, Adam, I think that long voyages such as the *Swallow* makes should be for unmarried men. Clem has been home so little since the baby was born, and when you see him and Kate and little Clem together—the *Belinus* makes the shortest trips of all and never goes on from Ireland to Iceland as the *Brennus* sometimes does."

Adam burst out laughing. "I see it is a woman's head on your shoulders after all, Crede."

"That wasn't my only reason," Crede protested hastily. "The *Belinus* is our smallest and slowest and has none of our senior men, so if we want to reward one of our own he has to come off another ship. Clem is young, but he has worked up fast on the *Swallow* though you know Master Burns is not easy to please; and, if you move Clem, Harry Blanket who is a good man, too, can have a promotion there."

"Your head is as good at finding reasons for your heart as it is at figures." Adam's eyes still twinkled. "But Clem is a good lad. I taught him navigation when he sailed with me for a while, and I found him quick at it and smart about other things. He will do well enough with the *Belinus,* I think, if you want to try him. And I'll have a taste of Pepper Burns's famous tongue when I tell him he's a favorite man short! I may as well get that settled now."

Adam got to his feet with alacrity, and Crede suspected that after the restraint he had been obliged to use at Spicer's Hall it would be a pleasure to deal with Master Burns.

"Won't you stay for dinner, Adam?"

"I have to be all over town today, and I think that by stopping in at Spicer's Hall I can persuade them to hurry things through for us in the morning when we turn up with our ten marks. But Mistress Mona expects me for supper. These suppers," Adam chuckled, pausing in the doorway and pretending to measure himself equal to its width, "have put a stone on me already."

He came nearly every night for supper, encouraged by Mona who liked to have at her table a man with an appreciation of good food. Though Cousin Allie had been persuaded by Philip to live in the house during his absence, Mona found her talents wasted on a guest whose head was usually far in the clouds above his trencher.

As soon as Adam had gone the boys' pens began to move with their usual slowness.

"Finish copying the *Swallow*'s manifest before dinner," Crede said, "and you may take the afternoon off to go to the Coulson obit."

This had the desired effect. Obits were popular with them because of the penny paid from the donor's estate to those who came to pray for his soul's repose, and even an obit, Crede thought, might be a step in the right direction. For it appeared that, although the boys had been sent to St. Mary's at some one of the canonical hours every day, they had too seldom got there. It had been made plain to her this morning by a visit from Father Ambrose, her confessor, that the boys' piety was one more of the things she must attend to; and dear old Father Ambrose was so easygoing that a matter which brought him out to administer reproof might cost more than a lenient penance if others noticed it. She would have to insist that the boys get up in time every morning to go to Prime with her and Mona, but that battle could be deferred until tomorrow. She went out by the house door now, leaving them to loiter if they chose since, under Adam's eye, they had already done more than usual.

Cormac followed her, but when she turned to the back of the house, the domain of women and kitchen cats, he went upstairs to lie across Philip's door. She found old Jed Alsop, the itinerant candlemaker, surrounded by a pile of rushes and a smell of hot tallow in the kitchen. Kate was cooking dinner while gossiping with Jed, but Crede decided that the news of Clem's good fortune should come first from him. She paused only long enough to admire little Clem, asleep in his cradle, and to pet Ginger, the more approachable of the two mousers, who was enjoying a nap in the sunny window, before joining Mona in the stillroom.

The stillroom was Mona's special province. All summer it had been full of scent and color as food was stored for winter, and in this sunny

October Mona was continuing to find things to put away. There were herbs to be gathered still for physic and seasoning and flowers to be dried for strewing or for making pastilles to burn when one could no longer pick fresh blooms to sweeten the air of rooms. Additions could still be made to the garden nosegay, a subtle perfume which they had been distilling since spring by one of Mona's most complicated recipes.

This morning the table was heaped with late roses and waves of their fragrance came from the stone mortar in which Mona was crushing their petals. For you could never have enough rosewater. Not only was it a pleasant drink—especially when, as sometimes happened, the well water tasted queer—but it was also good for the complexion, especially good for the eyes, and it could be made into a syrup which was beneficial in rheums and against the bleeding of wounds.

"You can take a turn at this, Crede," Mona said. "I had to let Sadie off to chase that rabbit. It's out again."

There was a certain relish in Mona's tone. The coney had long ceased to be a secret and, after several such escapes, it was likely that there would be a litter of coneys, none of them to be eaten; but Mona was enjoying an attitude of aloofness from the whole affair. She set about arranging crocks on the shelves, while Crede tucked up her sleeves gladly and got to work.

The stillroom delighted her almost as much as it did Mona. As she pounded rhythmically, the scent of the bruised petals mingled with the room's delicious blend of the sugary heaviness of honey and preserved fruit, the faint tang of dried herbs, and the mellowing sweetness of apples and pears. When Mona lifted the cover of a crock to stir its contents, there came a spicy whiff of pickles and Irish limes which no one else could put down so cunningly. The small room was as shining-clean as the rest of the house, and the jars which Mona was arranging pridefully on its shelves stood row upon row. The sun, streaming through the high window, picked out a few of these which were of Suffolk glass and showed the rich color inside: ruby, amethyst, topaz. It danced on strings of dried fruit and herbs suspended from the beams. It darkened the shadows cast on the stone floor by crocks and wooden tubs which held pickled or salted meat, baskets of winter fruits and nuts and rushes and strewing grasses.

On Quayside and in the counting house, Crede's mind flew to all the strange ports of the world. But she loved as much to be here with Mona, deep in the heart of the house, wrapped round with layers of careful housekeeping, hoarding stores like a squirrel against winter. She began to sing as she worked, bringing another richness into the room, Mona thought, for the clear, golden voice might have been her mother's; this one part of her mother's great beauty lived on in Crede.

She had not sung often lately, and Mona watched her anxiously as she worked. The child was too thin and was carrying a heavy load. Mona would gladly have driven Kate and Sadie harder—she herself being still, thank the good saints, tireless—to release Crede from all responsibility in the house just now, but she could not, with good conscience, do this entirely. For Crede was still far from being well trained in housewifery. It would be a shame all her life and a shame upon her father's house if she was not, and Mona was not sure how long she might be spared to pass on her knowledge. There were many skills yet to be mastered in the kitchen and buttery and stillroom and brewing house—in spinning, and needlework, and the care of linens. Crede had many more things to learn about garden herbs—in what phases of the moon the wild ones must be gathered for greatest potency—and the making of dyes and pomades and simples and possets, and the dressing of wounds and the treatment and physic for each disease. If she was ever to manage this house or any other proper one, she must understand the division of work that filled each month with its appropriate concerns and kept the household rhythm moving smoothly with the seasons. No one else could teach her these things so well. Some of them, such as the pomade which was better than myrrh and vinegar and honey to keep your teeth sound into old age and the paste for shining silver and the compound of a dozen things besides beeswax to rub into oak paneling, were Mona's own secrets, jealously guarded for Crede alone.

So Mona had demanded that Crede spend a little while each day with her, and there had been an occasional day of special moment when Cousin Allie had to be cajoled into presiding over the counting house while Crede dived more deeply into housewifery. All summer and autumn they had done everything in its appointed order, and there would be nothing slack or neglected in the house when its master returned.

They were working so agreeably in the stillroom that Sadie's liberal interpretation of a half hour's leave passed unnoticed by Mona. Since the coney and Sadie were mysteriously *en rapport* it would scarcely lead her much of a chase, Crede thought, but the child was probably pottering about the garden with Will, for she had struck up a queer but close friendship with the old man in which neither seemed handicapped by their common shortage of words. As a result, Will's crabbedness had noticeably lessened, and Sadie was a changed child. She stole freedoms like this with a daring which would have been quite beyond her a few months ago, yet even Mona noticed that meanwhile she did her work much better. She came into the stillroom at last, with her cheeks even more burstingly-red than usual, and announced that Kate had dinner ready.

Dinner was what Kate had chosen to make it today, and it was all on the table; for it had gradually become a meal of less ceremony than supper when Adam Bell joined them. Ned and Bob and Niles stood waiting, their eyes on the pasty which Sadie was setting down, and old Jed shuffled in from the kitchen behind Will.

"Master Bell sent for Clem to go to Quayside," Kate said, "and I have called twice up the stairs for Master Lusted."

"He never hears the gong when he is measuring the earth," Mona said, "nor eats enough to stay on it long."

Crede ran upstairs. When her father had asked Cousin Allie to live in the house during his absence he had offered his own room, but Cousin Allie had preferred the small one which had been Tony's and had moved from his cottage the things he thought he would need. Its door stood open upon a confusion of map making which had become Cousin Allie's major interest since Philip's voyage was first planned. No one was there, however, except Fand who was romping merrily among the loose papers.

Fand was her elfish self again and Crede was led a dance before she captured her and stood holding her close for a moment. She had so nearly lost Fand. A fine late summer night had lured her out to some dark encounter and a too-early adventure in motherhood had ended prematurely and almost cost her life. It was ridiculous, Mona said, for an animal to have such trouble and it came of getting one from heathen parts, but she had bent all her skill to the nursing. For days, Fand had been a limp bundle of lusterless fur and heartbreaking resignation; then, with an animal's enviable suddenness, completely well again. Afterward she had added Mona to the beings she was graciously aware of, and to her affection for Crede she had added all that she had briefly learned of passion and maternal yearnings. She could not have kittens again, Mona said, and a good thing too. Even with her own kind Mona was not indiscriminately maternal. She had loved her daughter and was fond of her granddaughter; Crede's mother had been the core of her heart, and Crede had inherited that devotion; but in general Mona was of the opinion that replenishing and multiplying had been a mixed blessing upon the earth.

Crede came downstairs with Fand chasing her skirts just as Cousin Allie entered the hall, smiling above a large, untidy bundle of papers.

"I found the ones I was looking for had been left at home in the cottage," he announced. "Dear me, I am keeping dinner? I am afraid Win will be even a little later."

"Master Perry!" Mona's glance swept down the board—one meat dish only and Kate's pasties, though good enough, were undistinguished fare for a guest. "When did Master Perry come to town?"

"He rode in this morning, a while ago." Cousin Allie beamed upon them as he imparted this timely information. "Nobody else was around, and I got him to help me bring some things from home. He can't be long. He merely had to turn back for another book I remembered needing."

Crede rescued the bursting bundle and set it on the sideboard. Mona and Kate made some hasty additions to the table and then, in a minute, Win Perry came through the door and they forgot their flurry and enjoyed themselves, for he was a favorite guest.

He had ridden in from Dalewood several times, and Mona as well as Crede looked forward to his visits even though a good deal of the time was spent in Cousin Allie's little room. Win's devotion to scholarship went far deeper than Crede's quick curiosity or Philip Canynges' leisurely browsings. He and Cousin Allie could sit for hours upstairs, buried to the neck in a litter of papers and miles away in some learned abstraction. But he could also be very good company, and he was friendly with them all. Mona's instant liking for him had been most unusual, and she smiled approval now as he enjoyed his dinner and gave them the news of Dalewood. Though she still yearned to fatten him, he had gained color and weight since coming to this favored part of England, and no longer bore signs of his illness.

Their cottage was already in good shape for winter, he said in answer to Crede's questioning, but his mother still had him making benches and shelves and was recklessly cutting up her petticoats for cushions and things. Though it had looked so dilapidated at first that Stephen thought it hopeless, its timbers proved to be sound enough and they were grateful to Master Bell for riding out just after their arrival and advising them to keep and repair it. The sheep they were raising on shares with him were thriving on its pasturage. Now if they should ever want to sell the place it would bring a fair price.

This revelation of Adam Bell's hand in their affairs came as a surprise to Crede, for she had not yet found time to visit Dalewood and Adam had said nothing of his interest there.

"But my big news," Win said smiling, "is Stephen's. The wedding is finally set for Martinmas and I am to bid you all come."

All conversation was of wedding plans then. Win, besieged by questions from Crede, Mona, and Kate, proved a very satisfactory source of information with an eye for more details than might have been expected of him. Bessie, who had no mother of her own, had made fast friends with Alison Perry and so much wedding talk between them buzzed about his ears, Win said, that he could tell you the number of frills on every cap and chemise in Bessie's dower chest. The party at Brookdale would take in half the shire, he thought. Food enough for the whole of it was in preparation, and afterwards Bessie was to have her pilgrimage.

After Win's visit, the wedding and plans to attend it gave them all something new to talk about while they were pretending not to count the days that might remain of good sailing weather. As they talked it over, it seemed that the occasion would provide an opportunity for several different kinds of holidaying, according to different tastes.

It could not have come at a better time. Because of the difficulty at Spicer's Hall, now happily settled, the ships had all been in port at once, and now they were all away together. This had meant a spell of heavier work than usual, but had made it possible to promise everyone both on Quayside and in the counting house a holiday of several days at Martinmas. Under this spur even Ned and Niles and Bob had worked with phenomenal speed and had been rewarded with leave to go home for a week. Crede and Adam could take a few days off too, while after a busy summer and autumn Mona had not a thing left in the house to clean and not an empty crock in the stillroom.

It was decided that Crede and Mona would ride to Dalewood two days before the wedding with Will as escort. This was Mona's suggestion. She did not particularly like Stephen Chalkraft, but the condition a bride found Dalewood in seemed to her a family matter, and she looked forward to the challenge Stephen's bachelor establishment was sure to present.

One day of wedding junketing would do for him, Adam said. He would ride out for the day of the ceremony, but he wanted to spend some time upriver here in his skiff, and he was hoping for some hawking and a morning of duck hunting on Treem Pond. Crede suspected that he knew she would leave home more readily if he remained on watch for news of the *Brigid*; indeed, she could scarcely have persuaded herself to go otherwise.

Cousin Allie was not attracted by the proposed entertainments at Brookdale—still less by the prospect of getting there on horseback, since he distrusted horses as thoroughly as boats. But the chance to be left undisturbed at his map making had come just when he needed it. Win had told him of seeing a curious chart in London. Drawn as long ago as 1448 it showed a far western shore marked, "an authentic island fifteen hundred miles across the Atlantic," and this had excited him greatly. He felt sure that, when William Canynges had been supreme in England's Iceland trade, the discovery must have been made in a Bristol ship. Yet he could find no mention of it in the town registers or the annals of the Kalendars Guild. In restoring what they could of the records after the disastrous fire of 1466, Bristol's ancient and unique fraternity of Kalendars, who maintained the first public library in England, must have been as careless as the city fathers. They seemed to have omitted matters which he considered of greater moment than ordinances and deeds and taxes. Cousin Allie felt it his plain duty to remedy this as far as possible.

He was determined to provide maps and the best account possible of voyages westward, and to have all this in order by the time Philip returned to add a new chapter.

Kate would see to it that Cousin Allie paused sometimes to eat, for she was happily staying at home too. The prospect of being in charge here, with no direction from Mona and nothing to do except cosset little Clem and enjoy her new dignity as the wife of a shipmaster, entranced her. But Sadie, to her unutterable joy, was going with the travelers, at least part way. The plan had been Crede's, and Sadie was now going about in a daze, more speechless than usual except to commend the coney hourly to Kate's care during her absence. She was to spend the holiday at home, for Thornbury was on their way and they hoped that her uncle, who was a weaver there, would take her up to her father's hill farm while the rest rode on to Dalewood.

Mona was spending the last morning before their departure packing their best clothes, while Crede was finishing odds and ends in the counting house. Without the boys it was temptingly hers to put in order. She tied an apron over her gown and a kerchief round her head and pulled the whole place apart with Mona's thoroughness. When the bell at the street entrance rang in the midst of this, she went rather crossly to answer it for she had felt safe from interruption. To her complete surprise the door opened upon Robin Thorne.

"I didn't mean to startle you," he said.

It did not improve matters to know that she had shown her dismay so plainly. Before she could collect herself she had left him standing too long in the doorway.

"I have just got into Quayside." He was still standing there awkwardly. "Master Bell said that you would be here and I—Father charged me to bring news of you all."

"Do come in and sit down, Master Thorne." Crede looked about her unhappily for something one could sit down upon.

He helpfully cleared two stools of a pile of office litter which in this exposure seemed to have decayed beyond any respectable use, and when Crede had sunk upon one of them he tucked his long legs under the other.

"Father sent me to make that trip through the Cotswold wool towns we planned last spring," he explained.

"All of you are well at home, I trust, Master Thorne?"

"Very well, thank you. We had word, though only lately, of your father's voyage, and I hope to take back the news he brings."

"We—we have not set any time to expect him"—the answer they all made now.

"Of course not," he said quickly. "Your father will want to bring back

[81]

a full report. And the weather is very favorable. It helped persuade Father that the roads will still be good in the hills. I shall have to ride out tomorrow or the next day."

There was a pause while Crede struggled with her conscience and with Mona's code of hospitality. Finally, he said, "Master Bell has told me how well you are managing here."

"We aren't often in such disorder."

It had not been necessary to make excuses. The trivial circumstance of being caught by Master Robin Thorne with her father's office in confusion and herself done up like a scullery maid had upset her more than was reasonable.

"I am sure our counting room needs such a turning-out, but it is so far from the house that a woman's hand never reaches it."

He glanced at the work of her hands in the chaos around them and smiled suddenly. Anyone might have found this insufferable, let alone a member in her own right of the Guild of Merchant Adventurers of Bristol.

Crede's temper rose and she said, too quickly, "I could find time to tidy it because we have just got three ships away at once."

His eyes met hers with a glint of laughter still in them, but he said with sober politeness, "Indeed, Master Bell told me what a rush of work you have had. I have much less responsibility, you know, and have never managed anything without Father. But if I—if there is anything I could do to help until your father returns—"

"That is very kind," Crede said, "and if Adam should need help—"

A faint red tinged the tan which he had gained since spring, as he got to his feet. He took a step toward the door and then paused.

"My friend Win Perry came to this part of the country. Have you chanced to meet him?"

"Win is my cousin."

"Perhaps you could tell me how to find his cottage." He had not pretended surprise. "We were at Oxford together, and I hope to see him before I go home."

"When you ride toward the Cotswolds you will find the road to Dalewood well known in Berkeley or Dursley," Crede said. "Win and his mother are at the Chalkraft farm there."

It would have been the merest courtesy to tell him that they were riding to Dalewood tomorrow. When you were riding in a party, not to offer company on the road was simply uncouth. Mona, and Philip too, would have been shocked by such behavior, but Crede could not seem to help it that these Thornes brought out the worst in her.

"Thank you," he said. "I expect to go that way as soon as possible." At the door he paused again. "Our fathers are old friends, Crede. Since

I am going to be around for a while, I'd like to think that if I can be useful at any time you will let me."

Without seeming to expect an answer, he made her a quick bow and went out.

Since he left so abruptly it was scarcely her fault that he had not been asked to break bread at her father's table.

NINE

Beyond Aylward's Gate, Broadmead stretched eastward, and just outside the town wall a straggling suburb lay between St. James's Priory and Blackfriars, with Castle Village to the south across the Frome. The Frome turned Castle Mill here, and above the weir and the witch's ducking stool it was a pleasant stream for bathing and fishing with wooded walks and pasture land along it. They rode for a while near its bank with the sun coming up ahead of them in a yellowing band across the horizon to promise another day of almost summer mildness. As it lightened, a smoky haze to their right marked the lower Cotswold edge, and at their left a slight milkiness tinged the bluing sky toward Severn.

They kept an easy pace. The horses would have taken their heads, but Will said that they must be held in because they had been on grass all summer with too little exercise. He was on a nag hired from a posting inn, while Crede rode Philip's Grey Knight with Mona on her Bess, and Sadie, her cheeks scarlet and her eyes shining, rode fat old Matilda.

From the moment they left town Grey Knight had been burning to leave this motley cavalcade behind, and without Philip's hand on the rein he felt free to put on a show as they came upon an encampment by the river. He was a good and dependable horse as a rule, but when they were all being saddled this morning he had thought that it meant a gallop with his master on his back again—he had to take his disappointment out on something. He carried Crede suddenly away from the rest and shied and danced as he neared this camp which had a smell he did not like.

Half a dozen dark-faced strangers rose as if out of the bushes to watch. They were obviously those strange Egyptians only lately seen in England, probably the same band who had been mending pots and telling fortunes at St. James's Fair. They were horse thieves too, it was said, and the nearest pair were moving closer, though perhaps this was only because they thought that Crede needed help.

[83]

"Keep on ahead, Will, I'm coming!" Crede shouted, letting Knight plunge and rear as he chose for a moment.

Will would know that a dozen louts could not touch Knight's bridle when he was roused, and Crede was too good a horsewoman to be thrown easily. She let Knight's antics hold their attention for a moment and then gave him his head to bolt through them and overtake the rest of her party who were safely past and had halted just out of reach.

Mona was white and crossing herself, but Will was grinning.

"Young Anthony couldn't have bettered that," he said.

Will had taught both Crede and Anthony to ride and had often amused himself with their rivalry.

They left the Frome now and bore north to join the main road through Berkeley Vale toward Gloucester. Here they passed a stream of carts and pack horses headed for Bristol, and as the country flattened out along the Severn they could look across marshy meadows and see the river barges making their way down. The road and the river were twin streams feeding the wharves of the great port.

On the east side of the valley the Cotswolds were rising higher and bolder, their beechwoods still thinly veiled with gold, and across the river was the darker bronze of the oaks of Dean Forest. Even so far into autumn there was green pasturage in the marshy river meadows. Fat cattle browsed there and the farmhouses were built on platforms above Severn floods.

As the valley narrowed, the spire of Thornbury Church rose ahead, and Sadie became suddenly voluble with directions. They rode up the wide village street between cottages, every one of which, it was said, housed a loom. The generally neat and thriving appearance of the cottages contrasted with the castle towering behind the churchyard; for the castle looked out of care and use, as if the village no longer had need of its supervision.

Sadie pointed out a small cottage, built of warm-colored Cotswold stone and roofed with slates of it, beside a large chestnut tree. She scrambled off Matilda's back to pound on its door.

The little old woman who popped out of it was as unlike her as possible. She had bright black eyes and a tiny, wrinkled, brown face with a long nose and a chin which rose up to meet it. Despite this she did not look like the witch of a fairy tale but like one of the good gnomes disguised in a full-skirted pink gown and a frilled cap.

"Marry come up! Is it you, Sadie, child?"

"And the mistress," Sadie said and left explanations to the rest.

"Is it Mistress Canynges then? Come in, all of you, come in! It's proud I am to have you. Tie your horses under the tree, master, and come in. There's a bucket by the well to water them."

The main room with a loom at the window was clean and tidy, though its mistress vowed as she dusted dustless benches for them that it was a sight and if she had known—Jud, too, would be proud to see them but just now he had gone with their cloth to a neighbor's—the packman calls there for us all, you see. But here she was chattering when what they needed after their ride was a bite and sup.

Crede protested as she began bustling about, but Mona did not. Mona had a test for quality and Sadie's aunt had met it: she must have been agog to know what had brought them, but above all she was mistress of her hearth and priestess of its hospitality. Although Mona's kitchen baked manchet of fine white flour she asked the secret of these delicious oat cakes; although she brewed many fragrant concoctions which she liked better than her own excellent ale, she drank ale with relish, stirring it with an herb stick upon Mistress Tupper's advice that "Sage, and with it herb of grace or rue, make drinks both safe and sound for you," and showing an amiable interest in this very elementary bit of herbal lore. Mistress Tupper beamed upon them, and since her cupboard seemed abundantly furnished they did full justice to her fare, meanwhile explaining their errand.

Yes, indeed—Jud would take Sadie to the farm now that the cloth was packed off, Mistress Tupper assured them, and she might go along too, for she had been promising herself a visit before winter.

"There will be great doings in the Dale this week," she said, her black eyes sparkling with curiosity. "There's talk of it all around the valley. Dalewood Farm is growing mighty great—the changes there would surprise Goodman Chalkraft if he could rise up to see them which I dare say he can't till Judgment Day, however much folk say he is turning over in his grave. To think that Master Stephen is marrying Squire Annet's girl, and his new house bigger than Squire's, they say, with chimneys and window glass all over it."

Sadie's aunt was not only unlike Sadie in appearance but turned out to be such a great talker that it was with difficulty they got away at last.

After their rest the last few miles went quickly. They left the Gloucester road for one that veered toward the Cotswolds and ascended until they could overlook the low plateau where Berkeley village clustered beside its little stream in the shadow of the great castle built centuries ago—when William the Norman set Roger de Berkele there to command the vale. The valley narrowed here between the Severn and the outthrusting Cotswold edge, which rose to the rugged heights of Nibley Knoll and Stinchcombe Hill. They climbed among the lower beechwoods and turned off onto a track between scattered farmhouses and sheepruns which brought them into the Dale.

Their first glimpse of the new order of Dalewood Farm was a fine

[85]

stone gateway between the hedges and a stone bridge across the brook. Inside the gate all was new prosperity. There was a fulling mill by the stream, and half a dozen new thatched cottages strung along it with pasture stretching on either side. Beyond the apple orchard, which was all that Crede could recognize of the old place, were the new farm buildings, a newly-laid-out pleasure garden, and then the new house. The old house with its built-on stable had been low and homely, but this one, as Mistress Tupper had said, was full of windows and chimneys. It rose three stories, part stone and part half-timbered, to its gabled roof. The new whiteness of the plaster and the high-peaked gables above its staring windows gave it, Crede thought, an air of shocked surprise at its own grandeur.

Win came hurrying from the barn, and then the front door of the house burst open and Alison Perry was flying across the terrace to them, running like a girl with her lavender-colored skirts gathered up.

"Crede, I've hoped so that you'd come before the wedding day! We moved over here for your visit, and I've had your room ready and Mistress Mona's for a week." Her arms were around Crede almost before Win had her feet on the ground. "My dear, I have been looking forward to this visit so much you will laugh at me." She laughed at herself, a clear little peal. "Ever since that day at the inn."

Crede slipped her arm through this almost-unknown cousin's and walked toward Stephen's strange, staring house with the oddest feeling of homecoming.

The kitchen was the nicest part of Stephen's new house, Crede decided on the day before the wedding. It looked out on the hills rising beyond the pasture, and it smelled of sugar and spice as she and Mona and Alison, with their sleeves rolled up, bustled about a gigantic baking while Stephen's awkward young kitchen-and-dairy maid obeyed orders distractedly. His elderly housekeeper, a relic of the simpler establishment, had taken to her bed yesterday with a combination of lumbago and resentment, and Mona had brewed her subtlest possets to keep her contented there while she and Alison, who had taken an instant liking to each other, put Dalewood into the state they considered fitting for a bride's homecoming. An unexpectedly fortunate circumstance was that they met with no interference from Stephen. He was out about the place most of the time, trying to put his various enterprises in shape to manage themselves while he turned his mind to the wedding and the threatened pilgrimage. Whenever he came into the house he seemed slightly dazed and more pliable than usual.

So yesterday they had cleaned and polished, and today they were filling as many crocks as they could in the ill-furnished stillroom. Win, looking as if he enjoyed this immensely, and Will, looking as if he might speak his mind at any moment, were in and out with wood and water or sent to the barn for eggs. All this happy activity was at its height when into it came the bride.

"Yum!" she said, sniffing the hot, scented air as she ran forward to receive a floury embrace from Crede.

Bessie had been a pretty little girl, Crede remembered, and now any-one would have called her a beauty. You did not need to wait for an expression or a trick of movement to decide. She took the eye as instantly as the sweet briar bloom her coloring suggested.

"Why everyone is working as hard here as at home, which is a complete madhouse, I can't imagine," she said, "but I suspect you are all being very sweet, and it's a secret or something. I came over to welcome you, Crede, but I also have to see Stephen, right away."

"Try the mill," Win said, emptying an armload of wood, "or the wool house, or the sheep pens, or the back pasture. Stephen had something on his mind about the cottages, too, before he goes on this pilgrimage."

Bessie wrinkled her perfect nose at him and ran out.

"Haven't we got those shelves nearly filled?" Win said. "When we have, would you like a ride, Crede? And would you let me try Grey Knight? We could go up Stinchcombe."

"Oh, I'd love to!"

Swept into the holiday mood of the Dale, Crede was ready for all its diversions. But they would go riding after dinner, she decided, since Alison had promised to show her the cottage this morning as soon as the baking was finished.

She and Alison slipped away by themselves, for both of them had been looking forward to a little time all of their own.

At first sight of the cottage, Crede fell in love with it as she had with Alison. It stood beyond the pasture, nearer the hills, and the brook which wound on through the sheeprun trickled beside its small garden where there were still a few bright flowers. It was old and tiny, built of the golden-gray Cotswold stone, and everything about it shone; in the main room there were fresh rushes on the stone floor and bright cushions on the benches and the chest-bed; on the homemade table and shelves were pieces of woodenware scoured silky white; on the clean hearth, apple-wood with sweet herbs scattered over it lay ready for kindling.

"There is a little scullery behind," Alison said, "and Win has his books and his bed in the loft. Sit down, Crede, while I light the fire to welcome us. Do you know, this is the first home Win and I have had in his mem-ory? While he was at school I stayed with Cousin Lisbet in London."

"You've made this beautiful," Crede said sincerely.

"We love it." Alison got the fire burning brightly and sat down to enjoy it. "With the garden and the sheep we have our living here, until

[87]

Win's chance comes to use his scholarship. I believe that it will come in time, though he begins without hope of preferment."

It was the grace of this contentment which had from the first drawn Crede wistfully to Alison. She knew why Win could expect no preferment and what this gentle white-haired woman put behind her with that brief statement.

Alison had been as young as Crede when her father, a Kentish squire turned scholar with no more worldly wisdom than Cousin Allie and his taste for unsettling speculations, had burned at the stake for heresy. Cousins had taken her in out of charity, and when she was past the usual age for marrying, Win Perry's father had chosen a bride without a dower, giving her the few years she knew of security, for he was prominent in the victorious party of the White Rose. But soon after Win's birth the White Rose went down on Bosworth Field and Master Perry with it in King Richard's bodyguard—a case of such flagrance that even though Henry Tudor had established his new dynasty with remarkable toleration, the Perrys were left without property or prospects.

"What matters," Alison was saying, "is that Win shall do what is in him—the need to spend oneself is stronger in some than in others. Your father has felt it, Crede, and it is your good fortune that you could help him."

No one else had spoken in this way of Philip's venture. Those interested in it reckoned what advantage it might bring and those who could foresee no advantage regretted that it should have disturbed his comfortable way of life.

To Alison Crede admitted what she had not dared admit to herself: "He has been gone too long."

"I don't think you need be anxious yet." Alison had not answered too quickly. "Philip always takes time to do thoroughly whatever he sets out to do. And," she hesitated for a moment, her hand touching Crede's, "fear is the one thing we must never step ahead to meet—even for those we love we must not. We must not put that burden on them to chain them to us." Then she added cheerfully, "I have wanted to hear more of Philip's purpose, for Win tells me it is not just to discover new trade routes."

Crede found herself talking of Amerike as she had done with her father, recapturing the sense of greatness in the western prospect which had seized her imagination that day on Quayside, and drawing some reassurance now from Alison.

Win had to call them to dinner, and after it he and Crede set out on Grey Knight and Bess for their ride. It was a glorious day, crisp and bright, and to be riding through it was sheer joy that needed no words. Win led the way through gold-carpeted beechwoods, skirting past

Dursley and up to the sparse top of Stinchcombe Hill, where the turf was marked with outcroppings of limestone.

"We'll leave the horses here," he said, "for I'm taking you to my siege perilous."

They scrambled to a ledge of the cliff where it projected above the Severn plain and sat down to get their breath. The valley lay at their feet, and its loveliness in this autumn sun and color held them silent. Far upriver they could faintly see the towers of Gloucester turned to gold in the silvery blue sky—Caer Glow, the Fair City of ancient Britain, the Roman Glevum. The eye could trace almost the whole sparkling course of the river down from it: past the loop and the narrow ford by Newnham, on as it widened by the fat valley farmlands below the hanging beechwoods at their feet, and then on past the outstretching headlands of Aust and Beachley until it lost itself in the far sea blue of Bristol Channel with the downs above.

They were on the highest point of the Cotswold edge; south of them rose lesser hills with their beechwoods and bald tops, their sheepruns and worn paths and ribbons of old stonewall. In the valley farmlands, among the orchards and winding hedges, from the hills and everywhere, rose the spires of church and convent; no other county of England had so many—"as sure as God's in Gloucestershire," the saying ran.

But He must have shown Himself at different times in different ways. Across the river, Dean Forest and the hills rising in hazy distance beyond held things older than the Church. Today was so clear that they could see May Hill far northwestward, where tribes whose names were forgotten had gathered for fire worship and where there was still an eerie touch of pagan things in the May-Day games. Dean Forest had been King Arthur's hunting ground, and the Romans had worked its iron mines and felled its oak for their ships, as was done today; but no one knew with how much more remote a past were linked the special liberties of the small dark men of the Forest, who were unlike the larger, fairer, people of the rest of Gloucestershire and who took their most solemn oath upon a holly branch.

Win spoke of this and added, "There are old things on this side too. This hill and Nibley Knoll are marked with ramparts and were probably outlook posts since men first walked the ridgeways of Britain. On Nibley Knoll there is a great mound built—I think perhaps the earliest Gloucestershire men brought their dead to rest near this far view. Perhaps the farthest view they knew answered some need in them beyond a watch against hostile tribes."

"As we look farther to see new islands," Crede said thoughtfully, "I suppose there is some question in us so strong that it may be our essence. It is that, more than the profit of new trade routes, that drew Father westward. Do you think that Amerike may be a larger island than our own, and not the fringe of Cathay but a great new world?"

"Perhaps," Win said. "I think that what stirs us in a far view, some promise of greater things than we know, is more than a hope of new lands. Have you heard of Erasmus, Crede?"

Crede had not.

"He came often to Oxford and is a friend of Thomas More, whom we knew in London, and Dean Colet of St. Paul's. At first sight you would think nothing of him—a little, long-nosed clerk from Rotterdam. But if the New Learning is bringing in a new age, then I think that Erasmus is the first man of it. Everything that stirs men's thoughts now is seething in him. Somehow he makes you believe in his dream of a world that is wider, yet all one—he means more than the finding of new lands and trade routes. The printing press he calls our greatest discovery, because it spreads thought farther and faster than ever has been done before. What divides men, he says, is ignorance. If we teach every ploughboy to read, and if we put into his hands the great books of the world—the New Testament above all—we shall learn to deal fairly and peaceably with one another, and our kings will be ruled by the wisdom of scholars."

"It sounds like a world of Cousin Allie's invention," Crede said. "What will he do with the Turks and their armies?"

"If Christendom were bound together in a strong free commonwealth instead of being divided into quarreling kingdoms, we need not fear the Turks. We might meet them with a vision that would touch them too; for the highest hopes of all men between the mysteries of birth and death are the same, Erasmus says, and if any be lifted up they will draw other men unto them. He wants the Church to lead a great crusade to free men's minds instead of preaching a crusading war. He says the Church should clean its own house instead of hunting heresies. Yet he would not divide or weaken the Church, for it is the union we have above nations and their quarrels, and he rails as much against bigots who narrow what Christ meant to be broad as against some priests and bishops who act, he says, as if Christ were dead."

As Win talked Crede caught familiar echoes of Cousin Allie's enthusiasms and her father's speculations, but they were being knit into something more complete and revolutionary. If such ideas set men afire, they might indeed discover a new world.

"Tell me more about Erasmus," she said.

"He calls his philosophy 'Humanism' and calls himself a man of no country except the free commonwealth of men's minds. Yet he loves England best, I think. He spends most of his time here, for he says that the flame of the New Learning burns brightest in our universities and that the Church has nowhere a more enlightened head than Archbishop

Wareham. He loves all things Greek, too. In the ten years since he was drawn to Oxford by Thomas Grocyn's first lectures in the Greek language, it has spread like quicksilver through the colleges. It is a magic language, Crede. Somehow it frees the spirit to roam, as the stiffer Latin sentences do not. There is a stir of new things at Oxford lately, as there must have been long ago when Friar Bacon stung men to use their minds boldly, or when John Wycliffe stung their conscience. This time more may come of it—it seems so, at least to us younger ones."

Win had set a picture in Crede's mind of a town buzzing with the sound of those strange characters in Cousin Allie's book and swarming with new ideas, fuller of marvels than a traveler's tale.

Her imagination was diverting itself pleasantly when he said, "My best friend at Oxford was Robin Thorne."

This was tiresome, for Crede had conveniently forgotten to mention an incident she preferred not to discuss. Win was busily tossing pebbles at a rock and waiting for her to say something. He could not know of her recent lapse from gentility, so it must be that he had heard of that awkward first visit to Bristol—no doubt he had been given a full and amusing account of it.

"I have met him," she said. "But with so much stirring at Oxford you must have had many interesting friends. Tell me—"

"Robin and I did most things together. He was much more outstanding, of course."

He seemed not to notice her complete lack of interest in this subject. "I am sure his father can make quite a good man of business of him," she said magnanimously—dismissing it lightly again, she hoped. "Win—"

"Robin will do very well anything he makes up his mind to do." Win dropped the pebble he had picked up and turned his attention upon her. "You can't describe Robin easily, you know. At Oxford he was considered one of the most promising students of law, but he found time for all sorts of things. He could get as interested in some civic affair as if he were one of the burghers, or he could throw himself into a game as if he hadn't a thought beyond it. And he was always wanted for masques and interludes because he can play any kind of person. Perhaps it is because he could sweep me into things I'm apt to stand outside of that I miss him most—but it's not easy to say what draws one most to a friend."

At first Crede had thought that Win must be amusing himself for some reason with this fanciful picture of Robin Thorne. But he seemed to be presenting it quite seriously. Friendship is an odd thing, she reflected; it was a mystery to her what Win, with all his charm and talents, could see in a friend who must appear entirely commonplace to any unprejudiced person.

But her conscience stirred uncomfortably when he added, "I'd rather see Robin than anyone I left behind in Oxford or London. There was a chance I'd been hoping for that he might come this way before winter."

"He is in Bristol now," she said with compunction. "I—told him how to find you."

"But not that he could ride here in company? Upon my word, Crede, I thought better of you!"

Crede would have liked to think better of herself. And now she had got into a quarrel with Win over the wretched Thornes! He looked really angry.

"I don't suppose," he said, "that Robin is afraid to show you ordinary politeness because your fathers hoped—"

"Oh—!" Crede jumped up, her face scarlet.

"Aren't you acting as if you thought he had come here to bother you?"

"I'm not!" Crede cried furiously. "I don't think about him at all."

"I wish you would think of him as my friend then, and be reasonably decent when you meet him."

Win had got to his feet too, and they stood glaring ridiculously at each other. Then his eyes softened and he said, "Please don't be so angry, Crede. I'm very fond of you, you know. I've begun to feel as if you were my sister, and I've never had one. Doubtless that is why I thought I could scold at you."

His smile was quick and disarming, with the slight wryness there sometimes was in Philip's for the unreasonableness of things in general and himself in particular. Crede could not hold out against it.

"I needed scolding—that's why it made me so cross," she confessed.

As they climbed down to the horses and set out for Dalewood she took pains to show that she had not only recovered her temper but had put the unimportant cause of their disagreement quite out of her mind.

Next morning was still mild and sunny, and they walked across the fields toward Brookdale with no fear for their fine clothes. Alison had not, as Win predicted, cut up everything she owned for curtains and cushions; Crede thought her lovelier than ever in a blue and silver houpelande which was rather old-fashioned but became her perfectly. Mona looked very handsome in her best violet silk, and Crede had a new gown of stiff pink brocade which rustled elegantly. Each of them carried a nosegay of rosemary, bergamot, and southernwood for scent and a few late blooms from Alison's garden for show. Their new gloves, Stephen's traditional gift to his wedding guests, were trimmed with silver love knots. The guests of Dalewood would do it credit.

Stephen and Win had gone ahead, and the cottagers were streaming toward Dale Church in holiday dress, the musicians among them already tuning up. Crede and Mona had waited until the last possible moment expecting Adam Bell to ride in, and Alison had stayed with them.

Now as they reached St. Swithin's, the churchyard around the square old Saxon building was already thronged, and the flutes and tabors of the bride's minstrels could be heard across the meadow from Brookdale. There would not be time left to reach the house and march with the other guests, so they stayed where they were.

Presently Adam found them. "My horse cast a shoe and I was delayed at a smithy," he explained. "Mistress Mona, I vow the bride will be no handsomer! It is your ribbon I mean to snatch for my cap."

Mona smiled tolerantly, for Adam was permitted liberties few would venture upon.

"What news at home, Adam?"

Of course if the least news had come he would have told it first. Yet Crede had thought that perhaps some word of the *Brigid* detained him. She had wakened this morning lighthearted, with some sixth sense that her father was near.

"Why, all is well there. But I'll ride home tomorrow morning in case the *Brennus* gets in from Ireland. I've a packet of letters from London for you and Win, Mistress Perry. Robin Thorne brought them. I wanted him to ride out with me today, but he said he would come this way after the wedding."

Alison tucked the letters hastily into her reticule, for now the church bell began to ring and there was a thrusting forward in the crowd as the wedding procession crossed the meadow.

First came a young cousin of Bessie's carrying the silver knitting cup filled with Squire Annet's best wine and decked with a gilded branch of rosemary, the herb of constancy. Behind him walked the bridesmen, two younger cousins, holding the ends of ribbon fastened to Bessie's russet gown. Nothing could have enhanced Bessie's own vivid coloring more than this shade favored by fashion for wedding gowns and the wreath of wheat binding her bright brown hair. The minstrels following her, adding the merry din of flute and viol and lute and tabor to the pealing bell, could not have saluted a more beautiful bride.

After the minstrels came six bridesmaids bringing Stephen, and after them Squire Annet and the wedding guests. Besides conducting Stephen, who, it had seemed to Crede when she last saw him, was going to need the support of all six, the bridesmaids had to carry the huge bridescake, garlands of wheat, and branches of rosemary. They fluttered gaily across the field in their bright colored gowns.

Stephen, in the midst of them, with a bunch of rosemary at his belt, looked still a little dazed but as if he might be getting his second wind, and his new mulberry suit was very handsome. Earlier this morning it had seemed unlikely that his appearance would be so creditable. None of the many successes he had carefully planned and achieved before had suddenly got into the control of other hands than his own and whirled him into a maze of complications beyond anything he had foreseen. He had begun the day in a state of uncharacteristic flurry, depending upon Win to get him into his wedding garments and produce him at Brookdale, and the Dalewood ladies sighed with relief now to see him in his proper place and in better command of himself.

The procession crossed the churchyard, and as many as could crowded after it into the church porch where Father Dunstan waited to perform the ceremony. The pledges were given; the gimmal ring, a half of which Stephen and Bessie had each worn since their formal betrothal, was clasped together on Bessie's finger; and then everyone followed them into the church for the nuptial mass. The wedding homily would not be preached until the following Sunday, at the end of the Brookdale festivities. Therefore, as soon as mass was over Stephen and Bessie and their witnesses drank from the knitting cup, and then the cup was passed on to as many as could reach it, and the bridescake was broken and scrambled for.

A scramble for Bessie followed, all the younger men snatching the ribbon knots fastened about her dress to wear as favors in their caps, the two bridesmen defending their right to her gloves. She was pulled about and unmercifully kissed, until she could get to the protection of Stephen's arms. After that Squire Annet was the center of attention, for he was dispensing bride's ale in the church porch and distributing pence. During this diversion Bessie and Stephen escaped from the church, but they had to run the gauntlet outside. All the girls were caught and kissed. The bell ringers kept the bell dancing, the minstrels played their loudest, the air was sweet with crushed nosegays, and the bitter tang of rue mingled with it as the herb of grace was trampled by the gravestones. Out of this confusion the wedding party straggled across the meadow to Brookdale.

Brookdale had been the big house of the Dale for generations and, though the new splendors of Dalewood outshone it now, the look of that usage was still upon it. The great hall, by whose entrance old Squire Annet waited to welcome each guest to what seemed likely to be the last Annet marriage, could, in the rough old days, have stood a siege and housed all the laborers and tenants of the farm. It was scarcely crowded by the throng of guests and the long trestle tables set up to feed them. The din of voices and the vigorous performance of the musicians in the gallery lost itself among the high, smoke-blackened rafters.

As soon as Squire Annet took his place on the dais the procession from the kitchen began with the musicians at the head of it, outdoing those in the gallery; and a group of jugglers and tumblers followed, doing their turns between courses. Since each of these was a long succession of fish, flesh, and fowl, it was as well that the guests were under no necessity of entertaining themselves with conversation. Mona considered that the sauces lacked imagination, but there was no denying the lavishness of Brookdale hospitality.

It cleared the head somewhat to move out to the garden for the banquet of sweets, and after that the younger ones were ready for such romping games as Blindman's Buff and Nuts in May. Crede was swept into them and it was fun for a while, but Dale play was rougher than she had been accustomed to. She was breathless by the time she found herself with Win as partner and glad when he suggested a rest.

"I wanted a chance to talk," he said when he had led her through the herb garden to a seat beside the well. "Crede, do you think Mother would mind too much if we have to leave the cottage? You know how hard she has worked on it."

Crede looked at him with astonishment. He had not said a word of this when they were alone yesterday.

"There was news in a letter Master Bell brought me," he said, and Crede could see that he was holding down excitement. "It is from Dean Colet of St. Paul's—do you remember I spoke of him yesterday? He is one of the best from Oxford whose minds have been stirred by the New Learning. He's a friend of Erasmus and Archbishop Wareham and Thomas More."

"Win, he has found a chance for you!"

"I didn't know he thought so well of me," Win said, his eyes shining. "He is using the fortune left by his father, who was a rich London merchant, to refound the old school for boys at St. Paul's Cathedral, with the new ideas that he and Erasmus have about teaching. Master William Lily of Oxford, the noted Greek and Latin scholar, will be its headmaster, and Dean Colet has offered me a place under him. I think that Robin has done more than carry the letter, of course. He knows Dean Colet, too, and he was there in London when this plan was forming."

"Your mother will be wild with joy, Win. Yesterday she said that a chance must surely come to use your scholarship. How could you think that she would mind?"

"It is just that I'd like her to enjoy what she has made here for a while longer," Win said slowly. "Mother would never say so, but she has worked like a slave to make a home of that cottage."

"It was the doing of it she loved, Win. Yesterday, when we were at the cottage, I thought that Alison must always put the most she has into any moment she has, but she wouldn't cling to it. You see, I felt so drawn to her from the first that I had to wonder why, as you don't with someone

[95]

you have always known. She doesn't make any claims with what she gives, she just wants to give it—especially to you."

"It hasn't been much of a life for Mother at her cousin's in London, you know. You are right in saying that she gives more than she takes—she was a servant without pay there. Of course I'd get a little place of our own as soon as I could, but I shan't be earning much. Here we have a home, and if I kept on with the sheep and learned some of Stephen's shrewdness we might have a fairly comfortable living."

"Anything you could afford in London would be enough to begin with, Win. Whatever it is, Alison will make something of it as she did of the cottage, and she'll be even happier because you have the chance she has wanted for you." Crede began planning excitedly. "You have a share in the sheep and you can arrange with Adam about that while he is here now, and I am sure you could sell the cottage and land for enough to make a start in London. You could find a place to rent at first—"

"Stop, I'm dizzy!" Win laughed. "What a little whirlwind you are, Crede!" But he put his arm around her.

"How soon should you go?"

"As soon as possible, I suppose. The new school won't be built for a while, but they are beginning with a few pupils left from the old foundation, and they want to plan new and better books to teach from."

"The place here ought to be worth more now than when you came. Stephen—"

"Stephen did offer something out of kindness then, though he couldn't see much in it. But lately Squire Annet said that if we ever wanted to sell it might do for a young nephew he means to set up. He put a higher value on it than Stephen had done—as high as Master Bell thought it might bring."

"Then there's nothing to keep you, Win. You will go, won't you?"

"There's no question if I tell Mother, of course. I suppose I could hardly bear not to go. But you helped clear my mind, Crede."

Crede walked rather soberly beside him to join the others. Now that there was time to think of another side of it, she knew how much she would miss having Alison and Win within reach, but she did not mean to spoil what she hoped she had learned from Alison by saying so.

It was growing dusk and chill outside, and one group after another began to move into the hall where a log was burning in the great fireplace. The table on the dais had been loaded with cold supper dishes for those whose appetites revived, and the rest of the room was cleared for games and dances. But everyone was ready for an idle hour first and now, while the firelight flickered and the hall grew long with shadows, was the time for songs and storytelling.

For a while the lute passed from hand to hand, and then there was an

Interlude got up by the tenants in honor of the occasion; but by candle-lighting time everyone had been sitting still long enough, and the musicians tuned up for dancing.

Everybody knew the rollicking country dances which followed in breathless succession, and everybody wanted to dance them, singing with the minstrels: "Nobody's Jig," "Dusty my Dear," "Flaunting Two," and other favorite tunes. The floor was crowded with a merry confusion in which it was hard to keep one's own place. Crede, whose feet could not stay still when there was dancing, stood up with everyone who asked her and was swung in the turns by these country boys till she was dizzy.

Suddenly in one of the changes she found herself opposite Robin Thorne! He looked tired and dusty, and how on earth had he got here? When their hands crossed he whirled her out of the set just as the circle joined for the romping hay-de-gay and carried her down the room with him before she could get her breath to speak.

"Crede, the *Brigid* is back."

"Father—he's—"

"All well!"

She stumbled and would have fallen, but he held her easily and swept on through the dancers to a space by the hearth.

She had not known until it was taken from her how heavy the burden had been of waking every morning to hope, of telling herself at night that it was too soon to be anxious, with the fear of November storms always growing. For a moment she felt lightheaded.

"Sit here," he said. "I am a clumsy oaf! Sit still and hold your head down while I get you a drink."

"I'm all right now. And how can I thank you! I can start home right away—could you please find Adam and Mona?"

"But you couldn't possibly ride this road at night—I mean," he said hastily, "nothing would be gained by going now. If you leave in the morning you'll be in time to see the *Brigid* get in. They stopped at Cork for a repair, and your father found the *Brennus* there and sent word with her that all are safe. That was good enough news, I thought, not to wait for any more."

He had ridden over strange hill roads past dark to bring it—a neighborly kindness she did not deserve.

"How did you manage to find us?"

"Why, it is an easy road to Thornbury, and after that everyone could tell me how to get to Brookdale. Here comes Master Bell."

Adam and Mona had seen them and were the first now to get the news.

"The saints be praised!" Mona said and sat down beside Crede. "I always knew it would turn out all right, *mo mhornin*."

[97]

"If the *Brennus* got in on the late tide," Adam said, "you must have ridden like the Demons' Hunt, Robin."

Probably he had not known enough about hill country to realize the hazards of the Dale road after dark, but by the mercy of heaven he had blundered through.

"It was a very kind thing to do," Crede said. "Adam, can't you and I start back now? The moon will soon be up. And if the *Brigid* makes the morning tide she might be in before we could get back tomorrow." She was in a fever of impatience.

"I have more care of our necks in these hills," Adam said. "Besides, they won't be in right on the heels of the *Brennus,* Crede, if Philip thought it worth while to send word ahead."

"Let me hear of no more night riding," Mona said severely. "There is not the least need of such folly!" But she tempered her remarks with a very friendly smile for Robin Thorne. "We will go back to Dalewood as soon as we can, and be ready to set out early tomorrow."

The dance now in progress was a slow dompe, and with the floor in less confusion Win caught sight of them and hurried Alison toward their corner.

"Robin! Where ever—?"

But all explanations waited on the good news. Alison hugged Crede and whispered, "I couldn't have borne to leave you, dear, until Philip was safe home. Win tells me you know about London."

It was Mona who remembered that Robin Thorne might be hungry.

"Take Master Thorne to the table, Win," she said, "and see that he has food and wine. You and I must find the wedding party, Crede, and take our leave."

A pause had come in the dancing, and others were moving toward the dais to refresh themselves. Most of the guests still here would stay the night, pallets would be spread in the hall for the overflow after a merry procession had escorted Bessie and Stephen to bed. Then the feasting would go on tomorrow. A riotous group surrounded the bride and groom now, breaking bridescake over them and scrambling to find their fortunes in the pieces. The bridesmaids untied Bessie's garters, throwing them as far as they could, and the young men raced for these trophies while the girls plucked myrtle leaves from the garlands round the hall, trying to make them crackle in their fingers to prove their loved ones true.

Through this confusion Mona shepherded her party to make their farewells. Then they followed the path to Dalewood in bright, crisp starlight while the music from the hall grew faint behind them and a light breeze chilled the air.

If the *Brigid* had left Ireland she could keep sail on tonight.

[98]

TEN

They had reached home none too soon for by afternoon the news was all over Quayside that the *Brigid* had been sighted in the Channel and might make the tide.

The ride from Dalewood in the morning had been as swift as Crede's impatience could make it. They had paused only long enough in Thornbury to leave word that Sadie could stay at the farm until next week and come back with the Perrys, who hoped to settle their affairs in the Dale while Robin Thorne visited the neighboring wool towns so that they could return with him to London.

Their arrival at Mary le Port Street had put an instant end to Kate's holiday for Mona had plunged at once into preparations of the utmost magnificence and was still busy with them now while Crede, with Adam and Cousin Allie, waited among a crowd on Quayside as the tide brought the incoming ships upriver.

"Listen!" Crede clutched Adam's arm. She had caught the first note from the bell of Clifton Church. Sebastien Cabot who had gone to watch from Giant's cliff had promised to set it ringing as soon as he caught sight of the *Brigid* and now St. Stephen's by Quayside, the mother church of the Bell Ringers' Guild, answered it and then all the bells of Bristol joined in. For though it was ten years ago that they had pealed to welcome the *Matthew* home, the safe return of a ship from Amerike was still a marvel and a score of families besides Philip's waited anxiously for their eyes to prove that the message "all well" truly meant the one they watched for.

With the din of the bells in their ears they strained their eyes against the sunset for what seemed ages. Then Adam shouted, "There she is!" and made his broad shoulders a bulwark behind Crede to hold her at the front of the crowd. Crede, whose eyes found Philip while he was still only a dot on the *Brigid*'s deck and were held fixed there, noticed nothing else until his arms were around her.

The crew were singing the Salve Regina, sung on all ships in Christendom at sunset, as they made the *Brigid* fast and the crowd on Quayside joined in. Philip kept his arm around Crede while he took Adam's hand and Cousin Allie's and greeted several old friends and neighbors. He was very thin but this was nothing she and Mona could not mend.

"My darling!" he said. "Crede, child, have you been worrying? You aren't much of an armful!" They were surrounded now by the other

[99]

merchants concerned in the venture and he turned to them with a smile, "Give me an hour, friends, to convince my daughter that I am alive and then have supper with us."

It must be wonderful, Crede thought even in the midst of her thankfulness, to be a man and enjoy this happy confidence that whatever commotion one's sudden return from the ends of the earth might cause along Quayside, a sufficiency of joints and pasties for any hospitable impulse would appear upon one's table.

But Mona had foreseen something of the sort and was equal to it. Short as the time had been since her arrival at the house Philip had no cause to blush for her provision and it could have fed twice as many as he had bidden. After supper they sat in the hall with Cormac stretched across his master's feet and there were questions from all but it was only what her father answered that caught Crede's ear.

The weather had favored them all the way, brisk sailing weather in which the *Brigid* could show her mettle, and many starlit nights through which they could hold their course. Only a month past sight of Ireland they had seen the far western coast.

"I was making for John Cabot's landfall at Cape Britain," Philip said, "but we had taken a straighter course west and the land we saw first was north of it, as we discovered later; sailing coastwise along it we concluded it is an island. We found harbor and rested to fill our casks and to fish. There are fish in abundance, but the shore is bleak. Below it we found a great bay and coasted along it and this coast is part of Amerike, for later we found John Cabot's mark in the harbor he named St. John's."

Cousin Allie sat with his sea cards around him. But he was too much excited to make marks on them; his cheeks were pink and his eyes, like Crede's, fastened upon Philip. Several who had not come to supper had drifted into the hall later, Sebastien Cabot among them.

"In the bay there is a great channel," Philip said, "that at first we thought must be the end of Amerike. But the land goes on below it and I think that what we passed must be the mouth of a mighty river. There must be more than one such river in Amerike for we found another wide opening farther south—and yet the land stretching on beyond it. Everything about Amerike is so large that it passes belief. There is land enough there for every landless man anywhere and there are so few inhabiting it that we scarcely saw them."

"One or both of what you took for rivers," Sebastien Cabot said sharply, "might be a passage to Cathay. I'd have left everything else to follow them."

"I still think they are rivers," Philip said. "As you sail down Amerike, the feel of the land comes to you as of one great mass, vast enough to have such rivers reaching far inland."

"How far down it did you go, Philip?" Master Robert Thorne asked.

"We got into the warm south as you did with John Cabot, but we could see no more signs of the land ending when we decided to try for home before winter. We had taken time for a good many landings, and our shore parties found things of such variety, although no gold or spices, that Amerike seems less like a country than a whole new world—it goes beyond our understanding that so great a part of creation has been left near empty."

He tried to make them see it then; and as he talked, Crede, leaning against his shoulder and feeling the strain of months relax, forgot whether she was listening or was part of the story.

All around Cape Britain the woods rose dense and endless, he explained. "The forest soil when you crumble it is black and rich and nourishes hardwoods as great as those of Dean Forest and evergreens whose tops rise above them. It's a good land for northerners, though hotter than here at noon, with more sudden changes; these stir the blood and at times the air is like wine. Fruits we know, plums and grapes and a sort of crabapple and most of our berries, grow wild there, and red and white roses. It seemed to me that a peninsula which curved like two outspread arms, very densely wooded, might be Markland, the tree land of the Iceland sagas.

"I may have given this matter as much thought as trade routes," Philip confessed with the smile which poked fun at himself. "My head has been full of those old tales since I was a boy hanging around Cousin William's Iceland ships, and I kept wondering whether we were choosing the same harbors as Leif Erikson found five hundred years ago for his long ship. We lived as well as they did, for you have only to throw out a line to get fish, and on shore there were wild fowl of all sorts, and coneys like ours—only their fur is grayer, more like a hare's—and deer like ours, except that their horns curve differently. Once we found a fire still smoldering with a haunch of venison roasting and beside it a basket of flat cakes, ground coarsely from no grain we know but very good. Our hosts did not appear, however, and it was not until much later that we saw any of the inhabitants."

"Did you find no spices at all?" Richard Amerike asked.

"Only sassafras trees farther south. The profit in this region, I think, is not spices or even the gold that Spain has found in the southern islands, but land—far more land than there are men to claim what a man may work—land which God has held out of time, free of overlords and rent."

"Spices and gold would take men there sooner, Philip," Robert Thorne said. "The patient man who wants his hide of land to work is slower moved. What did you find further south?"

"When we came to the end of what it pleased me to call Markland, we followed a coast of much the same country and climate, curving southwestward until a spit of land ran out so suddenly that we were almost wrecked on it. Down its side, I think, is Leif Erikson's 'Wonderstrand,' for I have never seen a beach more silvery and, if this is true, the end of the hook where we so nearly ran ashore must be where he found the keel of that ship which was before us all. Two islands lie south of the spit—on that side it is almost cut off at its base by a deep bay—and here, I think, may be Vineland the Good. Everything I can remember the saga telling of—the island and the point with its white sand, and the wooded bay, and an abundance of grapes—seemed to fit this place."

He had caught their imagination now, and even Sebastien waited without a question for him to go on.

"We rested here, and then, for two days' sailing, the coast bent westward until we came between it and a long, narrow island. We thought at first that we had found the western passage, until it narrowed so that we left the ship and took the long boat. Then we saw that the island comes to an end, and the mainland goes on, and what opens out of it here is, I am sure, the mouth of another great river like the one we had found farther north. Below the island the coast straightened out again, and we followed it almost due south for three days' sailing.

"I was watching for signs of Ireland the Great," Philip said with a smile for Mona. "We had found so much to match what Leif Erikson reported, and he believed that St. Brendan's City lay south of Vineland where natives had told him there were towns of fairer, white-robed men. But the shore was still wild and empty.

"We came next upon a very large bay and found that it curved back northward, long and narrow and full of islands and inlets, and here the country was quite different from Vineland or anything else we had yet seen in Amerike. It is a hot, moist country with ranker growth and many fruits we did not know.

"We harbored at a river mouth and stayed a week, and the first natives we had seen came out to greet us. They seemed honest, friendly folk with skins about as dark as a Moor's and high noses like a Spanish Jew's. They had a village, built with poles and a sort of matting, and they make boats by hollowing a log with fire. They showed us what fruits and nuts to eat and gave us some of the corn they grow—it has a head many times larger than ours, with larger kernels colored deep gold and sometimes red or blue. There is also a wild plant whose wands grow near water and whose seeds are mild and mealy when boiled. We brought some of these grains home, and I wish we could have kept some of the stranger fruits.

"But the natives knew nothing of any towns larger than their own settlement, and we soon had enough of the damp heat; even in September it was so hot that I doubt it is fit for an Englishman to work in. If we were to risk the voyage home before winter we had to give up trying to find the end of Amerike this year."

All their questions had stopped long ago. It seemed that the others had been carried with him as Crede had been, seeing the new land with his eyes. As Philip paused now to sit staring into the fire, his hand on Cormac's head, Crede saw that he looked tired. She was pleased when Master Thorne said that he would, no doubt, be glad of a bed ashore and carried the others off with him.

Philip's return changed everything. Like Cormac, the house seemed to stir itself again as if for months it had been merely passing time. The round of work took on a new briskness and purpose, while in the counting house the industry of the boys was something to marvel at.

Crede sang in the kitchen and stillroom, her feet moved in dance time as she went about Quayside, as close to Philip's elbow as Cormac was to his heels. She found him well pleased with what had been done in his absence.

Today, while she gathered the late green of rosemary and myrtle for the hall, she was romping with Fand in the garden as if the brisk November air and the crackle of dead leaves had set the same sort of spell upon her as sent Fand tearing through the hedges and borders. Today the Perrys were expected, and Mona had been making extensive preparations. Crede's last assigned task before she tidied herself to greet guests had been to put fresh garlands in the rooms, but she and Fand had forgotten the time and were still in the midst of their game when Alison and Win rode into the lane with Sadie and Robin Thorne.

As she ran to greet them Will came hurrying from the stable. Sadie tumbled off Matilda and hurled herself upon him before anyone else could speak.

"Is it all right, Will?" she demanded.

"The coney is right enough, you may as well go straight to see it. But another time, my girl, don't be putting yourself ahead of everyone—and leading guests in the back way!" Will said severely as he stepped forward to take the horses.

In the midst of the greetings Philip and Mona came from the house, and then Crede took Alison to her own room which Alison would share.

"We are going to have a wonderful visit," she said happily, taking Alison's cloak and bringing warm water for her to wash before she began pulling off her own crumpled and earth-stained gown. "There is time to rest a little before supper. What a sight I am to greet you!"

"I've never before seen you with such roses in your cheeks, dear. Any gown would do with them."

"I am so happy and thankful, Alison. Do you need anything out of your bags, or shall we wait to unpack them later?"

"Don't unpack them, dear—just a few things on top. Robin and Win hope to sail tomorrow or the next day."

"Oh not so soon!" Crede dropped the comb with which she was trying to bring some order to her wind-tangled hair. "I thought we were to have a visit!"

"I hoped we might have a few days. But it is getting late for good weather, you know. Robin found the cloth he wants in Stroud, and when it reaches here by Severn barge there will be nothing more to keep him."

So the feast which had been prepared to welcome them was full of their plans for leaving. Philip had invited Robin Thorne to stay, and when Crede and Alison came downstairs Adam Bell had joined the others. Questions about Amerike and Win's new prospects occupied them at first. Then the news that Stephen and Bessie were off on their pilgrimage but had compromised on one to the holy hand of St. James at Reading Abbey instead of to the shrine of St. Thomas at Canterbury (a journey which had the advantage of being shorter and also of allowing Stephen to do a little business on the way in the wool towns) lasted them through supper and on into the green parlor afterward.

When they were seated around the fire, Crede found herself beside Robin Thorne, and this was unfortunate because although she wanted Win to see that her manners had improved and wanted Robin Thorne to know that she could appreciate a kindness, she had thanked him again when they met this afternoon and was unable now to think of anything else it could interest them to talk about. Luckily she need not try for the moment, because Cousin Allie was still questioning Win about the new school at St. Paul's, and they were all curious.

It would be really new, Win said; for the old foundation was much decayed and Dean Colet was a man to cut away dead wood wherever he came upon it. The Dean had studied in Italy where scholars escaping from the Turkish conquest of Constantinople had brought back to the West the arts and sciences of ancient Greece and Rome, but the rebirth which John Colet hoped most to bring about was of the spirit of the early church in the light of the New Learning. When he preached from the Greek text of St. Paul's letters, Win told them, the apostle seemed as close as one's neighbor, the vision of Christ as fresh as if no time had passed in theological quibbling since He came to be the Light of the World. In London where it was commonly said that if the devil had murdered a monk a jury of citizens would acquit him, people who could not be forced to church even by fines crowded the Dean's weekday lectures on St. Paul. Now he meant their sons to have a school that fitted the times. He had given Erasmus the opportunity to plan a modern school building and books, while the headmaster he had chosen was equally advanced—Master William Lily, a noted scholar of the New Learning.

Cousin Allie shook his head doubtfully. "Among children only one in ten is worth the time of a learned man, and fewer still will add a jot to learning. Surely Dean Colet is going from great things to small, when the world is opening so swiftly that we can barely imagine what changes may come in our own lifetime."

"It's hard to say what fits the times in London," Robin Thorne said at the same moment.

But he had spoken only loud enough for Crede to hear, so that the discussion begun by Win and Cousin Allie went on without them. Though she was most interested in it she was obliged by politeness to give Robin her attention.

"London grows overnight. And you find as great a stir of new things there as in Oxford, though they don't put names to them so readily. I wonder what you would make of it," he added unexpectedly. "I wish you could see London. If your father comes that way again—"

"He seldom does," Crede said. "We don't ship east, you know."

"And there is nothing you need come to us for, of course. But I—" he hesitated, and Crede had a fleeting glimpse of something between amusement and ruefulness which she could see no reason for. She could not guess whether it made fun of himself or of her. "Your Cotswold cloth must continue to bring me back, I suppose."

Wherever his mind had wandered, it seemed to have returned quickly to this scheme for improving Thorne profits, and now he looked entirely serious, pausing for a moment as if reminded of trade secrets.

"I wanted to spend longer here this time," he said finally. "But we shouldn't miss this favorable weather with Mistress Perry aboard."

"Indeed you must not."

Crede's glance crossed the circle where Alison sat between Philip and Adam. For a few days she had been able to forget the lateness of the season for sailing, and she had wanted so much to keep the Perrys longer.

She had lost the thread of the conversation when Adam's voice caught her attention. He was saying something about the *Brigid*, and this touched off an uneasy question.

"She won't be refitted before spring sailing, Philip, for whatever you mean to use her for then. For years I've talked of seeing the north country again, and I've been thinking that this would be a good time to go."

"You have talked of it whenever you have had a foot on land for more than a week," Philip said with a quick smile for Adam. "Both feet have been tied ashore for months, and now it's my turn to manage for you. Take all the time you want."

Adam too was going, and perhaps he would never come back. There was a valley in the north country which his ancestors had called their own before the Normans came and, although he had been sent as a boy out of a house overcrowded with brothers to learn his letters from the monks of Jervaulx and then south to make his own fortune where silver was more plentiful, he still thought of himself as belonging to those hilly acres. Stories he had told Crede of their stubborn defense, through centuries changed by larger issues, made a long tale of violence; even yet, he had said with a pride strange in one so hard against lawlessness in Cornwall among Tony's relatives, there were valleys in Cumberland and Yorkshire where the king's writ did not run; and Englewood, south of Carlisle, was a remnant of the great English Wood of the north country, which had been a familiar refuge for many of its old stock when they were at outs with Norman laws and overlords. One of the oldest ballads told of an Adam Bell who had led a band there before the days of Robin Hood, and Philip began to sing it now with a teasing glance toward Adam who had taught it to them.

> *Merry it is in the green forest*
> *Among the leves green*
> *Where that men hunted east and west*
> *With bows and arrows keen.*

If Philip feared that Adam might not come back to them, he was not showing it. He had picked up Crede's lute as he sang and now meant the party to end pleasantly with music, for he passed it on to Cousin Allie.

But Adam had said, "whatever you mean to use the *Brigid* for next spring," and Philip had not answered that question. Lately, Crede had felt something disturbing reach through to her in his talk of Amerike. He had seemed to lose the air of detachment which had been his reassuring charm, the hint of something inwardly secure from change. Amerike had set a spell on him—he spoke, with an eagerness which seemed restless to drive events against time, of building towns and farms in that great emptiness, of seeing a new England rise there with opportunity for every man. But who could match a land so limitless—so out of the world's long tale of struggling and hoping—so ominously unchosen and unpeopled when other lands were filled with the clamor of men and church bells and friendly animals? For Crede, the charm of the unknown which she too had felt was becoming a vague fear of its strangeness, and of this new urgency in Philip.

Cousin Allie had been trying chords, and now a plaintive tune with a broken, restless rhythm was taking shape. He could compose his own airs and liked to fit them to something old and forgotten. These verses, he said, came down from English tribes who crossed the seas to Britain; and a monk of Malmesbury Abbey, where they kept many curious manuscripts, had helped him decipher them. His voice which was thin but still true began to follow the lute in a haunting minor key.

> Hungers my heart now for the high seas
> For Ocean's rough play.
> Stirs my soul now in the strait heart hold,
> Tide called to the whale's ways
> To the sea surge
> To earth's end.
> Back to me, back again
> Flies the lone seeker
> Calling me, driving me
> Down to the sea.

It fitted too well a growing unease. Cormac lay content at Philip's feet, while Fand merrily chased shadows—yet, here in the room she loved best, Crede had an odd moment of homesickness. Firelight warmed its soft colors; it fell rosily on Mona's white cap and painted violets on Alison's blue gown, and it touched the gold of the portrait with life. Crede had never before been so sharply aware of holding happiness to her. Was it only in childhood that you could feel the things you wanted unquestioningly safe around you, and could you never truly secure them? Once the room had held its own loveliness as confidently as a sunny glade kept its golden secret at the end of a forest path, but now all paths seemed leading away from it—the path of Alison, who had somehow become part of it, of Adam, who was like one of their own family.

Anthony had been the first to go, and it was at his going that things had begun to change. All summer and autumn no word had come from him. Crede's hands moved restlessly in her lap until she noticed that Robin Thorne was watching her and held them still.

Mona picked up the lute when Cousin Allie set it down, though even when it passed to her in turn she seldom took it, and only now and then could Crede coax her to remember her old Irish songs.

"It's no heathen spell I'll sing to you like Master Perry's," she said, "but this is as old. We were Christians in Ireland then, with the blessed saints keeping our souls where they belonged. I'll give you our own Saint Patrick's hymn for your journeying."

"Saint Patrick," Philip said, "was only an Englishman settled upon Ireland."

His glance toward Mona held his old gay teasing. In its easy lightness things growing strange and frightening could promise to find their own familiar shape again, whoever was leaving them, and Crede's spirits rose.

Mona merely sniffed and tried the lute. "These were the sainted Irishman's own words when it was put upon him to go abroad among foreigns, every last one of them outside of Ireland being savages," she said.

When her fingers had found the air she wanted, her voice which was sweet and high carried it.

> *I bind me today*
> *God's might to direct me*
> *God's power to protect me*
> *God's wisdom for learning*
> *God's eye for discerning*
> *God's ear for my hearing*
> *God's word for my clearing*
> *God's hand for my cover*
> *God's path to pass over.*

ELEVEN

After the London party had gone, Mona and Crede had nothing to distract them from putting their heads together to fatten Philip, and so resourceful were their imaginations and so dazzling the succession of dishes which appeared on the table that even Cousin Allie occasionally noticed what he was eating. Indeed, Crede thought that he was making an effort to do so and to lead them on.

As November advanced there was no talk of his return to the cottage; though Cousin Allie's mind might seem generally absent from everyday affairs, his heart never forgot its loyalties, and these were for Philip and Crede. He had stood by Crede to the best of his ability while Philip was away and, now that the boy had come home looking fine-drawn and too old for his years, Cousin Allie began finding jobs to do in the counting room and in the evenings let Philip talk his head off about Amerike. It had not escaped his notice that Crede and Mona avoided the subject.

Cousin Allie did not himself think Amerike a fit place for even the most destitute Englishman to settle in—it had no link with the civilized world except crazy boats and stormy water, and he hoped to get Philip tactfully over that notion. But he did think it offered a most interesting field for scholarly observation and speculation, and he found endless questions to ask in support of his own theories of cosmography and natural history. It was a pity, he said, that Englishmen seemed to have lost the taste for such subjects, which had once led them to increase the world's knowledge of itself; for it was the Venerable Bede who had revived, ages ago, Greek speculations that the earth was round and King Alfred, in his busy life, had found time to translate Orosius's history of the world and to send out expeditions with the disinterested purpose of gathering new information.

But the Bristol merchants did not see themselves in this role. With the exception of Master Robert Thorne they grew lukewarm when the *Brigid* reported no immediate opportunity for trade. Though Sebastien Cabot maintained that Philip had overlooked a passage to Cathay and went about pursuing them with offers to pilot an expedition next spring for the purpose of finding it, no definite plans were being made. So far, Philip had not suggested going again himself.

St. Catherine's day passed with the pageants and processions devised by the Weavers' Guild in honor of their patron saint, and now autumn was closing in to winter.

Crede spent almost as much time in the counting house as she had spent before Philip's return, and she often went to Quayside with him. He liked to have her beside him, and it amused him to take her among the other merchants. "I have better than any of their sons at my elbow," he told her, rendering her speechless with pride. "Besides, aren't you the Merchant Venturer?"

He had not been at all put out by that deal with Spicer's Hall, saying that Crede had jumped a hurdle he should have taken himself and that she had shown good judgment. He praised her also for Clem's appointment to the *Belinus,* and this seemed to be working out very well, for Clem was still, so late in the season, making quick, profitable trips to Dublin. Down in the Marsh, Tim Arden was working on the *Brigid* in a passion of love and anger; she had been roughly driven, he said, and he did not still his grumblings in Philip's presence. Nothing less than as-good-as-new would satisfy him, and he was making a long job of it, exasperating the men by his fussiness and scolding at every scratch he found, but Philip enjoyed him, Crede thought.

She thought that he enjoyed, almost deliberately, every small thing which touched his old humor yet, behind it all something remained unsettled, something he waited for with less than his usual sureness. She was with him so much, not only because he wanted her and they had months of separation to make up for, but because, as she suspected of Cousin Allie, she was watching him anxiously. It was quite unreasonable of them, for it must be expected that even a man who was so strong would be tired by such a voyage.

But there was little protecting numbness of surprise in the swift anguish of secret fear which took shape when Philip fell beside his desk one December morning.

After a long moment when they thought him dead—Crede, Cousin Allie, and the frightened boys—he opened his eyes and pressed Crede's hand.

"Happened before, dearest," he said. "Don't worry," and closed his eyes again, his mouth twisted with pain.

"Don't move him!" Cousin Allie said sharply.

They sent Bob for Master Gilfroy, the herbalist, and Ned for Master Hoare, the barber surgeon. Upon their arrival, Philip was bled and carried to his bed. Mona, white-faced and entirely competent, received their further instructions with her lips set and closed the door behind them.

"There will be no more bleeding," she told Crede. "I would have stopped this had I got there in time. It is not less blood he needs but more rest and food and the herbs I know best how to brew for him. Don't look so frightened, *mo mhornin*—you and I will make him well."

Crede found her hope in Mona and her refuge in work. Philip, when the sharp chest pain which had conquered him eased, smiled with his eyebrow lifted in its old humorous twist at the elaborate preparations for his comfort.

A saffron pillow had been put under his head, red curtains had been hung about the bed to ward off fever, bunches of pungent herbs were strung about the room, and something fragrant burned in a brazier. Crede was bathing his forehead from a vial so tiny that the essence it contained must be extremely holy, and Mona stood waiting with a steaming posset. He sipped it meekly and said, "Two such determined women will keep me living to a hundred, I expect, with my character eternally ruined."

In the next few days he took all the remedies they brought and swallowed the broths and custards, though he often insisted that Crede have a bowlful too and watched while she downed it.

"We'll make a bargain to fatten each other up, Kitten," he said, "for upon my word you look nearer a ghost than I do."

A little color was beginning to come into his face, and one morning he told them that his illness was passing off.

"It happened once before, in Amerike," he said, "after we had made a long day's journey in the hills, but within a week I was as good as ever. It may never happen again."

"This time," Mona said, "you will have proper care. You will keep to your bed for much more than a week until good food and herbs have restored your heart, for I judge the trouble to have its seat there. But there are herbs to heal each member of the body, and the blessed saints have given me knowledge of them."

With Crede's eyes hungrily searching his face for each day's gain,

Philip let them have their way with him. Even when he said that he felt as strong as an ox he let Mona forbid him to test his strength yet by getting out of bed. Crede spent most of her time beside him, and Mona brewed and cooked tirelessly with the air of a priestess of mysteries.

"I think she stirs my broth to dark Irish incantations instead of a paternoster," Philip confided to Crede and Cousin Allie.

He knew better than to venture the jest if Father Ambrose happened to be making one of his visits, for this could be a serious charge; it was part of a learned frivolity he shared with Cousin Allie, an atmosphere in which Crede had grown up, that they could be amused by it. But any nonsense was delightful when Philip was able to enjoy it.

He really did look better. He sat up in bed now, and although Mona still forbade visitors, except of course Father Ambrose, the family began to make his room their gathering place. Cousin Allie drew sea cards at his table, Crede and Mona brought their needlework there, and Cormac, who could be coaxed away for meals now, spent the rest of his time stretched contentedly across his master's feet instead of drearily upon the floor. Even Fand had found out where the new center of the house was; she had come in cautiously at first, but now she was often curled among the pillows.

"I feel like a graven image surrounded by its priesthood and sacred animals," Philip teased, but he liked to have them there.

Crede and Cousin Allie between them were easily able to give all the time needed at this season in the counting room, where the boys had only light tasks to perform among many holiday dispensations. Philip's suggestion of keeping Clem on Quayside for anything that needed managing there was working out well. Clem was eager to help and quick to learn anything he set his mind to. They had much to be thankful for, and Crede felt humbly grateful; in those first anxious days so many gifts of kindness and so many neighborly services had come to their door that she, who had never lived with trouble before, knew that she had never even thought to give the sympathy her family now received in such generous measure.

Soon Philip was sitting up in a chair, and even Mona said that he would be downstairs for Christmas. They would keep that holiday quietly, however. This meant that they would not hold open house for all the feasting and merrymaking which lasted until Twelfth Night. They would also have to forego their usual party for all Canynges workers and their families on St. Stephen's Day. However, they would not forget any of the traditional observances within the family. Mona and Kate carried on the usual preparations, and Philip said he had never before had a chance to sit and lazily watch the stir this made.

Will and the boys had chosen the huge Yule log and gathered holly

and ivy. The boys were in a fever of excitement. Not only had they been
given leave to go a-wassailing and were practicing carols at all hours, but
their improved attendance at St. Mary's had earned them a place among
the shepherds in the Nativity Play. They had not been chosen by the
Lord of Misrule for his court which was permitted the utmost license
to roister about the streets throughout the twelve days of Christmas, since
the supervision of apprentices in Philip Canynges' household was strict
enough to keep them from being intimate with the wilder element, but
they had their share in enough other diversions for which the town was
merrily laying aside its business.

There were Twelfth Night gifts to think of too, and Philip was in
everyone's secrets. Crede worked on her gifts in his room, with Fand
making a tangle of the wools and silks and sounds of the boys' minstrelsy
floating upstairs, generally a little off key:

> Herod the king in his raging
> Charged he hath this day
> His men of might in his own sight
> All children young to slay.

A woolly lamb which Crede was making for little Clem turned out
quite well, but Mona's gift was less to her liking although it had been
more ambitious. She was making a night robe, a new fashion which she
thought would please Mona who liked elegant innovations, and she was
putting her most painstaking embroidery stitches on lovely purple velvet.
But she was not an accomplished needlewoman. Mona had pointed out
more than once that Crede preferred to learn the things one might discover rather than those one must practice, and now Crede's stitches
seemed to grow perversely more crooked with her anxious care to make
them as fine as Mona's own. It was fortunate that this was the last gift
she had to make.

Philip's, which had to be done outside his room, had been finished
by candlelight last night. He loved the old Irish songs which Crede's
mother had first sung to him, and Crede had written down in a handsome vellum-bound book all that Mona could remember and had added
the little songs she herself sometimes made up, which he liked too. No
new songs had popped into her head for a long time, with all the other
things it had been full of, but now one was running in her thoughts between bursts of the boys' singing. If she could get it right she could add
it to the book with a design of green rushes in the margin, which would
be easy to paint. Some songs which she had made before the idea of the
book came to mind had led to extreme difficulty in illumination.

The hall door banged as only boys could bang it when escaping to a
larger freedom. Fand settled down for a nap between Cormac's paws

with a streamer of pink wool in her tail, and Philip picked up his book. The fire crackled and danced and the tune in Crede's head began to come clearly:

> *Green among the bushes*
> *When the leaves were young*
> *I found a clump of rushes*
> *Only one—*

The tune was a merry one and Philip would like it if she could manage the words which kept getting out of line like the pansies on Mona's gown.

> *I set me down to weaving*
> *My fingers flew*
> *To put into one pattern*
> *All I knew—*

Her needle began to move with the measure, and while she struggled with limping words and stitches the gay little melody that came without being sought danced on. Philip glanced up from his book and smiled, and the afternoon sun slanting through the window found healthy color in his face.

Christmas, when it came finally, was all that even the boys could have hoped. Philip was downstairs for it, and early in the new year he seemed so much himself again that neighbors could gather round the hearth fire in the evenings.

But after one such evening Crede returned from seeing Master Amerike and Sebastien Cabot to the door, to find her father slumped in his chair and Mona calling for hot bricks and cold cloths. These roused him and they got him to bed, still as white as the pillows, his face drawn with pain, until at last Mona's possets eased it and made him drowsy.

"It means only," Mona said, her mouth set firmly, "that we were too impatient. We will do it again more slowly, the good saints helping us as they did before."

But through their sleepless night Crede struggled with the fear that what touches us to the quick may be beyond what our will can reach—even, perhaps, beyond what the good saints can help us change.

In the morning Philip looked better and smiled at Crede when he woke, though Mona would not let him talk. For a longer time, she said, he must take the possets that made him drowsy, and they kept his room quiet. She and Crede shared the nursing.

Cousin Allie took over the counting house. He was determined to free Crede from that responsibility, and he kept his mind loyally upon it. But as they grew busier with preparations for spring she had to give him some help, for the business had expanded beyond his experience of it years ago. Yet even when she turned her mind to problems of the coming season's trade, with all the men who depended upon it for their living, she felt oddly out of the world. Their household seemed to have closed in upon itself like a castle besieged, cut off from the life around them by the anxiety within which they lived.

This morning in the counting room, while the boys worked with their new and touching diligence, the sense of isolation swept over her. If only Adam could have walked in from Quayside to the partnership she had depended upon more than she knew! But as the figures she was checking blurred before her eyes, it was not Adam's face which came between.

If only Tony were here to share her anxiety and take the son's place Philip had once given him! She had never ceased to miss him, but she had never before missed him with the desolation which seized her now. During those lonely days when Philip was in Amerike, Tony's absence in Cornwall had somehow become linked with Philip's, as if both would end in homecoming. The expectation that at any time Tony might surprise her again had never quite failed, nor the thought of what it would be like if he stayed to help her, making work the gay adventure everything had been when they shared it, contending together in their old friendly rivalry to surprise Philip with their achievement. Now she could no longer hide from herself that Tony could have sent some word in nearly a year if he ever meant to. She could have buried her own pride and sent a message that might call him back, but she knew in her heart that he would bring no peace of mind to Philip. The terms he refused had been fair.

She sat very still for a moment while that sudden, unbidden image faded, and she told herself that it would not come again. She would put Tony out of her mind.

January seemed to drag on to twice its length, but by its end Crede and Mona could assure each other that Philip was gaining. Although Mona said that he must not try his strength for a much longer time, Crede could sit and talk with him and his smile was his own.

On St. Brigid's day, which was Crede's birthday, the saint's own crocus brought its promise of spring. Crede, returning from the garden with the first blossoms to take upstairs, answered the door and found Robin Thorne waiting outside.

"How is your father?" he asked before she could speak.

"Better." Crede had felt sure of it today. "He is much better," she added, and as she brought this unexpected guest into the house she asked, "How did you know?"

"The Perrys had a letter from Bessie. You should have sent us word at once," he said, pulling off riding gloves.

There were not many traveling in wintertime to send letters by, and for weeks they had scarcely thought of anyone outside their own little circle. It seemed part of today's first promise of spring that the world outside should break through to them now, though its messenger was only Robin Thorne.

"How do you happen to be here?" she asked, feeling honestly glad to see him.

"Why I—we thought I should make another Cotswold trip before the busy season. It is a little early to ride the back roads yet, but I'll be here ready. It is shrewd business to be forehanded," he said with the quick smile which could so suddenly give life to his face.

Mona, carrying a tray from the kitchen, paused in surprise. But she looked extraordinarily pleased to see Robin Thorne and gave him her warmest greeting before she continued on her way upstairs.

While Crede was taking his mud-stained cloak, which was in a shocking state, and he was telling her how good the Bath road with its convenient posting inns was for winter traveling, Mona returned to say that Philip would like to see Robin. It would do him good to see a fresh face and hear news of his friends in London, she said, and apparently forgetting her own prohibition of visitors she led the way upstairs.

Crede did not go with them, for they were careful not to crowd the room. She sat down beside the fire, feeling oddly relaxed. It was weeks since she had felt lazy enough to sit anywhere doing nothing.

She was still there when Robin Thorne came downstairs, and she tried anxiously to read his face, not daring to ask how Philip seemed to someone who had not seen him since his illness.

"I think a wonderful job of nursing is being done," he said. "Your father seems much better than we feared."

Crede felt weak, easy tears filling her eyes. She had not cried before, but now she could not help letting them roll down her cheeks. Robin Thorne seemed not to notice. He pulled a stool to the other side of the hearth and stretched his muddy boots toward the heat.

"If you will let me, I think I could be a little use while I am waiting about here," he said casually. "I can't go far into the hills yet, and time is going to hang on my hands. If I could do a few of the things Adam Bell would help you with if he were here, you might more easily persuade your father not to fret that you are working too hard. And it would be a favor to let me do something for my lodging, since your father has very kindly offered me Adam's rooms on Quayside."

Anything which kept her father resting with an easy mind would help to cure him. Crede knew that he liked Robin Thorne, and she was humbly ready now to take a favor from anyone if it could do Philip some good.

She was still winking those silly tears away, but without waiting for an answer Robin Thorne went on to give her messages from Alison, messages that seemed to bring Alison close again until Crede began to feel some of the reassurance it always was to be near her. Win was working on new school books with Master Lily, he said, and he went on to describe the little cottage which Alison had found and told what she was doing to it, until Crede could almost see her flying about. When he left to get his bag from the inn and settle himself in Adam's rooms, she ran up to Philip with a lighter step.

It did them all good to have the pattern of their days change a little, as someone new to those weeks of strain entered it. Robin Thorne seemed in no haste to try the hill roads; he could do better there later, he explained, and his father was so well now that he need not hurry home.

He was at their door first thing every morning and fell into the way of taking Philip's breakfast up and having a short visit with him. Then he came into the counting room ready to do any errands, and he and Clem got on very well together at Quayside. Mona began to make supper more of an occasion again and expected him to stay for it, and Crede could not feel jealous of the pleasure Philip took in his visits. She could spend more time with him too, because of the number of things Robin Thorne found to do, and the restlessness which Philip had not quite been able to hide from her lately and which had made her afraid he would try to get up too soon seemed to have left him. He had her bring her lute upstairs and sing to him; she found new books which they read together; and Cousin Allie sometimes got out his sea cards again.

Suddenly, on the day that February ended and the excitement of Temple Fair began to stir Bristol, Crede realized that this routine had become fixed with no sign of further improvement. She had come into the room when Robin Thorne was sitting with her father, and her uneasiness, just stirring beneath thought, was touched by something between them.

"You look tired, Kitten," Philip said. "I have put a lot on your shoulders for a long time."

"I'm not a bit tired, Father. You know there is nothing you need bother about until you are quite well again."

Philip's eyes met hers, and there had never been anything less than truth between them.

"I thought once that Amerike was calling me, dearest," he said. "But it is a bigger venture, I think. It is a good enough one if only I leave you safe—I had hoped you would be older—"

"Mona and I are making you well!" Crede tried to keep fear out of her voice, but she could not meet her father's eyes. She dropped on her knees beside the bed and buried her face in his hands. They were strong and alive. How could they possibly slip away from her? She would never let them go!

Robin Thorne might not have been in the room. But Philip had meant him to be there.

"Robin has told me that he would like to marry you, dear. There is no one I could trust better to take care of you."

None of this mattered, for all that mattered was Philip. Crede's hands clutched his.

"I have never meant to bind you to any plan of mine," he said slowly, "and I will not now. Whatever you choose, dearest, you have my trust. But if there is a choice that I can help you with—while I have time—"

All the world had seemed full of choices only because she had looked out upon it from the security of Philip's love. Now nothing counted but the dread that he was going from her, the hope that somehow she could keep him. Pressing her face against his hands she cried as she had never cried before. For a moment she forgot even that she must not draw from his strength to help her. She was crying for him to kiss and tease her out of the fear of his death, as he had used to comfort her when the fearsome thing was a shadowy bear under her bed.

"Dearest—" Philip said.

"Crede!" Mona stood in the doorway, a bowl in her hand.

If Mona thought that she was fighting a losing battle she gave no sign of it—in any case, the quality of Mona's fighting was bred in her bones. It was part of her campaign that no one, not even Crede, should worry Philip, and here was Crede with her eyes red and swollen and Robin Thorne who had stayed more than long enough. She gave them both a cold glance. "If Master Thorne will be good enough to help you, Crede, the hall fire doesn't draw, and Will is not about."

Crede, banished from the room, could have hugged Mona for her wrath. Mona had not given up! Mona meant still to cure Philip. And perhaps—perhaps if his mind was fully at rest . . . there was nothing Crede would not do for that "perhaps."

Robin Thorne was peering up the chimney.

"I don't think there is a thing wrong with it, or with the way this log burns."

He turned his back on it and faced Crede.

"I meant what I told your father, Crede," he said abruptly, "but I didn't know he would speak of it yet. I didn't want you taken by surprise."

"It makes no difference," Crede said absently.

"Could you feel differently if you had time? I—hoped to make you like me better, and to ask you myself."

"I don't need more time, if you don't."

[117]

"Crede!" He took a quick step forward and then checked himself. "I won't have you pushed into anything! Your father did not mean to push you. I had rather you thought it over."

"I am thinking it over," Crede said slowly. "Father would never force me to do anything. But most marriages are arranged by families and turn out well enough."

"That's not—" he stared into the fire for so long that Crede wondered whether, after all, there had been some misunderstanding about his own readiness to do what their fathers thought best for them both.

"I hope I am being fair," he said, oddly, at last, and put his arms lightly around her. "When shall this family marriage be, Crede? You shan't be hurried."

"Whenever you like." Crede raised her face for a kiss to seal the bargain. "Shall we go and tell Father now?"

He drew his arms away suddenly. "Crede, you know, don't you, that I will do anything I can to help, without a promise? And so would Father. Your father knows I meant that. You don't have to—take me like a bitter posset for him."

"But I'm not!" Crede cried. "I've learned how kind you are, Robin, and I can see why Father and Win think so much of you."

"It might be better to have had less recommendation," he said. But then he laughed and took her hand as they went upstairs. "We may with care live it down. Crede, we can get a dispensation in Lent if you are willing to be married soon. Shall we tell your father that?"

They went in together, and Philip's face brightened when he saw them.

"You have my blessing already, Robin," he said. But he drew Crede close, and his eyes searched her face. "This is your own choice, dear?"

She knew what the anxious question in them was and could meet it honestly.

"There is no other choice I want to make—truly, Father," she said and saw the relief he could not hide.

TWELVE

Philip was determined to have the wedding downstairs in the green parlor; he said that Robin and Will could surely get him there without damaging any one of them, and Mona made no objection. It seemed that she felt able to relax her strict rules a little. Indeed she was in a mood of general indulgence except toward Kate, who was having one of her sullen spells, and she must have noticed that Philip's interest in the simple preparations appeared to be doing him good. Crede went about with a thankful heart. Her father had been overanxious, she thought, which was so unlike him, because he was tormented by the possibility of leaving her to manage alone, and now with his mind at ease he was getting better.

They had not used the parlor all winter, but for two days Will kept a fire burning in it so that it was warm and fresh and smelled sweetly of herbs and applewood. Philip's couch was near the portrait from which the other Crede seemed to step into the room beside him, and Crede and Robin and Father Ambrose stood close to it, with Kate and Clem and Will and Sadie in the gallery.

Without its pageantry and merrymaking a wedding seemed astonishingly short. Crede stood for a moment with her hand in Robin's, expecting Father Ambrose to say something more. But everyone began kissing her. Sadie was scattering leaves of rosemary over them, and Cousin Allie was holding the knitting cup for them to drink from. When they had taken the first sip they carried it to Philip; and Philip, keeping his arm around Crede when she bent to kiss him, gave Robin his hand.

"I can wish you joy with all my heart, dearest," he said. "I am very happy in my son."

Philip had insisted upon a wedding feast too, and they had set the little table in the room with their best linen and silver and had taken as much care to have everything perfect as for a great party. It was so pleasant to be gathered together here that they sat about afterward, until Mona said that Philip should go back to bed. But he said that he would rest here for a while first. When the others had gone out Robin slipped away too, and Crede sat on beside him. She sat quietly on the edge of the couch, hoping that he was falling asleep, for he looked tired now and had been awake early.

But he opened his eyes and said, "You didn't seem interested in the marriage settlement, dear, but I wanted you to know that by Robin's wish it is uncommonly generous. I could have trusted him safely, but he wanted to have not only your dower portion but everything that will come to you kept in your name so that you may do as you like with it. He found out how it could be drawn up that way. He said that you have been a son as well as a daughter, and so you have, my darling."

"I didn't need even a dower, Father, when I have you always giving me more than I can spend. Don't let us bother about anything now. I don't want today to tire you, when you are getting along so well."

Philip's eyes turned from her to her mother's picture. "I wanted to give her today," he said so low that she scarcely caught the words.

Then his arm tightened around her. "Dear heart, you are too much like me. I should have taught you that there are things we cannot do by willing. Crede, I hoped you were not still so set. I meant not to worry you today—but if I let you blind yourself until I can't help you with this . . . I know how hard it comes."

"Father, you are getting better, I know you are! If you will be content now and let Mona and me—"

"You must be content, dear. Crede, you must listen to me now. There are things Robin is too young to help you with, and I know you so well. I can't leave you to Father Ambrose's comfort only, naming and measuring too much that your mind can pick holes in. Darling, don't be driven bitterly, as I was once, to take the whole thing for a miracle play. Behind it—Truth is the nearest word I know for what we seek, though no word of ours reaches to it and we each find parts of it in different ways. There are moments, if we meet them quietly, when we know that it strives in us and in the world, and it is not purposeless for us. We need not know fully where the venture leads to know that it is good enough. Dearest, I believe that love . . . the noblest part in us . . . answers to something within it . . . cannot be lost."

Crede's mind had narrowed to one fear and one purpose. It could not follow thought, but her ear caught a change in Philip's voice which had begun so clearly, and all her will roused itself.

"Father, don't tire yourself! If you will only rest—"

Philip raised himself, and his arms held her so strongly that what he had been saying could not be true.

"Dear God," he said, "help me to help—"

He caught his breath sharply. In his face was a faint surprise, a slight change of color, as his arms slackened and he slipped from her hold.

She got his head on the pillow, calling for Mona, and held fast to his hand, trying to feel some life in it.

Mona was there, and Mona was doing nothing. Crede dared not slacken her grip. She was desperately holding Philip. "Father!"

"Hush, dear, he has gone."

Mona eased the pillow away, for feathers hamper the freed spirit, and the room turned black.

It was dusk, and the fire in Crede's room was burning. They had lit it for her to dress in the pink gown made for Bessie's wedding. She was dressed now, lying on her bed with the covers heaped over her. She moved to get free of them, and Robin was swiftly beside her.

"Stay quiet, dear. You're cold as ice still. I'm heating—"

From below came a heart-shaking sound. Cormac! Cormac had found his master and lifted his great voice in his tribe's age-old lament.

Robin threw his arms around her, pressing her head against his shoulder as if such a sound could be shut out. She turned to him as blindly as one caught in a tempest seizes any hold, while the storm of tears that broke at last swept over her like a violence outside herself. Cormac's terrible cry ceased, but Crede could not still the trembling that shook her.

"I killed Father, Robin!"

"My darling, you gave him everything—except more years of life, and no one could give him that."

"He was gaining! He didn't believe it yet—he had been patient so long. But I could see it! I meant him to have such peace of mind—"

Now that words had begun to come they rushed unchosen. "I thought there was nothing I couldn't do to give him that—I thought nothing, whatever I felt, could make me worry him and set him back. But I did! He wanted me to be content, and if I could have pretended—he killed himself trying to comfort me."

Robin sat very still for a moment. Then he said, gently, "There was nothing for you to worry about, dear. I am sure your father could trust that. And you did not harm him. For a while he thought that he might be up again, but before that day when he tried to prepare you, Crede, he had tested himself only a little. When I found him I thought that it was the end. He knew that it was. Somehow he stayed a while longer because he wanted to use the time for you, and the end of it came with you beside him as he would have chosen."

Words could not bring Father back, and now they beat upon her unbearably. She pulled away impatiently and sat up, though there was nothing now to hurry for.

"It is Mona you would like to have, isn't it? I'll send her."

As soon as he had gone, Fand crept from some corner of the darkening room into Crede's arms. The cat's small body was tense, as if she felt the desolation of the house, as if the primeval strangeness of Cormac's cry had driven her to seek the reassurance of her god. Crede stroked her gently until, trusting her universe again, Fand began to purr. But Crede, for a terrifying moment, imagined a loneliness deeper than her own. Did God yearn over a world which asked him for a safety that was not in it?

She was getting up when Mona came into the room. But it was night, Mona said, and bedtime. She unfastened Crede's gown and then, through the long, dark hours, Mona lay beside her as she had not done since Crede was a small child and would not let her leave the bed.

In the days that followed Crede's mind could sink sometimes into the numbness of exhaustion, but then some small familiar thing would prick with unbearable sharpness. All the familiar things had Philip as part of them. Not only the happier things had changed beyond recognition, but even the anxieties of his illness had left a void. She was separated even a little from Mona, for Mona was finding things to do with Father Ambrose to help her. The Church had mercifully established a round of duties to perform, candles to light and prayers to offer, services that Philip still needed from his household, binding them together and making even death homely and familiar. Although Crede went faithfully with Mona on these errands, they brought her no relief. As Philip had feared, Father Ambrose's comforts were too literal for her, yet she could not find the courage of his own faith which did not need them. When she tried to reach him she touched only the bitter, blank wall of her own grief.

Cousin Allie would have helped her if he could. His love for Philip and Crede was the human element which had kept him from soaring completely into abstractions, and the loss of his cousin who was so much younger was a blow he had not expected to have to bear. Yet in Cousin Allie's philosophy, knowledge was an end in itself, and in its service he could find consolation. He often put aside the easement which learning gave his own grief, to try to draw Crede toward it, but her trouble was too consuming.

She tried herself to dull it with work, hoping to find comfort in keeping together what her father had built and assuming his responsibility for the men who had depended upon him. But a toll had been taken of her physical strength by those months in which she had felt tireless. She worked slowly and stupidly.

She was still bent over a ledger in the counting room after the boys had left and twilight began to darken it, when Robin came in so quietly that she did not hear him and put his arms around her.

"Dearest, I must help you," he said. "Crede, there must be something you can let me give you now."

She had passed that stormy weeping which clung to any support, but her weariness was a frail hold above it. She could not bear anyone, even Mona, to touch her close now, and she drew away.

"Don't be frightened of me," he said. "You need not. But—don't go so far from us all, dear. Come to supper now. We'll finish this tomorrow."

It was he who had, indeed, been managing everything. Crede knew that and was grateful. But though they worked together and he came for his meals and spent the evening, he was no more real to her than anything else.

The first help to put some ground she knew under her feet came without warning. She and Mona returned from St. Mary's to find Adam Bell with Robin in the hall. He took Crede into his arms, and there was still rebellious disbelief in his face.

"I thought Philip looked tired," he said, "but I—Good God, how could I have left him!"

Adam, who was still close to that first bewilderment, eased Crede's numbing pain as no one else could have done. He was still in muddy riding clothes and had meant to stop off at Quayside, he said, but what he had heard there sent him straight on.

"I found I had stayed away from the North too long, and this is home," he said. "I came back—to explain this to Philip."

Adam had come to stay, and there was more comfort in this than Crede had thought could be found anywhere. Changed as things were, he gave them some substance, coming from outside when even Mona had no new help to offer.

Almost without discussing it, it was settled that Adam should take charge here and that Robin could be back in London for the busy season. He would make his trip through the Cotswold villages first and return in a few days to arrange shipment of the cloth from Bristol. And Adam said that if Crede agreed he would move someone else to the *Belinus* and let Clem, who had so quickly proved himself their best man, take out the *Brigid*. He made the suggestion with no sign of regret.

"I am of more use ashore," he said.

With Adam flinging himself savagely into work, all such matters were arranged and the ships away while Robin was still in the Cotswolds. With Adam striding into the counting house every morning from Quayside, things fell more familiarly into the shape of their old partnership when Philip had been only in Amerike, except that Adam took more responsibility. The truth was that Crede still found it hard to make even the smallest decisions. Adam knew every part of the business, he had scholarship enough for the counting house, and he seemed to find solace in carrying everything he could on his own broad shoulders. With Adam coming again for supper even the house was less empty. Even Cormac roused himself to greet this one return and began to follow Adam about.

It was an early spring. Lent lilies were over and Mary golds were out before Lady's Day, and wild asparagus was coming in from Berkeley to vary Lenten fare. Crede brought a basket of golden gorse into the house, and when she had put a great bunch of its prickly branches in the hall she hesitated. They had liked it best of all in the green parlor, but she had never gone back there since Philip's death.

She could not leave it waiting this spring for its own special flower. She carried the best of her picking there, and when she had arranged it the lonely little room seemed begging her to stay, and she sat down by the portrait.

Robin found her there. They had not expected him today.

"Mona thought you were here, and I hoped to find you alone," he said. "Crede, I have finished all I can do here just now, and I should be at home, at least through the summer. With Adam Bell here, and Master Lusted who would help him—will you ride to London with me?"

She had known that something must be decided soon. And Robin had the best right to say what it should be, for she had taken all the help he offered and used it as she needed.

"I know how tired you are," he said. "It must seem like a mountain ahead to decide anything at all. But Crede, you need not try to yet. We can just think of this as a holiday for you and not plan farther than that, leaving everything as it is here. We could ride by easy stages, making it a rest for you."

"I am out of the way of riding," she said desperately. "You will need to travel faster than I could, now you have stayed so late."

"You can set the pace." He met her eyes with the smile which at odd times seemed to change him into someone she knew better. "That's a promise. I wish you would try it. It might be good for us both, I think."

"I'll come," she said, surprising herself.

Instantly, she wished that she could take the words back. But he began at once to make plans. They could leave as soon as she was ready, he said, but they need not hurry along the way and would break the journey whenever they felt like it.

How could she leave all that remained of familiar things, and how could she do without Mona for the months until autumn, or Mona without her? Yet Mona was past riding so far, and hated strange places, and lived to hold the household together here.

But when the news was broken to Mona she took a surprisingly cheerful view of it.

"Robin shows good sense," she said and set about at once, deciding what Crede needed and could take with her.

The preparations seemed likely to extend indefinitely, however, for Mona sorted and resorted what could be carried on horseback and would have nothing packed that a stitch could improve, while Crede found any excuse now for delay. This morning when she should have been busy packing, she loitered in the kitchen helping Mona prepare dinner.

Robin came through on his way to the stable, and Mona who gave no one the run of her kitchen was evidently accustomed to seeing him there. Things which went on in the household before Crede had to rouse herself for this journey had passed her unnoticed, but now it occurred to her that a sort of informality Mona seldom permitted seemed to have grown between her and Robin.

He paused to help her lift a heavy crock to the table, and instead of reminding him tartly that she was still able-bodied, Mona smiled and said, "That Will hardly touches a stick of wood these days. All he does is fuss over the horses, and now he'll be telling you again how to treat them. In Ireland, we don't mistake the hands and voice of a good horseman."

Robin laughed and went out the back door, leaving it open on mild April sunshine. Every morning now he and Will gave Grey Knight and

Bess some exercise, for he had suggested riding them to London since there was no need to hurry by changing mounts at the posting inns.

This had helped a little to make their journey seem the short distance out of Bristol and back again that Crede wanted to think it. But when Mona tried to send her upstairs now, promising to come and help her as soon as Kate and Sadie got back from market, she kept finding things to do in the kitchen and was still there when the two girls came in with their baskets.

Kate set hers down on the table, looking a little flustered.

"We're late, Grandmother, but Sadie and I can do everything here now and let you get to the packing—if Crede would just stop a minute to help me put away what goes into the stillroom."

Mona gave her a sharp look. Crede had an orderly way in the stillroom while Kate's arrangements seldom pleased her, but generally Kate resented this. She had been in one of her provokingly contrary moods all through the London preparations, too, and had come out of it very suddenly. It must be counted a favor of the good saints, however, that she had turned helpful, since Crede seemed not to care in the least whether she went suitably furnished to London. Mona, who had a dozen things on her mind, hurried upstairs.

As soon as she had gone, Kate sent Sadie to the garden for greens and threw her arms around Crede.

"I've word of Anthony," she said, with an air of such portent that Crede sat down suddenly on the kitchen stool.

"Old Tom Barker from their home farm was at market. They've had a letter at last—Tony's cousin has promised him a ship, and he means to come this way as soon as he can."

Tony had always fascinated slow-moving Kate. When they were children she had been content, although she was the oldest, to wonder and applaud while he and Crede planned adventures, and now she was pink with excitement.

"Crede, I knew he'd come back in his own ship! He was only waiting for that, to prove it to you."

"Oh, Kate, if only he'd come when I needed him so!" At any time this way of returning was not the one she had hoped for, but she could remember only how long she had hoped—her hope a dream of their old happy circle unchanged and unbroken. She put her head against Kate's plump shoulder and wept for things that could never come again. "It's too late now!"

"But Tony is coming home!" Kate said, as if this changed everything. "You can't go away now, Crede, when he's coming soon."

"I have to go to London, Kate." She was back in the present now. Kate gave a start, and Crede looked up to see Robin in the open doorway. He stood there as if brought to a sudden stop while Kate, looking silly and frightened, scuttled into the buttery.

"I'm not forcing you to London, Crede," he said.

"Crede!" Mona came into the kitchen with Crede's gray woollen dress over her arm. "This is too crumpled to wear traveling. Put the irons to heat."

There was no telling from Mona's face how much she had heard. But she spread the dress on the table without seeming to notice Crede's reddened eyes, when such things seldom escaped her.

"We can be ready for you to set out tomorrow," she said blandly. "Last night St. Brigid came to me in a dream to bless that day for it."

"Crede must say whether we go." Robin came forward.

"Crede will heed her own saint." Mona pushed the irons into the fire. "You can press your gown, *mo mhornin*, while Kate gets dinner." If Kate's name had brought a betraying sharpness into Mona's voice it was smooth again as she added, "Robin, will you come upstairs with me now? I need—"

"Do you want to come tomorrow, Crede?"

Robin was still waiting, and Crede turned toward him uncertainly.

"If you are ready," she said finally, and managed a smile. "Mona will make us heed St. Brigid anyhow." After all, it was easier to be pushed into it suddenly.

"No one will be ready if we don't get to work," Mona said briskly. "Will you help me move a chest, Robin?"

She waited determinedly until he followed her out of the room.

III

London, thou art the flower of cities all!
Strong be thy wallis that about thee standis.

DUNBAR

Here in England a wondrous harvest of learning comes to flower. . . .
no light thing but profound and exact and based on the classics, both Latin
and Greek.

In my friend Colet I seem to hear Plato himself. Who would not marvel
at the range of Grocyn's knowledge, the keenness and accuracy of Linacre's
judgment? And when has nature formed a happier, kinder, genius than
Thomas More?

No country entire has yet discovered to me friends so true and high
minded, so enlightened and scholarly, as this one city of London.

(*From letters of* ERASMUS)

THIRTEEN

Crede and Robin rode Bess and Grey Knight out Temple Gate to the
Bath Road with Mona's carefully packed bundles around them and Fand
complaining from a basket strapped beside her mistress. In the moment
of departure, Crede had felt unequal to this separation and had assured
herself that Fand would prefer the discomforts of travel, a conclusion
which at present seemed doubtful.

The Bath Road, like other roads the Romans had built across Britain,
was still the best and shortest way. Taking their time as Robin had
suggested, they could have reached London in four or five days by it,
but he seemed in even less hurry now. Although he had worked as hard
as Mona yesterday to get them ready, as if St. Brigid had been prodding
him too, they had both been in so much easier humor this morning that
when he had proposed taking a longer route through the Cotswolds,
Mona, who had often compared them unfavorably with the lush plains
around Dublin, had agreed that the hill country would be delightful at
this time of year. Bess followed Grey Knight off the straight Bath Road
now into one which wound up toward the beechwoods.

Crede dared not turn her head to look back at Bristol, which she knew
was held gently by the curving downs as if in the palm of a hand, and
nothing had been said since they set out except by Fand whose remarks
were not cheerful.

After a while, Robin let Grey Knight loiter on top of a rise, and he
said, "Cousin Allie promised us a welcome from his friends in Malmesbury Abbey tonight, but we need not ride so far. On my last trip through
the hills I noticed an inn that I think you would like, at Chipping
Sodbury."

It had been near noon when they got away from Bristol, and they had
come at an ambling pace. When they reached Sodbury the sundial by
the church slanted a long finger toward its warning, "so passes ye glory
of ye world." There were several inns on the market square, but Robin
turned down a lane by the Cloth Hall to one at the edge of town which
was smaller and newer. Its stone was still a fresh honey color, the sign
swinging above its chequered door was brightly painted with a golden

star, and several chimneys gave it a look of modern comfort. The inn-keeper himself came out as they rode through the open gate of its courtyard. While Robin waited to see that Knight and Bess would be comfortably stabled, the mistress of the house made Crede welcome.

The inn's parlor smelled of clean rushes and fresh whitewash, and on one wall the star of its sign hovered above worshipping shepherds and sheep that bore a homely resemblance to sheep and shepherds of the Cotswolds.

"If you will rest here a minute, my lady," Mistress Megan said, "your room will be ready."

It had not escaped the notice of her hostess that Crede's cloak was of fine wool trimmed with fur and that although these travelers were with-out servants and carried only saddle baggage, Knight and Bess were handsome, pampered animals. "The Rose Room is our best," she said hopefully. "You could have a fire there and supper brought up. I promise it will be good."

A cup of broth and a clean place to rest were all that Crede wanted, but she could not disappoint Mistress Megan's eagerness to make dis-tinguished guests of them when everything here had so obviously the look of a brave new venture. The hostess had the same bright expectancy about her. She was young, though shaped already like a soft bolster, with strong black hair and quick-moving black eyes such as one saw oftener in Dean Forest than on this side of Severn, and words poured from her more easily than they do from paler-colored folk. Though she kept run-ning out to give orders to someone called "Tillie," Crede knew in no time at all that they were the first travelers who had taken the Rose Room, that her host and hostess had been married for only a year, and how Mistress Megan had met her Bert and each of them inherited what they were risking in the Star.

She found herself hoping fervently for its success, a friendliness not shared by Fand who had been cautiously taking stock of things through a chink in her basket and had decided against them. Fand interjected a remark so ill tempered now that Mistress Megan was stopped in full flight.

"*Bonne Deus,* what is it!"

"It's my cat. Generally she is well behaved," Crede said, hopefully.

"Whatever you had time to bring with you, my lady, is welcome."

Before Crede could try to make sense of this, the host and Robin appeared with their bags. Mistress Megan's quick black eyes turned to-ward them, and when they returned to Crede they were curiously softened.

Their host was as unlike their hostess as could possibly be. He was rangily built, as fair as Robin, and even taller. While he was bidding

Crede a slow but kindly welcome beneath his roof, she thought that the first words would always be spoken by Mistress Megan and the last by him but that without her less care might have been lavished on the Star Inn. Both of them conducted their guests upstairs to an open gallery above the courtyard and past several doors, each painted with a flower, to the door of the Rose Room which they opened with conscious pride. First there was an antechamber furnished for a personal servant and then a very pleasant room indeed, where a fire burned brightly and roses had been embroidered upon everything possible.

Robin and the innkeeper, who was apparently very short of servants, set down their bags, and Mistress Megan, taking Crede's cloak, said, smiling, "There's not many so near tall enough to touch shoulders with my Bert. I fancy you are safe enough on the roads without servants, my lady, and as the old song says, a bonnie lad's worth a long ride. But I can see it has done you out," she added briskly, "and I'll send something up right away that will put color in your cheeks. You'll be safe here."

She bustled off with an air of mystery, her Bert following more slowly. Crede, unfastening the top of Fand's basket, supposed that she must look tired, and indeed she felt tired enough to have ridden much farther. But why shouldn't they expect to be safe here? Whatever misconception their hostess's lively fancy was diverting itself with, she was giving them her best; the rooms were charming though Fand could find no favor in them and, announcing this, retreated under the bed. Crede looked up and met Robin's eyes dancing with laughter.

"A wild ride from a pursuing brother or guardian, I think," he said. "We seem to have traveled too light for the cut of that cloak of yours, Crede. And you do look rather an exhausted heroine. Are you very tired, dear?"

Crede began to laugh and discovered that she could not stop. If it had been Tony, who looked the part of some reckless adventurer—who could have made anything an adventure—a sob choked her, and she clung to the bedpost, her shoulders shaking.

Robin was piling Mistress Megan's embroidered pillows onto the settle by the fire. "Curl up here, Crede. You need that hot drink, too. I'll hurry it."

When he had gone Crede found that the pitcher beside the wash stand had been filled with lavender-scented water, and the towels were snowy white. By the time he returned she felt fresher. Fand had been coaxed out from under the bed and after being shown that nothing hostile lurked in the rooms or even on the gallery outside had been persuaded to take a more cheerful view of things.

The big innkeeper came in at Robin's heels. Explaining that they were shorthanded yet, he set up a table by the settle and spread a white cloth on it, then brought a measure of claret and dishes which smelled of good cookery. This was Lenten fare, but there were elvers with almond butter, and Severn salmon which was at its best now, and a sallet of purslane and mary buds. The fresh, crusty bread would have won praise even from Mona and there were saffron cakes and honey.

Crede filled a dish for Fand and sipped Mistress Megan's prescription of mulled cider which was so heady that it seemed wise to take little of the claret. She set it down to break the loaf, and Robin raised his own mug. *"Hfladige se cwena deor!"*

"Is that Greek?"

"Didn't Cousin Allie teach you Old English as well as Greek?"

She could not remember telling him about Cousin Allie's Greek, but he looked teasing. "What does it mean?" she asked.

"Hfladige is our word 'lady'—it means loaf-giver."

"And the rest?"

"Se cwena? His companion—that got turned into 'queen.' I only know a few words of it."

Crede was finding the cider an excellent restorative. She was only a trifle lightheaded and began to take an interest in food, while Robin talked of things that had taken his fancy on rides between the wool towns hereabout.

"These hills seem to me the heart of England," he said. "They hold our Golden Fleece, and all the while that our fortune grows upon the sea, rain falling here flows down to our two greatest ports. We are only a few miles here from a stretch, scarce longer than Robin Hood's bowshot, between springs that feed Bristol's Avon and those that are the source of the Thames. Less than a day's march from that little dingle, Alfred won his victory over the Danes at Ethandune and began to build the English kingdom."

Such things made a story for him, Crede thought with surprise. But the pictures he drew were only of the meaning to be found in them, not, as Tony would have made them, a background of high color for enterprises of their own.

When they had finished supper, twilight was fading. Robin moved the table outside the door and sat down by the fire again.

"Would you like to lengthen the journey a little and swing round by Oxford?" he asked suddenly. "We could still travel as slowly as we choose."

Towers and spires of an enchanted city which Win had once set before her took misty shape in the firelight—Oxford, where the New Learning was a flame to kindle men's thoughts and warm their hearts with a vision of shaping the world to a new pattern! It shimmered with airy lightness in her mind, and her face brightened.

[132]

"I thought you might." Robin looked pleased. "You'll like Oxford."

"Did you love it as much as Win did?"

He had, of course; he had wanted to stay longer there. But he had let his life be changed rather easily and had ended by accepting old Master Thorne's plans for him.

He was looking into the fire, and she waited for his answer with an anxiety to understand him which had not troubled her before. Everything between them had seemed to follow chance, to move with things so urgent that their own part in them was unimportant, to an end where nothing had reality. But, lying awake through last night, she had put other things behind her and faced her bargain. The word of Philip Canynges' daughter must be as good as his had always been; whatever Robin wanted to make of the promise they had given Father Ambrose, she was ready for now. Yet even now, when she made an effort to see him more clearly, she could not get that dominant impression which gives personality. He must be too indeterminate for it, she thought, and none of the scattered things she had learned of him could be related to a picture someone might have drawn at this moment. With the fire highlighting the strong bones of his face and his fair coloring, he looked more like some ancestor who might have gone a-viking to bend his fortune to his will than the sort to let things happen to him.

"Oxford puts a spell on one," he said thoughtfully. "It's easy there to think that it is all the world. But there is no lovelier old town. Crede, I've wanted to show it to you."

He began to plan their journey then. Tomorrow they need not leave here unless she felt rested, or they could ride only as far as Malmesbury, and Cirencester was only another dozen miles or so away, with a Roman road from it toward Oxford. They did not have to make even the gossipy twenty miles a day of a pilgrimage, and he would show her the Oxfordshire side of the Cotswolds.

It was past candlelighting time, but the firelight was more restful. Fand, curled up among the cushions, was sound asleep, and Crede was growing drowsy. She had been nodding when she heard Robin moving about and sat up.

"I was afraid you'd be sound asleep where you are, if I didn't rouse you," he said and crossed toward the anteroom. "But open-air tiredness is good for other kinds. Sleep well, dear. Nothing can reach your door except through mine, and this is a good, safe inn."

Not for months had Crede felt a wholesome tiredness of body so overwhelming her that she could scarcely keep awake to unfasten her gown and slip into the soft bed.

They were far enough from Oxford on Saturday, which was Easter

Even, that they would have entered late, so they kept Easter a few miles away at Woodstock. The village straggled down a hill and even kings had found its situation pleasant. Henry Tudor had recently improved the old palace which had been the favorite of England's first Henry, William the Norman's son, who had brought his Saxon bride here. Here too that restless genius, Henry the Second, had sometimes escaped with Fair Rosamond from the irritations of hammering Saxons and Normans into a nation. Long before there had been Normans in England, King Alfred had rested here after lifting his country out of barbarous war and confusion, to translate the noble philosophy of Boethius into its language and to found a school—so Oxford claimed—in the nearby town.

Now, on Monday morning, they were riding toward Oxford at the end of a spring shower, in company with a number of folk on foot, a farm cart decked with wreaths of flowers, a band of minstrels, and an old man with a sorrowful bear, all of whom they had overtaken.

"We haven't managed very well to come in on a holiday," Robin said.

They had been riding across country that rolled south to the city wall with rivers on either side of it, and beyond the eastern one the sun was finding its way through rain clouds over Shotover Woods. Crede checked Bess and let their noisy companions move away from them because, just at this moment, the towers and spires of Oxford rose through a golden mist.

There were few buildings north of the Wall to distract the eye. On their left, one river meandered southward around the eastern bastions. On their right, Whitefriars convent, once Henry Beauclerc's palace of Beaumont, overlooked the other river which curved past Oxford's West Wall, past its Norman castle and the Port Meadow where burghers of the corporation grassed their cattle, to Osney Abbey at the south of the town. Just now it carried back to them the chime of the Abbey's seven lovely bells.

As they drew close to North Gate they found that not all travelers had gone through it into the town. There was a sort of encampment outside by St. Giles Church where, Robin said, an important fair was to be held later in the year. Players' carts and flower-decked country carts with crowds of holidaymakers in them had been drawn up here. Peddlers were doing a thriving and illegal business in a variety of things under pretense of offering texts and tokens suitable to the holy season, and a band of Egyptians had ventured to display their attractions.

North Gate was a passage under the town gaol. At the end of it they were in Cornmarket, with the solid old tower of St. Michael's Church which was part of the Wall's defenses looking down on them, and Cornmarket was in a lively uproar as Oxford celebrated the end of Lent. In the space down its center, reserved on market days for stalls, various diversions drew crowds; students released from the rigorous discipline of Lenten observances jostled apprentices, making the most of this holiday; and riotous processions conducted Jack of Lent, attended by his priest and physician, the devil, and the ubiquitous Turk, to execution again and again. Whoever had to pass up or down the street pushed as best he could between the overhanging housefronts and the open kennel to whose mixture of smells was added that of a tannery, undoubtedly close.

Through the din, Robin shouted, "Knight will clear a path for us. Keep Bess at his tail, and we'll get to the Cross Inn."

Grey Knight rather enjoyed parting a crowd, which he could do with no loss of his usual affability because of his size. But Bess snorted nervously as she followed in his wake while Fand, who had seemed lately more reconciled to travel, from her basket shrieked disapproval of Cornmarket. The street was leading them into a carfax which seemed even more crowded, and just as Robin headed Grey Knight toward the gate of an inn near it, one of Jack of Lent's disorderly processions came tumbling out. Bess set back her ears, and nothing could turn her. She had no room to bolt, but having decided upon a straight way out of this she kept to it stubbornly, carrying Crede on past the center of town until the crowds had thinned and a bridge gate lay ahead of them.

It was possible to bring her to a stop then, and Robin caught up with them. Fand had been jolted into a silent rage, but Crede was laughing; Bess's tantrums never lasted long nor impaired their friendship and it was some time since they had enjoyed a tussle.

"I wanted to show you Broadgates Hall," Robin said, "but I've never hoped to come down South Street with such dash."

"Your college?" Bess was quiet now, and Crede looked about her.

"Broadgates Hall is not a college." Robin sounded rather shocked. "Halls are much older. The oldest of all, of course, is St. Edmund's by St. Mary's Churchyard, where the first scholars lived in huts, they say, until it was built—Broadgates can't claim anything like that, but it's a nice old place and has the best library for civil law." There was affection in his voice. "The library is over St. Aldate's Church here and the Hall at the side."

The church he pointed out stood beside Oxford's south gate, and the building west of it was in a pleasant garden. Across it they could see above housetops the crumbling battlements of the Norman castle, and beyond the Wall rose the twin spires of Osney Abbey.

The gardens on the other side of South Street were large and beautiful; by a postern cut in the Town Wall they opened upon the river meadows, and their trees shaded rambling convent buildings with a great church rising among them. St. Frideswide's Priory, Robin said, was Oxford's first foundation, begun by the Saxon saint herself. It had been centuries old by the time, so long ago, that Roger Bacon had come to Oxford, and the buildings he could have looked out upon from the little room over Southgate which he was said to have used as his study must have been much the same as now.

"We could turn into Broadgates," he suggested, "and wait until the streets have cleared a little at dinner time, before we ride back to the inn."

They led Grey Knight and Bess under a clump of trees in the garden, and Crede sat down on the soft grass with Fand's basket beside her, while Robin went into the Hall. In what seemed a very short time he was back.

"Everyone is out making holiday," he said, "except a strange boy in the room that used to be mine who has a toothache and looks scarcely old enough to have teethed at all. Anyhow, those I knew best were leaving at the end of the year, and it is another year since," he added as if this had just occurred to him. He stretched out on the grass looking thoughtful.

The quiet was shattered by a clamor in South Street. It drew nearer, and Robin seized Bess's bridle as a noisy group of boys swept across the lawn toward the Hall. Several had their short, bright-colored students' gowns torn almost off their backs, and one had a bloody nose, but all were exuberantly celebrating victory in some street affray.

With an odd expression on his face, Robin stared after them. "They must be sending them up younger every year," he said, and he laughed suddenly. "While others like them go home to their dinners the streets should be clear enough for sober citizens. Let's get to the inn."

"You could leave me there this afternoon while you go about to see your friends," Crede suggested. She thought that he seemed not quite at home here yet and that without her he might more easily find the Oxford he knew.

"There are some I could hunt up still, of course."

He hesitated, although before this he had been ready with plans for every day of their journey, and he showed her something more personal than he had ever done before when he added, "I've been feeling rather like a ghost here. Perhaps it's too soon, and after more years I'll enjoy it again. But there are things I'd like to show you."

Crede had been feeling some disappointment too. As they rode back toward the center of town there was much to remind her that many trades besides the scholars' guild of learning flourished here. Bristol had as fine buildings and its streets were unquestionably cleaner and better smelling—where was the dream city that Win had made her long to see?

The crowds which had filled Carfax earlier had thinned. Robin drew rein and said, "Look back and then eastward, Crede."

The towers and spires were there, some new and unweathered, some the gray old age of Cotswold stone. But this morning, riding toward Oxford, Crede had seen them for a moment rising above the river mists, bold towers of thought and slender spires of faith, gold-tipped in a clearing sky. Lovely as these were now, they were built of common stone, and in that far view had been something she wanted to keep from this earth-bound one. Perhaps what you could find at the end of any far view was only what you brought with you then, not the magic answer to your own uncertainties it had seemed to promise. Yet the promise might wait, and some time you might find it.

"We can walk back this way after we've got settled at the inn," Robin said.

"I saw what you and Win had made me want to see here as we were riding in. Nothing could be lovelier than that. Robin, the streets will soon be crowded again, so why don't we keep on our way?"

"On out of town? You'd rather?"

She had guessed that he would too. This morning he had let her see for the first time some unease in himself, and she wanted to prove that she could be a good companion. Indeed, they had been sharing a very satisfactory companionship on this journey, she thought, and she could understand why he had proposed it. Both of them had felt obliged to set other things ahead of their own free choices, but he had seen that they must find together how to make the best of their bargain. They had been finding enough each could offer to get along very comfortably. And riding had become a joy again. After each day's journey in the fresh spring air sleep had swooped down upon her like a healing spell, so that now she was beginning to feel a reserve of strength and a need to use it.

"I've loved our rides," she said. "I'm as eager now for a gallop as Bess is."

"We'll go on then."

Robin looked so cheerful that she knew he had welcomed her suggestion.

"Where have you stopped on the road?"

"I used to go on to Wycombe, but that is rather far for a late start."

"We could take our supper with us. It would be fun to eat like tramps along the road and find a place to stop when we choose, some village inn—or on to Wycombe, maybe."

It seemed an adventure after their carefully planned stages. She spoke eagerly, this quick rise of spirits a warmth she had almost forgotten, and he seemed ready to match her humor.

"I hadn't suspected you wanted to be a vagabond! If we eat in the

[137]

inn's ordinary we can have our dinner as quickly as the horses are fed, and they will pack us something to take along."

It was only a little past noon when they got away, and the sky had cleared so brightly that light would hold late. They rode out of Carfax toward Eastgate along the handsomest, gently-curving street Crede had ever seen. In an odd way it reminded her of the street of ships in the heart of Bristol, although there was no real likeness for the eye between these towers which thrust upward among the trees and that line of tall masts in Bristol whose furled sails awaited the tide.

The newest building and the finest tower of all was by the bridge at Eastgate, rising above the river meadow in the midst of gardens older than the fresh beauty of its stonework, which seemed to have just discovered the most graceful forms that stone could take.

"Bishop Waynfleet's dream," Robin said, "but he did not live to see it finished. When I was here the last work on the tower was being done by order of a young clerk, Thomas Wolsey, who was Magdalen's bursar."

This last bit of Oxford stood at the very edge, with woods and river beyond, and it seemed an afterglow from that first fleeting vision as they had come toward the town. Their road ran on past river meadows and climbed among hills where the beech trees were leafing, and sunshine rippled through them on violets and anemones, then led into farm land with pilewort starring the roadside and the hedges coming into bloom.

On a level stretch Crede gave Bess the gallop she was spoiling for and did not check her until she was breathless herself, her cheeks tingling. Robin and Grey Knight who had come thundering after them paused, too, and Robin said, "What siege do we ride to raise, Sir Knight?"

Crede caught her breath and laughed, "I haven't ridden just to ride for ages!"

He let her lead again, and the road flattened by meadows and wound among hills, while she held Bess now to a pace that would not tire her because she wanted to ride on and on through this shining afternoon.

They ate supper beside a brook and rested the horses, and let Fand out of her basket since they had discovered that she would not lose sight of Crede in any strange place. When they had ridden a short distance farther they passed a village with a small, clean-looking inn where Robin thought they should stop.

"But I'm just getting the feel of the road again," Crede protested. "And the horses aren't tired, we've made such lazy stages before."

"You do look better, with color in your cheeks."

"I could ride all night."

"And ride down highwaymen too? I believe you're ready for some mad venture!" Robin laughed. "The first time I saw you—you are enjoying this, aren't you? We can keep on a while if you like. There's another inn I've heard well spoken of, not too far along, I think."

The sun had slipped over the hills and the sky ahead was turning pale amethyst when they reached the crossroads whose inn Robin remembered. There was an air of dilapidation about it, and he said, frowning, "Wait here on the road, Crede, while I go in."

In a moment he was back, swinging himself into the saddle. "It has changed hands, and I don't like the look of mine host. We may have to make Wykham."

Now they met few travelers on the road, and the only inns they passed he did not even inquire at, nor did Crede like their appearance. He had quickened their pace, and as dusk fell he set a very hard one and made sure that Bess and Knight left no distance between them. It was almost too dark to see the road when they got to the edge of Wykham, and without slackening he pushed on through the outskirts into the center of town.

"Thank heaven we have no farther to go," he said. "Are you done out?"

Crede was a little tired, but she had not felt so timid in twilight on the road as he had seemed to be. He had set the horses galloping past every clump of trees until now they were in a lather. They rode into the yard of an inn on the High Street, but the ostler gave them a doubtful welcome.

"We're filled to the roof, sir."

"Can you tell us where to try—fit for a lady?"

"They'll all be as crowded. Seems like the fine weather over the holiday has set everyone on the road." He looked at the coin Robin had put in his hand. "I can't find a room even for that, sir. But I'll see that you have a clean corner in the ordinary, and a fresh pallet. You won't do better anywhere else so late."

"We can't go on." Robin looked anxiously at Crede. "I've been cursing myself this last hour. That road and some of the inns have a bad name after dusk."

"We can manage very well in the ordinary," Crede said cheerfully. She did not quite know how one managed in the common rooms of inns, but she thought that their mild escapade would have been amusing if Robin had any taste for adventure.

The ostler promised to find stable room for Bess and Knight and to rub them down well and assured Robin that the inn's horsebread was made of the best beans and peason. They were approaching the open door of the ordinary, whose bush proclaimed it a tavern too, when he ran after them to point out a smaller door just inside the gate near the kitchens.

[139]

"If you go in by the service way, sir, you won't land right on top of them and can pick out a quiet corner for the lady."

By following his suggestion they had a moment to get their bearings inside, for their entrance was scarcely noticed by the other travelers. They were gathered about the fire at the far end of the room in the midst of a rollicking song, interrupted by arguments about the verses while ale mugs were refilled, and it was plain that these had been refilled often.

"This corner is the best we can find," Robin said, after a quick glance about the room. A window bowed out near the entrance they had used, making a small alcove. He looked it over carefully, testing the framework of the lattice and making sure that the door could be bolted. "It will be cold here before morning, but we'll get better air."

Crede set Fand's basket down and spoke reassuringly to her. Poor Fand would have to stay shut up and forgive them for an outrage she could not understand; fortunately she was keeping remarkably quiet. The other end of the room was lighted by the fire and rushlights in sconces, but the window corner was in shadow except for the faint beam of a street lantern outside, and from it they could observe their fellow travelers.

The man strumming on a mandore had come alone, Crede imagined, and he looked as if he could pay the price of a room but was feeling rather dashing to be without his comforts. For the rest of them this was probably their usual way of traveling—except for the black-haired girl and the red-faced young countryman in a homespun smock who kept his arm around her; both of them looked as if to travel at all was the wildest adventure. The others were peddlers, Crede decided, with here and there a countryman journeying to some fair.

"I dare say they are decent enough people," she said. "The black-haired girl is showing off a little in company, and they are playing up to her for the fun of it, but she is keeping quite close to the red-faced boy she is with. It might be a good idea," she added practically, "to pick out the best pallets while they are all busy."

Robin burst out laughing. "I continually underestimate you, Crede." Looking more cheerful, he chose two straw pallets from the pile and spread them in the corner with Fand's basket and their cloaks, to mark possession. He folded Crede's cloak carefully, so that the rich fur trimming was inside. "Better give me your brooch and rings," he said, and tucked them into his doublet. Without these jewels Crede's gray dress was plain enough to attract no attention.

"It is as well not to seem richer than one's company—or too proud for it," he observed.

Putting his arm around her, he drew her toward the fire. They slipped into an empty place but were not quite unnoticed. The buxom black-haired beauty who was called "Jill" was performing a jig amid shouts of encouragement, and suddenly she brought up before Robin and Crede with a great flurry of petticoats and a curtsy that was none too steady.

"We're all friends here tonight. Aren't we all?"

"That's right, Jill!" Whatever she said drew applause.

"We've all told our business on the road right friendly. What's yours, my master?"

"A poor scrivener can maybe fill his purse better in London," Robin said with a sigh. "In Oxford every donkey can use a pen."

"And knows his neck verse!" The man with the mandore joined in the laugh at his own wit. "You travel late for an honest clerk, Master Scrivener."

"I could have outwalked the bag of bones we hired to carry my wife, sir. And by the saints it was thirsty going!" He felt in his purse and counted out a few pence with a care that suggested its leanness. "If you will drink to London with me, friends, it may bring luck there. Here, Boy!"

He paid for a round of ale even for the two who were dicing in a corner and, as Jill proclaimed, they all drank it right friendly and wished him happy.

"And now," said Jill, who had made herself mistress of ceremonies, "do you know any new songs, Master Scrivener?"

"By your favor, Mistress, I'll choose an old one," Robin said, smiling. As he began it there was a shout of laughter for his choice, and they all joined lustily:

> Of all the maidens mild as mead
> There's none so gympt as Jillie,
> As any rose her cheek is red
> Her brow is like the lily.

Jill giggled at the compliment and buried her head on the red-faced young man's shoulder. After it she was persuaded to do another dance while they all beat time and sang,

> Skip it and trip it nimbly, nimbly
> Tickle it, tickle it lustily—

and the red-faced young man continued to watch all that she did with admiration in his fuddled blue eyes.

"She will get tired soon, I should think," Robin whispered, "and things will quiet down. They will all sleep near the fire."

"Where did you learn to be so much at home in these places, Master Scrivener?"

"A traveling student gets into queerer company than this. Especially in some French and Italian inns."

When Jill stopped, panting but still determined to have no dull moments, and called for more songs, Robin joined in them again and in the rough banter as heartily as anyone. He seemed a different person—strung to some heightened tension. Crede felt it in the arm which he kept between her and her next neighbor on the bench, a hideously pock-marked man with a toothless grin for every sally, who was noticeably dirty and smelt, predominantly, of a tannery. She could not explain it by supposing that he had overdrunk; for all the show he made of honoring every round his ale mug had been refilled only once, she noticed.

It had seemed completely out of character for Robin when Win said that he was good at mummery, but it was undoubtedly true, and even though he had confided his purpose the readiness with which he played his part astonished her. He could even make her share in an odd way some excitement he felt in it. Like most people, Crede supposed that she could act very well herself if she chose. She joined in the songs and tried to fit in with this odd collection of strangers whom chance had shut up together for the night.

"Don't I make a good Mistress Scrivener?" she whispered. "It's fun, isn't it?" Except, she thought, for the overpowering aroma of her neighbor, and she moved closer to Robin.

The mandore player had a good voice and carried the air strongly. Crede had already noticed the quality and cleanness of his clothes and an assurance of manner which set him apart here, although he was making himself a boon companion. He did not look like a strolling minstrel, and although he seemed ready to please them with his talents she thought that it was his humor not so much to amuse the company as to amuse himself. He began to play songs of his own choosing, softer airs and some which not everyone knew. Some of the group were past singing anyhow—voices had thickened and one or two heads were nodding. The rushlights were burning down, and nobody had bothered to trim them. Even Jill was offering no new suggestions but was leaning rather heavily against the red-faced young man.

The mandore player struck a rippling chord. "This would suit your voice, Mistress—do you know 'Mannerly Margery'?" He looked directly toward Crede, his eyes meeting hers with a boldness she did not like. She shook her head, but he was not discouraged. "It's a new song of Jack Skelton's set to music by Master Cornish of the Chapel Royal. I'll teach you if Master Scrivener will change places."

Robin's arm stiffened, but Jill spoke before he could. Although she was yawning hugely she had not forgotten that this was her court and it was her place to choose the entertainments. She got to her feet unsteadily.

"You've been putting us to sleep with those sickly tunes. Why don't we kiss a friendly goodnight all round and find our pallets?"

This was followed by a good-natured scramble to kiss Jill. The English kissed on all occasions with a freedom which foreigns found diverting, yet even if there had been strangers here it would have been generally understood among them that the undisciplined ways of English women were accepted naturally in their queer island and did not mean what might have been expected elsewhere. Although the manners of this company were rougher than Crede was accustomed to, she was merely amused by Jill's fling this evening.

But one of her neighbors was looming over her! Merciful saints, was this what play acting got you into? One of these unwashed louts—the one with the toothless grin—!

Suddenly Robin was between, his arms closed tightly around her, and his lips pressed hard on hers. "They shan't touch you," he whispered.

Drawing her out of the firelight he lifted her off her feet and carried her swiftly across the room. In their own dark corner he still held her close.

The others were more concerned with Jill, and even the toothless one, thank goodness, was not following.

"It's all right now, you can let me down. Wasn't he awful!" Crede got her breath and slipped to her feet. "I'm afraid I'm no good at play acting," she confessed ruefully. "You were quick-witted, Robin."

"No, I'm just a fool."

There was such bitterness in his voice that he must be magnifying a little inconvenience again and blaming himself unreasonably.

"It wasn't your fault that we rode on." Crede lowered her voice, for the noise at the other end of the room was subsiding. The other travelers were drawing their pallets around the fire as Robin had predicted, and they would not disturb this corner. "It's not going to be so bad, after all. And it was rather fun until that last mix-up." Crede could laugh about it now. "You were as good as a play, Robin! Win told me you could act any part."

Robin seemed not to hear. He had turned toward the window and stood staring out, his shoulders blocking most of the faint light from the street. The room smelled stale and close, but when Crede opened the door it was a still, clear night with stars, and the quietness of a late hour had fallen upon the inn yard. She ventured to let Fand out but Fand climbed meekly back into the shelter of her basket and, when it was set close to Crede's pallet, mewed only a little and settled down, deciding apparently that these circumstances were beyond anyone's control. Crede did not expect that she could sleep here, but she lay down wrapped in her cloak and glad of its warm fur. Apparently Robin still felt wakeful, for his shadow across the window did not move. Crede was growing drowsy. Tomorrow they would be in London. . . .

They rode past Holborn Bar and rested their horses for the last time by St. Andrew's Churchyard, with late afternoon sun at their backs and London ahead. Behind them was a broad road lined by country houses and market gardens, travelers' inns, and inns of the law students, with open country beyond.

Below the fields south of the road, Fleet Street also ran busily toward London. And south of Fleet Street was the busiest highway of all, the Thames. The Thames curved between low banks, past the Abbey and Royal Palace of Westminster and the village of Charing, flowing for two miles beside the town houses of bishops and courtiers, whose gardens sloped down to water stairs. From this high spot Crede could see the constant stream of barges that rounded the bend, past the new hospital which King Henry was building on the ruins of the old Savoy Palace. They moved on, below the Temple gardens, and inns of law, and the small tower of St. Bride's Church, to the mouth of the Fleet River. Here some of them turned up, between the convents of the White Friars and the Black Friars, to hold a water market under London's West Wall, while others followed the Thames toward the Bridge.

Ahead of them their road ran down two steep hills and crossed Holborn Bridge over the Fleet to enter Newgate. And there the church towers and red-tiled roofs of London rose above the Wall. The tall spire of St. Paul's with its gilded cross pointed heavenward from their midst, and, across the city, the grim battlements of the Tower loomed in the east.

St. Andrew's looked northward across the road to the Bishop of Ely's palace, whose gardens sloped down the hillside. Beyond this, open fields stretched farther north and east to the Priory of the Knights Hospitalers of St. John and the low-spread cloisters of the Carthusians and the village of Clerkenwell. From these, straggling suburbs spread around the open space of Smithfield and the Augustinian Hospital of St. Bartholomew, up to London's North Wall.

Crede had always thought of London and Bristol together, since they were the two great ports of England, and she had supposed that London would seem only somewhat larger and grander. But now it seemed that half the people in England must be gathered here, and Bristol's population of six thousand could be lost in a suburb, she thought, staring.

The grandeur she had expected was not immediately apparent when they rode in. As they crossed its stone bridge the Fleet River smelled abominably. South of them, on its east bank, a slimy moat enclosed the

King's Prison of the Fleet. They entered Newgate, which had Mayor Whittington's famous cat carved upon it, and were passing under the city's prison where wretched faces at a barred window begged, "I pray you bread, for the love of God."

Crede put all her small coins into a cup held out on the end of a stick. It was a dreadful sight to come upon first, inside London. And down the middle of Newgate Street were the shambles—crowded sheds and mean houses in whose cellars London's meat supply was awkwardly butchered.

But then the wonder of St. Paul's towered on their right, its precinct wall long enough to enclose a small town, and the fine buildings of the Grey Friars and the College of St. Martin le Grande rose on their left. They rode past a handsome public fountain into Cheapside, where it was said that everything the world had to offer could be bought.

At first the famous West Chepe seemed only crowded and dirty, an offense in comparison with Bristol's clean streets. Except for an occasional guildhall the north side was lined by rather ordinary houses with clumsily-built shops projecting from their fronts. It was broken by narrow lanes filled with the stalls of different trades. But as they rode on past a number of taverns and a tall Queen Eleanor's Cross, the south side became magnificent. It contained a handsome church with rows of tall houses and good shop fronts. The buildings in one long row, which seemed all new—half-timbered fronts lavishly carved and pricked with gold—were finer than anything Crede had imagined. Through the low shop windows one caught glimpses of jewels and silks and goldsmiths' work, and it was possible at last to believe London's boast that Cheapside alone contained more wealth now than there was in the whole of Venice.

The wide street led straight on past another and larger water conduit, built of stone with a battlemented top, into an open poultry market. From this they passed between two churches into a street of handsome houses which brought them to a wide carfax, and by this time they must have come the best part of a mile straight east from Newgate.

"The main crossroads of London," Robin said, "and St. Peter's hill here is the highest point within the walls. Grasschurch Street runs south from it to the Bridge. We shall turn north along Bishopsgate Street and be at home."

Crede's heart sank suddenly. She saw nothing more of the square or of the street they turned up, except to notice vaguely that there were fine buildings and gardens. While riding through London her eyes had been so busy that she had almost forgotten she was coming into a strange house and family. Robin had described it to her but without the power to make her see it—not as she could have made a picture of her own home, loving every part of it so that it must have come alive for anyone.

[145]

There was Dame Serena Fenton, she knew, Master Thorne's widowed sister who had kept his house since the children were small, and there was Susan, the maidservant, who was a treasure, and Dick, Susan's brother, who had been with them for years. The only person Robin spoke of often was his little sister Madeline, who, he said, was a nice child and would love Crede. He had bought Madeline a pretty girdle of old Irish silverwork in Bristol and then had asked Crede just before they came away to find some gift for Aunt Serena which would be noticeably handsomer, because her life had been unhappy and her feelings were easily hurt.

They came to a substantial house, larger than the Canynges' house though not so modern; its sign a flowering thorn which was repeated again on the door knocker.

"This is it," Robin said.

When they had dismounted Robin paused with his hand on the knocker.

"Aunt Serena may be in a tizzy because she didn't know what day we'd arrive, but don't let it bother you, dear. It's just her way."

The door was opened by a little gray-haired dumpling of a woman whose rosy face broke into smiles.

"Master Robin! Oh, I've been hoping I'd be the first to say, 'Welcome home' to Mistress Thorne!"

"This is Susy, Crede." Robin gave Susy a hug and a hearty kiss.

"Don't you be setting my cap crooked," Susy scolded. "I've my proper curtsy to make to the mistress."

But Crede kissed Susy too. The unmistakable warmth of this greeting had touched her, and impulsively she made a friend for life.

"Come in, my pretty, come in!" Susy said. "It's a real lady you've got, Master Robin, and you are letting her stand at the door. Will you take the mistress's cloak now, while I send Dick to the horses? Come over to the fire, my pretty, you'll be cold and tired. Master Thorne and Mistress Madeline are out, and indeed they will be sorry, but I'll find Mistress Fenton." She bustled away and they could hear her calling, in a voice that sounded shrill and nasal to Bristol ears: "Dick! Dick, will you let horses stand all day in the street!"

Robin stirred the fire which was merely smoldering. "Do you feel chilly, Crede?"

She did, rather, and kept her cloak. The house had a dampness never felt in rooms Mona had charge of, and the hall was ill lighted compared with the Canynges' many-windowed house. While this must be considered a large, handsome room, Crede thought it gloomy. But before she had time to notice much about it, Dame Fenton appeared.

She was a tall, large-boned woman with a fresh color who looked, in

[146]

spite of her severe dark clothes, neither elderly nor delicate, as Crede had imagined her.

"We thought you had forgotten us, Robin," she said. "I am glad to see you, Crede." But she was not glad, Crede knew instantly. Dame Fenton took her cloak and remarking, "You are not much like your mother, are you?" kissed her as an afterthought.

"I am sure I should have been glad to have a welcome prepared for Robin's bride, Crede," she said with the effect of a pronouncement, "if he had told us what day we were to see you at last. We shall just have to manage as best we can now, with most of the house torn up for the spring cleaning."

Housecleaning should have been done before Easter, Crede thought. But however inconvenient their arrival, surely any house welcomed travelers to the best it had without apology. I do believe she has tried to have things upset so that she will seem put upon, Crede thought, and since she had no real reason for her petty suspicion and was naturally ashamed of it she felt doubly uncomfortable.

"Do please let us do whatever will cause least trouble," she begged.

"I expect Crede would like a chance to tidy up first of all," Robin said cheerfully.

"I am afraid your room looks rather bare with the curtains down, Robin, but it can't be helped. Take Crede upstairs, while I see what can be done to make a more suitable supper. I will have water heated and sent there—unless," Dame Serena sighed and then continued bravely, "unless I should give up your mother's room to the new Mistress Thorne."

"Good heavens, Aunt, do you suppose anyone would think of that? Shall we go up, Crede?"

Crede picked up Fand's basket and followed, feeling tired, unwelcome except for that blessed Susan, and dreadfully homesick already. The upper floor had a long gallery running across the house above the stairs, with windows at the ends and the rooms opening off it as at home, but it seemed larger and gloomier, like the hall. Robin showed her the way into a good-sized bedchamber which was rather untidy.

"This one used to be Walter's," he said, "but I moved into it. The smaller one next it was mine, and you shall have whichever you like for a lady's bower and get anything you like to make it prettier."

"I'd like the smaller room, please," Crede said quickly. She had almost forgotten Walter and the recollection added gloom to this place.

Robin opened the door and said, "It seems in fair order, at least. I'll bring your things up."

He left her there and, after carefully closing the door, she opened Fand's basket. While Fand ventured out to make her usual cautious survey of new quarters, Crede too looked about. The furniture was dark and massive, as in the other rooms she had seen, but the confusion of housecleaning had not penetrated here, and the window overlooked a very nice back garden.

The knock at the door was, she hoped, to announce that a servant had brought water.

But the young girl who burst into the room hugged her impulsively and exclaimed, "Dearest Crede! I have been waiting so long to see you! I was ready to wring Robin's neck if he didn't bring you soon."

"You must be Maddie!"

Crede looked at her in astonishment, for Robin had spoken of his young sister as if he considered her a child still, but this lovely girl was far taller than Crede and could not be much more than a year younger. She was almost startlingly beautiful, Crede thought. She was slim, without the large bones of her brother and her aunt, and her fairness was a warm honey color. Only about her eyes was there a likeness to Robin, and it was hard to say what suggested this because they were hazel brown while his were blue.

"You look just as lovely as I thought you would," Madeline said happily.

Crede, remembering her dusty face and the clothes she had spent a night in, felt that this could come from only the kindest heart.

FOURTEEN

The day after their arrival in London was the last of the Easter Week celebrations, and Master Thorne said genially that they would all make a holiday of it and show Crede the town. Crede had hoped that someone would send word to Alison and Win or take her to visit them, but Master Thorne had the day planned before she could ask.

After breakfast he had to show her the garden which was of a fair size, with more open space to be seen behind the house than she had expected in London, but he said that most houses and Company Halls in the north had good grounds while churchyards and the precincts of religious foundations spread over a third of the land within the city. There were fruit trees trained along the wall, and the borders were so well kept that Dick must have a thumb as green as Will's.

They came upon Dick in the stable, a small wizened man with merry blue eyes whom Knight and Bess seemed to have accepted as well intentioned. Their only stable companion—for the Thornes did not keep a cow—was a rangy bay named Saracen which Master Thorne rode when he went hunting with other burghers of London in the forests that were their preserves. Saracen was stand-offish, but Bess and Knight coaxed for petting, and Crede loitered with them until it was time to set out for the preaching at St. Mary Spital.

They were all going, and this preaching seemed as curious a custom as Crede had ever heard of. Somebody in the dim past had endowed five sermons on the mysteries of Easter: the first, on Good Friday, was given at Paul's Cross, and the next three at the cross of St. Mary Spital outside Bishopsgate, while on Low Sunday following there would be a final sermon at Paul's Cross criticizing those which had gone before. The sermons were attended by the mayor and aldermen in full livery and by crowds besides, for London (disputatious enough already) found this an excellent opportunity to sharpen wits.

When they came out the front door onto Bishopsgate Street a stream of people was already heading north along it. The street, as Crede had noticed when they crossed it to early mass at St. Helen's, was hand-somer and more spacious than anything in Bristol; on their side were a number of well-kept houses, and on the east side was Crosby Hall which they told her had been built a generation ago by a wealthy mer-chant, Sir John Crosby, and was still the finest house in London. Except for its grounds and the ancient chapel of St. Ethelberga by the gate, all that side of the street was part of the nunnery of St. Helen's. The parish church which the Thornes attended was separated by only a screen from the church of the convent whose Benedictine sisters had been, since early Christian times, the daughters of London citizens. The benefac-tions of their families through the ages had made St. Helen's and its wide gardens very beautiful.

Bishopsgate itself was an imposing structure. The statue of the Saxon Bishop, St. Erkenwald, looked down benignly from it, and the present Bishop of London could still collect his tribute of one faggot from every cart of wood which passed through it. St. Erkenwald was a popular saint among Londoners nevertheless. During his lifetime he had inclined toward practical good works, such as putting aside his robes of state and wandering outside the gate to perform deeds of piety among the charcoal burners of the forest—in those days the forest reached down to London's North Wall—and his bones still performed satisfactory miracles of healing from their tomb in St. Paul's.

Outside the gate on the Great North Road was a chapel where travelers might offer a last prayer to St. Botolph, patron saint of wayfarers, and the Dolphin Inn for their bodily comfort. Then the North Road ran on, broad and straight as the Romans had built it for their legions to pass to York and the Great Wall. There were a few scattered houses along it. Ahead, beyond a circle of religious foundations, were the hills of

[149]

Hampstead and Highgate, the domain of London citizens, where they could go hunting like lords or gather firewood thriftily.

West of the road, Moorfields, which also belonged to the citizens for pasturage and pleasure, came down to the North Wall. It stretched by marshy streams and wooded walks past the archery butts and Finsbury Field, where the Trained Bands drilled, toward the fairground of Smithfield and the suburbs around St. Bartholomew's Hospital. Above Moorfields was the Hospital of St. Mary of Bethlehem—pronounced Bedlam in London's queer dialect—whose monks in their piety cared for the mad. All along the east side of the road opposite, stretched the grounds of St. Mary Spital which was beloved of London, for the good brothers brought the city's sick here to be nursed in fresh country air.

By its wayside cross the mayor and aldermen were already assembled, wearing scarlet robes. On Good Friday at Paul's Cross they had worn their violet ones, Maddie said.

As they edged through the crowd to find a good position, Master Thorne bowed to a gentleman standing a little apart. His bow was returned less deeply, and the stranger permitted himself rather a long look at the party. Then he took a step forward and Master Thorne, all smiles, performed introductions, for it seemed that none of the rest knew Lord Hertley.

Lord Hertley's bow for the ladies was a model of courtliness now. He followed it with the suggestion that by moving to the edge of the crowd they could sit on a knoll under a tree and hear in comfort what this fellow had to say. With another bow for Mistress Fenton, he spread his cloak for her under the tree. Apparently he had invited himself to join them, and Master Thorne's gratification was obvious.

Crede thought that they would have done better to move closer if they meant to hear much of the sermon, but Dame Serena had already settled herself, and Lord Hertley was now engaging Maddie's attention, openly pointing to people in the crowd with manners that would not have been considered good in Bristol, occasionally bowing to a passer-by who was always someone richly dressed. His own clothes were in the extreme of new fashion: his short, saffron-colored doublet was slashed and puffed so that it swelled like a pumpkin above long, parti-colored hose; his shoes were absurdly broad-toed, and his gloves were stiff with jewels; a round hat, like a smaller pumpkin, sat upon his head. Such foppishness became him ill, for he was past his youth and rather scrawny.

The sermon had begun, and Robin made a place for Crede to move closer. She soon gathered that it was going to be very learned and rather dry. The preacher moved cautiously from point to point with copious reference to the Church Fathers, and was too obviously aware of that sermon of criticism to come at Paul's Cross, and of the pitfalls of heresy.

[150]

Since the attention of London was more easily caught by a number of interesting heresies, the crowd became restive and began to drift toward the diversions of Moorsfield.

Crede found Maddie at her elbow. "Let us move a little farther along," Maddie said, glancing uneasily over her shoulder where Dame Serena, still enthroned upon Lord Hertley's cloak, held him in conversation.

In the shifting of the crowd, Crede caught sight of Win and Alison, and with a cry of pleasure she hurried toward them. Oh, it was good to see them again, to feel Alison's arms warmly around her! She would have forgotten any sermon then, and with all of them talking at once they had moved óut of earshot. Win and Robin were exchanging news, and Crede and Maddie and Alison seated themselves under a tree. Crede asked and answered questions with Alison's hand still holding hers. In what seemed no time at all they discovered that the sermon had ended and that those who had stayed through it were moving away.

"Could you come home with us for dinner?" Alison asked, but Robin explained that his father wanted to take them on the river to watch the water quintain, and Maddie promised to take Crede without fail for a visit tomorrow.

"I usually drop in on Alison if I am out on any errand," Maddie said when they had separated. "Their cottage is not far from Chepe, and I love it better than any other place I know."

"Couldn't they have come with us on the river?" Crede was struggling with disappointment.

Maddie looked uncomfortable. "Aunt Serena wouldn't come in that case," she said. "Alison seems to upset her."

It was extremely important, Crede was already learning, that Dame Serena should not be upset. But when they entered the house, which Master Thorne and Mistress Fenton had reached before them, she seemed to be already in what Robin called a tizzy.

"I don't know where you have been," she said, "and I must say, Maddie, that you slipped off in a very rude and sly way."

Her glance rested upon both girls, and it was clear that her disapproval included Crede.

"Now, now," Master Thorne said easily, "they just got lost in the crowd."

He seemed in high good humor and did most of the talking at dinner, for Maddie fell silent under her aunt's continued criticism and Crede felt a sort of discomfort so new in her experience that she could think of little to say. It was Robin who joined in the conversation with his father and endeavored to persuade Dame Serena that the headache she felt coming on would be benefited by the river excursion.

Finally she announced that she would not spoil their pleasure by her own suffering, and they set out feeling rather selfish. All London, apparently, was abroad again. The carfax at the end of Bishopsgate Street was crowded. In front of St. Peter's Church some noisy apprentices in blue smocks and white gaiters were playing leap frog, while across the street more dignified citizens were enjoying the gardens in front of the roofed market of Leadenhall and children were rolling Easter eggs under the elms of St. Benet's Church by the Grassmarket. They followed the crowds moving along Grasschurch Street toward the Bridge, and coming down Fish Hill they passed through the dirtiest and most congested part of London which overflowed toward the bridgehead and the quays and warehouses and taverns below Thames Street.

Boatmen hovered about water stairs running down to the river. They shouted for fares, and while Master Thorne was bargaining with them, Robin took Crede a few steps along the Bridge.

Like Bristol's bridge it was built with tall houses and had a central chapel, but an open space had been left near the entrance, and from this she could look down-river. Crede caught her breath. For as far as the Tower the river was a forest of furled sails that made Quayside seem a narrow pathway.

"You like this about London!" Robin said, watching her face.

"All the ships of the world must come here!"

"From most parts of the world, anyhow. They have been coming, I suppose, ever since the Romans made London their chief port of the North—but never before so many as now. Sometimes it seems to me that you can feel a surge in Thames tide, as if it had not even yet reached its full."

Across the river, Southwark crowded against the bridge-head and was packed with inns, Robin said, for travelers from all the south roads. He went on to explain that downstream the fishing villages had grown together in almost a solid line around the bend to the Royal Palace of Greenwich and King Henry's new shipyard at Deptford. All the while Crede could scarcely take her eyes from that great flock of folded wings that had paused to keep Eastertide in London.

A moment later Master Thorne was settling them in the boat he had hired. Here above the Bridge many of the barges were handsomely painted and had bright awnings and pennants bearing the devices of wealthy owners, making a brave show on the sparkling blue of the river. A space in the middle had been kept clear for the water quintain which was one of the events of the Easter season. Besides those in the boats, crowds lined the shore to watch it. On the river there was much juggling for position while boats bumped and boatmen cursed with a fluency which even Bristol's waterside could not outdo. Master Thorne observed with satisfaction that they had been lucky in their boatman: he could not only outshout most of his neighbors but he maneuvered his party into a spot near the quintain without quite upsetting them.

The game was just beginning. The first boat was coming up, rowing full tilt for the target—a tree trunk anchored in the river—with a boy standing nervously poised for the moment when he must shiver his long lance against it. If he missed, or struck so that his lance caught without breaking, he would lose his precarious balance and fall into the river. A rescue boat waited nearby to fish him out if he should so disgrace himself. The first contender made a good strike, and his boat shot on past the quintain amid cheers. Other boats were coming up in turn, some carrying the colors of a London school or guild, some with obviously homemade devices. Robin called encouragement to a boat from St. Peter's, which had been his own school, and Maddie shouted with him, but Crede had already chosen one with only a red kerchief to mark it. It waited quite close to them. The boy who was perched like an eager bird in it seemed one of the youngest contenders and dreadfully in earnest; she could see the set purpose of his face. When his unskillful boatmen carried him on too wide a course to strike, she cheered as loudly as she could for him above roars of laughter while they rowed back to await another turn.

Now his boat was coming up again and she could see that every line of his skinny little body was taut with excitement. This time they were going to make it! She felt her own muscles tense with the effort of his, as he thrust. Alas, he had not broken his shaft! He shot out of the boat, a terrific splash for so light a projectile, and amid shouts of derision he was fished up half drowned. They were taking him out of the game now and, as the rescue boat passed theirs, Crede gave a solitary cheer for her champion. She could see his face again and guessed that he was yearning for the watery grave he had been plucked from—her consciousness met his in that flash of understanding which can link strangers, and she knew that winning or losing touched him too close, as it did her. The other contestants looked big and competent in comparison, and she could not care whether they won applause or jeers—in fact, she hoped that a lot of them would fall in too and quickly enough to offer consolation. Since no one immediately obliged her she began to lose interest.

Her eyes turned shoreward. London, as seen from the river, rose incredibly dense from its waterfront. The great mass of St. Paul's on its western hill brooded over the maze of the lower streets and the line of rooftops dipped and rose again at St. Peter's hill in the east. Many of the buildings along the river were low and rather mean, leaving unhidden a tangle of crooked streets and lanes climbing the rise with trees and spires above, and all along shore water stairs ran down to the river. Robin, seeing where her attention had wandered, named for her Paul's stairs, waterbearers' stairs, laundresses' stairs, the stairs of the stews, or bath houses, Puddledock where carters watered their horses, brewers' dock, fishmongers' dock. . . .

The docks at Queenhithe surrounded a natural inlet where ships had unloaded from earliest times, and the inlet east of it, Dowgate, had been the mouth of the Walbrook which was once an open stream that carried boats into the heart of London between the twin hills of St. Peter and St. Paul. Between Queenhithe and Dowgate were the wine vaults of the Vintry, and east of Dowgate the warehouses of the Hanse League were enclosed by the massive walls of the Steelyard. Within, these Baltic traders lived by their own laws, with privileges resented, often violently, by native merchants but confirmed since ancient times by royal charters. The fine old mansion which rose among meaner buildings east of the Steelyard was Coldharbor, where the Black Prince had once lived. It was owned now by Lady Margaret, the King's mother. But in answer to Crede's eager question whether he had seen this famous lady whose scholarship Cousin Allie had so often held up to her as an example, Robin replied that she made few public appearances and spent most of her time at her favorite country house in Surrey.

The water quintain had come to an end, and the barges were jostling to get out of the press. Maddie wanted to stay longer on the river. In particular she wanted to shoot the Bridge for she had got into conversation with their waterman who assured her that she would never be in a safer boat to try it. But the others positively forbade this; it was difficult enough at any time to steer between the pillars with their outbuilt starlings, and only the most foolhardy cared to attempt it when the tide changed and roared through the arches as it was beginning to do now. Besides, Dame Fenton had begun to worry about supper. Susan and that new flibbertigibbet Polly had no doubt been gadding all afternoon, she said, and there had always to be someone for whom feast days were no holiday.

She could not, however, be brought to agree with Robin's suggestion that they row across the river to have supper at the Bear Tavern, whose water stairs ran down at the Southwark side. She said that he must think very poorly of her to suppose that she would roister with holiday crowds in a common alehouse.

"Do you good, Serena," Master Thorne said. "But if you won't, we'll take something home from the cookhouses, so you needn't fuss."

He had furnished the boat for their refreshment during the game with a basket of oysters and a half gallon of sack, and there was no question but that he had become slightly carefree.

"Do I run your house so ill, Gilbert, that we are driven to the cook-houses?" said Dame Serena with chilling dignity.

[154]

Master Thorne's face flushed. "Sacred bodkins, Sairy, spare us a long face for once! I want to go to the cookhouses. Haven't been there for ages."

Dame Serena seemed for a moment frozen with astonishment. Then her gaze traveled significantly from her brother's flushed face to the wine cask. Obviously, her expression proclaimed, Gilbert was not himself, and his drunken abuse must be borne among her other crosses.

"Let us go to the cookhouses," she said with Christian forbearance, and folded her lips.

Lower London, east of the bridgehead, surpassed anything Crede had yet seen of crowded disorder. Warehouses, tenements of several stories called flats, houses, shops, and taverns elbowed one another in a tangle of narrow lanes through which Lower Thames Street ran beside the wharves and Eastchepe threaded its way toward the Tower. The holiday crowd in which they had to push their way was rougher here. Dame Serena pointedly refused her brother's arm, requesting Robin's, and Crede and Maddie clung together, keeping close behind Master Thorne in the path he cleared for them.

The cookhouses were in Eastchepe. Although the cooks were bound to observe holy days as strictly as other tradesmen, provision had been made for members of the guild to take turns in keeping a shop open for London could scarcely do without them. Not only travelers and transients used them, but any house caught with unexpected guests might send out for good hot food. Strangers to London were amazed by its excellence and variety.

Master Thorne found an open shop, and Maddie followed him inside, but Mistress Fenton refused to take any part in the proceedings. Since they could not leave her alone in the street Crede and Robin stayed beside her. Her complaints robbed even a boisterously jovial holiday scene like today's of color and savor—Mistress Fenton, Crede thought, could take the gold out of sunshine. She was beginning to find something frightening in this discontent with everything. It sucked at your toes like quicksand and threatened to drag you down with it.

Eastchepe was an ancient market street, the only one except Cheapside where street peddling was allowed, and a few vendors were risking the stocks this afternoon by discreet solicitation upon a holy day. Crede felt her arm nudged.

"Buy eel pies, Mistress, fresh and hot! Two for a penny."

Something about the young peddler was familiar. Crede stared at him for a moment and recognized her knight of the quintain. He was taller than he had seemed in the boat, but there was no mistaking him now, for he was so much the cleanest young ragamuffin on the street, his hair still wetly plastered.

[155]

"I'll take one," she said.

She fumbled in her purse for a silver shilling, a staggering overpayment and quite illegal, but his clothes were so ragged, his face so pinched and eager.

"Sweet Mary and all the saints give you good fortune, Mistress!"

He stuffed the shilling hastily into his smock and dumped the greasy pie into her hands just as Maddie, looking highly pleased, and Master Thorne, looking indulgent, came out of the cookhouse with a basket between them.

"Eel pies today! Stale and warmed up from Lent, I'll be bound, you young rogue!" Master Thorne cried indignantly. "Be off with you!"

The boy made a sudden swoop past Crede and disappeared in the crowd. She had felt a tug at her girdle and glanced down. Oh, he couldn't have—but her purse was gone!

There was over five shillings in it. Theft of it was a hanging matter—branding, at least. Did they hang them so young? Hanging was the remedy for so many errors that Crede could not be sure. And he might be older than he looked.

Robin took the pie from her and set it on top of the basket. "Is something the matter, Crede?"

"I—it has dripped on my gown." She dabbed at the greasy spot.

She was thoughtful during the walk home and was not especially hungry for supper, though Maddie, free for once to exercise her own judgment in a household matter, had let her fancy rove in the cookhouse.

She must not let anyone miss her purse, not even Maddie. For while Maddie's sense of public duty was likely to be as flexible as Crede's own, she might let something slip, and it was just possible that the purse, which was a handsome one, could be traced to the boy. The Watch did catch a number of malefactors, as the crowded gaols proved and the city officers strove valiantly by means of stocks and pillory, whipping carts and the rope, to keep London honest and orderly. Even the Church, though it gave sanctuary to fugitives from justice, to the exasperation of the courts and the king, did not hold that crime should go unpunished; it was better that the body be broken than the soul hardened in sin.

What right had she to set herself against them all to protect a young ruffian who had rewarded her generosity by snatching her purse? Her generosity—it had been no more than a sentimental indulgence, worth no more than his glib thanks. Even the purse had cost her no more than that. This, when she remembered the boy's pinched face and dreadful earnestness, was a disturbing thought. It set them worlds apart, yet she had felt an instant sympathy at the quintain which had shown them to be somehow alike.

The color and movement had gone out of this first crowded London day. After supper Robin piled logs on the fire and kept them burning brightly, yet the big hall was still gloomy, somehow comfortless in spite of its handsome furniture. Nowhere in this house was there a room which seemed to have grown companionably about the family circle to enclose them with its content whether they talked or fell silent. Crede's own thoughts went on separately and uncomfortably.

Surely she could have found something better to offer that boy than a careless lavishness which tempted him to steal. Conscience, so dolefully named in old English "the agen bite of inwit," found other tender places: in the firelight the boy's face mingled with the faces of those children grubbing in the midden near Bristol's Castle, and those desperate, hardened faces at Newgate.

During her first few days in London Crede became increasingly grateful for Maddie. It was Maddie who helped her to unpack and found things to make her room comfortable, who admired her clothes and advised her on London fashions, whose open adoration of Fand won over that captious beauty and persuaded her to come out from a royal retirement under the bed. It was Maddie who gave Crede a place in the household by sharing her own duties with this eagerly welcomed sister, for Dame Serena found nothing that new hands could do—although she complained daily of being overworked herself and kept Susan and the little housemaid, Polly, hurrying from one task to another, expecially if ever she found them with Crede.

Master Thorne claimed most of Robin's time. He had been away so long that things he should have helped with had mounted up and Crede, supposing that he must have known this, wondered at the leisureliness he had seemed content with on their journey. Now that the busy season had begun he and his father were away all day at Thames Street. Since the counting room was there too and the apprentices lived with the chief clerk above it, the exciting world of ships and trade did not reach into the house as it had always done at home. Maddie knew nothing of her father's affairs, and it was plain that he would give Crede no opportunity to help here as Robin had helped her in Bristol. It was also quite plain, she thought, that however much he depended upon Robin his own hold upon his business was as authoritative as Dame Serena's upon the house—that Maddie and Robin had no experience of the easier relations with their elders which she herself had enjoyed.

An anticipation of companionship with Robin which had grown pleasantly during the ride to London had only been part of that holiday, she thought now; it was only because they had been separated for a while from their own concerns that they had found interests to share and even the heightened comradeship of adventure. There had been a quickness and gaiety in "Master Scrivener" at Wykham which she had not expected. But it must be that Robin could be gay only in play acting, for he had not been at all like that since. Perhaps throughout their journey he had acted the part of enjoying a holiday which his kindness had offered because he thought she needed it. Now, although he was still friendly and considerate, she no longer felt as she had sometimes then that he was unclosing something in himself for her understanding.

He need not feel that he must entertain me here, she decided, and she found reasons to keep busy with Maddie. They began to do everything together, delighting in a relationship neither of them had experienced before and finding a pleasure in it which Crede had not even known she had missed. Full and perfect as the days had seemed when she was growing up, Cousin Allie's lessons had kept her from close association with girls of her own age. Anthony had been her chief playmate and, except for stolid Kate, and Mona, who was two generations older, she had been almost always with men—devoted men whom she loved but who never made small amusing secrets of quite ordinary things or burst into peals of laughter over simply nothing at all.

"How have you and Maddie lived apart before?" Robin said.

He had got home a little early and had been lounging on the window seat in the long gallery, playing with Fand and watching them sew. They had been altering, on Maddie's advice, the sleeves of a gown Crede meant to wear to supper, and Maddie had just left them with Crede's choice between a green and a yellow snood in her hand.

"I lost my heart to her at first sight, you know. She simply stepped into it." Crede smiled as she remembered how impulsively Maddie had done just that. "It made all the difference here."

"Here is a new ballad for the rhymesters!" Robin laughed oddly.

But when Crede looked up, puzzled, he did not seem to be laughing at her. His expression was thoughtful. "I suppose," he said, "you were no more than Maddie's age when I first saw you. At the moment you look even less."

"Are you so greatly aged?" She was not sure, after all, that he had not been making fun of her.

"I think perhaps those four years more have been pressing too hard and fast on me." Looking as if he had made a discovery which pleased him greatly he added, "Both you and Maddie were cheated of some of your playtime. I should have seen to it that Maddie had more—and I might have remembered that you had to grow up very suddenly."

After this he was always finding things that Crede and Maddie could do together. Before leaving for Thames Street in the morning he might think of some delicacy for supper, something Master Thorne had a particular fondness and an instant longing for, which meant a special trip to the exciting market district around Cheapside. When Dame Serena reminded them how heavily burdened her shoulders were without such inconsiderate demands, he would suggest sympathetically that she ought to spare herself and Susan the errands when two girls together could go quite properly through a respectable district. He managed also to persuade Master Thorne that Bess was gentle enough for Maddie to learn to ride, so that the two girls and Dick could give the horses the exercise they needed.

Without entering the crowded parts of town they could ride north through Bishopsgate or cross below the grounds of St. Helen's to Aldgate. This led them out over Houndsditch, a section of the moat on whose banks citizens kenneled their hunting dogs, to the flat countryside down Thames. Riding this way they had the busy life of the river beside them, but Crede could never quite enjoy its diversions until they were out of the shadow of the Tower which seemed to hold still a darkness that this new age was comfortably forgetting, a long memory of violence whose storm centers had broken here. In comparison with the reassuring dilapidation of Bristol's and Oxford's castles, its fortifications were grimly efficient. The Town Wall, which was the corporation's responsibility and was maintained by a levy of one day's work a year upon the citizens of each ward, had a decidedly patchy appearance. It was completely gone along the river side, but the royal upkeep of the Tower was no such haphazard business. William the Norman had not felt easy on his throne until he had set the White Tower there as a warning to London and had provided a royal residence within it for moments of strain. With all the additions kings had made since, it kept close watch over the strong-willed giant beside it. But there had been fewer executions for treason in it under Henry Tudor than for many years before, Robin told her. Sometimes it was he instead of Dick who rode Saracen, but this was not often because in addition to keeping long hours at Thames Street Master Thorne frequently brought things home with him to worry about and kept Robin with him after supper.

Her father's enterprises, Crede thought, had been conducted with far less strain. And certainly Mona had never made the management of their house such a burden. Somehow, while life kept its pleasant course, Mona had got things done in a regular succession of household events, each bringing its own interest and pride of achievement. But this belated housecleaning of Dame Serena's stretched drearily on and on.

Just as a job was hopefully nearing its end, Dame Serena was apt to say, "We'll leave that for today. I'm sure I am ready to drop."

No matter how one's fingers itched to finish it then, it had to be left hanging over Mistress Fenton's martyred head in a cloud whose gloom the rest of them could not escape. It was not advisable to do otherwise than obey, Crede discovered at some cost.

On the day that the spring washing of linens came in from the bushes she and Susan and Maddie and Polly ironed swiftly in the steamy kitchen, and it began to look as if they could finish, when Mistress Fenton decided that things would have to be left as they were until tomorrow and, directing Susan what to prepare for supper, went to rest. Polly looked mutinous, for she had been half promised tomorrow with her young man whose sea-coal barge was in, and now she would probably not be spared.

"Drat!" Susan said. "Supper is well enough along. We could have finished and got out of this mess."

It might be a pleasant surprise for Dame Serena, Crede thought, if they managed it, and the others needed little encouragement. Then while Susan and Polly hurried with supper she offered to put the linens away in the cupboards. Because she enjoyed bringing order anywhere, she made a loving job of it, taking care that they had cooled, sorting the fresh-smelling piles neatly, choosing the best arrangement, and spreading lavender and southernwood with a lavish hand.

The result was a storm of tears from Dame Serena. She was being put out of her brother's house in her old age, she said, and the scene grew into a recital of slights which Crede could scarcely have dreamed herself capable of committing. Amazingly, Dame Serena was able to eat her supper after it, though Crede's stuck in her throat.

She had no experience of scenes to fortify her, and this particular one left her shaken and remorseful, for one accusation was true enough—she did not love Dame Serena. It was also true that she offered her no confidences although, as Dame Serena pointed out, she and Maddie were always chattering together. She did not know how she could amend even this, since with Dame Serena her tongue became hopelessly tied, and its unaccustomed awkwardness grew worse instead of better after accusations of unfriendliness. She had not known that Dame Serena wanted anything of her, and it was rather dreadful to find nothing to give; she knew that they could never talk intimately and easily as she did with Maddie, yet her efforts to find something to say about more general things did no good at all. Dame Serena did not appear ever to have had a general idea, and it was not this she wanted of you. It seemed to Crede that she was like a prisoner locked in herself; when she made a pathetic effort to peer out it was only to try to see into someone else's lockup—she had a frightful curiosity about what you might have shut away there.

After the housecleaning upheaval was over Crede and Maddie were able to get a good deal of freedom out of their errands. When anything really important had to be done Dame Serena felt obliged to go herself, but she did not enjoy walking, and fortunately she had no idea how much entertainment the girls found when they offered to spare her. Nor did she know how long they stayed away on many such commissions, since she always took an afternoon nap.

"It helps pass the time," she would say drearily, for though she found work a burden leisure was apparently an equal one to her.

It was strange, Crede thought with aching remembrance of her father's interests, that Dame Serena seemed likely to have more than the usual allotment of time on this earth which she found so wearisome. Though she was older than Master Thorne she did not look it, and her deepest depressions, even when they caused scenes and an atmosphere in the house which left Crede physically ill, did not harm her sturdy body. It looked fit for many years yet. Perhaps, Crede thought, the angels had pleaded for this extra time to improve paradise so that it might possibly please her.

This shocking blasphemy did nothing for Crede's state of mind except to warn her that she must keep her thoughts as much as possible from Dame Serena until she could reform her own character sufficiently to have more creditable ones; but whenever she and Maddie escaped to enjoy themselves about London it was easy to think that she could manage this. The streets were an unfailing amusement. They were dirty, and their smell was so much stronger than Bristol's that Crede learned to carry a posy of the more pungent herbs under her nose. But in these streets was the deep undercurrent of a city that had been a metropolis for ages and the rising excitement of a port that was suddenly bursting its bounds. There might be half a hundred thousand people living here, Robin told her, not counting the many in religious houses, and those on business who could get a permit to stay only thirty days, and the foreigns in their allotted quarters, and the suburbs which were growing like mushrooms outside the Wall.

The growth of London frightened the five thousand or so registered freemen of its corporation of guilds which ruled it and paid its taxes. They were liable for its responsibilities and had to keep some sort of order in it. They passed laws against new building; they and their apprentices sometimes sallied forth with spades and picks to demolish the houses of squatters on the commons. But London continued to grow monstrously. The voice of the giant was the roar of Thames tide through the Bridge arches, which could be heard as the persistent undertone of street noises and the bells of church and convent and guildhall. That tide brought to London the ships of the world in increasing numbers, and it could no more be stayed than the tide which King Canute could not halt.

Crede, going with Maddie on her errands, learned to know the streets of the different trades off Cheapside, the licensed seldes where citizens were permitted to buy foreign goods, the roofed stalls of Leadenhall where workmen outside the corporation could sell their wares, the poultry and butter market near their own corner, the meat and vegetable markets near St. Paul's. And nearly every day they managed to stretch some errand into a visit with Alison.

FIFTEEN

The cottage which the Perrys had taken was in Cordwainer Street below Cheapside, and their neighbors were mostly hosiers since, for some reason, shoemakers were moving from the district which bore their name to one near St. Martin le Grande and hosiers in a small way of business had been replacing them. This shifting about had given Win the chance to get a small house which he and Alison had restored from a rather tumbledown condition. They had weeded and planted its tiny garden, freshly whitewashed its walls inside, and gaily painted its door and the sign of a griffon which swung above it. Their great extravagance had been a window with panes of Flanders glass to close the open shop front, and this gave them great comfort and the lightest, most charming room imaginable. It was almost as large, though not so high, as the hall in more pretentious houses for they had taken down the partition between the workshop and the kitchen-bedroom, which had a fine big fireplace. This left them no other rooms except the loft above a narrow stairway. Win had divided this into two bedchambers. The shed at the back they had turned into a kitchen, and that was all they needed. Win had cleverly made furniture and shelves out of the workbenches and the lumber from the partition, and Alison was still happily contriving curtains and cushions and inventing substitutes for this and that, as if she were playing a game.

She had some new improvement to show or plan whenever Crede and Maddie dropped in, and she let them share the fun. Helping with anything about the pretty, tiny cottage had the charm for them of playing house, and the joy which Alison found in bringing beauty into it was infectious. They slipped away on many afternoons while Dame Serena took her nap, to put their stitches beside Alison's fine needlework, making curtains of cheap Norfolk worsted as gay with embroidered flowers as the costly tapestry and arras cloth which, Alison said cheerfully, kept out draughts no better. Maddie was never ready to leave. She found such happiness here that it seemed to glow from her, making her lovelier than ever.

Sometimes Win came in when they were working, and would stop to talk for a while before going upstairs to his books. He had been given a small part in preparing courses for the new school while helping with classes that would be the nucleus of it, and he was able to tell them a number of interesting things about Dean Colet's battle with tradition.

To the outrage of his bishop he had put the new foundation under the governace of lay trustees, his father's associates in the Mercer's Company, remarking that although there was corruption in all human affairs he had found less among them than most. Even its headmaster, William Lily, was not in priestly orders. And Dr. Erasmus, who was the Dean's chief adviser, had nothing tactful to say about the salutary discipline of his own boyhood. The classrooms he was happily spending the Dean's fortune upon were to be light and airy, with nothing resembling a cell of punishment in the whole building. A gracious figure of the Child Jesus joyously conferring with men of learning in the Temple was to set the tone of instruction. And he had conceived the startling theory that textbooks for children ought to make it as easy as possible to acquire knowledge.

The problem just now was to get such a textbook for Latin grammar, which was, of course, the basic subject in any school. Dean Colet had asked the renowned classical scholar Dr. Grocyn to prepare it, but Dr. Grocyn's views were not entirely in harmony with those of Dr. Lily. Dr. Lily himself was an eminent classical scholar and, after all, he was the one who would have to teach from it. Dr. Erasmus had some still different ideas which he held as strongly as the others held theirs. Even Win had ideas, though he was not famous enough to be listened to and so was not seriously embroiled in the dispute. How Cousin Allie would have enjoyed this learned argument! Crede thought with a pang of homesickness.

Maddie listened to Win's accounts with rapt attention. You might suppose that theories of education were her first concern, although Crede knew that Maddie had been a lazy student going not much farther than her hornbook and an ability to read ballad sheets and broadsides. A suspicion which had been taking form in her mind emerged with sudden clarity: Maddie would have listened with equal pleasure to a recitation of the Statutes of Westminster if Win had been making it.

If Win came home during one of their visits with Alison, Maddie was radiant. And Win, who was as charming to her as to Crede and his mother, was married to the New Learning as unmistakably as Cousin Allie was. It seemed as unlikely that the thought of any other attachment crossed his mind as that, if it did, he could ever ask Master Thorne for a daughter who could be the means of cementing some profitable business alliance.

Was it wise to come here so often? Crede wondered. Yet she no more

[163]

than Maddie could bear to miss their happy hours at the cottage. This afternoon they had come again. A rose flowered on the curtains under Maddie's fingers, while Crede labored with a bluebell, and as Win came through the door Maddie's rose bloomed on her cheeks.

"The family plate," he said, setting down a bundle.

He had a dozen wooden trenchers and mazers such as poorer households used instead of pewter or silver. Alison looked at them happily.

"The idea came to me of painting them like the old roundels," she said. "I am going to use my needlework patterns and paint them with flowers and fruit. Don't you think they will be pretty? We haven't enough dishes, and now that we are settled it would be so nice to give a party."

"Settled!" Win groaned. "I thought we had the curtains up at least, but you girls sit under them forever stitching. You egg Mother on, and every day she thinks of a new shelf for me to put up."

Alison laughed. "I want one down now. I have a wonderful new idea!" She jumped up and ran to the other end of the room, her movements as quick as a girl's. "We don't need this cupboard here—the side ones are enough. Win, dear, I'm sorry you had to make it, but you can have it for books in your room. Will it be a great nuisance to move it?"

"Think nothing of it." Win sighed. "It almost knows how to move itself by now. But what," he added with sudden suspicion, "do we have to build in its place?"

"You don't have to make a thing," Alison promised gaily. "After I've practiced on the trenchers I am going to paint that wall. It came to me just now—it's exactly what is needed to finish the room."

"Finish is a word I had not hoped to hear." Win's expression was teasing, but he added, "I can get you some good colors from a friend in the Painter-Stainers Guild, Mistress Leonardo."

"Oh, Alison, can't we help?" Maddie cried. "We could come first thing tomorrow and begin practicing on the trenchers."

Should they? Crede wondered again. Here in this happy house, so different from anything she had known before, Maddie was unfolding joyously, her loving, impulsive heart unguarded. Win treated her like a child, but surely Alison had noticed. Crede looked toward her doubtfully.

"Do come if you can," Alison said serenely. Alison who loved Maddie too did not fear for her, and in a swift flash of intuition Crede realized that this was because they were alike—Maddie, like Alison, had to give, without counting return. Crede had grown up in a happy house, but Maddie was finding her native air here for the first time, and who should tell her to be cautious?

Although Dame Serena did not guess how many errands included a visit to Cordwainer Street, she guessed enough to protest to Master

Thorne when the announcement was made next morning that Alison had invited Crede and Maddie to spend the day. But Master Thorne saw nothing wrong with it. The Perrys were among their oldest friends, in spite of his sister's dislike of them, and he felt moved to say now that surely the girls could be spared sometimes from a house supplied with servants. Crede felt sure that no question of Win and Maddie had ever entered his head; marriages were suitably arranged among people of substance, and their children knew better than to let their thoughts stray in unsuitable directions.

Nor did even Dame Serena think of this objection. Her resentment was because she thought herself slighted when Crede and Maddie had other interests, and because on general principles she objected to people traipsing about to amuse themselves. In particular she disapproved of Alison Perry, for in her judgment a woman who could be happy after so many misfortunes lacked proper feeling.

But with Master Thorne taking this stand she could not forbid Maddie to go, and she did not expect Crede to show the slightest consideration for her opinion when even her own family had so little regard for it, in spite of the many occasions she could point to when they would have done better to take her advice. She could only suppose that this was because she was a poor widow with the most niggardly of fortunes, who had merely devoted her life to them.

"Do you propose to go through the streets dressed in that way, Crede?" she asked when Crede and Maddie, having hurried through their morning tasks with amazing speed, were escaping out the door.

Crede paused to inspect her neat gray dress which seemed to be in order. She had her cloak over her arm and pattens to protect her shoes from street mud.

"Have I forgotten something?"

"I think so. Have you ever seen me or any other respectable married woman without a coif?"

Of course Crede had not. She had never seen more of Dame Serena's head than her pink face and an inch of neatly parted gray hair above it under her cap. Only unmarried girls wore their hair flowing, and brides put on a headdress as the first badge of matronly dignity.

But on Crede's wedding day there had been no time to think of such trifles. With all that came hard upon it she, and even Mona, must have forgotten. The swift anger which shook her now was out of all proportion. It flared because the criticism reached back to that time and she could not bear to have Dame Serena touch anything which touched her so close.

"It's my own head," she said and slammed the door behind her.

[165]

"Oh, Crede!" Maddie said, catching up with her furious pace. "Don't let Aunt Serena fuss you! Its just her way."

Robin said that, they all said that. But nobody could help being upset. They couldn't help it themselves.

"I think your hair is lovely," Maddie said loyally. "I'd never put an ugly old coif over it."

"I ought not to be conspicuous, Maddie. I just hadn't thought about it. We'll have to go to the shops soon. But not right away," she added rebelliously. And then, because they were free for the day and on the way to Alison, she could laugh at herself. "I do believe," she admitted, "that Dame Serena annoys me most when she is right."

Alison already had her embroidery patterns spread out, a trencher painted with cornflowers, and a smudge of blue paint down one cheek.

"Put on these old smocks, girls," she said, scarcely greeting them. "You have no idea how this color spreads or what odd shades you get by mixing. We'll try more patterns on the trenchers and then begin on the wall."

It was not so different from making sampler patterns, and they had done that since they could hold a needle, except that painting went so much faster. It frightened Crede at first to work so quickly, but as she grew bolder it was magic of a most exciting kind. She could add a leaf or a bud as quick as thought, and this tempted her to follow the patterns less closely and begin to invent her own. Trenchers burst into flowers and fruit under her fingers, and soon she was eyeing the large, smooth surface of the wall with longing.

Alison took a deep breath.

"We'll begin on it!" she announced. "After all, we can whitewash over if we spoil it. I thought we might have a tree full of birds and fruit in the center and then spread out vines and flowers. Perhaps we should try those first in the corners."

She and Maddie each flew to a corner and Crede began at the very bottom of the wall with ground ivy and little pink and blue stars of hepatica. It was going beautifully. She bumped along on her knees and did not know that she was singing as she worked, until Maddie said crossly, "Do stop, Crede! You are putting me off."

Crede looked up in astonishment. Maddie was never cross, and Maddie was always begging her to sing.

Maddie had a tip of pink tongue stuck out one corner of her mouth, a wrinkle down her forehead, and she was painting far differently from Crede's small, cautious work. Her corner had spread from a low tangle of gorse to a great straggling may branch with a light violet-gray behind it like a moody April sky.

"I am putting a linnet on the branch," she said in an awed voice.

Alison stepped back from her corner where a little holly bush was springing up in full berry. "Why, Maddie!" she said. "Maddie, you must do the tree in the middle! Crede and I will do background."

"Umm—" Maddie said. "Just let me finish this!"

The others returned to their own work, and after a while Maddie stepped back. She moved to a space one side of the center and stood frowning.

"The tree should be here, and there is a pale, greenish light behind it, because it is early morning and the light comes low behind other trees— but they are not close enough to show, for this is a special tree that stands by itself—"

She seized her brush and began to paint furiously.

Crede ventured upon a bank of bluebells and then found that she could crawl no farther without bumping into Maddie. Alison was working her way steadily across a flowering glade on the other side, but Maddie's method was different. On her part of the wall nothing was finished, and it seemed to be splashed messily with colors. Maddie would suddenly step back and glower at it, then rush forward with a violence which made it seem probable that anything which got in her way, even her dearest Crede, would be trampled upon. Crede moved prudently out of reach and went into the kitchen to see what she could do about dinner, for although they had been too much occupied to heed any bells it must be past noon, and it was fortunate that Win did not come home in the middle of the day.

She found that Alison had made provision beforehand and set the kitchen table. While she looked about for anything that needed doing, a knock came at the door, and just as she opened it upon six small girls Alison came hurrying from the other room.

"Oh, my dears, I had quite forgotten you!" she cried. "I'm afraid we can't have our lesson today—you would get all over paint. Will you come back tomorrow? Wait—you shall have your honey cakes at least."

When they had gone, she turned merrily to Crede. "Yesterday there were only five. I shall soon have the dozen I hope for."

"Have you some other wonderful new plan?" Crede said severely.

For surely Alison, who had not even a scullery maid, when the poorest tradesman's wife had usually some help, need not add to her work by minding the neighbors' children.

"Yes, I have, dear. I think girls should learn their letters, too—all these schools for boys, yet only daughters of the well-to-do are given anything to awaken their minds besides housewifery. This is my contribution to the New Learning." She dimpled in the way that made her look sixteen. "I suppose it ought to be called a Dame School. Win made me hornbooks for them, and I tempt them here with honey cakes."

Crede threw her arms around Alison and kissed her. Alison made life still full of promise, since she would never be too insecure or poor or overworked to have something to give joyously out of an abundance she found.

"I'd like to help you if I can," Crede said suddenly.

It was a moment before Alison understood that she was speaking again of the Dame School, as they had named it, and accepted gladly; for the children's visit was long past and in the meantime Maddie had been tempted out for food, and then they had all returned to painting.

Crede and Alison had to find corners to fill in where they would be out of Maddie's way. This strange, fierce Maddie seemed possessed and could not even be spoken to. The tree had taken shape now, spreading widely and bearing fruits and blossoms of all sorts and seasons and sheltering a variety of birds. Watching it grow under Maddie's reckless strokes was so fascinating that the others did not mind when they had to move back out of the way or even when they were stepped upon.

Finally Maddie stood back and stared at it. She was pale with a red spot on each cheek. After a moment she reached for a stool and sank down on it, all her fierceness gone.

"Alison," she said in a very small voice, "have I spoiled your lovely room?"

"It's beautiful!" Alison moved beside her and stood looking at it. "It is much lovelier than I was able to imagine it, Maddie."

Crede thought it beautiful too—strange and crude but with something that caught the imagination in its pattern while the colors mingled oddly yet did not clash. "How ever did you do it, Maddie?"

"Is it really going to be all right?" Maddie laughed shakily. "I've always liked to make my own tapestry patterns, but it wasn't exciting like this." She looked again at her tree, doubtfully. "It needs a lot. But I can't do any more now."

"Indeed not!" Alison said firmly. "I've let you work far too long. But it would have been a sin to stop anyone in the mood you were in."

"Do you toilers know that it is past five?"

Win stood in the doorway surveying the clutter of trenchers and paint pots. He saw the wall then and came to stand in front of it, while Maddie turned paler.

"Why, it is charming! It's—as if the room opened out into some sort of fairyland. It beats me, though, how you got so much done."

"What is charming?" said Robin's voice from behind them. He came into the room and looked about him with some astonishment. "You do let them muck your place about, Alison! Aunt Serena—"

"Would be in a tizzy," laughed Maddie.

She was bubbling over with high spirits now because Win, too, had liked her tree.

"Is in one," Robin said. "Supper is waiting, and Aunt Serena thinks that you have both been run over, slugged in an alley, drowned in the moat. She has gone to bed with a headache." He stopped to regard the wall with rather a puzzled expression.

"Maddie did the best of it," Crede said.

"Did you really, Mad?" His glance moved from the painting to his young sister, losing none of its speculation. "If ever I can get to Italy again I'd like to take you round Florence."

Maddie stood speechless with gratification. Then she turned a questioning look upon her achievement and her face fell.

"There's such a lot wrong," she said anxiously. "It's not near finished."

"I think we should have a party for Maddie when it is finished," Alison said.

"Oh no, for your birthday, Alison," Maddie begged. "Can't we have a party on your birthday?"

Crede added her persuasions to Maddie's, for it occurred to her that if they made an occasion of Alison's birthday she could bring a gift to the house. You could not give Alison and Win things they needed, but for an occasion she might get something, not just useful and not obviously costly. She turned this over in her mind as they set out, not too eagerly, for Bishopsgate Street.

It was quite true that Mistress Fenton had taken to her bed. Yet instead of being touched by this manifestation of her anxious regard for them, Crede told herself crossly that Dame Serena had always to find some club for people's backs and make her feelings their first concern. Maddie went dutifully to her door and reported that Aunt could not come down because worry had brought on such a headache that it would be impossible for her to sit at table, but that Polly had been encountered in the gallery with a well-filled tray. Even Maddie did not show the remorse that could usually be wrung from her and, as a matter of fact, supper was a pleasanter meal than usual.

Master Thorne was in particularly good spirits. He filled his glass oftener than when under his sister's eye, and though he seldom talked of business matters before the women of his family, he was too full of a new and favorable prospect to contain his pleasure. This opportunity he told them with satisfaction was likely to come through Lord Hertley.

Apparently Lord Hertley was sniffing enviously the favoring trade wind of England's new source of wealth, and it had occurred to him, as it had done to Stephen Chalkraft in humbler circumstances, that the sheep pasturing on his estate might yield him more than the single profit to be found in raw wool. He had done Master Thorne the honor of seeking his advice in the matter.

"If he carries out the plan of developing a weaving village on his Essex manor," Master Thorne said, "we can deal directly with him for cloth and share between us the profits skimmed off by the great cloth merchants. It would be a nearer connection than you have made in the Cotswolds, Robin."

Crede found the subject interesting and listened attentively. She had not realized how much she was missing problems of trade in which she had been able to show herself competent.

"I don't like Hertley much," Robin said doubtfully, "or what I have heard of him."

"I can't see why." Master Thorne looked surprised. "He could not be more agreeable. And he moves in the best circles."

"And is a friend of Empson and Dudley, Father. All the judgments for enclosures near his estate seem to go his way, and he can't be pinched hard by taxes if he has the means to make it into a cloth village."

"Well," Master Thorne said wryly, "a friend of Empson or Dudley is not to be despised."

The names of these London lawyers who had risen to a high place in King Henry's service were familiar even in Bristol and in the opinion of most Englishmen were a monstrously-growing blot upon the best administration the country had known in many reigns. They had gained the royal favor by devising a number of ingenious ways to curb feudal pretensions and to tax estates for the benefit of the royal treasury.

At first the majority of King Henry's subjects had watched this strengthening of the central government with complaisance. Henry Tudor was not the colorful sort of leader crowds shouted for; but the new dynasty which boasted that it was merely English had succeeded in ending civil disorders at home and showed more interest in keeping the island prosperous than in claims to continental possessions which had distracted its rulers since the first Norman came. Sensible folk who wanted to get on with the business of making their own and England's fortune approved of him. Most of the men he gathered about him were from the universities and inns of court, and their interests were bound with his against the old feudal families. After the anarchy during the long Wars of the Roses brought about by their quarrels and pretensions, most people had been thankful to see the King's strong hand reach down into all departments of administration. He had ousted corrupt officials and freed local magistrates and courts from intimidation by armed retinues of nobles. His newly reorganized royal council of the Star Chamber reviewed as many cases for common men as it did for the Crown against overmighty subjects who had taken the law into their own hands.

But it seemed to many now that the law was no longer safe in the hands of Empson and Dudley. Their arrogance had grown with the royal favor; and the King's greed to fill his treasury was growing too, blinding him to their methods. They had gone far beyond the clipping of a turbulent aristocracy; every man with something taxable or with a deed to prove felt their exactions, while the occasions for fines had multiplied into a network hard to escape. Their agents pried everywhere, trumping up breaches of regulations or flaws in titles, and if a jury voted for the defendant in such a case it was frequently fined for a false verdict. In London, more secret wrongs were whispered about, too: the houses of these upstarts in St. Swithin's Lane were no better, it was said, than the castles of the old robber barons; men were haled there on false charges which never reached the courts and were terrorized into paying their private extortions. Few believed that King Henry knew all the evil ramifications of their power, but his ear seemed deaf to any complaint against them. He was in failing health, and for his soul's sake it was hoped that his judgment was honestly deceived in his favorites. Meantime men went in fear of them.

"If Lord Hertley finds it wise to keep on the right side of Empson and Dudley," Master Thorne said, "few men can criticize him. Who does any different, Robin?"

"There are degrees of difference, I suppose. And that is not entirely what I was thinking of," Robin said slowly. "What we are doing in the Cotswolds seems fair enough to me—small men helping each other against the monopoly of the cloth merchants. Their capital is breaking up the trades, so that spinners and weavers and dyers work for wages instead of in their own guilds for the profits of their crafts. If a great landowner sets out to do the same thing, a man who is already rich through flocks and enclosures, it means gathering still more power into fewer hands."

Master Thorne laughed. "Sometimes I think you have a good head on your shoulders, Robin, and sometimes I think that it has been addled by Oxford nonsense. I can tell you that if a man doesn't move with the times they won't stop for him. Lord Hertley has as much right to see how the wind blows as another man—except that you have something against him you can't give a sensible reason for."

"I don't know anything more definite, Father, but—"

"Of course you don't," Master Thorne said good-humoredly. "Lord Hertley has been most open and agreeable, and I consider his confidence an honor. And the association could be valuable in more ways than one," he added, smiling. "Sometimes I think we have let your aunt keep us living too quietly, when families no better or richer than ours move into society nowadays. And Maddie is growing up—"

"Father," Robin said quickly, "you will take time to consider all this, won't you?"

"Have you ever known me to rush into anything?" Master Thorne showed the first sign of irritation. "I was thinking aloud in my own family about matters which are scarcely in the air as yet. There is a good deal to be looked into, and I am an old-enough hand not to scatter my men about the board until I know the other's play. But I thought you young people would be taken with the idea of a little entertainment."

"The Perrys are giving a party next week." Robin seemed suddenly anxious to discuss it. "Quite a large one, I believe—Alison's cousin, Lady Featherstone and—"

"A very fine woman," Master Thorne said. "Alison is well connected on her mother's side, and she moved in the best society when she lived at Lady Featherstone's. Well, we must go, of course. It's time Maddie saw a bit more of life if—" He kept to himself the rest of some reflection which apparently pleased him, and opening his purse he gave the astonished Maddie five marks. "Buy yourself a new gown," he said genially. "Upon my word, child, you've grown up on us. And don't let your aunt choose it—you could carry off something richer."

Maddie seemed incapable of speech. Crede knew that she never had spending money of her own beyond a few pence, and this was a fortune. Master Thorne must be quite beside himself.

Although she had never managed to be comfortable with him, Crede felt a moment's sympathy now. His interests and capacities were limited compared with her own father's, but she suspected a misgiving in him sometimes that success was not enriching his life as it should and a discontent under Dame Serena's joyless regime, without finding resources in himself to improve matters.

"You go shopping with Maddie, Crede," he said. "See that she gets something fine."

"Father," Maddie said breathlessly, "may I spend some of the money for paints? May I take down the tapestries in my room and paint the walls?"

"Eh?"

"Maddie paints beautifully," Crede said. "She painted a beautiful tree on Alison's wall, and that is why we are having the party."

"Some new fashion, is it?" Master Thorne looked slightly bewildered. "Maddie can do what she likes to her room, I suppose. But mind you get something handsome in a gown."

"Why don't you get a blue gown for the party, Crede?" Robin said suddenly. "You used to have a blue gown."

Crede had not worn her father's favorite color since coming to London. No doubt she had made herself as drab for people to look at as Dame Serena. Well, she would go shopping with Maddie and get a blue gown.

"Four large walls," Maddie said dreamily. "Crede, we must go shopping first thing tomorrow."

Poor Dame Serena would have done better to conquer her headache tonight, Crede thought, and restrain her household from straying in so many new directions.

The next ten days were busy ones, and Crede and Maddie had so many affairs in hand that they hurried through their part of the work every morning and scarcely heard Dame Serena easing her mind. Since it must be supposed that Gilbert had lost his own mind and appeals to reason were wasted upon him, there was little Dame Serena could do to prevent them from rushing out of the house as soon as they had finished, with their heads full of this folly at the Perrys'. They ran back and forth to Cordwainer Street while Maddie completed the painting and Crede and Alison made preparations for the party, all in a pleasant fever of haste, and they went shopping every day. Their previous shopping errands had been paltry in comparison.

London mercers' shops were bewildering and contained every sort of material devised by weavers and dyers anywhere. Some of the shops were on London Bridge and others in Chepe; Painted Seld in Chepe was the largest of all. When you entered it there were rows of smaller shops inside, whose open fronts showed as many colors as a flower garden, and you could pass from one to another comparing and choosing.

Finally they chose a green brocade for Maddie with threads of gold and a soft shade of blue in Lyons silk for Crede. They had then to find a shop in Threadneedle Street to make the dresses in a hurry. They took pieces of the material to a chaucer near St. Martin's who fitted them for shoes, and then Crede spent some time ordering a headdress. When all this was done, Maddie, who had commissioned Win to buy paints rather lavishly for her, was shocked to discover her purse empty.

Crede's purse had rapidly emptied too, but she had only to refill it at the Sign of the Salamander in Goldsmiths' Row where Robin had taken her when they first came to London to deposit a Bristol Goldsmith's letter of credit for running cash. She would gladly have shared this convenience with Maddie, but Maddie could not contemplate the meanness of buying Alison a present which cost her nothing after spending fabulous sums on herself.

"I simply don't know where it all went to," she said. "We'll have to go to the fripperers, Crede. I shan't really need my other best gown now."

So they had to smuggle her Sunday gown out of the house and carry their bulky parcel along busy Cornhill Street to an open market which was held by the stocks and whipping post and spread into the grounds of St. Mary Woolchurch. The fripperers' corner was the noisiest part of it, for the trade in old clothes seemed to stimulate the most vituperative bargaining, but Maddie plunged through it with determination and opened her bundle at one of the stalls.

"How much?" she said hopefully.

[173]

The fripperer—Crede thought that Maddie could not have chosen a less prepossessing one—fingered the material and released a torrent of comment so rich in street slang that they could make nothing of it.

"Ten shillings?" Maddie suggested. "It is good cloth."

This called forth another torrent, but fortunately for their lack of skill in such encounters their confused silence passed for stubbornness. Finally the fripperer held out eight shillings and they seized it and fled toward Chepe.

Crede had already thought what she would like to buy for Alison, and Maddie had agreed that a few pieces of Venice glass in Alison's cupboard would enrich the room with its jewel-like colors. After savoring the wealth of choice as long as possible, they settled upon some lovely goblets in shades of amber and amethyst and rosy red.

As they were coming out of the shop with their purchase, they noticed that a few doors farther along Goldsmiths' Row several richly dressed and splendidly mounted horsemen waited beside a litter.

"Someone from the court," Maddie decided, and they joined the curious, edging their way through the crowd which in Chepe could always gather at a moment's notice.

A slight man who looked pale and ill came from a goldsmith's, leaning on the arm of a youth whose height and breadth of shoulder would stand out in any crowd and whose fresh color and red-gold hair were enhanced by a violet doublet.

"The King and the Prince of Wales," Maddie whispered. "The cheers are for Prince Henry—London loves him."

Evidently he loved their approval, smiling and raising his hand, giving them plenty of time to admire him as he mounted his horse and let the splendid beast prance for their amusement. He was not quite seventeen but already known as one of the finest horsemen in England, a champion of the lists and the butts and all games of strength and skill. He was also a talented musician, whose songs lilted from the court to the people, and a scholar who had been intended for the Church before his older brother's death. His attainments in the New Learning had won the admiration of Dr. Erasmus. And he was as handsome as a fairy-tale prince.

Beside his glowing youth the king looked the more sickly and prematurely aged—an insignificant figure in plain dark clothes who might have been taken for a pettifogging lawyer. They passed quite close and Crede thought that there was wry humor in the older man's slight smile. He had a sensitive mouth for all the grim set of the jaw. For a moment she seemed to meet the glance of very clear, large, gray eyes and was startled to discover that this colorless figure had one great beauty.

It was the King she watched, then, as he stepped into the litter. Her father had thought him a great man. Even though England was finding him less and less heroic, he had succeeded in one of the maddest ventures in English history, and after it had met sterner tests than seemed likely ever to try the glittering young prince. Henry Tudor had begun with nothing. He was the grandson of a penniless Welsh squire and Queen Katherine of France and England, the widow of Henry the Fifth, whose liaison had been a court scandal. On his mother's side he had inherited a claim of equally doubtful legitimacy to a kingdom disordered by the Wars of the Roses, and his youth had been spent perilously in exile. But he would leave Prince Henry the acknowledged heir of both the Red and the White Rose of England, acclaimed by a reconciled Wales as a descendant of the ancient British line, and allied by his sister's marriage with Scotland. He would leave Prince Henry a full treasury, prosperity and orderliness at home, and profitable treaties instead of wars abroad.

The King's party rode away, the crowd shifted, and Crede suddenly saw her boy of the quintain. Forgetting everything else she made a dash for him, but he saw her and took to his heels, wriggling through the crowded street toward St. Martin's Lane. The precinct of St. Martin's College of Black Canons was sanctuary ground. Within it a warren of outlaws lived safe from royal or city authorities, for this was one of the few absolute sanctuaries. It did not enforce even the forty-day limit after which a fugitive must surrender to the law or travel under Church protection to the nearest port and abjure the realm.

Crede might have been rash enough to venture into that unsavory labyrinth if she had not lost sight of her quarry on its outskirts. It would be hopeless to try to find him. At least he knew that she had not raised a hue and cry, and he might take that as a small gesture of good will—a small and rather useless one! What she could do if she caught him was still an unanswered problem, and its attendant discomforts returned to plague her as she went back to find Maddie.

SIXTEEN

The new gowns came home on the morning of Alison's supper party, but Maddie took them at once to her room and said that no one was to see them until she and Crede were ready to appear in all their glory. They began their preparations early, and when the last point had been tied they surveyed each other with great satisfaction.

It was too bad that Maddie could not see how really beautiful she was, Crede thought, holding her polished metal hand mirror at the best possible angles. The stiff green and gold brocade which opened upon an underbody of pale primrose spread to the floor with the sweep of Maddie's slender height, and enriched her own bright coloring.

Crede's gown was much plainer—an untrimmed bodice and full skirt of soft, sea-blue silk. While helping to choose Maddie's she had realized that she could not carry off such fine clothes and had dared to have the costly material fashioned as simply as the everyday dresses she made for herself. But Maddie said that it was perfect and needed no ornament except her rings, both of which were handsome. On her right thumb she wore her father's heavy gold signet with his seal of a gorse blossom, and on her left hand was the ring which Robin had provided because they had no betrothal rings to join at their hasty wedding. Philip must have told him that she liked pearls above all other jewels, for not only was it set with a very fine pearl but the carving was delicately frosted with them.

"We do look nice," Maddie said happily. "Your eyes are the exact shade of that dress, Crede. Will you fasten my snood?"

While they had only to tie a green ribbon in Maddie's hair, the adjustment of Crede's new headdress required anxious consultation. It was elegantly made of velvet in the latest version of the coif, and it had a stiff crescent sewed with seed pearls in front and a pouchlike back into which they had to bundle her long curls. The effect so disappointingly resembled a stuffed mealsack that Crede seized the shears and shortened them recklessly. After that the coif fitted better, but Maddie still looked doubtful.

"It seems too heavy for your small face," she said. "Crede, you looked lovely before. I'd leave it off."

Crede was not entirely pleased with it either, but she had counted upon it to add a modish touch to her costume, and it was annoying to be told that she could not wear any of the things which seemed to become everyone else. Holding up the mirror, she was assuring herself that it looked quite stylish, when Robin appeared at the door, very neat in his best buff suit.

"Aren't you girls ready to be admired yet?" he called. "Holy saints, Crede!" The glance which swept over her wasted no time on her new gown. "What is that black bag on your head? You can't mean to wear it!"

"It's what everyone wears," Crede cried, the more crossly because of her own misgivings.

"It can't be, surely." Robin came closer. "Do take the ugly thing off."

"It's the very latest fashion!" Making an effort to recover her temper which was indeed being sorely tried, she said with dignity, "You must have noticed that everyone wears a headdress. Surely I can look like other people."

"I've never thought you did." He seemed to find this amusing. "Nor like your grandmother—why do you want to?"

"I intend to look respectable—"

"Has Aunt Serena been at you?" He gave the headdress a tweak which dislodged it suddenly and tumbled Crede's short curls about her head. She faced him angrily, her cheeks flushing.

"By George!" he said. "This becomes you marvelously. So does that blue dress. This thing—!" he held the offending object out of reach.

"Give it back to me!"

He continued to regard it curiously. "Ladies in Italy don't wear these clumsy affairs," he pronounced after a moment's cogitation. "I remember that some of them had little, round, flat things. Haven't you got anything like that?"

"Of course I haven't. What are you doing!"

With a fatal sound of ripping, her costly headdress came apart. Maddie who had been hovering uneasily on the outskirts of battle, torn between loyalty and her own conviction, gave a gasp of outrage now, and Crede took a furious step forward. He had bent the pearl-sewn crescent into a small cap and offered it to her. "That's what I meant. Sometimes it is made of gauzy stuff."

Crede surprised herself by bursting into laughter. Robin, with the little cap in his big hands, intent upon his role of bonnet maker, looked utterly absurd. It was impossible to remain angry when the whole thing was so ridiculous. Besides, she felt curious to try this Italian style.

With Maddie anxiously holding the mirror, she fitted the tiny cap to her head—and, odd as it seemed, it looked rather well. If this was enough headdress for respectable ladies in Italy it must be quite proper too, for everything there was highly regarded by the rest of the world.

"There, leave it just so," Maddie said, standing back to get the effect, her expression brightening as when her tree had pleased her. "Crede, it's exactly right for you—so is your hair that way."

"That's from the artist of the family!" Robin said complacently.

"Aunt Serena can't say you have nothing at all on your head!" Maddie giggled.

But Crede prudently drew up the hood of her cloak as they went downstairs. She felt sufficiently reassured to face Alison's party but not, she knew, to face Dame Serena's comments on this Italian style.

Master Thorne was ready and waiting in the hall, and Dame Serena was with him though she was not dressed for the party, since she had from the first refused to go. Why everyone should make a fuss over Alison Perry's birthday she could not see and, besides, it was foolish for the Perrys in their circumstances to give a party. But she was waiting magnanimously now to see them off.

"Well, you will all have a gay time, I am sure," she said. "No doubt you will have a much better time without me."

Oh dear, Crede thought, her spirits diminishing, I believe she wanted us to coax her to come. But why on earth did we need to? She knew that she ought to put her arms around Dame Serena now and say any of the pleasant things which came so easily with Maddie and Alison, say that she must come and they would wait for her . . . but as usual her tongue was frozen. With Dame Serena she could not, it seemed, make any natural gesture.

They set out with Robin carrying a lantern to light them home and found other guests already assembling at the cottage. Its big room glowed with firelight and late sunshine and was fragrant with the tang of mint and bergamot crushed underfoot and the sweet scent of may boughs from every corner. The painted wall seemed to lead, as Win had said, into a fairy garden beyond it, while here within the circle of the hearth the light found soft colors in the broiderie of the curtains and the sheen of Venice glass.

"The cups are treasures and make the room perfect," Alison whispered, taking their wraps. "How pretty you both look!"

She was wearing the blue and silver houpelande she had worn at Bessie's wedding, and it still looked elegant beyond any changing fashion. It could not be spoiled by comparisons any more than the cottage could. There was no room for measuring such things in Alison's joyous hospitality.

Her cousin, Lady Elizabeth Featherstone, was immeasurably grander than Alison. She wore puce velvet with a very stylish headdress almost like the one Robin had torn from Crede's unworthy head. Crede thought that she was a little bewildered by the company, and that for all her training in high society she was unable to decide upon the proper attitude to take here.

No mixture of company could have disconcerted Alison. On one side of Lady Featherstone was Mistress Budge, a hosier's widow who had been kind when the Perrys were moving in, and on the other was Dean Colet who was London's idol of the moment—though he was not, perhaps, quite sound in doctrine, and was so careless of Church traditions that it was said only his standing with the King and Archbishop Wareham could restrain his Bishop from trying him for heresy.

Crede had heard some of his weekday lectures on St. Paul, and though Win said that he was not considered a great theologian by learned churchmen he had made her feel the New Learning as a living thing, freshening the world. He could make men step alive from the books of the Bible, as real as your next-door neighbor, men who struggled and hoped and sinned and feared, with problems like your own. But he could also shake your easy acceptance of a round of ceremonies and dues and penances as a sufficient duty to the Church. Crede bowed to him warily as to a force that might undo you, although he looked very harmless and benevolent at the moment. It had been kind of him to honor Win by coming, she thought, noticing that his face, out of the pulpit, showed contradictory features. It had the long oval eyes of a dreamer, the brow of a dreamer, with a nose that extended straight and purposeful from it, but there were deep lines of determination and high temper about his sensitive mouth.

Before she recollected her manners she had missed the names of several guests, but then she caught some which conversations with Win had made familiar to her. The elderly man in clerical habit was the famous classical scholar, Dr. Grocyn, rector of St. Lawrence Jewry. The youngish one with a look too carefree for a schoolmaster and a fashionably short doublet was Master Lily who did not see eye to eye with Dr. Grocyn in the matter of the new Latin grammar. In the group about them were Dr. Linacre, the well-known physician who, besides holding very advanced views on the practices of his own craft, was as obstinate as his friends in his opinions about Latin syntax, Win had said, and, next to him, Master Thomas More, London's favorite lawyer. He had brought his wife and also his guest, Desiderius Erasmus of Rotterdam.

Crede caught herself staring at the sharp-nosed little man who was the most celebrated scholar of the New Learning and the final authority for Win on any subject under heaven. His face looked both petulant and kindly, and his eyes were the brightest, most inquisitive ones she had ever seen. You felt that at any moment they might discover things even more exciting than Humanism and the Commonwealth of Man, and you feared to miss the revelation. This explained, perhaps, why eminent scholars everywhere endured a good deal from him and sought his company. The Church also showed him forbearance, even when he accused it of confounding learning with heresy and fearing to walk in the light of day as Christ had done. Though he had taken Augustinian orders he managed to stay out of his monastery by means of various dispensations. He was teaching and writing books, preparing a more correct Latin version of the New Testament from Greek manuscripts, railing against those who thought that the exact words of an older translation must be inspired, and proposing the radical experiment of putting it even into vulgar tongues and having a copy in the hands of every plowboy. As he traveled about, taking a very lively interest in this world and criticizing with sharp wit whatever he found amiss in Christendom, he liked England best of all parts of it, Win had said proudly. He had spent a considerable share of the last ten years at English universities or with congenial friends like Thomas More and Archbishop Wareham.

Crede felt a hand on her arm and found that Mistress More, whom she had scarcely noticed in the greetings, was smiling rather timidly at her. Mistress More was not a noticeable person. Beside her brilliant husband she looked neither very handsome nor very clever but she had a sweet face, though her purple gown and headdress could not have become it less.

"Do come and sit by me," she said. "These clever people will be talking in Latin soon. Dr. Erasmus uses it even at table, you know, except when he and Thomas practice their Greek—indeed, he speaks English very badly."

She sighed, and Crede realized that visits from this bright star of the New Learning might be a trial. She had meant to help with supper, and Maddie and Alison were already moving toward the kitchen, but Alison made her a sign to stay, so she sat down beside Mistress More on the window seat.

The men still stood around the fire while Dame Budge and Lady Featherstone, who had settled themselves near, were absorbed in the coincidence that both were martyrs to headache and discussed the measures each found most effective. Dame Budge in her best saffron gown was doing the party credit. She and Lady Featherstone and Master Thorne, who soon found his way toward Alison's fashionable cousin, became so happily occupied with one another that Crede and Mistress More were left undisturbed.

"Your husband seems to have been at Oxford too," Mistress More said. "Tell me, do you find it hard to talk to a clever man? Should one try to learn things to say?"

The thought of struggling to find conversation profound enough for Robin's ears was so extremely odd that, instead of answering Mistress More, Crede found herself studying the group of men by the fire. Robin was not a noticeable figure in it, and as usual he seemed to listen more than he talked. The two whom you watched were the center of the group, as you felt they would be of any group. Whether Erasmus talked or listened, his face had that quick curiosity which Crede had first noticed in it. Master More's changed oftener. When he was not speaking it was thoughtful, almost sad, but when he spoke it lightened and all the faces about him lightened too. Often a ripple of laughter interrupted him, and Crede longed to hear what had been said.

A slight movement beside her made her realize that she was being very rude to Mistress More.

"Please forgive me," she cried. "I was thinking of what you said and watching them talk. There is a flood of words in the New Learning, isn't there?" Meeting Mistress More's earnest eyes she decided that she liked her very much, though it was strange that she felt so much older when Mistress More was undoubtedly her senior and had been married several

[180]

years. "I think you must make Master More as happy a home as can be," she said, "in spite of the Latin."

Mistress More laughed suddenly, and her laugh was charming. "Oh, my husband wears his learning very lightly. But we have such clever guests. I suppose I can stand our baby beginning to lisp in Latin, considering that Dr. Erasmus is as good for Thomas as a dose of bitters in spring. I don't mean," she added hastily, "that he is like bitters really. He is very pleasant company and as fond of fun almost as Thomas is. Last night when my sister-in-law Elizabeth and her husband had us for supper they all made a play. The Rastells are mad about play acting and have a stage built into their house. And when Thomas is in the mood he can devise the action instantly and needs no prepared lines. But the Doctor surprised us all. They chose to make him the devil, and I fear the devil has never had a better advocate. We laughed sinfully."

So Master More liked play acting too, and he did not look like it either.

"I don't mean that Dr. Erasmus is not a pious man"—Mistress More seemed given to hasty revisions of her confidences—"but he often expects you to know that he is taking the wrong side out of drollery. Just now he is planning a book called 'In Praise of Folly' and has worked the name More into its Greek title in a way that might not seem a compliment yet, from what I can understand about it, the whole thing means exactly the opposite of what it says."

Alison and Maddie were setting the long trestle table which Win had put up at the end of the room. Maddie, looking, as Erasmus said to her confusion, like a radiant Hebe, brought the finger bowls around. Then they gathered at the table and Dean Colet, on Alison's right, blessed the food, and Alison filled the almsbasket from the first and best of it as she always did. Crede and Maddie had helped prepare the dishes, and though they were simple, none of them, Crede thought with satisfaction, could have been tastier. But this company could have made a feast of bread and wit and in order to sparkle did not need the Malmsey, kindly provided by Lady Featherstone.

Alison never seemed to lead the conversation. Yet in a sense she spoke through them all. Master More improvised a fable in his merriest vein, Erasmus coined a shining new epigram, Mistress More found courage for a shy remark, and the lines about Dean Colet's mouth softened. Master Thorne, Lady Featherstone, and Dame Budge found one another increasingly entertaining. This lovely room was Alison's creation and you could not be in it without catching its mood. A saying of Crede's own Saint Brigid came into her mind: "I should like the Men of Heaven in my own house. I should like rivers of peace to be at their disposal."

Sometimes the talk became general, sometimes a group pursued its own ways—in Latin if it included Dr. Erasmus. Crede, between Dr. Linacre and Master Lily with Mistress More and Maddie on either side, strained her ears to follow two or three conversations at once, even while Master Lily was talking most entertainingly about a visit to Rhodes, where the Knights Hospitalers of St. John still held an island of Greek civilization safe from the Turks, and about a pilgrimage he had made from there to the Holy City.

Win, who had been drawn into a discussion across the table with Dr. Erasmus, suddenly blushed scarlet.

"One finds the youth of every country eager to call it the true heir of Athens now," Erasmus said, smiling.

"I do think there is something between Greece and England, sir." An idea meant more to Win than any embarrassment, as it did to Cousin Allie, and he continued earnestly: "Some hold that the Celts who migrated here were kin to the tribes that moved down into Greece and found a long coastline there, too, and could live nowhere far from the sea. Perhaps those who do so are restless for distance always and long to see the shape of things more than the exact detail of their parts. Architecture in which the Greeks wrought so nobly is our best art too, one for men who design largely. And nowhere else, I should think, except in ancient Greece, can the hope of finding some whole of justice have persisted so and kept ordinary men watching their laws and politics so jealously and arguing so stubbornly about rights and charters. Sir, I know I spoke conceitedly about our language being ready for great flights of thought and poetry like theirs, yet it seems to me that it is becoming richer and more flexible than Latin, as theirs was."

"Master Thorne, you too are lately from Oxford," Erasmus said, looking mischievous. "Do you also think your country readiest to be the new Greece?"

Robin, sitting near the famous scholar, had taken no part in this discussion but to Crede's surprise answered without confusion. "Win would admit one difference, sir. They kept themselves a small caste which used slaves and despised commerce, but here an old family will send a younger son to be apprenticed to a town guild. Everything is fluid here, and what we make of philosophy or art, even of justice, will have to take account of a greater and commoner mixture, rather a seething one so far."

"We have what the Greeks did not have to bind them together," Dr. Grocyn suggested. "When our friend Thomas lectured on St. Augustine's 'City of God' in my church, he drew London. And unless all Christendom draws together again in that ideal," he added, "with faith that once launched crusades, the Turk will leave us small time to consider our arts."

Master Lily had noticed where Crede's attention had wandered. "I see you have Latin," he said in an undertone. "Our friend Tom More could charm London by reciting the alphabet, and so could the Dean. But Father Grocyn mistakes their mood if he thinks they hope to see the world settle back under the temporal rule of the Church. Dean Colet knows better than that."

"It must be gratifying to believe that crowds are eager to strengthen the power of the Church in England," Dr. Erasmus said dryly. "Is that the answer for the new age that you young men have put your faith in, Master Thorne?"

"I don't know, sir." Robin hesitated. "As the world widens it seems to contain more different things than we knew, and yet to bring us closer together so that our paths cross and tangle more. Perhaps we can't make a set pattern for it."

"I thought that youth at Oxford knew more answers," Erasmus said, his eyes twinkling. "Now I am still young enough and rash enough to hope that there is an answer for both the Church and the world. Don't you believe," he added, becoming serious, "that men can grow wiser than the ignorant superstitions which set us at odds and still darken the Church? And that when learning spreads to all, we shall be like enough to live together in one great commonwealth?"

"It is a noble hope, sir," Robin said.

"But not yours?" said Erasmus sharply.

Robin flushed, looking as if he would be glad to escape.

"I have not been sure," he said slowly, "whether learning makes one man more like another. Sir, I haven't the conceit to differ from you and I think that it is only in words, for I know the value you set on each man's freedom and variety. I've found that I can't think broadly enough to fit that into systems. But they say here in London that the common man can be roused quickest by shouting, ' 'Tain't fair!' I've hoped we may get somewhere just heeding that."

Dean Colet leaned forward, a smile making his face seem much younger. "Even if the Doctor makes them learned enough to shout 'It is unfair!' in elegant Latin, you have hopes of them, Robin, I take it?" He laughed boyishly. "I have too, you know. And here is another Londoner who bristles at the word." He turned to Master More beside him. "It can always send you tilting into court or parliament, Tom, against enclosures, benevolences, or what not."

"And is likely to send me packing abroad again," Master More said wryly. "Empson and Dudley practice law more to the King's liking, if not to London's."

"There is a new reign coming," Dr. Linacre said.

"And you can tell us nothing but good of the Golden Boy," teased Master More.

"Well, isn't he worth praising?" demanded the doctor. "Mens sana in corpore sano—as physician or teacher I have never seen them more promisingly combined. When I was at court teaching his older brother I'd rather have been in Jack Skelton's shoes teaching him. With the young prince as king, and the men of the New Learning he will gather around him—"

"Why, Thomas will not have to weave us fables of paradise on earth in some western isle!" Erasmus laughed, but his eyes were brighter than usual.

It was dusk when they left the table. Alison lighted candles and Win offered Master More his lute.

"Have you some merry verses of your own?" he begged.

"Nothing that suits our occasion so well as a song by Dr. Linacre's Prince Charming." Master More took the lute and sang:

> Pastyme with good companie
> I love and shall until I die
> Grouche who list but none deny
> So God be pleased, thus live will I.
>
> For Idleness
> Is chief Mistress
> Of vices all.
> Then who can say
> But mirth and play
> Is best of all?

Lady Featherstone then gave them "The Thistle and the Rose" which had been composed by the Scottish poet Dunbar on the occasion of the marriage of Lady Margaret, King Henry's oldest daughter, to the King of Scotland—an alliance that, it was devoutly hoped, would end border wars.

The lute went on around, for everyone was so glad to sing on all occasions that travelers called England "the land of song." In her turn Crede sang,

> A handy hap I have y-hent
> I wot from Heaven it is me-sent
> From all others my love is lent
> And lights on Alison.

At the end of the quaint old melody she had chosen, Master More moved beside her.

"Will you tell me a little about Bristol?" he asked.

No one else seemed to care much about Bristol in this great, bustling town which was a world in itself. Between the songs Crede found that she could talk very easily to Master More for, though he was so brilliant and witty, his questions were put not to display his cleverness but to show his interest in what she could tell him. He wanted to know about Cotswold wool and whether many small farmers were being ruined by enclosures there, and about the weaving and dyeing villages. But especially he wanted to hear about the western voyages.

He knew a good deal about the Iceland trade of William Canynges, and he knew too that Robin's Bristol cousins had been concerned with western routes for as long a period. He wanted to know whether Crede could remember the *Matthew*'s return after finding the new land at last and what was reported in Bristol by the ships that had visited it since.

"Robin told me," he said gently, "that your father was one of those who risked a good deal to see it."

"He was a merchant, but it was not Ind or the Spice Isles he cared most about finding," Crede said. "It was Vineland the Good he wanted for landless men."

As she repeated things Philip had told them about Amerike she could almost hear his voice again.

"I should have liked to know your father," Master More said thoughtfully.

Her father would have liked him, Crede thought.

She was finding herself attracted to this London lawyer who seemed interested in so many things outside his own trade. He was younger than she had realized, younger than most of his friends here—might be still under thirty. His skin was very fair and fresh, though his hair was dark, and his gray eyes were tinged with brown. Like Philip, he was of no great size but of good proportion, with the same fine balance in his movements. It seemed to her that this habit of body expressed something significant about him and that his charm of manner might be a balancing of humors it had not been easy to reconcile.

"We have not many in London with your father's vision," he sighed. "But I should like to have you and John Rastell, my brother-in-law, talk together. He and I have both thought that our new-found land, though so much less rich than Spain's Islands, might be more than a barrier on our way to Ind. It might be," he added whimsically, "a land of second chances."

Crede smiled too. "People in western ports have always set their wonders somewhere there."

She told him about Prince Madoc who a thousand years ago had set out to build a New Wales across the Sea of Darkness, and about Mona's still older tales of Saint Brendan's Blessed Isle and Ireland the Great.

"My friends would say that I am no more sceptical than your foster mother," he replied with a laugh. "Sometimes when I am out of sorts with things here I make up fables of a perfectly-governed island in the west. I'm advised to call it Utopia, since Nowhere sounds more impressive in Greek. Robin tells me that in Bristol the new land is called Amerike for a friend of John Cabot's, but I could wish that he had kept for us one of the old names men sought it by."

Win was standing beside them. "Mother begs that you will tell us one of your animal fables, Thomas."

Master More thought for a moment and said, as obligingly as if he had not been brought back across half the world, "I know one that would make a masque, I believe. That will be merrier than listening to my voice."

Instantly he was on his feet and had gathered Win and Robin and Master Lily into a corner. In a very short time they were out of it again, disguised with Alison's towels and sheets, to set the rest laughing at the ridiculous adventures of a sheep that would not be enclosed, a woolsack which made maundering pronouncements, a bumbling lawyer who was Master More himself, and a wolf whose name was Empson-Dudley.

When the masque was over Lady Featherstone's chair had arrived, and the rest lighted their lanterns for the walk home. None of them had far to go. Dr. Grocyn lived by St. Lawrence's Church just north of Cheapside, the Mores in Bucklesbury south of it, and Dean Colet and Master Lily in Paul's Yard. The Thornes, who were the only ones to go east, parted from them all at the door.

Crede had not yet been out so late in London. Most houses were shuttered and had their night lanterns hung up, but sometimes they could see down a dark alley a door opening in a sudden patch of light to let out revelers and a burst of noise.

"There is a scandalous amount of late dicing," Master Thorne said. "And not all the Rorers who sneak out of such dives to rob back their debts get picked up by the Watch."

Sometimes a dark figure slipped past the beam of their lantern, but its light showed that Master Thorne carried a stout staff and Robin a sword, so no one troubled them. Crede went through the shadowy streets in a dream. For all the glittering show of London she had lived in a closer circle here than at home where their house had seemed linked by their ships with the world. Tonight she had felt its restless tides again: the new age, the new learning, the commonwealth of man, the Turk, the western land. . . .

IV

I have desired material for the use of my faculties that my talents might not be hidden away . . . for every good gift and power soon groweth old and is no more heard of if wisdom be not in them . . . it has been my desire to live honourably while I was alive and after my death to leave to them that follow me, my memory in good works.

KING ALFRED

SEVENTEEN

Mayday, when the houses were decked with garlands and Morris dancers went up and down the town, had been scarcely over before the excitement of planning Alison's party kept them busy. After that, summer seemed to come suddenly with roses in the gardens and London in holiday mood again for Whitsuntide.

Whitsuntide was a great season for plays. Besides the special mystery play of each craft guild, given from platforms drawn in carts about the streets, the parish clerks gave a whole cycle on an open stage in the village of Clerkenwell, marching out past the Thornes' house from their guildhall in Bishopsgate Street with wreaths of roses and lavender above their vestments.

Their corner was also the gathering place for the finest procession of the holiday on Whitmonday. In the morning the Fishmongers' Guild came, in full livery with banners and musicians, to St. Peter's, and after mass there they marched across town to St. Paul's to offer a staff and a red rose at the altar and present a rose to the Lord Mayor as rent for their Guildhall land. They were led by choristers and a hundred priests in cloth of gold; then came the clerks of each parish church in their vestments, the parishioners carrying white rods, the Mayor and aldermen in scarlet, and, last of all, in the place of honor, the choir and clergy of St. Peter's—for St. Peter's was the oldest parish in London and tradition said that its church had been founded there on the highest spot of Roman Londinium little more than a century after Christ's mission upon earth.

After the service at St. Paul's, Master Thorne as a representative of his ward attended the Mayor's banquet at the Guildhall and wanted Robin with him. Crede and Maddie and Dame Serena were making their way through the crowded churchyard toward home, when an elegant figure placed itself before them with a sweeping bow.

"Fortune smiles upon me! Mistress Fenton in radiant beauty attended by the Graces."

For a moment Crede had not recognized him but Maddie, clutching her arm, whispered with a fierceness unlike her, "That old nincompoop, Hertley!"

"My dear Lord Hertley!"

The gloom which had been gathering upon Dame Serena with each manifestation of everyone else's holiday spirits lifted and when Lord Hertley begged the pleasure of escorting them home she bestowed it graciously.

"Rather a mixed crowd," he said in his affected drawl. "But it's the thing to see it, of course. Look, there's poor dear Princess Catherine."

He made a grand bow to an empty space beyond which a small party moved with a sort of protectiveness around a young woman in her middle twenties. She was rather above average height, and her full-cheeked, fresh-colored face showed a parting of auburn hair beneath a very tall headdress.

Crede watched them with interest, for though Princess Catherine had been kept living mostly in retirement during the years of her widowhood she had become a lively subject of controversy. Her marriage with Prince Henry's older brother had brought advantages King Henry had been loath to relinquish upon Prince Arthur's untimely death so soon afterward; it had not only added the sensible precaution of a family tie to the useful Spanish Treaty, but King Ferdinand and Queen Isabella had been induced to provide a dowry in keeping with their daughter's prospects as future Queen of England. This dowry had been comfortably absorbed in King Henry's treasury. Ever since, King Ferdinand had been debating the advisability of getting his daughter and her dowry back for some other investment, and King Henry had been exploring means of keeping both by removing her brother-in-law from the prohibited degree of kin— or even her father-in-law if this proof of devotion to England and the treasury should be required of him, for he was now a widower. Unfortunately, neither of these convenient arrangements could be sanctioned if the first marriage had been consummated. Princess Catherine said that it had not, and while Pope Julius and Archbishop Wareham consulted their consciences London consulted its imagination as to what had happened on that brief honeymoon. To add to the confusion in everyone's mind, Archbishop Wareham's meditations reached a different conclusion from those of Pope Julius; over his opposition in Council a betrothal to Prince Henry was tentatively announced and then, more recently, Prince Henry had suffered a qualm of conscience, or his father one of polity. The prince had been allowed to make a public protest, and that was how matters stood now.

"It does the dear lady no good," Lord Hertley sighed as if sharing with them for a moment the burdens of one in the confidence of royalty, "to keep that crowd of black crows from Spain around her, always prodding the King about her dowry."

Princess Catherine's party moved on, and he offered his arm to Dame Serena. But whenever Maddie, who showed a disposition to loiter, fell a step behind, he slowed his pace to address one of his high-flown compliments to her or point out some notability with an added tidbit of court gossip.

Since he paid less attention to Crede she was able to pursue her own interests in the scene about them. On highdays such as this she realized how much St. Paul's was the heart of London, the church of every Londoner whatever his own parish, and the center of the town's teeming life.

It was counted one of the finest Gothic cathedrals of the world, its towering spire rising high above the city, its nave so large that only on great occasions was it filled. Through the ages during which it had been a-building, so many nameless artists had put their dreams into it, so many gifts of piety or penance had enriched it, so many chapels and cloisters and offices in its service had spread around it, that it seemed to have grown beyond any plan human wit could devise. It was a mixture of beauty and ugliness, like London itself, and strongly alive.

Generations of London had brought it the pageantry of special days. From earliest times the Moot Bell in its tower at this east side of the churchyard had summoned townsfolk to hear good news and bad from the steps of Paul's Cross. And on ordinary days they came through the eight gates of the precinct wall to use the great church familiarly: there to make devotions in one of the chapels; to loiter with friends or keep business appointments in the nave; to solicit trade or to deal with the scriveners and printers and beadsellers in the yard; to hear a sermon or lecture from the outdoor pulpit of Paul's Cross; or to take a shortcut for their carts and their beasts across town.

Today all the motley that was London could be seen here: prosperous merchants with their well-dressed families and apprentices, friars, laborers, law students, a sprinkling of great folk from the court—rich man, poor man, beggar man, and even thief. Outlaws from St. Martin's sometimes ventured across Chepe into the sanctuary of the graveyard to beg alms or whisper of bargains. St. Martin's beads and similar wares of spurious glitter or doubtful ownership were produced in that hive of vagrants, foreigns, and masterless men who had failed to find any status in the closed corporation of London or had got on the wrong side of its laws.

A ragged boy was sitting on a gravestone now—with a start Crede recognized her young thief.

While the others passed on—Lord Hertley claiming the attention of Maddie and Dame Serena—Crede stepped aside and was soon out of sight in the crowd, coming close behind her quarry before he noticed her. He turned a frightened face then, but her hand was on his shoulder and she said, "I only want to help you. Tell me how."

"I didn't steal it! It fell. Let me go!"

"Do you want to start a commotion here?" He saw wisdom in that and stopped wriggling. "I haven't told anyone about the purse," Crede said casually, "and if you will tell me without any more lies why you needed it so badly, we might be friends. My name is Crede, what's yours?"

"Davie—Penryn." There was a slight glimmer of hope in the sharpness of his young face. How old was he? He was as skinny as an unfledged bird and, although nearly as tall as she was, must be tall for his age which seemed not more than twelve.

"By tre pol and pen, ye shall know the Cornish men," she said, smiling. "The West Country is in your voice too. How did you get here?"

"Father and me we came in service with a Cornish gentleman and then he went back home. But Father, he's sick and we couldn't go along."

"The gentleman should have looked after you both!" Crede said indignantly. "Have you friends still in Cornwall? Where did you live?"

"Grannie's at St. Just, Mistress. Up from Falmouth it is."

"Near Falmouth?" Crede cried. "It's thereabouts the Jestyns are. Davie, you must know of them!"

But Davie was looking frightened again.

"Come home with me, Davie," she said persuasively, putting her hand on his arm. "We'll think of some way to help you."

Then she saw that what had drawn Davie's attention was an older boy, a hulking lout who was edging toward them.

"I dassent," Davie whispered. "I was brought here to beg. And there's things I could squeal—if they thought I was squealing now they'd take it out on me and Father." Plucking at her sleeve he began in a whining singsong, "For the love of the sweet saints, Mistress, a penny for bread."

Crede took a penny hastily from her purse. "Davie," she whispered, as she put it into his hand, "whenever you can do so safely, come to Master Thorne's house in Bishopsgate Street and ask for me—just for me," she warned with visions of his encountering Dame Serena. "Get Dick, in the stable at the back, to call me."

There was nothing she could do for him then except to go. It was like stepping back from a burning house, horrors within lighted for a moment, and leaving him there. But surely he would come soon. Her mind began to busy itself with plans to help him, shrinking away from that glimpse of misery which was more than a single misery, and beyond reach of any comfort one could take in mending a little part of it.

She walked almost into Desiderius Erasmus and received an elegant Latin greeting from him.

"I came to watch this bustle," he said, "and my tongue was feeling rusty in a babel of English. But at the Perrys' I noticed that Latin, the one gift most of your charming countrywomen lack, seemed not unknown to Mistress Thorne."

So he had seen her listening that evening across Alison's table. There was not much those sharp eyes missed, Crede thought, flushing.

They were twinkling now as he said, "Your husband may bring my Commonwealth about sooner than he expects, if he makes learning the fashion for ladies. Did he teach you Latin?"

"My cousin taught me."

With the thought of Cousin Allie and how eagerly he would have plunged into the controversies of these London scholars, she forgot her shyness and found herself telling Dr. Erasmus about him. He seemed really interested in Cousin Allie's enthusiasms and had the art of asking questions which led her on, until, without her quite knowing how it came about, they were strolling very companionably through the churchyard, as if he were an old friend instead of a famous wit.

"Your cousin must be a gifted teacher, and more than that," he said. "God give us others like him. Sometimes I think I am too much at the center and it is those tending a spark in odd corners who—" he broke off suddenly and Crede followed his glance. "God give it to us at the center too! There's Dr. Linacre's Golden Boy."

Crede had only a brief glimpse of Prince Henry, for with several young companions he moved easily through the crowd, as much at home in it as any Londoner yet with the air of being somehow larger and more glittering than life. By that she would have known him again anywhere.

"A common streak in the Tudors, which would undo them most places outside your island, seems part of their strength here," Dr. Erasmus said thoughtfully. "But for all that the young Henry would be as uncommon a man anywhere as the old one. And his father and grandmother between them have seen to it that he has time for the New Learning. If his ear stays open to things stirring in it here—I am talking like the schoolmaster I am," he broke off, laughing. "But like Thomas Linacre I'd like to have had Jack Skelton's chance to form Prince Henry's mind."

He went on to give her a lively description of a visit he had paid years ago with Thomas More to Eltham Manor, a country house of the Tudors near Greenwich Palace, where Prince Henry and his two sisters had lived under the tutorship of Master John Skelton. Master Skelton had been the poet laureate, but the Lady Margaret had got him into holy orders before entrusting her grandchildren to him, Dr. Erasmus said, and had rewarded him when his teaching duties were over with a vicarage at her manor of Dis in Northumberland—"where," he added slyly, "he has as many verses and sons to his credit, I hear, as sermons." But the Latin letter written in Prince Henry's own hand to acknowledge a poem presented on the occasion of that visit had been no common effort for an eight-year-old.

They had reached the east gate of Paul's Yard by this time, and he paused to say, as if the oddity of it had just occurred to him, "Did you come into this crowd alone?"

"The rest of my family can't be far ahead," Crede said reassuringly, "and it is only a short distance home. You should turn down here, sir, if you are going to the Mores' in Bucklersbury."

He obviously hadn't known what he ought to do with her, and it was amusing for her to take charge of so much brilliance. But when she had replied to his ceremonious leave-taking in Cousin Allie's best Latin, which (unlike his Greek) seemed fortunately quite reliable, she went on reluctantly toward Bishopsgate and Dame Serena's reproaches.

The restlessness Crede felt after Whitsuntide was partly, she supposed, because Dr. Erasmus and the talk at Alison's party had unsettled her. It had opened the world as wide again as it had seemed when she was close to the busy seaways at Quayside and the variety of things outside their own concerns which had always interested her father and Cousin Allie. Part of it, however, was her own idleness. She had drifted from day to day in a sort of playtime with Maddie, and this was what she had needed at first. But she was used to more demands upon her than were made by the narrow round of Dame Serena's household, demands which she could meet with more pride of achievement than she was able to find in helping Alison with her pupils.

Though she had kept that resolution, her attempts to arouse as much enthusiasm in her classes for the hornbooks as for Alison's honey cakes were unrewarded. She wondered gloomily whether the efforts of each generation to improve the next might not be quite against nature. Maddie got along much better with the children. Indeed, Maddie was finding life very full and interesting. Besides helping with the Dame School to whose curriculum she had added lessons in needlework, she had taken down the tapestries in her room and was painting madly.

Robin seemed to take it for granted that Crede's time was satisfactorily filled, and now that the summer season had reached its peak he was even more closely tied to Thames Street. Master Thorne was a man who needed to keep the threads of everything in his own hands, Crede thought. He seemed to find some special satisfaction in the pace he set while Robin, who looked rather tired and was quieter than usual, apparently had to follow it.

But for Crede, the days had begun to drag. They brought no news of Davie either, and helping him was an interest she had looked forward to. He was so much in her mind because she had good reason to feel anxious about him, she told herself, without admitting how much stronger the link between them seemed since he had mentioned Cornwall. Davie and Tony had a way of coming into her thoughts together now. Tony was there oftener than she had permitted him to be for a long time, and every plan that formed for helping Davie had Cornwall at the end of it and took on the color of something she and Tony planned together.

She should have made Davie tell her how to reach him instead of depending upon him to find her, she thought with growing disappointment, for there seemed little chance left that he would come. In the one demand made upon her here for resourcefulness, she had failed. This, added to the real concern she felt for the boy, merged in a nagging sense of futility.

They had left home at Eastertide with no more definite plan than Robin's suggestion that she needed a holiday. That had suited her own weary indifference then, but now she wanted to look ahead more purposefully. They were to ride back to Bristol in the autumn, but autumn —when she measured the days with increasing homesickness—seemed a lifetime away.

She had sent letters home, and Cousin Allie and Adam had written to her. Cousin Allie's letters concerned mostly his books and discoveries, for other things went on under his nose unnoticed, but Adam had turned out to be a very good letter writer, giving her news not only of the business but of the household, and messages from Mona and Kate, who had never learned to hold a pen. Only today a letter had come from Adam, and she took it to her room to read and re-read.

"Dear Crede," it said in the clerkly hand which the monks of Jervaulx had taught Adam and which was so unlike his voice. "Mona especially sends love as do we all. Kate's son is born, a healthy child who is to be called Philip and is uncommonly well-favored, Mona says. Do not worry about Mona who is in good health and finds ways to busy herself. She will have me to sup with them every night.

"Master Lusted charges me to say that he will write you as soon as he can tell more about a new discovery. He spends much time lately at Master Thomas Norton's house where they work upon something that is to benefit mankind and smells vilely. Will's garden was never better and this is lucky for Sadie has more coneys to feed but he is less crabbed with her than with others. Cormac follows me everywhere and nothing that you have entrusted to me of your father's brings such comfort. Sometimes I think there is a between-worlds which animals are free of and that he may hear Philip's voice still as well as mine."

Crede sat with the letter in her hand while Fand, startled by a tear which dropped onto her nose, stirred in her lap and began one of her low, murmurous conversations.

"Mona wishes to know whether you eat well. In case she did not teach you the draught against a listlessness in warm weather she has had me write it down to send with this and also a new way to make a pomander against sweating sickness. You are to carry it always and to remember that the rue used must be without fail the narrow-leafed herb of grace and the rosemary from a hallowed spot.

"I miss talking business with you though all goes favorably. If you should wish me to I could safely trust Clem to manage here with Master Lusted's help the while I bring his ship with some cargo that way. No more for now. God rest you all. Adam."

She read the letter over until it seemed that Adam's voice and Mona's and Cousin Allie's each spoke their written messages and others unwritten. Then she moved restlessly to the window. She could not settle herself yet to write a letter back as she had intended.

The house was quiet and outside it was raining. Dame Serena was having her afternoon nap, and Maddie had gone to her room to paint. But Crede did not want even Maddie just now. She wanted Adam and Cousin Allie, and Mona most of all.

She picked up her cloak and went out of the house. If she had been in Bristol she would have been drawn to the bustle of Quayside, and instinctively she walked now toward the river, though Robin had warned that she and Maddie must not go without him near the slums and disorderly taverns around Thames Street. It was not like Quayside in Bristol, he had said, where she was never out of sight of people who knew her. But when she found herself at the waterside with its familiar sights and smells, it seemed homelike and reassuring.

Before she had walked far, however, the rain became more than a shower, and everyone who could was taking cover. Crede had never been inside the Thorne warehouse, but she had been shown where it was and she hurried there. Part of the same building was the counting room, and the clerk nearest its door summoned Robin.

He came from an inner office, looking anxious, "Crede, is something wrong?"

"Only that I was idle and lonesome," Crede said, feeling rather foolish now.

"My dear—!"

"Whom have we here?" Master Thorne bustled from the inner room. "Crede, child, what a nice surprise! We don't often have a young lady visit us. And how pretty you look, my dear. Is this some new finery to show us?"

It was her old street cloak now splashed with mud. He was making her an elegant stranger to these surroundings, when she could feel at home in them if he would let her.

"I was curious to see the docks and warehouses," she said awkwardly.

"A dull business!" Master Thorne smiled indulgently. "But when you do us this honor Robin and I must make holiday and show you round."

He did just that, taking her through workshops and storage rooms which were much like their own in Bristol, and pointing out such things as might amuse a child. He was very good-humored about it, but the occasion was plainly being made a special one. Obviously Master Thorne considered it unsuitable for her to slip in and out of here and still more unsuitable that anything here should interest her seriously.

"The rain is over," Robin said suddenly. "If you like, I'll show you round the docks, Crede."

"Why yes, take her home that way. It's getting on towards four o'clock," Master Thorne said as if he had just noticed this and found the hour important. "Don't bother to come back, Robin. There's nothing more you need do here before the holiday. I'll be going home myself as soon as—quite soon."

He seemed suddenly anxious to be rid of them both and hustled them to the door, but when he had got them there he was all smiles again, calling after them indulgently, "Show Crede the big ships below the Bridge, Robin. And mind you don't let her go home alone. The streets will soon be full of roisterers."

The burst of rain from which Crede had taken shelter had been the clearing shower. Now the sun was out, making a warm wet stench of the littered streets and dancing on puddles in the narrow lanes that ran down to the river. And Thames Street was awash with its human tide again. Children ran out of the tenements to play in the puddles, porters trundled barrows among red-capped seamen swaggering from the taverns, water bearers climbed up from the river stairs with leather jacks balanced on their shoulders, bargemen shouted for fares—"Westward Ho! Eastward Ho!" An increasing number of idlers began to fill the streets, a pushing but good-natured crowd already in festive mood, for tomorrow was St. John's Day and a holiday. Tonight there would be the finest show of the year, the torchlight march of the Watch.

Robin seemed in as high spirits as the crowd, in the mood which had surprised Crede sometimes during the ride to London but seldom since. They loitered to enjoy each diversion as if the teeming streets enclosed them carefree and foot-loose in some holiday island, although she had expected him to lead her by only a short walk from Master Thorne's counting house to Dame Serena's supper table. He tossed a penny to a street musician, asking him to play "Come over the Burn, Bessie." That was Master Skelton's merry new song, and it set a group of children dancing on the cobbles. Then he filled Crede's hands with spice pinks from a flower seller's basket.

"You'll need a posy as we go by Billingsgate, my lady from Bristol," he said. "Crede, was it only lonesomeness for a waterfront brought you down?"

"I shouldn't have come." Master Thorne had made such a fuss of it that Crede still felt foolish. "Your father—"

"Oh, Father thinks you are just made for pretty gowns. I think—but you haven't answered my question."

"I just wandered out." The wretchedness which had driven her from the house returned past hiding it. "I'm so homesick here."

"Crede, why didn't you tell me!"

"There's nothing you could do about it. I thought I could hold out till autumn."

He walked for a moment beside her without speaking. "I thought that you and Maddie were still enjoying yourselves together and it was what you needed," he said finally. "I should have known we can't work it out here."

He was admitting that he, too, knew they had failed to find any real interest together. But in Bristol she had work to do as he had here. They could carry on their separate responsibilities, as often turned out to be the most agreeable way in marriages made to strengthen family holdings. They could profit by the association when Robin came to buy Cotswold cloth, or Canynges' interests could be served in London. They could remain better friends than sometimes happened in such cases, for Robin was always reasonable and considerate.

"There's nothing to keep me here all through the summer," she said. "Adam could bring a ship this way, but I've thought that I could ask at the Goldsmiths' when a party is riding west."

This plan had only now formed in her mind. It seemed as if cobwebs had blown away and she was able again to look ahead and make decisions.

Robin stopped short. "I brought you here. You don't have to ask Adam or anyone else to take you back."

He sounded angry, and it occurred to her that there had been a lack of consideration on her side.

"You won't have to manage it for me, Robin. I shouldn't have bothered you with my plans when you are so busy. I have noticed lately that you seem to have something worrying you."

"Do I?" He glanced at her sharply.

"Is it something about that business with Lord Hertley?"

She thought that he looked surprised. Without answering, he piloted them through the crowds by Billingsgate Market to the wharves that lined the Thames from the Bridge to the Tower. Here the tall-masted seagoing ships, moving upriver on a rising tide, found their berths among fussing wherries and lighters but carried distance with them still.

"Do you want to sit here a moment and watch them coming up? This is the wharf we use." Robin made room on a barrow and looked downriver. Then he said suddenly, "Crede, are you too homesick to wait through summer? By September, even, some things may be settled well enough that I can ride west."

Talking of going home and making a plan of her own about it had brought it so much nearer already that two months more did not seem impossibly long to wait. But she said in some surprise, "I hadn't supposed you would go to the Cotswolds as soon as September. Have you something to do there then?"

"I hope I have. I can't see how to get away earlier." He paused, frowning. "Crede, that Hertley is a worry. What have you guessed about it?"

"I thought that your father inclines to deal with him and you don't."

"I've been doing anything I can against it. I have to keep trying."

"Lord Hertley seems remarkably silly to me, and I know you don't like his friends. But if it suits your father to ship his cloth, need it matter so much?" Crede said practically.

"It would matter to Maddie."

"Maddie?" Crede stared at him, and then understanding came with an unpleasant shock. This was the secret of Master Thorne's indulgences, his elation—a family connection for the whole cloth trade down to Lord Hertley's sheep, and the Thornes moving into Lord Hertley's circle as other families were rising at the new Tudor court.

"Maddie hates that simpering old fop, so she can't even be civil to him!" she cried. "Oh, Robin, your father wouldn't just use her to bind the bargain!"

But he would, she thought, all her own first antagonism rising furiously. And in the end Master Thorne's children did what he wanted of them.

"I'm afraid Maddie was the beginning of it. Oh, I dare say Hertley has been scenting profits in the cloth trade and thinks that Father could help him, but he's taken with Maddie. And you see Father thinks that it would be wonderful for her to make such a marriage. I'm afraid all that slows things down still is that he is a cautious trader. But while there is any chance that I might change his mind I can't risk going away."

"Oh, no! I can't leave Maddie, either. What are we going to do!"

"It may delay matters at least if I can persuade Father that he has to go himself to Antwerp. That's a worry I've been glad of," Robin said wryly. "The factor we use in Antwerp isn't handling our trade properly."

He stood up suddenly and looked down-river. "That is our *Pelican* coming in! She's made good time."

Crede followed his glance toward a carvel nosing her way upstream, and something seemed familiar. She had a good eye for ships, trained since childhood, and after a puzzled moment she knew where she had seen this one, would have known even without the yellow paint. It had been at Quayside a year ago, and she had reason to remember particularly.

"Robin!" she caught his arm excitedly. "It was the *Pelican* brought you and your father to Bristol. I didn't know she was yours!"

"Why, yes." Robin continued to observe the carvel.

"Have you a one-eyed seaman, a great swarthy fellow, as daft with the New Learning as Cousin Allie?"

"It sounds like a riddle!"

"Haven't you? He is so odd you would notice him, ugly and scarred, and he must have come down in the world, his speech and manners are above his station."

"They come and go, you know, especially oddities," Robin said carelessly. "I'm sure there is no one of his description on the *Pelican* now. Crede, we ought to hurry home. Father should be there by this time, and he will want to be on hand when the *Pelican* docks. We need Antwerp news badly."

Crede turned away with him but cast a backward glance toward the ship. She could not be mistaken in it.

"Surely it was your *Pelican*. Can't you remember him?"

"Your blackamoor?" He drew her arm through his as they entered crowded Thames Street again. "Why do you want to find him?"

"He must have belonged on the *Pelican*. He had a beautiful black cat—"

"Oh, that's Tasia. Our men call her the luck of the ship. You can see her tomorrow if you like."

"She gave me Fand. I mean the seaman did, because Tasia made friends with me. I—thought she was his to give."

In retrospect the queer seaman, the great black cat, and the yellow ship had taken on elements of fantasy, until Crede could almost believe that Fand had come to her through one of those cracks in the tangible world which opened to fairyland in Mona's tales. She had liked it so. It made Fand so mysteriously her own.

"I didn't know that it was a Thorne ship. And Fand—" Disenchantment was in her voice.

"You needn't owe Fand to anyone except Tasia," Robin said lightly. "Someone on the *Pelican* always finds homes for her kittens."

EIGHTEEN

The marching Watch would go from Chepe to Aldgate and circle back. All along the way householders had decked their windows with garlands and hung out their brightest tapestries, and the wealthy had set tables by their doors loaded with food and ale. Long before dusk the streets were in an uproar.

Since the Thorne house was not on the line of march, they would have to join the crowds to see it. But Win had been given a key to the Grocers' Garden near which it would pass, and he invited them to wait there. It was a fashionable resort on summer evenings, for the Grocers' Guild had the finest Company Garden in London, and those favored with a key tonight strolled through its famous orchard and tastefully-devised shrubberies conscious of privilege.

Master Thorne, with Maddie on his arm, bowed right and left to acquaintances, looking exceedingly prosperous in his best plum-colored suit and heavy gold neck chain, entirely recovered in humor from a brush with Dame Serena at suppertime. At a moment when Mistress Fenton felt sufficiently tried by the prospect of boisterous merrymaking in general and the composition of this party in particular, he had proposed having the Perrys share their holiday supper tomorrow as a return of Win's hospitality, and he had remained unusually deaf to his sister's objections. He had already invited Lord Hertley, he announced complacently, and Alison was at ease in the best company. Whatever pleasure Dame Serena might otherwise have felt in Lord Hertley's condescension, a combination so unsuitable in her opinion had only incensed her further. But Master Thorne had then gone off to enjoy himself, fortified with several glasses of wine, while she remained at home with a headache.

He showed no compunction now. There was about him an air of suppressed excitement, as if something highly gratifying waited only upon the moment of his choosing, Crede thought apprehensively. She wondered whether it was because of some final negotiation with Lord Hertley that he had wanted Robin out of the way this afternoon. He swaggered a little as he and Maddie led along a maze-like path, while Crede and Win followed with Robin and Alison. But he was steady enough on his feet despite his sister's parting thrust: it was not wine, apparently, which had given him confidence tonight.

"Win," said Crede, "I am dreadfully worried about Maddie, and I have never wished harder for anyone to be happy."

"I should think you have your wish then." Win looked amused. "I've never seen a happier child. She adores Robin and you, she adores Mother, she adores teaching Mother's brats, she adores slapping paint round—"

"I'm afraid Master Thorne is making a marriage for her."

"Already? She seems—but I suppose she is grown-up."

There was only surprise in his voice. Yet even if the news had touched him closer, what could any of them do?

"It isn't going to be what Maddie wants at all," Crede said desperately. "It's just what Master Thorne thinks would be wonderful for her."

"And he is fond of her. I imagine Maddie has always expected her father to arrange things for her, Crede. You had to make up your own mind, didn't you?" He laughed. "But Maddie has never been given such freedom, you know, and she seems happy enough without it."

"You don't know a thing about her." Worry was beginning to have its usual effect upon Crede's temper. Nothing tried it so much as to find herself helpless to mend matters that needed mending. "Don't you suppose everybody wants to choose what happens to them? You are doing what you want."

"Am I?" Win's tone startled her by its bitterness. "Watering down scholarship for children while real scholars—" He broke off with a laugh. "I was just putting on airs then, Crede, so don't get into a state over me now, you little fidget. Less than half of me would go wandering off after truth with a crust for baggage. Mother and I are as cosy as can be here."

But he had said too much to deceive Crede now. She had thought that Win was as happy as Alison. The little house in Cordwainer Street had seemed to her a sort of promise that you could find what you wanted and enjoy it single-mindedly. She looked at Win in dismay, and the sharp pang of disappointment she felt was partly for herself.

"Here comes Tom More," he said with obvious relief.

Master More was strolling along a path that crossed theirs, accompanied by a gentleman whose fashionable clothes were a contrast to Master More's own plainness, and he stopped to greet them with an exclamation of pleasure.

"I had promised my brother-in-law a meeting soon with the lady from Bristol who knew John Cabot," he said and presented Master John Rastell, a very brisk and bright-eyed gentleman. "He has gone as mad about Amerike lately as about play acting, we fear," he added solemnly. "Nothing would do him last night but to put his two obsessions together and give us an Interlude full of gusty arguments to prove the new-found land a quarter, no less, of the whole size and wealth of the world."

Master Rastell took possession of Crede at once and, wasting no time in polite conversation, shot a series of rapid questions at her concerning the western voyages.

"I wish our London merchants could see farther than Antwerp and Lisbon," he said impatiently. "A lawyer is no merchant venturer, but I have itched lately to send ships westward if I could find the backing. All our talk has been of finding a new route for the spice trade. But suppose what we have found is a new land suited to northerners, away from wrongs we weary ourselves trying to right here?"

The old dream of the Fortunate Isles of the West, Crede thought, must be in the blood of races whose migrations had always been westward.

"We were the Far West once," Master Rastell said, as if answering her. "Yet from the first Norman until Henry Tudor our kings tried to turn the course of history by looking backward to the Continent—no one since Canute has been great enough to dream of a sea empire of the north and west, with Britain at its center."

Master More caught up with them, his arm linked in Win's. "I should not have turned Jack loose on you, Mistress Thorne—he will wear you out. The bee that has stung me only a little buzzes incessantly in his bonnet."

"You weave tales about a commonwealth in the west, Tom, but I would build it. Why shouldn't there be as much profit in a New England as in a New Spain?"

"Meantime," said Master More firmly, "it is near dusk, and we came out to see the march."

They were overtaken then by Alison and Robin, and Maddie came back along the path alone.

"Father has just met a friend in the Grocers' Company," she explained, "and has gone with him for a moment into their hall."

Robin looked displeased. "I think I should find them. Oughtn't we leave here soon if we're to find a chink in the crowd to watch from?"

"We can offer you a window," Master More said. "A cousin in Cornhill who is out of town left us his key, and the others of our party are already there. We'll wait while you find Master Thorne, Robin."

But Robin insisted that the rest should go on. Promising that he and his father would come after them to the sign of the dolphin, which Master More said marked the house in Cornhill, he hurried away in the direction of the grocers' hall.

Outside the garden, crowds overflowed the poultry market and the neighboring churchyards, where bonfires had been lighted. Heads hung out of the windows of the Rose Tavern and the Angel Inn, and householders were fastening lanterns and candles among their garlands. The lanterns were still only pale blooms in the soft gray twilight. The fires crackled and scented the air with the musky forest smell of wood not yet burning briskly, and the crowds milled about, waiting.

The house of the dolphin had two large upper windows bowed over Cornhill, and Mistress More and Mistress Rastell and Dr. Linacre were there already. From here they could all look out above the heads of the people in the street. In a few minutes they could hear music westward in Chepe, and below them the crowd grew denser and jostled for better places. Its movement lapped the housefront, slipping under the bow of the window until they seemed to ride the stream in a barge. Crede and Maddie, leaning far out together, saw Robin and Master Thorne shouldering their way below, and as they called to them Win ran down to unbar the door and let them in.

"I see the torches!"

Maddie almost fell out the window which she and Crede and Alison were sharing with Robin and Master Thorne, and all of them leaned precariously. The light of seven hundred cressets stretched westward farther than the eye could reach. The velvety dusk melted away from them, and the voice of the crowd was swallowed in the blare of trumpets.

Minstrels and cresset bearers led the march, the Mayor's parti-colored livery behind them. Then came the painted giants of the Guildhall, Gog-magog and Corineus, mythical defenders of London, followed by the Mayor's sword-bearer, the Mayor's pages, the Mayor himself on a horse stout enough to bear the weight of crimson and gold. Minstrels and cresset bearers divided each section of the parade: the Mayor's stately pageant from the giddy Morris Dancers, the scarlet-robed aldermen from the lancers riding in burnished armor, the carbiniers in white fustian from the archers marching with drawn bows.

The archers drew the wildest cheers of the crowd, for every Englishman might be called a freeman of their mystery. English yew, which was grown in all churchyards, and the English trick of bending the body with the longbow which had to be practiced from childhood, had made their archery formation the world's deadliest invention of war for more than a century. By royal decree boys and men of all classes exercised regularly at the butts, and these descendants in London of bowmen who had mowed down the mailed chivalry of the continent at Crecy and Agincourt still thought their weapon superior to the uncertain tricks of gunpowder and the silly popping of carbines, which took so long to load and prime that a good flight of arrows could already have won the battle.

After the archers came the pikemen, and halberdiers, and a great host of billmen who needed no arduous training beyond the readiness of any London apprentice to rush headlong into a brawl. It was a long parade of the might of the freemen of London—"good, sad, and able men"—within the walls first built to defend a Roman city. The minstrels played lustily, but the rhythm which set the pulse throbbing was the beat of two thousand marching feet of grocers, tailors, vintners, hosiers, bearing arms: the centuries-old Watch of London.

Master Thorne explained every part of the procession to Crede in great detail, with a slight thickness in his speech which made her suspect that the grocers' hall was a hospitable place. The smoking cressets warmed the scent of roses and St. John's wort and greenbush in the garlands crushed against the housefront, and wafted it upwards. The march moved on toward Aldgate, and some of the crowd tried to follow, but more remained to await its return, for Cornhill was twice on the route. Across the street boys dared one another to leap the bonfire between St. Michael's and St. Peter's, and sweethearts made the test of leaping hand in hand. In its uncertain light Crede saw a face that she knew—the flare as a dry log caught framed it for an instant, fair and ruddy, a radiant young face, as untried and reckless as an angel's.

"Prince Harry, and in a 'prentice smock!" Dr. Linacre at Crede's shoulder laughed indulgently. "The young scamp has found a royal window at the King's Head in Chepe too dull for his humor."

Dr. Linacre was standing where Master Thorne had stood when Crede had last taken her eyes from the street below. At his voice Robin too turned his head and looked around the room.

"I thought that Father—"

"He is of the prince's mood," Dr. Linacre said, "and went below."

"He may need another arm to help him back when the street fills up again." Robin looked anxious and ran downstairs.

The march was so long that, although the last of the billmen had lately passed, the music at its head was drawing close again. Crowds that seemed denser than before packed Cornhill again. The line of scarlet and gold and flashing steel flowed down it again. Finally the last minstrels and cresset bearers moved on westward, and the uproar in the street below swallowed everything. The procession would disband at the Conduit in Chepe, but the crowd, let loose now, would amuse itself boisterously until tired. Neither Robin nor Master Thorne had returned.

"Most likely they have been carried along and will go home another way," Master More said finally. "It will be best for us to stick together and see the ladies safely housed in turn."

It was a mad business in the streets still, although Bishopsgate where Maddie and Crede were delivered first was a little out of it. Only Dame Serena was in the house, for those addlepates from the kitchen were gallivanting too, she told them. She wore her nightcap to emphasize the lateness of the hour, but she had not gone to bed because, as she said, no Christian could hope to sleep until she knew that ill had not come of such folly. At once she took the gloomiest possible view of the prolonged absence of Robin and Master Thorne and thought of a dozen mischances while they waited, by turns fidgeting in her chair and going to stare out the window.

There was no room for anyone else to worry when Dame Serena was about it. Crede who had been slightly anxious before was sure now that Robin and his father were merely staying out for the last of the excitement, as Master Thorne in his liberated mood might insist upon doing. She caught Maddie's eye and awaited with naughty enjoyment the reception being prepared for them.

Polly and Susan had returned, and Dick's voice could be heard with theirs in the kitchen. After a while the back of the house became quiet and the street outside was quiet too. Surely Robin and his father had been gone a very long time. Maddie got up from her chair and stood looking out the window.

"The bonfire at the corner has gone out," she said in a carefully casual voice. "There is scarcely anyone on the street now."

Crede's resistance to agreement with Dame Serena began to weaken. What could there be to stay out for now, when only the dregs of the crowd would be loitering, late roisterers from the gaming houses, or those who lurked in dark alleys for the unwary? Should they get a lantern and rouse Dick from his bed and go out—or call the Watch—what did one do?

Maddie darted from the window to fling open the door, and Robin came in alone.

"Gilbert—where is Gilbert?" Dame Serena cried shrilly.

"Father will be here in a minute." Robin leaned against the doorway. "He has been a little hurt. I came ahead of the litter."

Dame Serena got out of her chair more quickly than Crede had ever before seen her move.

"Maddie, turn down his bed. Crede, wake Susan and get water heating. Now, Robin, tell me what has happened. I knew trouble would come of this."

Crede set Susan to work in her nightcap and hurried back to the hall.

As she entered Robin turned toward her and said, "I couldn't reach Father before the parade separated us. Afterwards I hunted for him towards Chepe, and I don't know what I heard in the confusion that made me look down Scalding Alley. He was fighting two roarers off very stoutly, but just as I reached them he went down. We got to a tavern close by, and when the streets cleared they found us a litter. Meanwhile I had sent for Dr. Linacre, and he is coming with it."

"You are hurt yourself!"

The dark stain on Robin's doublet was not mud! Crede ran forward as he swayed suddenly, groping for the settle.

[206]

"One of them had a knife—it's just a prick," he said crossly, and slumped forward.

"Get his feet up, Crede."

Dame Serena caught Robin's shoulders and stretched him along the bench.

At this moment the litter arrived. Mistress Fenton ran to open the door, leaving Crede holding onto Robin while the litter bearers stumped in with their burden. Master Thorne's head was bound in a bloodstained bandage, and he looked limp and lifeless. The heavy gold chain which had probably been the cause of the attack was still about his neck and clattered against the frame of the stretcher as they set it down.

"Do not be alarmed, Mistress Fenton." Dr. Linacre came in as briskly as if this was all in the day's work. "Will you show them where to go?"

"Down this passage." Dame Serena, brief and composed, led the way. Dr. Linacre, turning to follow, checked himself.

"Dear me," he said, and seized Robin's wrist. "He's live enough, Mistress Thorne. But the young idiot should have showed me this. Bring shears to cut the cloth."

The gash was through the shoulder and bleeding copiously. Robin roused as they examined it.

"Too high by a handsbreadth to get you this time," Dr. Linacre said cheerfully. "But I'll have no call to bleed you for a while, my lad."

Crede had brought linen and a basin of water, and he dressed the wound carefully, not turning his head as the litter bearers passed through on their way out.

"I'm all right now." Robin sat up.

"Get to your bed then, and lie still." Dr. Linacre wiped his hands. "I don't hold with burning a wound if I can help it, but this must not open."

When Robin got to his feet he followed the doctor to Master Thorne's room, with Crede behind them. How much they feared there she knew because neither of them paused for her, and Dr. Linacre forgot that he had sent Robin away.

They had Master Thorne in his bed, and Dame Serena was bathing his face while Maddie brought towels and lotions. Crede could see no sign of life in him.

"Do not disturb the bandages," Dr. Linacre warned. "And keep him warmly covered."

"I know." Dame Serena added a soft coneyskin rug to the bed covers. "Maddie, send Dick to light a fire here, and hurry Susan with the posset —camomile and saffron to strengthen the heart, and then an embrocation of alder for bruises," she explained in acknowledgement of Dr. Linacre's presence. "We must get red curtains up at once in case of fever. The danger from wounds will be greatest in the next hour of Mars, and to-night that is the eighth from sunset."

"Folderol," said Dr. Linacre.

It was not usual for a scholar to have taken to his calling, and he seemed to put no faith in astrology, the one subject which made physicians more learned than housewives or barber surgeons. Yet Crede had heard him say that physicians ought to be as well educated as lawyers or teachers and ought to have a college of their own, whatever it was that he wanted them to study in it. He had maintained that most things done for the sick were nonsense, but now with Dame Serena's eye upon him he coughed.

"Hang red curtains if you wish, Mistress Fenton," he said. "The embrocation you speak of is soothing, and the posset will be beneficial if your brother can swallow. Put only a little on the tongue—and, above all, do not disturb him." His fingers moved gently over Master Thorne's head. "I do not look to have him rouse tonight. Tomorrow—we shall see. I will be back early, but send your man for me if there is any change."

When he had gone, Dame Serena turned to Robin and said with a gentleness that seemed strange in her voice, "How badly are you hurt?"

"Just a scratch." But his face was very white.

"Dr. Linacre ordered him to lie still," Crede said.

"Then see that he goes to bed, Crede. You have heard the doctor say that there is nothing to be done tonight except what I am doing, and it will not help to have two ill."

"I'll lie down for a while." He stumbled getting upstairs and once there stretched out on his bed with his clothes on. When Crede returned from the kitchen with a cordial of fern root compounded according to the book she kept with her of Mona's recipes and recommended as "sovereign whenever a man hath in a quarrel or hunting or such occasion suffered too much blood letting," she found him heavily asleep.

She set the drink down, for it seemed better to defer its benefits than to risk rousing him enough that he might insist upon sharing the night's watching. If she took the light away he might sleep through until morning, and possibly sleep was all he needed. As she drew a blanket cautiously over him she thought there was so much lean hard strength in the big bones under it that just a loss of blood could not weaken him seriously. Standing with the candle in her hand she was seeing him for the first time when he was unaware and defenseless. This even more than the pallor of his face, which revealed a childish sprinkling of freckles across the straight nose, made it strange to her, and for all the strong line of the jaw it had a sensitiveness she had not noticed before. Ashamed, as if she had been caught prying, she turned away and slipped out of the room.

Downstairs Maddie and Dame Serena were sitting quietly in the room behind the hall which Master Thorne had made half office and half bedchamber, and nothing had been changed there except that the fire was burning.

"I sent Susan and Dick to bed," Dame Serena said, "for there will be too much to do tomorrow to have them dead on their feet. But I think the red curtains should be up. If you will stay here, Crede, Maddie can help me get them out."

Maddie lingered behind. She put her arms around Crede and clung to her. "They were up when Walter died," she whispered. "Oh, Crede, what difference can any color make?"

Crede could only tighten her arms and feel the trembling in Maddie.

Dame Serena turned back. "When the curtains are up we have other things to do, Maddie. I have a vial of Canterbury drops, and the sacred blood of St. Thomas in them works miracles."

This was a new and surprising Dame Serena who took Maddie's hand gently and led her from the room.

Crede sat down beside the bed where Master Thorne lay like an effigy in the candlelight. His face held, as if frozen there, a shadow of jauntiness. Tonight he had swaggered a little, a knowing man whose affairs had prospered, whose hand was reaching toward what he wanted from life, and the blow must have come when he was still confident that his luck was too good to be changed by footpads, for satisfaction lingered oddly on his face.

Everything was carefully sealed against draughts. The air was heavy with unguents and burning wax, and it was overwarm from the fire. It seemed to Crede that the wings of death pressed close and breathless upon the room.

She dared to open the casement for a moment. From the garden came the sweetness of June blossoms, a whiff from the stables, and then the fruitful dampness—older than man, his gardens or his animals, his hopes or his fears—of summer dew upon the earth.

NINETEEN

The hours during which Master Thorne returned no nearer life and yet did not leave it seemed curiously unmeasured by time. While London kept the holiday of St. John, all the members of the household took their turns watching at his bedside. Robin, after sleeping until dawn as if drugged, declared himself perfectly well and shared this vigil with the others. Dr. Linacre came, Father Vincent of St. Helen's came, Win and Alison and others called with offers to help. But there were already more hands than things for them to do.

The first reminder that affairs outside the household went on as usual came late in the afternoon. Crede was alone in the hall after seeing a neighbor out, and she answered the door again to find Lord Hertley upon the step. They had forgotten all about him, yet it was only last night that Master Thorne had been planning his entertainment so gleefully.

"Mistress Thorne herself!" He made Crede a sweeping bow and, as he entered, his eye took in the empty hall with no signs of preparation for supper. "I trust I have not come too early?"

"Do forgive us—you should have been told, of course," Crede said. "Master Thorne has had an accident."

"Not serious, I hope?"

"We are anxious." Crede gave him a brief account and then waited while he expressed commiseration at great length and made no move to leave.

"I shall hope to be of service. Pray call upon me in any way. Perhaps I may offer sympathy to Mistress Madeline?"

"Maddie is—is suffering shock," Crede said hastily. "But you are most kind, and Robin will wish to thank you. Permit me—"

She fled rather hastily for Robin, first assuring herself that Maddie was safely closed in her father's room.

Robin was fortunately alone upstairs. "Damnation," he said. "Crede, the fellow shall have no footing here until Father himself gives it to him. But I must see how far things have gone."

Crede sat down in the Long Gallery and waited, her thoughts concerned with Maddie who was in no state for new worries. Finally she heard the front door close, and Robin returned.

"He thinks it would cheer Maddie to know the great honor he wishes to do her," he said, scowling. "The fool is so wrapped up in himself."

"You didn't—"

"I didn't let him see Maddie."

Robin eased himself into a chair. A cautiousness in movement was the only sign he gave of feeling his wound, except an irritability if notice was taken of it, for it seemed that he was one of those who cannot be ill gracefully.

"Even if I had the power to," he said slowly, "I could not undo anything Father has done, while he is helpless. But they have not signed any agreement yet. I managed to assure myself of that. And I need not take Hertley's word that a betrothal would have been announced tonight, or his opinion that this gives him an excuse to bother Maddie."

"Why is he so suddenly in a hurry?"

"It seems that he and Father may have come nearer to the point yesterday because he has to leave town. He wanted this settled, and now the conceited jackanapes is mostly concerned with his own inconvenience."

"Does he have to go soon?" Crede asked hopefully.

"In a few days. Perhaps for several months. He is connected with one of the embassies to Flanders."

"Then there can be no trouble for a while," Crede cried with relief. "Why are you so put out?"

"He ruffles me." Robin grinned ruefully. "Some time, I suppose, I may have to stand it. Not that it is much for me to swallow, compared with Maddie. Hell and damnation, these arranged marriages are the devil! When it comes to your own little sister, you see the wickedness of it."

"Robin"—Dame Serena stood at the top of the stairs—"see if you can persuade Maddie to take a rest. You stay with her, Crede."

It was Dame Serena who gave the days that followed some sense of purpose and progress. After the holiday, Robin went back to Thames Street, and his first question when he came home in the afternoon received the same answer. They still waited for some sign of consciousness from Master Thorne. But Dame Serena knew a dozen things to do for his comfort, managed everything, kept a succession of duties and watches for everyone, yet saw that they all had rest and food. She seemed tireless herself, as if her strong body had waited until now to throw off its headaches and minor ills. It was not only this new energy and resourcefulness which made her a different person—it was a friendly, uncomplaining Dame Serena who took charge of the disordered household.

Why did I never see before that there is this kindness in her? Crede thought guiltily. In trouble, Dame Serena seemed able at last to come near them without resentment—surely they ought to have found some way past it before.

On the third morning after the accident she came to call Crede, just as the bells rang for Prime.

"Robin is with his father now," she said. "If you and Maddie relieve him, I can make up some compounds in the stillroom. Break your fast first, child, and see that Maddie eats something."

She generally sent them in together, for Maddie was anxious to do her part but when alone grew frightened of the stillness of the sickroom. While Crede got into her clothes, Dame Serena sat for a moment on the bench by the dressing table, pushing back the close coif from her head. It was strange to see her there. But she made such gestures now as if feeling herself near to them at last, as if she had wanted to be near them before and could only find the way in this narrow round of anxiety which enclosed them—a world such as Dame Serena had always conceived it to be, from which the rest of them had continually made escapes.

[211]

She moved the things on Crede's table, the breviary, the enameled scent box, the silver mirror. Then she picked up the comb and ran it through her hair. In that instant all Crede's resolutions to be more understanding with Dame Serena gave way to swift anger and physical aversion. Her fingers fastening the points of her gown shook with it. How dared she—how dared anyone come past the decent barriers of intimacy? The old resentment which had shamed her lately returned unconquered. Was this what happened if you ceased to fight her—if the guard of hostility was dropped, could she leave you no private domain and no personal nicety?

"I am ready now," she said in a choked voice and hurried from the room, shrinking from Dame Serena's hand on her arm.

The curtains were only partly drawn about the bed within which Master Thorne looked composed and remote. The room was still candle-lighted and very stuffy, its window tight-closed against the danger of night air. Maddie seated herself by the head of the bed. Whenever she sat in the room she held herself stiffly as if afraid to move or breathe. Crede blew out the candles and parted the curtains to let in the early morning light, and the string of Canterbury bells fastened to them pealed a sudden, tinkling chime.

Master Thorne turned his head.

"Maddie," he said, "you startled me. Isn't it very early, child?"

"Quite early, Father." Maddie's voice shook.

"I was sure you would come home for Christmas," Master Thorne said, satisfaction in his voice. "Is my lord with you?"

Maddie cast a frightened glance toward Crede, and Crede came forward as naturally as she could, wishing humbly now for Dame Serena.

"Please, you must rest a while, sir. You—had a fall."

Master Thorne considered this. "Must have knocked myself out then. I can't remember." He moved his arms experimentally and then his legs. "No great harm done," he said cheerfully, "but I may as well rest a while. Crede, will you send Walter in?"

Crede felt the blood drain from her cheeks. She flew to the stillroom, and Dame Serena dropped the bowl in her hands and ran to her brother. In a moment Maddie burst into the kitchen.

"Father is hungry! Aunt Serena said to bring broth."

"There is some here." Susan filled a bowl from the kettle on the hob with her usual neatness. "I'll carry it myself. There is no call to shake so, dearie—and Mistress Crede white as a ghost! 'Tis the best sign in man or beast to want food."

By the time they had got Dr. Linacre, Master Thorne had taken his broth and fallen asleep.

"A natural sleep," Dr. Linacre said with satisfaction. "He will do nicely now, I think."

For further assurance he bled the patient and left orders that he should stay in bed for several days longer.

To this Master Thorne made no objection. He was the easiest of patients. He received their explanation of his mishap without any sign of awakened recollection, and it soon became evident that the blow had driven more than its immediate circumstances from his mind. The delusions with which he had awakened persisted, and the mood of optimism in which he had walked into his accident remained as a conviction that all his hopes and plans had become fact. It protected itself cunningly: Maddie's appearances were explained as visits from her glittering life at court; Robin was on holiday from Oxford; Walter was managing everything at Thames Street so well that Master Thorne might retire if he chose to enjoy his leisure. He would tell them of conversations with Walter who had come into the room as he was awakening in the morning or after work at night, and it seemed that his mind had shaped things in this mold and would make no inconvenient tests.

When his strength improved they attempted to bring him back to reality. Robin tried gently to explain things to him. Dame Serena made conserves of cowslips to clear his wits and got a topaz ring for his finger. Father Vincent held a service of exorcism, and Dr. Linacre bled him repeatedly. But at last he warned them against further efforts: this block in the mind had fixed itself so firmly that to break it down might derange Master Thorne completely.

Maddie had been shocked and frightened at first. It had been necessary to make some explanation of Master Thorne's delusion concerning her, but Crede, to whom this task had fallen, had left the expectations responsible for it vague. Master Thorne's own references to her exalted fortune were confused and nameless too, for he seemed to have no definite recollection of the recent past beyond an assurance of prosperity which had accompanied him to his accident and in which the fulfillment of his hopes of a brilliant marriage for Maddie merged now with all his earlier hopes for Walter and crowned his own success.

When first Master Thorne brought a ghostlike Walter to move among them, Crede had not understood that she was its companion, part of that accomplishment of his plans. Swift revulsion became panic when she did understand, and she escaped blindly from the room. Running upstairs to the one corner of the house which held something of her own, she found Robin at her heels and ran from him too.

"Crede!" Her hand was on the door of her room, and he put his over it. "This has nothing to do with you and me, dear. A sick fancy—you were in no shape for it, I know, or to live in an anxious house again. I'd hoped time was on our side—"

His hand tightened on hers but she pulled free.

"You can't be frightened of me, Crede!"

"Leave me alone, all of you!" she cried desperately and, wrenching the door open, slammed it behind her and drew the bolt.

She wanted only to escape from everyone here, from a net of Master Thorne's weaving which, it seemed to her hysteria, had been closing about her since first he came to Bristol. Even then she had felt something unnatural in his persistence to fit things to his own plans. She felt caught now in some monstrous projection of his will, all the more frightful, as a nightmare is more frightful, because it had slipped over the rim of reality. In its shadowy terror she was lost from herself too, no more substantial than that other vaguely horrifying figure of Master Thorne's obsession.

She flung herself miserably on her bed and after a moment felt a cautious stirring of it. She must have shut Fand in with her, and Fand, with her uncanny perception of moods, was approaching delicately. Her paw closed tentatively around Crede's finger. She was ready to offer an endearment, but she never fawned for attention, keeping the bounds of mutual respect between the human race and hers. Crede, who had found her own reserves too roughly invaded lately, took comfort in this unobtrusive sympathy. Holding Fand close, she seemed to find herself again—that intuition of something separate and timeless and unbreakable, which can stand outside the bewilderment of chance.

After a while she got up and, taking Fand on her knee, sat by the open window, steadying herself in the evening coolness which came flower-scented from the garden below. It was near enough bedtime, she thought, that she need not go downstairs again, for Robin had freed the others at night by setting up a cot in his father's room. Soon she heard Dame Serena and Maddie come upstairs, and then the house was quiet. The moon was rising above the trees along the garden wall, and she was beginning to feel sleepy at last, when something tinkled against the window frame. A pebble had been thrown up.

Leaning out she could distinguish a figure below, and someone whispered, "Mistress Crede!"

It was Dick, and his voice said softly, "Mistress Crede, there's a young lad with a message, he says, only for you. He roused me at the stable in such a state I shut him in my loft there—Davie something—"

"Davie Penryn!" Thank goodness the other windows did not look this way. "I must see him before anyone else does, Dick. I'll come right down."

"You'll see him with me there, Mistress Crede, or else wake Master Robin," Dick said firmly. "You're not up to the tricks of the kind I take that young limb for. But I suppose I can bring him into the kitchen."

Although Dick's voice sounded disapproving, it was part of the servants' general resentment of Dame Serena's iron hand upon them that they enjoyed favoring Crede.

Maddie's and Dame Serena's doors were closed when Crede opened her own cautiously, and in the faint moonlight coming through the windows of the Long Gallery she made her way down to the hall below and past Master Thorne's room, from which she could hear no sound of waking, to the back of the house. By the time she had a candle lighted in the kitchen and the outer door unbolted, Dick was there with a bedraggled Davie held in a firm grasp.

"I ain't talking to nobody but you, Mistress," he whispered, his eyes darting about the room as if every shadow in it frightened him.

"Sit down here by the table," Crede said, for he looked utterly exhausted. "Dick, will you bring a mug of ale from the stillroom?"

When Dick remained stubbornly where he was she brought the ale herself with some bread and cheese and then sent him across the room from where he watched suspiciously.

"Dick means you no harm, Davie," she said, sitting down beside him, "and no one can hear us now, if we talk low. Why were you so long in coming?"

"I was scairt they'd know." Davie was eating ravenously.

"But you had to risk it now. Are you in worse trouble?"

He looked terrified again. "You said you'd be helping me away, Mistress. I got to get away right now."

"You will have to tell me what frightened you so, Davie, if I am to find a way to help you and your father." Crede tried to look more confident of managing this than she felt.

"Father died." Davie rubbed his nose hard with a grimy hand. "And then they kept me with them. They need me on account of I'm small. But 'twasn't my doing, Mistress! I didn't do nothing but get in—Black Pete he made me—"

He burst into tears then, and the story tumbled out. Black Pete's band had planned the robbery of a shop in Lombard Street, and Davie's part had been to slip in during a busy hour of the day and hide himself in the basement so that he could unbolt the door to the thieves after dark. But they had been surprised at work. Two of them had been taken by the Watch, while the leader, after knifing his assailant, had got away, and now the hunt was on, barring escape to their hideout in St. Martin's. Davie had fled this way unnoticed.

Crede listened, her heart sinking. When she had made a secret of Davie's coming, it was merely because she did not want him frightened away by Dame Serena before she had gained his confidence and found

[215]

how to help him. She had not supposed that help would have to be given so immediately and underhandedly as seemed necessary now. Davie might have been noticed in tonight's affray, or his part in making the entry might be got out of those captured. In any case, the boy ought to be away from London and his evil companions at once. Yet it might not be safe for him to attempt passage of a gate, certainly not as he looked now. Could she manage decent clothes and some plausible errand? But then what?

Davie was watching her with the trust of desperation, and her mind began working furiously.

"Can you ride, Davie?"

"We rid from Cornwall." His eyes brightened. "Fresh post horses the gentleman had at every stage and Father and me had to ride fast ahead so the inns would be ready for him. Oh, Mistress, I'd know how to get back home. And Grannie's there! I wouldn't get in with such like as here."

He was sharp enough to look out for himself on the roads, Crede thought, if he had money for the inns and something to give him credence—a letter to carry, perhaps. But he was not out of London yet.

Suddenly she thought of Dick's brother who was chief ostler at the Crown Inn. They had stopped there sometimes on their rides out of London, while Dick had a word with Sam, and the Crown was a posting inn, not far away. She beckoned Dick nearer, and he came with alacrity.

"Davie is from Cornwall and must go back at once," she said. "He will carry a letter from me to—to one of my family there." There would have to be a letter now. "Dick, I want him to go by post as quickly as possible. I thought if I sent him to the Crown now, Sam could see that he has a bed tonight and gets off early tomorrow."

The chance of any search for a little ragamuffin at a respectable inn was so slight, she thought, that she need not fear Sam would be drawn into his trouble.

"I hope as he hasn't brought you bad news from them parts, Mistress Crede." Dick looked concerned and regarded this unprepossessing messenger with surprise.

"Oh, no," Crede said hastily. "This is just something I have to attend to, Dick. And Davie needs help to get home, because he has had a misfortune here."

She could not send Dick out into Davie's risks on the street and, indeed, he would do better alone at dodging any pursuit, yet he must have some proof of his errand for Sam. Crede wished heartily that Dr. Erasmus had got farther with his dream of teaching common folk their letters.

"You know the Crown Inn near Moorgate, Davie?" she said. "Master

Todd, the ostler, lodges over the stable, and there is a lane at the back. Can you get there?"

Davie nodded, wise enough to follow her lead and explain nothing unnecessary.

"You will tell Master Todd that you travel in haste with a letter from me and show him that you have it. And to prove that I sent you, remind him that I lost a silk kerchief at the innyard and he found it for me. When you give it to him, say that you have money to pay your way and that you are to have a place to sleep tonight and a horse as soon as the gates open tomorrow, with a postboy in the inn's livery to take you the first stage out of London."

Davie listened closely, his eyes fastened upon her with returning cockiness. He enjoyed the intricacies of this, she feared, and the wink he gave her expressed so much admiration that she wondered uneasily whether she was discovering a talent in herself for such shifts. But faced with so urgent a need to do good, even Mona's saints could surely not have paused to worry about the effects of deviousness on their own characters.

"Now you must wash and tidy yourself," she said briskly. "Dick, will you see to that while I get what he needs?"

A clean face and a brushing might improve Davie considerably, she hoped, and perhaps her light riding cape which was not noticeably a woman's would fit him well enough. As she tiptoed upstairs she calculated his needs—sixpence at most inns for bed and breakfast, say thrippence a meal at the ordinaries, for he needed good food, tuppence a mile for post horses. He would not need a postboy except to get him out of London with this added appearance of respectability. It was coming to a good round sum, and it was fortunate that she had drawn on the goldsmith this week. With her door closed and a candle lighted she found her cloak and the embroidered kerchief Sam would recognize, and then there was the letter to think of, the impressively-sealed letter with which Davie had to travel in such haste.

To whom except Tony in Cornwall could she send a letter? So often last winter she had longed to write and would not! Had he been in Bristol again this spring, as only Kate had expected, and found her gone? There was no time to think of such things. She seized her pen and wrote in the only way she could, as if they still helped each other and she had need of him. Davie's misadventure must be left vague on paper, but mystery would only interest Tony the more. She smiled and wrote faster—it was always so easy to talk to him.

"Help him if you can," she ended. "I'll hope for good news of him when next you come to Bristol where I shall be again soon."

It had not taken long. She sanded and folded the letter hastily, marking the seals with her ring, and when she had written under the address, "by hand of D. Penryn with all speed," she got safely downstairs again.

"Everything is ready, Davie," she said, drawing the first breath of relief. "Keep this purse inside your jerkin, always."

As she was adjusting the cloak, the door of the passage swung open. Pray heaven it was not Dame Serena! Dick blocked her view for an instant.

"What's wrong, Dick?" Robin's voice said sharply. "Was it you came downstairs?" He strode into the room gathering a night robe around him.

"I came downstairs. This was a message for me." Crede took a step forward, while poor Dick stood tongue-tied, looking as if such going on by night had become too much for an honest servant to bear.

"Crede! Why didn't you call me? What is it?" Robin's astonished gaze took in Davie and then the letter, lying plainly addressed on the table.

"It's all right, Dick," he said. "You can get back to your bed."

Reassured, Dick took himself off promptly. No sooner was the door closing behind him than Davie, who had stood as still as an animal freezes, seized the letter and kerchief and made a rush for it.

"Davie, you needn't be frightened—" But he was out, and Crede had only time to call after him, "Safe journey!"

Robin had scarcely turned his head, paying no more attention to Davie's departure than he had paid to Dick's. There was a streak of red across his cheek bones, and his mouth was set in a hard line.

"Couldn't you have slept on this for one night, Crede? What have you to write Jestyn about in such haste?"

This was too much. She had meant to explain something about Davie, but now she would not. Could she keep nothing of her own from these Thornes?

"I'll write what I please!" she cried. "You can't stop—"

"Do you suppose I would seize your letters? But if Jestyn comes here, there is one thing your father could trust me for."

The mood she had fought all evening became a fury of resentment, and now anger left her speechless. She had been completely fair about Tony, as her father had known. He would never have set Robin Thorne up for a watchdog. It was Mona Robin had listened to, Mona who had turned so hard against someone they'd known all his life that Crede had to be hurried off here among strangers at the first word from Cornwall. Indignation with Mona was the quick heat that can burn out, but behind this quarrel now something colder and more lasting sobered her. A growing estrangement here, in which all her first antagonism to the Thornes and their interference in her life returned, included Robin, separating him from anything pleasanter and more familiar that had grown between them.

"Crede!" Robin came toward her. "I didn't mean that as it sounded. But I know how he bothered you once. He shan't interfere here—when you have just been too much upset to understand—"

"I am beginning to understand a good deal. But I can still see my friends in Bristol."

She turned toward the passage door, and he put out his hand as if to stop her, then dropped it.

"We do ourselves no good talking now."

TWENTY

A call upon Sam at the Crown next morning relieved Crede's immediate anxiety about Davie. He had got off early and no further news of him was reassuring.

But she was finding it hard to occupy herself here. She was no longer frightened for Maddie; Lord Hertley had gone, and Master Thorne contented himself with fancies too vague to raise disturbing questions. His health had ceased to be a cause for concern though his delusions remained fixed; in Dr. Linacre's opinion there was so little hope of improvement that Master More arranged for Robin to take charge of his father's affairs; yet it seemed to Crede that the others were able to accommodate themselves comfortably enough. Master Thorne was in the happiest humor, and no one else appeared to find that terrifying. He had settled down to enjoy a prosperous retirement, leaving everything on Thames Street to Walter, while his memory for recent events became increasingly hazy. Since Maddie and Robin, in the roles he assigned them, merely came for visits, it was only Dame Serena he expected to have constantly with him, but Dame Serena made no complaint. She stepped into the center of his curiously restricted world, one that would have meant martyrdom to most people, Crede thought with compunction, and humored him in ways that turned her into a person hard to recognize. She showed none of her old dislike for the pleasures and amusements of life.

It was Crede who felt out of tune in the house she had always thought too gloomy. She was doing no one any good by staying in it. In her alienation from everything here, the quarrel with Robin over Davie remained deeper than the misunderstanding which had brought it about. She avoided him and would not discuss it. Only at home, she thought now with the desperation of homesickness, could she hope to get her feet under her again.

She would trouble none of them with her plans, not even Alison, who had certainly never run from anything. She left an inquiry with the goldsmith for a suitable party riding west, and after this reassurance that she could manage her own affairs her spirits improved. Now she spent every possible moment with Maddie and Alison, realizing how much she would miss them and sharing their interests without the restlessness which had plagued her lately.

They were together at the cottage one July afternoon. Alison, to the delight of their pupils, had decided it was too hot for anything more arduous than storytelling—when Win burst in upon them with an air of happy mystery.

"I have a present outside," he announced. "Open the door, Crede."

Crede opened it upon Adam. He stood there smiling, a little startled by the dozen of assorted ages who sat in a cricle with Maddie at its center looking like an expectant child herself.

"Adam! Oh, Adam!"

"All's well at home," he said anticipating her question, even before he bent to kiss her.

Nothing that she might have hoped for could have improved London more in an instant. She clung to Adam's arm while Alison welcomed him, while Win declared school out and shepherded their flock through the door.

Maddie stood forgotten until Adam said, "Surely this is Robin's sister, the likeness is so strong."

People sometimes said this though even Maddie's beautiful coloring was different from Robin's, and it always seemed to please her. She blushed and smiled and looked her loveliest and was instantly disposed to like Adam. Win and Alison could not have needed him as Crede did, but they made his coming an event. Only when he had been settled comfortably and wine poured, a precious store kept for occasions, was there time for questions.

He had met Win at St. Paul's, having gone there first to inquire for him because it was easy to find, and Win had known that Crede would be here. Indeed they were all well at home as he had written lately.

"I found soon after that I could carry a cargo this way to advantage," he said.

"And your feet itched for the *Brigid*'s deck," Crede teased, although she knew quite well that he had not come for that but out of kindness to bring her a bit of home.

"They didn't get on it! The *Brigid*'s speed profits us too much on her own run. I borrowed the *Swallow*."

"From Master Burns!"

Adam laughed. "The Lord gave him a quick temper but a quick hand too for the feel of any ship. I sent him out with the *Brigid* while Clem manages for me. We have everything in good enough shape, Crede, that I felt safe to leave him when Master Lusted offered to help with accounts. Clem seems to have a natural head for trade, and it will pay us, I think, to let men of promise prove themselves, for we are all riding such a swell now from the new routes of Spain and Portugal that we could branch out a little. It's matters such as this I wanted to talk over with you. We could afford another ship whenever we choose. I let Harry Blanket act as master of the *Swallow* on this trip, and after watching him bring her through a storm off Devon I'd trust him with one any time."

For Crede the familiar talk of trade and ships with Adam came like a fresh sea breeze to stir her mind. She felt eager for their old partnership again. But what she wanted first was news of home, above all of Mona. Adam gave it with the particularity which made him a good letter writer. He had even gathered a budget from Dalewood of Stephen's latest triumphs. Finally he got to his feet against their protests.

"It is time I found Robin," he said, "for what we do with the *Swallow* and her cargo must be through him. Perhaps I can still catch him at work. That would be better than surprising them at the house, from what I have been sorry to hear about Master Thorne."

"You will come back and stay with us here, Adam, we hope." Alison's hospitality was never limited by the size of her house.

But Adam meant to sleep aboard the *Swallow* tonight and later to find lodgings near her. He accepted only Win's offer to take him to the Thorne offices now.

Crede and Maddie returned to Bishopsgate, where they found that Father Vincent (a frequent guest since Master Thorne's illness) was expected for supper, and such preparations were under way that Crede wished she had felt free to invite Adam. However, Robin brought Adam back from Thames Street, and Master Thorne welcomed an addition to the party with so much pleasure that Dame Serena also accepted him favorably.

Adam was received as a friend of Robin's, for Master Thorne showed no recollection of him, and when Crede had a moment alone with him after supper she explained, "We don't tax Master Thorne's memory with anything he has forgotten, because it confuses him. But he is quite happy, really, and so is Mistress Fenton in humoring him. Adam, I want to go home with you."

Adam did not express the instant pleasure she expected.

"Robin thought you might say that, since he may be unable to bring you this autumn," he said finally. "But Crede, since I have seen how things are here, I doubt whether he will be free to follow even in the winter."

They were interrupted then, and next morning when Adam called to take her to visit the *Swallow* he invited Maddie to go with them.

This expedition interested Maddie greatly, for she knew scarcely anything about their own ships. She was like a child exploring a new world, and Adam proved an indulgent guide, patiently explaining the uses of things Maddie had not even heard the names of. The *Swallow* was a roomy ship, broader in the beam than the *Brigid,* though only the usual three beams long and without the *Brigid's* grace and speed. Adam showed Maddie how a square sail could be rigged to the high bowsprit to give her the advantage of a fourth mast in light winds, and how sweeps could be used from the waist if it was necessary to move her when becalmed. He let her climb to the lookout on top of the high forecastle and peep into the messroom below, where food could be cooked over a brazier set in a sand box, for men on Canynges ships had a good hot meal at noon.

"We keep good men by treating them well," he said, displaying a clean bunkhouse off the messroom for the petty officers, and pointing out that Crede's father had never been too greedy of cargo space to leave room for the men to find shelter to sleep between the bales and boxes and food stores and water casks, the spare rigging and anchors and thick flax cables, among which they picked their way now, round the hold and the covered lower deck.

The *Swallow* had three cabins in the high aftercastle which towered above everything except the masts. The master's cabin and one for his first officer opened onto the quarter deck, while a companionway between them ran up to a hatch on the poop deck where there was a third cabin, scarcely necessary on the *Swallow* though more pretentious ships carried a captain as well as the master. It was the little upper cabin she would choose for her own quarters, Crede thought, looking down from it. There she would feel like a bird flying over the waves.

Maddie examined the contrivances for living at sea with the delight of one discovering a new kind of housekeeping. When she had satisfied herself that they could sleep and eat, Adam let her stand in the helmsman's place, high in the stern under the poop deck, and showed her how the heavy wooden tiller was handled and how the helmsman, even though the forecastle and sails obstructed his view, could steer by compass and the directions shouted to him by the officer of the watch.

"But how can you teach them to do anything so difficult?" Maddie dropped her hands nervously from the helm of even an anchored ship and gazed at Adam with awe. "You have everything that goes on in the whole ship under your care! The only thing I could do here," she laughed, "would be the ship's boy's task of turning the half-hour glass and ringing the bell; perhaps I could remember to count eight turns of it, as you said, for a watch."

In the amazements of this floating world Maddie seemed to have lost the confidence in boats which had made her delight in a barge trip on the river and long to shoot the Bridge. It astonished her that Crede could estimate the value of the *Swallow*'s cargo and plunge into a technical discussion with Adam about refitting her after the storm's damage, and that she should seem on familiar ground anywhere in the ship, calling the crew by name and asking about their families at home.

Compared with London, Bristol was a small, friendly place, Crede thought. She was told about Tom Dawson's new cottage and Bill Lloyd's twins and how much Sam Easton's grannie missed her visits. Of them all it was old Nat Tillson, the boatswain, who made her most homesick; he was as much a part of the *Swallow* as her storm-battered figurehead, and not one grizzled hair of him had changed within Crede's recollection. He had always been there when she and Anthony played about the ship in port, scolding them impartially and grumbling with a twinkle in his eye at the trouble they made him. His manners had not changed in the least when an older Crede came down from the counting room to Quayside to make an owner's inspection and did not change now. He said that London had made her mighty fine and in the same breath shouted at her to keep her frippery furbelows away from his bucket of tar.

Adam was so busy after this that they seldom saw him except when Robin brought him home to supper, but this happened often, for his gift of storytelling so delighted Master Thorne that Dame Serena pressed invitations upon him. Through Robin the *Swallow*'s cargo was being disposed of, but Adam wanted the ship thoroughly overhauled and was in no hurry to reload for the voyage home. He spent all day on Thames side and Robin seemed pleased to have him.

"Robin gives me the run of the place," Adam said. "It is an advantage to know what goes on in other ports and whether it may profit us to send a ship sometimes this way. I may just as well offer a hand here."

He was greatly interested in the Antwerp trade, and he and Robin sat discussing points of it after supper, while the others played at cards with Master Thorne.

Crede was drawn to that end of the room and Adam surprised her by saying, "What would you think of trying the profit of one voyage there, Crede, while the *Swallow* is so far on the way? If we could use your Antwerp factor, Robin, there should be nothing about it young Blanket can't handle while I stretch my legs here, and it is a good chance to try him out."

It seemed to Crede that he was in no hurry to get back to Bristol. "It would delay us considerably," she said.

[223]

"Not so much," Adam said easily. "Robin's knowledge of the Antwerp trade and his connections at both ends would help us to furnish the *Swallow* for a quick trip, and I am not sure yet of a cargo here for Bristol. What do you think, Robin?"

"I think I've been taking more help from you than you have found in me. I doubt whether you should send an inexperienced man to Antwerp, because our own masters are having trouble with the agent we use there. We'd like to change our connection, and if you thought of taking the *Swallow* yourself, Adam, I'd ask you to look into it for me. Before Father's accident we had agreed that he or I should go over."

"I'd be a poor substitute for you in a port and trade that are new to me," Adam said thoughtfully. "But there's a debt to you from Bristol, Robin, if you want me to try."

"Adam, if you take the *Swallow* to Antwerp I think I will go too," Crede said. She had rather be going anywhere than wait here.

"Well," Adam said, "we don't have to make up our minds at once. I haven't needed Tim Arden to tell me that the *Swallow* took a beating in that storm we came through, and I'd like to have her in better shape before we ship cargo."

He seemed anxious to drop the subject then, and for several days he was never alone with Crede to discuss it. But the more she thought about the prospect of a trip to Antwerp the more attractive it became. To be on the *Swallow* would be the first step toward home, even with this lengthening of the journey, and no one could help feeling curious about Antwerp, the greatest of all ports.

Even though it was out of the general course of Bristol trade, Crede had heard about Antwerp all her life as anyone did who lived by shipping; for the story of this Venice of the North was one of the wonders of the age. Not much more than a generation ago it had been an inconsiderable town up a sluggish river. Bruges had been the great port of the North, center of the Hanse League's long monopoly of northern trade, while Venice, with her front door on the Mediterranean and her back to the ancient land and river routes eastward, had been greatest of all through the centuries before the new sea routes of Spain and Portugal changed the face of the world. There was more wealth now in London than in Venice, but incomparably more in Antwerp. It might seem that the sea itself, at the moment when it opened to Europe's dazzling new opportunities, had chosen to do Antwerp special favor. For while the harbor of Bruges was silting up, a season of violent storms had suddenly cleared the mouth of the Scheldt and given Antwerp a broad, safe waterway.

The old Baltic trade crossed there with the new Atlantic trade, and the burghers of Antwerp had been great enough for their opportunity.

They permitted such freedom to foreigners that trading colonies of all nations were established in the town. The great bankers of Europe, the Italian houses and the Fuggers of the German Empire had moved in to serve them. The harbor had cleared five hundred ships in a day, it was said, and everything that ships or caravans carried could be bought there. One of the two great yearly fairs was held in August, and Crede and Adam might see it.

But days passed before Adam offered to make definite plans. Then one evening as they sat talking he said, "If you are still of a mind to see Antwerp, Crede, I'd trust your eye as well as my own to discover anything of advantage to our Bristol trade there."

He was ready, it seemed, to welcome her back to work, though Crede had felt lately that he was holding her off. "I can be ready as soon as the *Swallow* is," she said eagerly.

"The *Swallow* is as sound as ever now," Adam said. "You have good men, Robin, though I notice that most of them wait for instruction more than ours do."

"They miss Father." Robin looked tired and anxious still and seemed to have drawn into himself, although whenever Adam came he roused from his preoccupation. "Father liked to keep his hand on everything."

"So I guessed. Your way, I notice, is more like Philip's which I have tried to follow—to let men who can take responsibility. You have some who are liking it. Smithson, for instance."

"Smithson is a treasure. He has been in the counting room for years and knows everything that goes through it. Purdy is just about as dependable in the warehouse. But we have all felt your help, Adam, more than I can say. I'll be still farther in your debt if you can straighten out this business in Antwerp, for that's our only real worry now."

"You know Antwerp and have connections there," Adam said, as promptly as if he had been waiting for this. "Since your chief problem at the moment is there, why not let me stay here with Smithson and Purdy to depend upon, while you and Crede make a trip over in the *Swallow*?"

Robin looked startled but could not have been more so than Crede was. What possessed Adam to take her so by surprise? He did not meet her quick glance of resentment and, before she could speak, he continued blandly, "I have been turning it over in my mind while I learned my way around Thames side, Robin. There is not likely to be anything we can't manage here, if you trust me, while you attend to things you can do best yourself."

He had addressed himself to Robin and waited for Robin's answer which was slow in coming, while Crede's amazement at his highhandedness left her still without words.

"I'll take your offer, Adam," Robin said suddenly, "and try sometime to thank you."

No one had consulted Crede. But before she had recovered herself Adam was discussing his plan as if it was all part of her proposal to go with the *Swallow* to Antwerp. She would be taking out a Canynges ship and cargo herself . . . perhaps Adam had guessed that she was beginning to need some challenge. Well, she would accept this one, she decided, and prove that she was equal to it.

TWENTY-ONE

Outside the low window was a neat little garden with a bricked path you could step out upon between stiff rows of red and yellow flowers; the room itself, except for a queer bed built solidly in the walls of an alcove whose curtains Crede had pulled aside when she waked, was furnished like a parlor. The tiny garden, and the blue door in its wall which led perhaps to a lane, gave it an air of independence. It might have been a small cottage instead of part of the Thrupps' house.

Recollection was coming back to her of being met last night by Master John Thrupp of the English colony in Antwerp and of traveling in a litter to his house, but it was rather hazy. She felt still a trifle dizzy as she dressed, for to her mortification her first sea voyage had proved her a very poor sailor. They had been no more than out of the Thames when she had been obliged to escape from Master Blanket's supper table and the sight of people who could be grossly concerned with eating. She had shut herself in the little upper cabin in misery and ill temper. While the *Swallow* continued to pitch through what Master Blanket tactlessly described as not much of a blow, she had prayed only to set foot on shore but had discovered upon doing so that seasickness can be followed by landsickness. She could only remember being received with great kindness by a yellow-haired Mistress Thrupp who spoke broken English. Then she must have fallen heavily asleep.

Now midday sunshine was coming through the window. There was a tumbled couch and Robin's sea chest, with no other sign of him. But just as she was discovering, to her surprise, an interest in food and a hope that someone would appear who knew a way to it, he came through the door that must lead to the rest of the house.

"I am afraid I have slept half the day," she said.

"Only until dinnertime. Mistress Thrupp meant to offer your dinner

[226]

in bed, but it is ready in the hall if you feel like coming out. You look more like yourself," Robin said with satisfaction.

He seemed exceedingly fresh and cheerful and was apparently so peculiarly constituted that sea voyages benefited him, for his face had lost lines of strain which had been growing upon it in London. Crede had not realized how much he was changing there, until she saw him now looking, it struck her suddenly, much as he had looked when the door of the counting house in Bristol had first opened upon him. Something as he came into the room had recalled that other entrance with the sharpness of first impressions.

"Are you quite up to dinner with the rest of them? If you aren't we could have—"

"There is nothing wrong with me now except hunger. But what a merchant venturer I turned out to be!" she added ruefully.

It was an apology for things she vaguely remembered . . . Robin in the cabin at intervals that faded and jumbled with a horribly bitter brew he made her sip while she scolded at him . . . an impression of scolding weakly but shrewishly returned with certain other humiliating incidents, and she flushed suddenly.

"Not all merchant venturers are their best at sea." Robin's voice was politely serious, but his eyes met hers with a glint which offered amusement.

Crede laughed with him in the sudden lightheartedness of commanding her wretched body again, and it was not only the uncomfortable voyage which laughter put behind them. They were closer again to the easy good terms they had found riding from Bristol.

"Mistress Thrupp has been exceptionally kind, when she is not even English." Crede glanced about the unfamiliar room which was as precise and high-colored as the garden, with shining tiles and light wood and bright tapestries that smoke seemed never to have touched, and a round pink stove, which might explain this, scrubbed as clean as everything else. Even though she thought herself dainty the immaculacy of everything here and the dazzling colors overwhelmed her a little. "I suppose she is of this country. No wonder Dr. Erasmus pinches his nose at us."

"We have almost a castle of our own and a sally-port, did you notice?" Robin came to stand beside her at the window. "The garden gate leads, I think, through the stableyard to the street we came along from the water front, Rue d'Orfèvres."

No doubt he could have made a map of Antwerp, though he had visited it only once before, and briefly! Crede had noticed in Bristol that he had seemed to keep a compass in his head through the twists of any road.

"The Thrupps have invited us to use this while we stay in port," he said. "John and I spent the morning talking business, and I think he is the man we want here. We lost touch with him years ago, but he heard lately of our difficulties and met us to make an offer. I hadn't supposed he would be enough established to represent us himself."

Master Thrupp, as Crede had learned when he met them so hospitably at the ship, had been a clerk of the Thornes years ago in London and had heard of their coming through the *Pelican* which had docked a day or two before them. He must have risen far from a clerk, she thought, as she entered his hall with Robin now. It was large and handsomely furnished, and the length of the table indicated a considerable establishment of apprentices and servants. He came forward with Mistress Thrupp to welcome Crede, and as soon as they had taken their places on the dais a bell summoned the rest of the household.

It was well that Crede had recovered her appetite, for the table was bountifully furnished and Master Thrupp was a solicitous host. It gave him great satisfaction, she thought, to offer the son of his old master lavish hospitality, yet his pleasure in displaying his good fortune was too frank to be offensive. Mistress Thrupp was more reserved. Her inquiries in uncertain English after Crede's health and comfort were friendly, nonetheless, and despite her shyness there was an air of some consequence about her. Master Thrupp obviously deferred to her, and Crede's misgiving that his invitation might have been offered without consulting her was relieved. As she tasted the unfamiliar dishes and looked about the hall which was as un-English as the room they had been given, she recognized that the command of this household was firmly in Mistress Thrupp's small plump hands although she seemed so much younger and quieter than the bluff, middle-aged Kentishman she had married. She looked very young, but it was not easy to measure time against coloring so brilliant that it seemed as indestructibly red and white and blue and yellow as these shining tiles.

Caspar Thrupp, the only child, resembled her. He had the same bright fairness which suggested something more structural than English fairness, as if the colors went right through. The slightest smut would have showed on him, and that it did not bore evidence of someone's strength of character since, otherwise, he seemed to be a normal eight-year-old. He was more composed, however, than an English child might have been and was, apparently, accustomed to dining in company and sharing the conversation. Sometimes his father, answering the questions by which Crede and Robin were piecing together an amazing picture of the mushroom growth of Antwerp, turned to the boy indulgently. "How many ships came in yesterday, Caspar?" or, "How long is the new Vleech Haus?" From his answers it appeared that Caspar went about town with his round, sky-blue eyes very wide open.

Now he turned his eyes directly on Crede, measuring her worth. "Were you seasick?"

"Yes," said Crede humbly.

"I have been on a boat to Brussels, and I wasn't. But"—the blue eyes met hers honestly—"it was only a trekshuit—river barge, I mean."

This scrupulous qualification of what must have been a major adventure revealed character, Crede thought. "Did you have a good voyage?"

"It was inter—interesting. Brussels is nothing to Antwerp, of course. Do you know that Antwerp is the biggest port in the world, and some days more than a hundred ships come in?"

"I need someone to show me the marvels here," Crede suggested. "Do you think that you could spare some time?"

"I could have spared all morning if you had waked up." Thoughtfully weighing this black mark against her possibilities as a companion, he decided, "If you don't always sleep so much we could have fun." But then his face clouded. "There won't be another holy day for quite some time, and I have to waste this afternoon going to grandmother's."

"Caspar!" said Mistress Thrupp. "Your grandmother would grieve herself to listen."

"It is because of time," Caspar protested. "Unfortunately I have a good voice," he told Crede regretfully, "so that I have to be in the choir school at Vrou Kirk on other days. But if I had not to go to bed so early, always, there is daylight after supper."

He looked hopefully toward his mother who met Crede's inquiring glance with one of gratification.

"He does not often so like strangers. Certainly he cannot disappoint his grandmother, but it would do his English goot if you wish to have times with him, and who knows that any language may not be of a usefulness? It needs only to disorder supper the half of an hour more late tomorrow, so he walks you about from school."

Crede had not supposed that anything could be permitted to disorder the shining precision of this household, but the way to Mistress Thrupp's heart was evidently through Caspar. Now she inquired whether Crede felt sufficiently recovered to go out that evening. Her husband had suggested taking Master Thorne to a reception at the house of Signore Vitelli—a Venetian banker, she explained, where he would meet many of the merchants they did business with. While she did not always attend these rather frequent entertainments, they would find a number of ladies there and Master Thorne had expressed the hope that they might all enjoy it together.

Crede was eager to see everything here. Dressed in her best that evening she found herself at a house fine enough for a palace, in a gathering which surpassed anything she had known of splendor and fashion, with a mixture of nationalities such as one might see on Thames Street or Quayside but not under one roof.

Mistress Thrupp was soon enclosed in a group of her own country-women who tried to make Crede welcome but with whom she could only nod and smile. The men who were in much greater numbers moved freely about. From Master Thrupp's description of these affairs held at a guildhall or hospitably open house Crede had inferred that they found useful rumors of trade and politics as well as entertainment, or might unobtrusively make a profitable connection. But the ladies, she noticed, soon drifted into little islands, for they could in most cases speak only their own language, while men who traveled had generally enough Latin to understand one another. After a short time, Master Thrupp took Robin off rather urgently and, between nodding and smiling, Crede looked curiously about her.

Signore Vitelli's house must follow an Italian style, she supposed, for it was as different from the Thrupps' as from anything at home: there was an airy spaciousness in its light colors, and slender columns divided the reception rooms through which this large company moved easily. Musicians played in a gallery at the end of the hall, and beneath it a long table had been set which servants refurnished as groups paused and passed on. When Mistress Thrupp's group moved in that direction Crede began to use her ears as well as her eyes, happy that Cousin Allie had made her free of a speech which like gold coins and a church universal knew no national boundaries.

The younger one of the two gentlemen who had made a place for them near the table was a Venetian and had gone by his city's old land route from the Adriatic to the east. He was telling his companion (a tall man of a grizzled, weather-beaten fairness, obviously a northerner of some sort) that he had lived for years among Turks who had not used him ill.

They were not speaking the Latin of books but a sort of mixture which you could make shift with if you knew the prayers and psalms of the daily offices and common words of various languages picked up in sea-ports. How could she fail to listen when anything about the Turks had a fearful fascination? They had drawn a heavy curtain over the half of Europe and of what went on in the once-Christian kingdoms behind it the West had only fearful rumors. Yet here was a man who had seen.

They had many arts and sciences, he was saying, and made govern-ment a science too, for which boys of any class were trained under severe discipline in the Palace School. Many of these boys, who could rise to the highest offices, were sons of slaves or of Christians in the conquered countries, like those taken to be trained as warriors in the Janissary Corps. Since their status among the Turks was derived solely from the Sultan, neither the army nor the government could be split by personal ambitions. Whoever attacked the Turk would find him united.

Crede shivered. In whatever language spoken, Janissary was a word that chilled Europe. Members of that corps were not only the spearhead of the resistless Mohammedan advance, an inhumanly efficient machine of war, but something even more terrifying. Parents praying in the Litany for deliverance from the Turk and other pestilences clutched their children closer, for by what dreadful necromancy had children snatched from Christian parents become willing slaves of error, fighting to spread its darkness over the world?

The tall northerner had noticed the interest Crede could not hide, and he turned to include her. He was old enough to be her father, and he had an air of bluff friendliness about him as natural as Adam's.

"You too are wondering," he said, "what there is in that strange heresy to bind every soul among them so strongly that they are spreading as one total power across the earth, when we cannot agree well enough together to defend Christendom."

"In my lifetime Christendom has shrunk to half its former size," said the Venetian, "and while we hunt new islands in the West, the Turk's sword, shaped strangely like a sickle, mows close to our backs."

"Reaping a harvest your city once gathered in the East," added the northerner. "Once we could reach down from Stockholm for a share of it, too. My grandfather remembered when silks and spices were brought by land and river routes to Novgarod, and every seafaring nation of the North had a factory at Wisby in Gotland to trade for them. Wisby was the richest port of the North then, and now it is no more than an out-of-the-way nesting place for pirates."

Someone on the other side of the Venetian drew his attention then, but the elderly Swede remained beside Crede.

"You put me in mind of Freya, my youngest, but I take you for English," he said, and began to use mostly English words. He had often been in London, he told her, and still had ships trading there, though nowadays he himself seldom traveled farther than Antwerp. He seemed well known here; others joined them from time to time, and when they drifted on, Crede felt flattered that Master Gustavson stayed talking to her of ships and markets, and that when she spoke of Bristol he remembered the name of Canynges in the Iceland trade.

Mistress Thrupp, seeing them in as easy conversation as if each had discovered an old acquaintance, moved on with her friends. They settled themselves a little distance away and Crede nodded and smiled in their direction but was not ready to join them yet. Who that had a coin of freer passage could be confined to nodding and smiling, when anyone beside you might come from a town you knew only as a name listed in your counting house and have seen things your eyes might never see?

With the curiosity which Cousin Allie had given her along with his Latin, Crede was floating happily upon a glittering stream of impressions, too much absorbed in their changing shapes and colors to look for her own reflection among them, unaware that Maddie as well as Cousin Allie had marked her out. Here, where gowns and headdresses were even more elaborate than at home, she was still wearing with Maddie's encouragement only a small patch of velvet for a cap, while the finest clothes she had were made simply. She knew that this lack of ornament became her best, but not how effectively Maddie had made the most of her, choosing with an artist's eye dull shades of green and blue and violet which heightened Crede's indeterminate coloring, and lines which suited her slight figure. She did not realize that flouting fashion successfully is an arrogance and did not suspect that anything about her could be noticeable enough to attract attention.

But ladies in their various groups had begun to share a conviction that the nice-looking young Englishman the Thrupps had brought with them was to be pitied for having such a wife. It was known, of course, that English women were scarcely civilized, as much out of their homes as in them, mingling with unbecoming boldness in the business and pleasures of men. Yet even in Antwerp, where visitors from below this rude northern fringe found the women of it shockingly independent, the behavior of young Mistress Thorne must excite remark.

"You have a listener's ear like my Freya," Master Gustavson said. "I count it as good a dowry for a maid as a quick hand on the distaff— though her mother does not."

Choosing a peach from a handsome silver bowl, he put it into her hand as if finding a reward after Mistress Gustavson's scolding, and then he noticed that a very large young man, fair enough to be another Swede, was trying to catch his eye.

"One seems to run into Vassily Petrov everywhere," he said. "A Muscovite is a rare bird so far west, and he has no colony of his own countrymen here, as the rest of us have, yet he seems not to miss them. You will find him odd but friendly as a puppy," he added as the Muscovite, taking the glance for an invitation, made his way toward them.

When Master Gustavson introduced him he began at once to talk to them in a jargon of very barbarous Latin, with phrases from all the babel of tongues to be heard in Antwerp. As he talked he bowed in various directions so that Crede was reminded absurdly of Lord Hertley, but this over-eagerness was more naïve and affable. Most of those he greeted smiled in return, and it seemed that he knew nearly everyone here and was accepted indulgently. Yet when Master Gustavson excused himself to go in search of a fellow countryman, the Muscovite turned toward Crede as anxiously as if he feared to be left alone.

He cried, "Mistress Inglish, you will converse me still? I am so what you call out of my sort."

Crede looked at him with astonishment, for his smile had faded in an expression of melancholy, and his melancholy seemed cut to as large size as his boots.

"Are you homesick?" she cried with quick sympathy.

There was scarcely another of the foreigns who could not find in Antwerp a man of his own town or someone who had been in its harbor or market place and could make them live a little here, but whatever had separated Vassily from his home must have carried him westward like a stray leaf on an empty wind.

"I amuse myself better here," he said flatly.

"But then why—"

"Why do I afflict myself tonight? Needs it reason?" His large hand made a hopeless gesture, and he turned a woebegone smile on her. "Is it not that a cloud arrives anywhere? I see you flit like the bee in sunshine, and I think that one swings low too when it comes—like Vassily."

Crede could not suppose herself in the least like this peculiar foreign and was sure that whenever she suffered from low spirits she had quite understandable reasons for feeling so.

"I think," she said severely, "that you are taking pride in the sin of accidia, which is the deadliest of the seven deadly sins."

Vassily looked interested. "You have only seven bad sins in your church and the worst is being sorrowful? But we discourse of me—do not hesitate to continue."

"Tell me about your city, your country."

Though Vassily's queerness disturbed her a little and she thought that the Venetian's wines might be stronger than he was accustomed to, she was not quite ready to escape to Mistress Thrupp. His strangeness might be some strangeness of the land he came from, which no one seemed to know much about, and the little she had heard of it teased her imagination.

She knew that it stretched vaguely east of the Europe which for ages had rubbed elbows in trade and had looked to Rome as the center of the Church, following a still older habit of looking to Rome as the center of government. None of these habits and their common groundwork of thought and custom had reached his country. Although its Church was admittedly Christian, it had separated itself long ago from the true faith.

Ages ago, Cousin Allie had told her, pagan vikings of the Baltic had followed the rivers south to Constantinople in the Roman Empire of the East. That had survived when Rome fell but had grown more and more unlike the nations that sprang from the ruins of the Western Empire—estranged also by a split in the Church. Trading posts built by these Norse adventurers along their way had developed into walled towns which ruled the local tribes and mingled with them and borrowed scraps of the civilization of the Eastern Empire. They were engulfed for generations by an invasion of Mongolian Tartars from far east, but when this finally receded the Prince of Moscow had begun to bind the area together by conquest. These Muscovites (who called themselves Russians or descendents of Rurik, the Viking founder of their town) now ruled most of their neighbors. When, in the memory of men still living, the capital of the Roman Empire of the East had fallen to the Turks, the Prince of Moscow had claimed to carry on the imperial title of Caesar and to be the protector of the Eastern Church.

What Crede drew from Vassily sounded more like scraps of extravagant and ill-assorted ballads than the history and description of a country. Magnificence and barbarism, rude privation and lavish indulgence, made a bewildering mixture that strained the terms beyond any usage she knew: towns like primitive forest outposts overlaid with fabulous luxury; lush river valleys and trackless forests and unmeasured wastelands, some icebound and some burning hot. The country seemed to have no natural bounds, and its history seemed to have blown over it, seeding only odd patches.

She felt that Vassily could not make a whole of it to carry in his heart as one does of something deeper than the local differences of one's country and countrymen; that from its vastness he could extract nothing which touched him closer than the patchwork of speech and habits he was picking up here. He was less interested, apparently, in what Crede's questions recalled to him than in displaying to her his fit of the dumps, which he regarded with odd pride as a mysterious visitation and which seemed to her as formless and extravagant as the picture he gave of his homeland. If he had been detached so lightly from it, was he less than those whose roots fastened deep in familiar things? Or was he, she wondered uneasily, the first of Dr. Erasmus's men of no country?

"You are not listening!" he said suddenly.

Crede's attention had been caught by a group near the door. Now her feet carried her down the hall, careless of those she brushed against and the notice her haste drew upon her.

Anthony was here! He separated himself from those who had entered late with him and came toward her. He was thinner. There were lines about his mouth, and his vivid darkness had grown swarthier. But nothing could really change him, and across any crowd, in any unexpected place, she would always discover him instantly.

"Cousin Crede!" he cried, his black eyes dancing, and he made an

[234]

elegant bow before he kissed her hand. "I've done better on Brandon Hill," he whispered. He added rather loudly, "What happy chance brings you here, Cousin? Ah, there is Cousin Robin—this is like home!"

Crede, overwhelmed by this swarm of cousinship, looked round without discovering Robin. But Anthony nodded and smiled toward a window corner as if greeting him and led her in that direction.

"Cats of seven nations watched you charge down the hall!" He had offered his arm formally, but he tightened it so that her hand was pressed close. "Cre, you are glad to see me! My sweet, do you know how much your face gives you away?"

The window corner was empty. "I don't see Robin anywhere," Crede said. "How do you know him?"

"Dear Cousin Robin? I don't, and how patiently I can wait." He drew her toward the window. "See, all the good burghers have turned back to their stuffy affairs. I could almost risk kissing you properly."

Crede hastily pulled her hand from his arm. She had run to greet him with the warmth of real affection, but he was making her feel silly and self-conscious, as if they had something to hide. He was talking in an extravagant way which seemed to set some high-flown pose of penny-ballad gallantry above their former naturalness.

"You are remembering them now, but you didn't a moment ago. Nor Robin. Cre, you little fool, didn't you know it would always be like this?"

He let her free herself and, leaning indolently against the window frame, laughed at her confusion as if he had provoked it by one of his schoolboy tricks for upsetting her deportment in polite company.

"You've made yourself prettier," he said. "Not that it mattered, somehow."

The change was in him. Crede could see it now. Under his appearance of ease was a wariness there had never been before. Anthony, who had been so carelessly confident anywhere, was not sure of himself here, and he was trying to hide his discomfort with affectation.

"Tony, what brings you here?" she cried.

"Isn't this open house tonight?"

"I mean, what brought you to Antwerp?"

If they had been like themselves at all they would have been exchanging news long ago without this sparring.

"Does it change anything where we are? You knew I'd come back when I could properly—yet the first word you sent me was from London."

This diverted Crede for a moment from their own affairs. "Davie got to you safely! Thank heaven!"

"Are you sure you and heaven take to the same sort, dear? However, the young limb is safe with his gammer now, and when I have need of a cabin boy I've promised to rescue him. I guessed why you might favor

[235]

him and send him to me—but I thought you would be in Bristol as you wrote."

"You've been in Bristol since!"

"Where Kate had all the news you had never sent me. Don't you suppose I would have come last winter to stop you making such a mess of everything?"

"We had no word at all of you, Tony."

"I planned to surprise you in the spring," he said impatiently. "And then, well, things didn't turn out as I expected, but I had made up my mind to ride back, just when Davie came."

"Tony, what are you doing here, so far from home?"

The uneasiness about him which news of Davie had driven for a moment from Crede's mind returned.

"Isn't this where everyone can get rich piously overnight? I thought you'd be pleased to see me in good company at last."

"You've left your cousin?"

"For good!" His face darkened.

"I knew you would!" Crede even managed to believe that she had not ceased to hope so. "Are you captain for a merchant?"

"I may do that," he said carelessly. "A friend brought me over to look about."

His manner offered no confidences. But he had not prospered, Crede saw now. Though his green velvet suit became him so that no one in the room had his distinction, it was a trifle frayed. Tony was made to be more splendid than anyone else, and this was so natural to him that in a shabby coat, at outs with fortune, he could only act a part, hiding anything that was really in his mind under a mocking pretense of their old ease together. If it had been more than a pretense they would be eagerly discussing his plans as they used to do, and he would expect her to help him. Now she would have to go warily.

If he wanted a merchant ship, Master Thrupp should be able to help him with connections in Antwerp, she thought swiftly. If Tony were master of a fast trading ship, his daring would make a legend of it, and if he had a share of its luck, his fortune would soon be made. Perhaps he would let her offer this herself when he knew that Philip would gladly have helped him to such a thing. Crede's mind began working busily. Perched on the window seat with one embroidered shoe swinging to and fro, an unladylike habit of hers when concentrating her thoughts, she let her imagination move ahead to see Tony a second and even more prosperous Adam Bell.

"You missed your best chance to tidy up my affairs, you know." Anthony was grinning wickedly. "I can still read your mind, Cre."

She was too intent to be diverted. "What do you hope for most, Tony? If it's a ship—"

"Can't you read mine any more? Suppose we say I'd like to sail to Wisby and find the lost treasure?"

"Wisby!" What Crede had heard of it lately did not fit her comfortable plan.

"The old story of the lost ship and the King of Norway's treasure is the sort of tale we used to play at."

She had been too clumsy with her offer of help, and he was turning it into their old make-believe.

Crede flushed and said quickly, "Tell me about it, and maybe I'll hunt it too."

"Once upon a time," said Anthony in Mona's best manner which had so often enthralled them both, "the wealth of Wisby was so great that pigs ate from silver troughs and the homeliest, crankiest spinster used a golden distaff. The pretty, amiable ones had countless rings and bracelets too, and in the three hundred churches of the town jewels were as thick as incense. The King of Norway thought this a suitable time to descend in war—I must remind you, Crede, that war is a quite different thing from piracy, and the King had high and patriotic motives. However, a ship which he filled with gold and jewels from Wisby sank before it cleared the harbor and there, so far as anyone knows, it still is. Shall we go treasure hunting?"

In this way they used to turn Mona's stories into endless adventures— so long ago.

"How much good you do me, Tony!" Crede cried. "I have grown so dull I thought for a moment you were serious about Wisby, and I hear it is no better than a den for pirates now."

"Its star sank with the old routes. Old ways are of no more account now than old names." Anthony's voice hardened, and he was no longer amusing himself with make-believe. "How do we know there is not fortune still in some of the old ways?"

"Do you really think it could be profitable still to trade to the east, perhaps to Moscow, from Wisby? If you have some plan, Tony, won't you—"

"Wisby! I had forgotten how your mind fastens on things, Cre." He laughed at her, teasing and careless again. "While the brave new spirits batter their ships westward, it would be amusing to sail east to fortune!"

Whatever it was that interested Tony would be an adventure against the common run of things. In this there was a spell whose half-forgotten magic reached through time and misunderstanding to an unbroken bond.

"There is Robin, now," she said, and she returned slowly through the years.

Robin was coming down the broad stair with their host and a stranger who was richly dressed in a Spanish style yet looked English. He looked, indeed, a little like Robin, though older and more distinguished. The three were deep in conversation, but Robin's glance about the room found her and, breaking from the group which immediately surrounded Messer Vitelli, he brought the Spanish Englishman to the window corner.

"Crede, I hadn't thought John's errand would keep us so long. But I have found someone you will like to see—your fathers were old friends in Bristol. My wife, Cousin Robert."

"Master Robert Thorne's son!" Crede recognized him with the delight of finding a link with home so unexpectedly. "I remember when your father sent you to be his factor on the Peninsula."

"You were the merest infant." Robert Thorne laughed, claiming the English kiss of greeting, although Crede offered her hand as she had noticed was done here. "Canynges and Thornes are well met in any port, Cousin Crede. I've just come from Bristol."

"Tony has just come from there too," Crede said.

And then, when she should have been able to introduce her cousin as easily as Robin had done, Robin's sudden stiffening had to carry her back to that stupid scene in the Thornes' kitchen so that she finished awkwardly, her color rising.

Although Robin's bow was the smallest courtesy required, Anthony was in command of his best manner, and to her relief he set out to be his most charming. He turned the conversation to Seville, making it an occasion to meet someone who could speak with authority of Spain's western trade, and he led Robert Thorne on with questions and a modest deference.

Robert Thorne talked well. He described the excitement of the Spanish ports—the riot of new wealth and color and rumor as each ship returned from the west that was opening island beyond island with Ind beckoning in the shore mists. He knew one Englishman who had sailed to a Spanish colony . . . his factor, Nicholas Tyson, was moving heaven and earth to be allowed one voyage on that jealously guarded route . . . he himself was using all the influence he had to get a map maker in his service aboard a Spanish galleon.

As Crede listened she was back in a world that had grown fresher and more eager, its colors as rich and bright again as when she and Tony had looked westward from Brandon Hill. It was no longer Robert Thorne's words which made her see the wonder of each treasure ship's unloading, the fabulous stream of gold and gems, strange fruit and birds —and still stranger captive men.

Spain was setting up a slave market to sell their labor, Robert Thorne said. Unwillingly now, Crede's imagination made a picture of it, though she had nothing to build it from except the hiring post in Bristol's market where servants bound themselves for a year and a day. Even though these were free men who made the bargain themselves, it had disturbed her vaguely to see them stand there to be appraised and chosen, and now she pictured bewildered red men there, making no bargain of their own. Portuguese ships brought back slaves too, black men from Africa. Yet to sell men must be against the laws of God.

In the dim past, according to Cousin Allie, Bristol had thrived on a trade with Dublin of captives in local wars, until the good Saxon bishop, Wulfstan, roused the power of the Church and the conscience of the King against it. Surely the Church (which had just shown the tenderness of its conscience by burning the monk Savonarola for an unsoundness of doctrine though he had brought crowds flocking back to it in Italy; and had shown its might in Spain by establishing a court called the Holy Inquisition to search out heresy in men's thoughts) would set its ban on this, even if it must threaten Spain with the dreadful weapon of Interdict. Some believed that God's hand was raised in anger already and that a strange new plague called the Spanish sickness was his warning.

How was it that evil had come from men's long hopes of the Blessed Isles of the West? And what of the noble vision Dr. Erasmus had that men of this age would use the new discoveries and the New Learning and the swift coming-together of the ends of the earth to make it one great commonwealth in which all could be brothers?

"My father talked most of the freedom of Amerike," she said. "It was free, empty land he wanted."

"Amerike seems empty enough," Robert Thorne said. "We have always guessed there is land northwest, and my father saw it before the Cabots, but the marvel is that John Cabot could get gold out of King Henry's purse for proving it to be such a huge grim barrier to the seaways. I heard at home that young Sebastien has got a royal charter to try this summer to find a passage through it, yet I have begun to think lately that England's route to the East may lie eastward."

Crede cast a quick glance toward Anthony. Behind the fairy tale he amused her with, had he been serious about something which seemed possible to Robert Thorne?

"You think that we can trade again from Wisby?" she cried. "Anthony was telling me—"

This did not please Tony, she sensed at once. Perhaps he was ahead of others with a plan which might make him famous! Quickening to a shared secret she met his eyes in swift reaffirmation of an old compact, while schemes for helping him to secure the interest of someone in the Baltic trade flashed through her mind.

"Wisby?" Robert Thorne looked puzzled. "The day of the old overland routes from the Baltic is gone. Even if the Turk were not astride them, the new seaways would be their ruin. But if we could find a seaway east across the top of the world it would be a shorter passage than sailing west to find Cathay, and we of the North should have it."

"I wish us Godspeed of the Ice Mountain," Anthony said lightly.

"If I had my will," Robert Thorne said, "the first thing I would attempt is whether our seas northward be navigable past the Pole."

As if anxious now to end the conversation, Anthony glanced across the hall where guests were beginning to leave.

"How late it has grown in pleasant company!" he said. "My friends are waiting on me."

"But we'll see you soon, Tony? We are stopping with Master John Thrupp."

"Indeed, yes." Anthony made them a general bow and moved away before Crede could ask when he would call.

Robert Thorne's eyes followed him. "Is your cousin related to the Cornwall Jestyns, Crede?"

"Distantly." It was the instinctive answer of solidly respectable Canynges, yet she felt perversely that Thornes were stuffy people. "He and I grew up together in Bristol."

"The Thrupps went home a while ago," Robin said. "John was about ready to leave when we met Robert, and I told him not to wait for us. You are coming to see us before you sail tomorrow, Robert? We'll say good night, then. Shall I find you a chair, Crede?"

"Let us walk home. It's such a fine night."

She was unwilling to bring the occasion to a close so suddenly. She felt restlessly excited still by the flood of swiftly-changing impressions which had swept her along all evening.

As soon as they were alone in the quiet street, however, she wished that she had taken a chair and postponed the quarrel she felt was coming. Robin could not have been stiffer with Tony and had found nothing to say since they had bade their host good night. When he finally spoke she braced herself, for she meant to see Tony and to help him.

What he said was only, "I suppose there is no town where the whole world meets as it does here. Did you enjoy it tonight, Crede?"

"I have a hundred things to tell Maddie," Crede said, thankful for a safe subject.

"I have been here only once before, you know, so we must discover Antwerp together. John can show us the working side of it. He didn't understand tonight, but I have explained to him now that you have responsibilities here too, and he is to take us both about."

He was offering the sort of working partnership Crede had thought once they could enjoy, and perhaps, after all, they could.

"I'd like to be busy again," she said.

"I ought to have seen long ago that idleness is no rest for you. Sewing a fine seam is not your work either, is it? Crede, this won't be like London."

They had only a short distance to walk along the Thrupps' own street which was lined with handsome houses, most of them darkened now with their night lights out, though the moon was so bright they were not needed. They turned down by the stableyard so that they could use their own entrance without disturbing the household, and Robin unlocked the gate.

"Come into our garden."

Moonlight whitened it and flooded the windows so that a candle would scarcely be needed, and in moonlight this garden was as stiff as if made of marzipan for a subtlety. Robin paused at the bench which was flanked by flowers in precise rows.

"Let's sit for a moment."

On an English summer evening after today's heat the scent of flowers and shrubbery would have lingered mistily, but this moon rode higher above a wider earth, flattening it and leaving it bare of fragrance and mystery. It was not for overtones to haunt the imagination that Antwerp led the world, but for ordering its affairs neatly and clear-headedly. Crede felt wide awake with a sudden determination to tidy her own concerns.

"Robin," she said, "I have thought of asking Master Thrupp whether he knows a merchant in the Baltic trade who needs a shipmaster. Anthony is interested in those routes, and he has left his cousin."

"With a recommendation from their service to an honest man like John Thrupp!"

This sounded so like an echo of Adam's prejudice that Adam must have been meddling too, and her impulse to clear things by straightforwardness had only raised another issue.

"They had a commission," she cried, "and kings have always kept their navies up that way. Anyhow, Tony has broken with them, and if he is ready to turn to trade whoever gets him will be lucky. Sebastien Cabot said nobody in Bristol is trained to handle a ship like the Jestyns. Father would have given him a chance. He has this notion now to sail east where our ships don't go, but I mean to help him however I can."

"Crede," Robin's voice surprised her by its mildness, "let's call a truce. Perhaps both of us want too impatiently tonight to push things that can't be pushed. Nothing presses on us that won't wait while we get our feet under us here."

It would always be his way to drift, Crede thought, and nothing could be more trying. Her mind, still restlessly active, concerned itself with schemes for helping Tony without letting him realize that she had guessed he needed help.

"Tomorrow," Robin said, "we should go over the *Swallow*'s manifest with John, and there will be merchants to meet."

He began to plan the whole day, and she had to turn her attention to the immediate problems of a merchant adventurer in Antwerp with her own ship.

Master Thrupp took them about next morning, and they were soon convinced that they could not have found a better agent. Whatever his rapid rise owed to a marriage that connected him with solidly established burghers of the town, his own honesty and shrewdness seemed to have won general respect.

While the business that had brought them to Antwerp made good progress, Crede gained no clearer idea of what Anthony was doing here. Although they met him at various public entertainments or open houses and he always sought her out, she could not get him to confide enough of his plans to give her an idea how she could help. Sometimes he dropped out of sight for several days, and she thought that he might have been out of town, but he was vague about his movements, turning aside questions with teasing or a rigmarole of gallantry. Her misgiving that things were not going well with him remained, but she could not persist in meddling when there might be as much vanity in her concern as pride in his refusal to let her help.

Impatience at having to wait upon events drove her harder into affairs at hand. She set herself to learn the ways of trade here, as eagerly as if Canynges ships were likely to make this voyage often. She plunged into the various diversions Antwerp had to offer, until each day was filled so full that they rushed from one thing to another.

"We aren't so pressed that we can't spend an idle hour now and then," Robin protested, but she wanted to avoid time for worrying.

Once he persuaded her to ride out of town. She found the low, uninteresting countryside of the Scheldt irritating to her unsettled mood, and an unexpected meeting with Tony did nothing to soothe her. He was riding toward Antwerp with two companions, and he was obviously ill pleased to meet her and Robin. He passed on with the barest greeting, while they continued down-river toward Hulst where Robin presented letters to a friend of Dr. Erasmus.

This elderly gentleman turned out to be a magistrate, and when he and Robin discovered a mutual interest in comparing the laws of their two countries he invited them to return for a longer visit. But Crede made no promise of her own.

Antwerp held her. There was something swift and breathless here. The maze of ships and markets was more complex and the lines threading it more tangled than when she had first felt their pull through her fingers in the counting house. She felt exhilaration in matching her wits to something hard, which promised definite answers not hopelessly mixed with feeling as one's personal problems always seemed to be.

It was the very heart of Antwerp into which they ventured with John Thrupp, the network of docks and offices whose pulse was the flow of the seaways toward ever-wider limits. They sucked back a seething mixture from all the adventurous trading nations.

To Crede's surprise, she learned that her own countrymen were considered the most turbulent and pushing. For ages English downs had given them the finest wool known to bargain with, supplying the famous looms of Flanders where coarse English cloth was thought fit only for windmill sails. Now England had more cloth than wool for sale, as good cloth as any, and Flanders had to beg for enough woolsacks to save its own industry. The English merchant adventurers were riding high on this new wave of prosperity. The wily Henry Tudor had taken advantage of the situation to win from the guardians of the young Duke Charles such concessions for English trade in the Low Countries that they were freer of tolls and restrictions than the native merchants were. Yet it seemed to Crede that the English were the least at home here and that the Europeans, whatever their disagreements, were more of a kind—as if England and the Continent faced in different directions. It turned her ideas upside down to discover that what she had accepted as the center of the universe, measuring from its bustling three million all the chances and promises of the new age, was thought of here as an outlandish island off the coast of Christendom.

She learned other things also which would have surprised anyone who knew ports and trading towns. Though Antwerp was growing monstrous —some said it had a hundred thousand souls and some guessed more—its burghers made no anxious effort to limit it or to guard their special privileges. A thousand foreign merchants had settled here. Portuguese, English, Spanish, French, Italians, Scandinavians, and Germans now made it their chief depot abroad. But instead of trembling at what their strange invention of free trade had brought upon them, the city fathers gave the newcomers representation in the Toll, where rules of fair dealing were enacted. To attract even more foreigns to their great six-week fairs at Whitsuntide and Harvest, they had promised suspension during them of imprisonment for debt, with a year to pay for what was bought, and freedom to take home unsold goods.

To keep trade whirling at an even dizzier pace the Corporation of Antwerp was forming a new sort of market called the Bourse, to which merchants brought only samples of their goods, sometimes only a manifest. Their written promises of delivery might be sold and resold, passing from hand to hand like coined money. A goldsmith would give letters of running cash for them, as if real gold had been deposited in his strongbox. German and Italian banking houses had developed a network of exchange and lending which narrowly escaped the Church's ban on usury.

From the fascinating intricacy of Master Thrupp's Antwerp, Crede stepped with Caspar into one that was simpler but even more colorful. With Mistress Thrupp's approval he devoted the hour between school and supper to Crede's instruction. As soon as he came out of Vrou Kirk he looked about for her, detaching himself from his schoolmates with flattering eagerness, and he took her into his confidence as an equal and trusted her to behave sensibly in adventures. Caspar counted the whole town his, with the mixture of familiarity and breathless discovery which had made Bristol a place of enchantment for Crede at his age. She could still move companionably in another child's wonderland of streets and ships and seaport bustle, while her eyes recaptured the sharp freshness of his in the Antwerp he showed her.

The huge Vrou Kirk with its seven naves was in the center of it. Although parts of the church were more than a century old, workmen were still busy on the great north tower. There were ways for the nimble-footed to climb up it, until the churchyard was a small patch of green and the whole hive of Antwerp lay uncovered below. You could look over the honeycomb of streets, swarming darkly, to the sluggish Scheldt which stretched eight fat fingers, laden with the gold of the seaways, among the clustering quays . . . past the ancient castle of the Lords of Brabant, rising north of them . . . or south over the flat fields with their windmills and slow rivers where everything lay open to the eye and yet, though you could see farther, had been robbed of distance.

Besides the lumbering carts that filled the roads (two thousand weekly, Caspar said), an endless procession of barges came down the river to feed the Queen of the North and bring the produce of a wide countryside to her shops and docks. Walks in this direction were full of interest because a family lived on each of the barges and seemed to inhabit a complete world of its own there. On the decks were small, neat gardens, and they hung their washing out like gaily-colored sails. Their goat, and cat, and dog, and their rosy-cheeked children looked as incuriously toward land as if they had never bothered to set foot on it further than the towpath, and the barges were clean and cosy beyond the common run of

English cottages. In this country which Crede learned had been plagued through most of its history by quarrelsome neighbors and jealous overlords, in contrast with the growing security of her own island, nothing surprised her more than the settled tidiness of everything.

There were more streets of shops to wander among than even in London and everything the world had to sell was crammed into them, yet Cheapside had prepared her for this. No town that Crede had ever before seen, however, prepared her for the stir of new building here. Wherever they walked they were within the sound of hammers. Round about Grande Place magnificent halls of the foreign companies were rising among the mansions and guildhalls upon which Antwerp citizens were spending their new wealth. Farther out whole streets, freshly built and neatly lined with young trees, looked as if someone had planned them whole and some careful housewife kept them unnaturally clean.

But along the docks which lined the river Crede could feel at home. It was not only because the *Swallow* was moored there and she and Caspar in their explorations kept under the eye of Canynges seamen. All the familiar bustle of loading and unloading, the mixture of dress and speech, the coming or going of ships, made this quarter just Thames Street or Quayside—spread wider, but part of the same seaport world.

TWENTY-TWO

The *Pelican* had gone home some time ago, the *Swallow* had taken on her cargo and was ready to sail. They were waiting until the *Mary Thorne,* due any day, should make port, for Robin thought that he might as well use this opportunity to put her master on good terms with the new agent.

Today he had ridden to Hulst for a last visit with the friend of Dr. Erasmus and would spend the night. Crede, as she waited outside Vrou Kirk for Caspar to come from school, knew that the walk which they had planned to take along the towpath of the upper river might be their last together. She would be leaving Tony behind in Antwerp, too, but she could not, she thought, be farther away than now from whatever it was that held him apparently unoccupied here. Misgivings about this and the expectation that he would in his own time confide in her had kept her still unsettled, but even the news that she must leave very soon had not brought from him any statement of his own plans.

She was a little early, so she left the fountain which was the usual meeting place with Caspar to wander about the churchyard.

[245]

"My only ane, she walks alane
And evermair has dune so."

She turned with a start to find Anthony close behind her.

"I saw you all forlorn by Matsy's Well," he said, "and before I could cross the street you had flown here."

Sometimes she hoped that he had planned to be where she was, but he always seemed to discover her by accident. If they had a few minutes alone, a word or gesture could summon associations so strong that time moved back, yet afterwards Crede knew that this bore little likeness to what it recalled, for then their common ground had been the present.

He stood smiling down at her. "Must you amuse yourself alone in churchyards, nowadays?"

She was suddenly angry. Neither she nor this Tony with the mocking smile were the same as they had been. He played a masque of a boy's careless teasing against her real concern for him and her wish to be simple and natural.

"I am not amusing myself alone," she said carefully. "I am waiting for Mistress Thrupp's little boy to come out of school."

"To play with you? Alas, that I am not ten again! Yet I hoped that we might run off to the fair together. Do you remember how we counted the days to St. James's Fair?"

She remembered—indeed she remembered—but she was not going to play a game of children at a fair.

"I am afraid I am too busy, Tony. And I must go back to find Caspar."

Brushing past him she almost ran across the churchyard. And as she hurried she felt angrier than ever because she had made this seem an escape and had left Anthony laughing.

He did not follow, and almost at once one small and three slightly older, rosy-cheeked choristers tumbled out a side door of the church. Caspar waved his larger companions off with an air of condescension as he hurried toward her.

"They wanted me to go to the fair," he said, tucking his hand in hers. "But of course we have all been there together several times, and it is much the same sort of jugglers and things every day. Don't you think so?"

"Did you want to go?"

"I am not allowed to go there without someone grown-up. Next year," he said wistfully, "I'll be nine, and I should think I could go anywhere then."

"Oh, I meant with me. Had you rather we went to the fair today?"

They had not gone by themselves before, but it had grown quite familiar to Crede now, and she wanted to give Caspar some final indulgence. After she had spoken she felt a slight misgiving but put it aside as she watched his eyes brighten.

He pulled at her hand. "Come on, we had better hurry. It's quite misfortunate that I was kept a little late—did you sometimes have trouble with verbs?"

The August fair was in full swing and, even if they had not visited it before, they could have found their way there without guidance. One had only to follow the crowds toward noise of a special intensity. For, besides merchants gathered from all over for the serious business of buying and selling, the six-week-long fair attracted more than the usual motley of entertainers and vagabonds, and idle crowds who came to be amused by them.

Caspar knew where he wanted to go today. In the same spot as before, at one of the sprawling edges of the fair, a slim, dark-eyed stroller was attracting a crowd with a marvelous combination of juggling and tumbling, and just beyond him idlers pressed even closer about a dancing bear. It always seemed Crede's fate at fairs to come upon some poor mangy bear with the rage in his little red eyes dulled to sick patience.

"Come away, Caspar," she commanded.

But Caspar, intentionally deaf, was edging to the front of the bear's admirers and, since she could not leave him, she turned her back and concentrated upon the juggler.

"Mistress Inglish!"

She swung about to face Vassily Petrov, who was smiling broadly and holding himself unnaturally straight.

"Mine friend!" he shouted. "We partake this affair in concert!"

Crede barely eluded the arm he threw out. She slipped aside, hoping to lose him in the crowd.

"Allons!" he cried joyously and took after her.

She had thought him over-drunk to follow, but his long legs were not too unsteady to cover distance, and it had been most unwise to offer him the merry diversion of a chase. Crede, running her fastest now, dodged between two stalls and found herself among a cluster of tents. She considered taking refuge in one of them until she might hope that he had given up, but the swarthy face she saw through the first opening frightened her more than Vassily. She turned into a miry passage at the back and suddenly lost her head. Behind this tangle at the seamy edges of a fair something sly and evil seemed closed in, and she ran on between the tents in unreasoning panic, until her foot caught on some obstruction and the ground flew up and hit her.

She had been stunned for a moment, she thought; her head swam wretchedly. She got unsteadily to her feet, feeling the sharp pain of a sprained ankle, and managed to limp out of this backwater until she was among the crowd again. But she had lost her bearings and could not remember which way she should turn to get back to Caspar. Then to her great relief she saw Anthony and made straight for him, calling his name.

He was a little distance away at the edge of a group which surrounded some attraction. Separating himself from two rather odd-looking companions he hurried toward her.

"Cre! Holy Mother, what has happened to you?"

Crede looked down at her skirts. "I fell in mud," she said unnecessarily and began to laugh. She had been in a ridiculous panic, but everything was all right now, if only her head would stop spinning. She raised a hand to it and found it as sticky as her gown.

"Your face is covered with blood!"

Anthony put his arm around her and half carried her to an open spot under a tree. He set her with her back against the trunk and drove away a pair of curious small boys.

"Let me see this cut on your head. Were you clubbed?"

"I suppose there was a stone where I fell."

She felt shakily for her kerchief.

"There seems to be more mud than blood, fortunately. How did it happen?"

Crede told of her flight. "It was foolish to lose my head and run, of course."

"You had no business coming here alone," Anthony said angrily. "You wouldn't come with me!"

"Caspar! We've got to find him." She tried to get to her feet, but the pain in her ankle was sickening.

Anthony bent down and felt it carefully. "I am pretty sure it isn't broken. But you shouldn't walk on it. I know where I can get a litter."

"Find Caspar first, Tony. A little yellow-haired boy—over where there is a dancing bear and a juggler—call his name."

"If there is a bear and a juggler he hasn't even missed you yet. When he does, an Antwerp boy can surely find his way home."

"Please, Tony. He is too small to be here alone, and he would be likely to stay hunting me."

Anthony hurried away, pausing only for a word with his two former companions who were still standing where he had left them. Crede leaned her head against the tree and fought dizziness.

When Anthony finally returned he had a chair but no Caspar.

"I couldn't find him," he said, "and I might hunt till dark for a strange child. It would be better to send somebody back who knows him."

"I suppose so." Crede tried her weight on her foot and realized that she could do no hunting herself. Anthony had to lift her into the chair. "It will give Mistress Thrupp a fright to have me come home looking like a brawl without him," she said unhappily.

The bearers raised the poles and Anthony walked alongside.

"I suppose you have sometimes taken Caspar to the *Swallow*," he said. "Does Nat Tillson know him?"

"Why, yes—"

"Nat had the watch when I happened to pass by a little while ago. We could just as quickly go to the *Swallow* first, Cre, and send Nat after Caspar. You could wash up a bit and take Caspar home with you then, without harrowing Mistress Thrupp's feelings unnecessarily."

It seemed a good plan, for they would not be expected at home yet, and Crede relaxed gratefully. Tony was always quick-witted.

Old Nat was leaning against the *Swallow's* rail. By his own choice he did more than his share of watchman's duty, for his dislike of foreigns extended to their ports and the diversions therein, and he preferred to live aboard ship while the rest of the crew, now that the *Swallow* was ready to sail and nothing remained to be done on her, eagerly took all the shore leave they could get. He turned his grizzled head and a face weather-beaten by years of Canynges' service as Anthony hailed him.

"Are you back again?" he said grumpily.

"That's gratitude," Anthony laughed. "I only offered to buy you a drink for old times' sake, Nat."

"And hung about bothering me when I'm on duty." Nat scowled fearsomely as if Anthony were still a mischievous small boy. "You're as full of tricks as a monkey, Master Tony, but you'll not get it on me that I went off my watch to a wine shop."

Suddenly his eye took in the litter and Crede. "Blessed St. Brendan! Have you two got in another of your scrapes?"

Crede could not help laughing, for Nat had set them back about ten years now. He stepped onto the dock and peered anxiously at her.

"I had a fall, Nat, but I'm more dirty than hurt. I want to tidy myself in my cabin before I go home."

"I can see you've a bad foot on you," Nat scolded as they helped her to the deck. "There's a fire going for my supper, and we'll put hot cloths to it right now."

"I can do that. Nat, I need you to do me a favor. Caspar Thrupp got separated from me at the fair—will you go there and find him? He is probably still waiting around near a dancing bear."

"I reckon that one can find his way home."

"I'm really ashamed to go without him, Nat. His mother trusts me."

"Send Master Anthony then," Nat said stubbornly. "I'm on watch here alone."

"But I'm here now, Nat. Anthony did look about, but he doesn't know Caspar—he just happened to be near when I fell, and he helped me. I thought you would help me too, Nat."

"Umph." Nat looked less balefully at Anthony who seemed blameless in this misadventure and then at Crede, and he weakened. "It's a silly bother. But if you're bound to fret yourself I'll get him for you," he growled, and stumped off.

"Only you could have sent Nat off his watch," Anthony said with a laugh. "Well, you're captain and I'm mate now, Cre." His eyes danced as they used to in some boyish prank that promised mischief and danger. Then he sobered. "I forget you aren't up to the fun of having Nat scold like fury and then help us out. I'll take you to your cabin and bring hot water there. Wait, I can carry you easier.

"Your head is miserable, isn't it?" he said as he set her down on the bunk. "I know what—" He disappeared and in a short time returned with a mug in his hand. "I still remember where things are kept here. A cup of wine is what you need first of all, Cre. Drink this and lie still for a few moments.

Crede drank it gratefully and felt the throbbing in her head ease. Even her ankle felt so much better that she decided she had made too much fuss about her injuries and that with a short rest she would be herself again.

She was floating on soundless waves, rising and falling gently . . . rising and falling endlessly. Only this gentle swell measured time—long, long time. Now she was borne above it . . . she could fly, mounting and dipping effortlessly . . . mounting, dipping . . . like a swallow. She must remember to tell Cousin Allie how it was done.

Crede opened her eyes. Her throat was dry and her head was light. It was clearing, however. She remembered now that she was resting for a few minutes in the *Swallow*'s cabin. But it was night! The light came from a lantern Tony was setting on the table, and this swaying motion— this motion was the *Swallow*'s!

"We're adrift!" she cried. "Tony!"

"I thought you were near waking." Anthony carried a bowl from the table. "Have some of Nat's pottage." He was putting on an air of casualness, but she felt his excitement. "Anthony, what has happened— what has happened to us? The ship is moving!"

"Very sweetly, for hours. We are slowing down now. Everything is all right, Cre. Take this, and your head will steady."

"Tell me what happened!" She pushed the bowl aside, her hands trembling.

Anthony set it down and put his arm around her. "I had to make something happen, dear, when you had muddled things for us so. This evening the chance came."

"You brought the *Swallow* out! You must be mad, Anthony. Oh, where are we?"

[250]

"Following a creek of the river where we will lie hid today. It's dawn now, and tonight we shall be at sea. You're safe away with me, Cre!"

"Tony, you can't mean this! You can't be—so wicked."

Fright and bewilderment overwhelmed her. She struggled to get to her feet, but Anthony tightened his arm.

"Is it wicked that we have always belonged together? We grew up knowing that, and it was the best thing in us both. Whatever gets between us is wrong. I tried to make you see that, Cre, but you kept mixing it up with things that can't matter, until I knew I'd get nowhere trying to talk you out of them. It's not my fault there wasn't much choice of ways left."

"You can give me that bowl now," Crede said.

"Good girl!" He freed her and brought the bowl and stood smiling down at her.

Crede forced herself to swallow a mouthful of the warm, thick broth. She must do something to get control of this shaking and clear her thoughts. In spite of the tightness of her throat she sipped determinedly.

"I knew I was right," Anthony said. "I knew last year in Bristol that this was the only way to make you see it, but things went wrong. This time I had to plan, knowing even less what chance could serve, and then everything went so marvelously that the stars must be with us. Cre, we'll live the sort of adventures we used to play at—you sailing with me always. Tomorrow we'll be toward Wisby, and I've friends there who will join the ship—"

"Wisby! From the first this plot was in your mind! You wanted a ship for Wisby—to join pirates!"

"Freebooters or venturers, what great difference is there? If hunting farther for treasure makes it so respectable we'll go as far as you like . . . help ourselves as Spain does in her islands . . . find the Portingales' secret way to Ind. We are free of the whole world, Cre."

He was moving restlessly about the cabin as if the *Swallow* could not go fast enough for him now.

"Put us back, Tony! I'll say that we drifted loose, that you saved the ship."

"Turn back, with the *Swallow* clean away!" Anthony laughed. "I've never known you to take fright, Cre. You'd match me at anything, always. And we are safe now." He stopped his pacing to perch on the edge of the table, one foot swinging, his eyes bright and restless. "Jock and Frank found this inlet days ago—it's a perfect hideout. Only a short run to sea after dark again, and time to get clear of the coast." Under his breath he hummed, "Haule and howe, rumbelowe. Stir well the good ship and let the wind blow!"

"Jock and Frank?" How could she clear her thoughts while confusions piled up?

"Did you think the *Swallow* was steering herself now? The three of us were kept pretty busy handling her down-channel, I can tell you. But we judged the tide right for this creek, and Jock knows the sounding. They have only to ease her up it. I told them to follow us from the fair and wait about for the turn of the tide after dark when we could slip out with it. If anyone had come aboard before then, why, you were resting and I was keeping watch for Nat. But luck was with us."

"Nat!" Crede cried, a new fear stirring. She had been so slow sorting things out. "You could not risk his coming back, giving an alarm—Anthony, what have you done with Nat?"

"Nat is safe enough. Do you think I would harm him?"

"What have you done with him?" Could this be Tony . . . herself . . . caught in a nightmare of distrust and fear! He had tricked her from the moment they met at the fair, perhaps he had followed her and Caspar for some such chance as she had given him. He had plotted unbelievable treachery with those villainous-looking men. "Anthony, did you set those men after Nat?"

"Only to overtake him and leave him where he would be held for a while. He wasn't harmed."

He had turned two ruffians loose on Nat and expected her to believe they had not hurt him. She could only pray that he was safe as she tried to collect herself and piece the story together. Nat had not reached Caspar, of course, and Caspar at least must be all right. He was a sensible child, and when he could not find her at the fair would go home before dark. When he got home they would begin searching the town for her. But even when the *Swallow* was missed, could they guess what had happened unless Nat were found?

"Did you," she said slowly, "put a drug in my wine—one you had ready for Nat if you could have got him to drink with you?"

"It was harmless, Cre. Nat would have had the sleep which has done you only good. I'd still have had to find a way to bring you with us."

The ship lurched so suddenly that Crede was thrown back on the bunk, and then it came gently to rest.

"We're in," Anthony said. "I'll have a look at our berth, Cre."

As soon as he had gone Crede got up and discovered that although her ankle was badly swollen she could walk a little. If she watched for a chance during the day could she slip ashore, find a place to hide, reach some farmhouse, perhaps? Yet she knew that she could not move quickly or cover any distance. And there were three to watch her.

Those two ruffians would take care that she did not escape to betray their hiding place. Even if she promised, they would be afraid to risk it;

even if she could persuade Anthony to let her go—and she had little hope of reasoning with Anthony in his present mood. He was in a fit of wild spirits which she knew well, carried along by the success of this reckless plan, sure that he could win her to it as he had done in childish escapades. Just now she would not be able to shake his confidence by the bitterest things she could say. He would put it down to annoyance at his trick and her quick temper but would remember how often they had quarreled and made up.

It would be better to avoid a scene, to keep her head and watch for any chance. She must try to think more coolly. When she had poured a drink from the water cask and washed and tidied herself as best she could, she felt fresher.

The curtain had been drawn across the cabin window. Pushing it aside she could see the sky taking color behind the dark trees that closed round the ship. She was standing there quietly when Tony returned.

"A perfect mooring," he said with satisfaction. "We had been well over the ground before, and this is a lonely spot. There is only the risk of a chance person stumbling on us, and not much danger of that."

He was taking her partnership for granted now, reassuring her of their safety.

"Frank is taking a post down-creek to keep watch, but we can expect a quiet day here while Jock goes inland for two friends who have kept in readiness to join us. With them, tonight will be easy."

He had carried in with him a measure of wine and a plate of cheese and biscuit, and he set these on the table and brought two mugs from the locker.

"We've been too busy to eat, but we have just had a look at the *Swallow*'s stores and we shan't go hungry or thirsty at any rate. Sit down, Cre, and let us drink our first cup to the venture." He poured the wine and raised his mug. "To Merry Fortune!"

"A pirate's fortune quite commonly ends swinging in chains at Thames' tide." Crede was making a last effort to sober him.

He only laughed and drained his wine. "Jestyns make most uncommon pirates. You look better already, Cre. Could Robin Thorne have carried you off under my nose?"

He was flushed with triumph. The bitter lines about his mouth which had been the first change she noticed in him were gone, and he looked a boy again, playing this as if it were a boy's game, as if the rules were no harder, as if he had grown no wiser. Yet he had managed the plan shrewdly and his reckless humor was more dangerous than a boy's wilfulness.

"If you mean to live this way, Anthony, why did you leave your cousin?"

"He has turned as cautious as a trader, and just because I took a chance he wouldn't have taken—well, we quarreled, but we'd have been bound to, sooner or later." He was eating hungrily. "I hardly noticed I'd missed my supper," he said between mouthfuls. "But we brought it off. You're my luck, Cre."

He filled his mug again and raised it to her, humming the catch:

> *Mistress Anne, I am your man*
> *As you may well espie.*
> *If you will be content with me*
> *I am merrie.*

They had heard no sound until the door was flung back. Anthony dropped his wine cup and was half to his feet.

"Keep your hand from your sword, Jestyn."

Robin's voice! How could it be?

A swift rush through the entrance, before Anthony could clear the bench to draw, pointed the other blade to his throat. Robin stood out of reach, his sword point keeping its advantage—and Anthony, hampered by bench and table, empty-handed, shouting furiously, "Let me up and fight fair, you damned shopkeeper!"

"Keep your hands on the table! Get back, Crede."

"You can't—not this way!"

Crede screamed, and tried to get between them.

Robin's left arm flung her aside, but the sword point was held steady. Her ankle turned under her, and she fell onto the bunk.

"We can't all be as open and honorable as pirates," Robin said. "If your man strays into woods, Jestyn, someone may be watching to sneak up on him, and if you light your cabin—" his glance took in the lantern, still burning, though scarcely needed now, and the window whose curtains Crede had left apart—"someone in a hurry to find you may forget to knock."

"Stop talking, curse you! Will you fight?"

"Shopkeepers like to know the score before they settle it." Robin did not change his position. "Nat got away from that dive your friends shut him in. Before he was knocked out he had recognized them as loiterers around the quay with you, and when he found the *Swallow* gone he chose a night ride to Hulst for me, though he was in poor shape for it, instead of giving an alarm."

And now, though Robin kept his eyes fixed on Anthony, Crede knew that he was speaking to her.

"It happens that I had done some riding out from Hulst and remembered this creek," he said. "And though I thought nothing of it at the time, a man we had once seen riding below Antwerp with you, Jestyn,

[254]

was loitering there. When I reckoned how much darkness would be left after you waited the turn of the tide last night, the convenience of this place to lie in through the day so seized me that I had to try that chance first. I wanted to know for myself, Crede, why Nat did not raise an alarm."

"Because I made Nat leave the ship. But I didn't know—"

She dared not say that! Huddled miserably on the edge of the bunk, she searched her wits in desperation. To say that Anthony had tricked her and stolen the *Swallow* could get him hanged. "I mean that I—"

"I was pretty sure you didn't. This—subtlety—seemed unlike your way of doing things. Well, Jestyn—" Robin lowered his guard.

"I mean that I am here by accident, but I had given Anthony the *Swallow*."

She got the words out in a rush, but neither of them was listening to her now.

Anthony was free of the table, his sword out, attacking furiously. They meant to kill each other, and any cry that she made now, any movement to hinder, might free one sword for a murderous stroke.

Robin was giving way! He seemed just managing to cover a retreat! Now he was through the passage, Anthony pressing him hotly, and Crede was on her feet, sick with terror but following them.

They had come to a stand on the afterdeck, and now Robin was holding his ground—yet not so much holding it as defending swift movements. He would not fight close, and every effort Anthony made to force it was evaded. There was none of the forthright cut and slash practiced in singlestick about this, and for a moment it seemed to Crede less dangerous.

Neither of them wasted a word, and in the quiet early light their engagement assumed unreality, the innocence of some measured pantomime. Since Crede had awakened in the *Swallow*'s cabin, each successive shock had seemed untrue and unbelievable. For a moment now the present slipped from her, and she watched not this scene but one long ago in Philip's Field. For an instant this seemed the same duel, the same duelists.

It was there she had seen this odd, dance-like advance with the sword point. Anthony, if it had been Anthony there, had already learned this Italian trick somewhere, while the other had been baffled by it. But now the other was Robin, who had traveled in Italy . . . and knew it very well! It was his choice that they should fight in such a way. Anthony kept trying to close and, always fended off, returned to this thrust and parry as something not yet natural. In the small cabin they must have fought at close quarters—had Robin purposely retreated here?

And his purpose was deadly. Crede was no longer bemused by a light swift play that had seemed almost like a game. Both were breathing faster now, the pace quickening. Oh Mother Mary, all these dreadful things had begun because of her stupid folly! And there was nothing she could do. She dared not move or distract them.

They were evenly matched for height, but Robin was quicker—his thrust seemed straight for Anthony's heart that instant! Anthony barely parried it, and before he could recover the darting steel was back again and easily, contemptuously, as if it had chosen the spot, pierced his sword arm.

Robin lowered his point, but Anthony snatched with his left hand for his falling sword. "Fight, damn you!" he cried. "I won't stop!"

Crede threw herself in front of him. An accumulation of anxiety, self-accusation, fright, was wiped out suddenly by anger. She was hotly angry with them both, with Anthony who had tricked her, with Robin who could make others fight as suited him so much better . . . both of them settling her affairs without her leave, and brawling, and killing each other under her nose.

"Get out of my way!" Anthony shouted furiously.

Crede kicked the sword he was reaching for across the deck and faced him. He had clutched his arm now and a bright stain was spreading on his sleeve. He looked down at it, his face dark with rage.

"It has to be bound at once," she said, tearing a strip from her petticoat.

Robin neither moved nor said anything. Anthony, watching the blood that dripped through his fingers, let Crede rip the sleeve back and bind the gash firmly. It was bleeding freely, but she saw with relief that it was not spurting and should do well enough without burning. Anthony saw this too, and his fingers moved toward his dagger. He swung about suddenly toward Robin, "We'll finish this, Thorne!"

"No!"

Crede clung with her full weight on his injured arm, knowing quite well how sharply this must hurt him. He whitened and caught his breath.

"I may choose to leave a pirate to the hangman," Robin said.

"What piracy is there?" Crede spoke clearly and coldly. "I gave Anthony the *Swallow*, and whatever papers have to be signed I will swear to. We will leave her with him and go back now."

Robin had turned whiter than Anthony, whose arm stiffened under her fingers.

"Your father's ship!"

"And mine. You have always said the ships were mine."

"Oh, what matter! Do you mean your father's ship to be a scourge to decent men in his own trade? You know what Anthony and that gallows bird I trussed up in the woods want it for!"

[256]

"It will not be used for an ill purpose. I couldn't give Father's ship for a wrong use—to anyone."

She was speaking to Anthony now, staking the best she had known of him on a desperate throw.

"Father did not care only for trade, Tony. What is brave and venture-some in you can feel the pull that took him westward. Our games used to be of new islands and seaways—you talked of them again today. I—I'll think of you sailing the *Swallow* in ventures I might have tried if I had been Father's son."

"Are you offering me a parting gift, and good wishes, Lady Bounti-ful?"

"The gift was made before. I am offering the good wishes," Crede said quickly.

With Robin ready to charge piracy, able to command here, and not only more violent but harder than she had suspected, Crede could see no course except the one she had impulsively chosen. It left her unable to make terms now or ask a promise. She could only cling to a hope of reaching Anthony through her trust in things they had shared. Despite the bitterness in his voice now she persisted, but the need to talk to him around Robin's hostility was a weight on her tongue.

"I still think you may have trouble with those two men you shipped first, Tony, yet I am not afraid you couldn't handle twice such and take on enough others more to your purpose to get the ship to Bristol."

Anthony started, but she kept her hand on his arm and hurried on. "I shan't forget to send a letter to our own office asking Clem to give any help you want to sell the *Swallow*'s cargo there. And Sebastien Cabot will welcome a captain, with his own ship, to the company he is gathering under King Henry's charter. Anthony, if you find the passage to Ind, the rewards and honors for it will be so great that all my life I'll be proud of this share in the venture."

"You are a fool, Cre!" Anthony put his arms around her suddenly and kissed her. "A sweet fool. I'll never again find anyone like you—for heaven's sake cut this short and go."

She might never see him again. He had deceived her shamefully, and she had been shocked and angry and frightened. If chance had not brought this escape she would still have been desperately contriving one —yet for a moment she clung to him in desolation. And the moment's anguish brought its own sharp clarity. She knew now what Anthony had always been to her. He was the brother she had never had, the one who grows up with you sharing things which the others you love across a gen-eration cannot share, and which no later love can find the dear familiar roots of. This must remain uncanceled and unchanged, but they were cut adrift from it. Anthony would follow his reckless way far from hers, and the women he loved would fit it. They would not be in the least like her.

She turned away from him, her eyes full of tears, and without looking back descended to the lower deck and stepped ashore where the ship's waist grazed the bank. The sun was loitering behind the trees, just touching the creek with a sleepy finger, and the marsh grasses were heavy-headed with dew, smelling mistily of night as she trampled them. She would not look back toward the *Swallow*. If she walked on purposefully, Robin would surely have to leave it too.

He caught up with her in a moment.

"Turn this way. I left the horse at the edge of the wood," he said briefly. "How bad is your foot?"

"Only a little stiff—it's nothing."

Determined to need no help, she limped along until they came upon the horse tied to a tree.

Robin led it out into a winding road. "This cuts back across country to Hulst."

Of course he would know the countryside, though he had visited it only a few times. His sense of direction no longer surprised her.

Instead of mounting her pillion fashion he held her in front of him. "The beast is quiet enough to carry us this way. Don't tell me you aren't dead beat. God, when I think—"

There was such roughness in his voice and in the grip of his arm around her that Crede shrank away from it. Among the many shocks of this miserable day the harshness of Robin's temper which it had discovered to her seemed more than she had strength left to face.

After a moment he said in a controlled tone, "When did you decide to give the *Swallow* away, Crede?"

She felt herself stiffen. It must be before Tony had done anything that could be called piracy. And she would have to watch every word, for Robin could be very sharp when he chose. The quickness with which he had pieced together tides and times and the memory of a face she had scarcely noticed had startled her as much as his impulsiveness in testing his conjecture alone.

"It was quite some time ago," she said unhappily.

"And then you went on to load her with what must be one of the richest cargoes she has ever carried?"

"You would think of that, I suppose."

"I have to think of a number of things I shouldn't choose to. When we called a truce, Crede, I thought you would deal openly. How long have you been conspiring with Jestyn in a way so underhanded and unlike you?"

"Conspiring! Because I decided to give—?"

[258]

"You know very well what I mean. Had you arranged to meet him when we came to Antwerp?"

"I—no I hadn't!"

"I didn't think so. But when he hatched this scheme—Crede, I trusted everything I have ever known of you that you didn't mean to be carried off with the ship. I know you didn't. It's not a way you could take out of anything. But the rest of it is hard enough to believe. I suppose you didn't know that Nat would be set upon?"

"Of course I didn't!" It was wrung from her without calculation. Before she could pause to reflect that when one has a lie to tell elaboration is dangerous, she said, "All that part of it was a mix-up. It began when I fell and hurt my ankle at the fair, because Vassily Petrov was drunk—when he spoke to me I lost my head and ran."

"Muscovites must be unlike anyone else. Vassily seems to have had an unprecedented effect on you. What happened then?"

"I went to rest in the *Swallow*'s cabin and—I fell asleep and got carried on here. Anthony was mistaken and thought I wanted to go."

This part was difficult, for she wanted to be as honest as possible, but having once diverged from truth it was not easy to join company again.

"I was planning how to get back when you came. We—it was only a short time since I waked and found what had happened. Anthony had just lately come in—"

She had been too eager to explain this and found herself flushing uncomfortably.

"I didn't doubt that he was kept as busy with an argument this morning as he must have been last night spiriting the *Swallow* out. There's one thing I could have taught him." Robin laughed shortly. "Do you think I know nothing at all about you? I even know how badly you lie. And I have to see at last how dear a cause must be to make you condone—you don't need to explain the rest." The anger had gone out of his voice, and it sounded as tired as Crede felt.

She was thankful to ride in silence. Using her foot had pained her more than she admitted, and she was beginning to feel lightheaded again. But her mind would not rest, and her thoughts scurried about distractedly. Sometimes they were with Anthony, praying that she had touched things he could not close his mind to. Sometimes they reached blindly toward her father, begging him to understand what she had done. At last they came to the gate of Hulst.

"You aren't fit to ride to Antwerp this morning," Robin said, "and neither will Nat be. I left him at an inn here, and you had better stay with him, while I go on to relieve the Thrupps' anxiety about you and calm Harry Blanket. He must by now have found the *Swallow* gone."

She had left the *Swallow*'s crew, Canynges seamen, stranded in a for-

[259]

eign port! Well, she thought, overlooking obstacles in the desperation of near exhaustion, there was all this business of paper credits in Antwerp, and Adam had said they could afford another ship, so it must be bought here.

As they dismounted in the inn yard, she said with compunction, "Robin, I haven't even thanked you! I hardly know how to."

"You could give me a ship, I suppose. You had better tell me to sail mine round Africa."

With a rudeness she had never before seen in him, he swung into the saddle and left her standing there. Now she had only to join Nat who since she was six had permitted himself the utmost freedom of speaking his mind.

TWENTY-THREE

The *Katerine* was a sound, clean craft, and although Master Blanket grumbled that she was as thick amidships as a Flanders mare and Nat had not a good word for her—and many that Crede would not have permitted him to say if she had felt less guilty—she had excellent cargo space and unusually comfortable cabins. Crede found her steadier than the *Swallow,* and since the weather was remarkably kind she suffered much less physical discomfort on this crossing. It was not agreeable otherwise, however, with everyone openly disgruntled except Robin who had regained his politeness but talked only of trivial things.

Since their early morning ride to Hulst the matter of the *Swallow* had not been mentioned between them. Before he took her and Nat back to Antwerp next day he had made some explanation of their adventure which apparently satisfied the others. And he had managed the whole business of buying the *Katerine* and her cargo, insisting with Mistress Thrupp that Crede must stay in bed until her swollen ankle was better, for it brought on a slight fever. As she had been anxious to cause no further delays she stayed there for most of their last week in Antwerp, fussed over by kind Mistress Thrupp and consoled by Caspar's devotion and his plans for sailing a ship of his own to England as soon as possible. She had done one thing for herself, however; she had written at once to Clem about the *Swallow* and Master Thrupp had got her letter on a fast ship clearing for Bristol. Clem would be furious, but she had made her instructions very definite, and he would have no choice in the matter.

They were far up Thames. All afternoon she stayed on deck as they made their way among the slow barges and fishing boats and tall seagoing

[260]

ships—past the Essex woods, past the Surrey fishing villages, past the Royal Palace at Greenwich. They passed the Isle of Dogs with the royal kennels, and the docks at Deptford where they saw in the slips the latest of the King's Ships which Henry Tudor meant someday to be a Royal Navy independent of privateers and merchants' loans. They came round the bend, the tide carrying them into London's forest of masts.

There was a sweep about the Thames, a restless drive of its tide to the heart of the port, which she had not felt on the Scheldt, for that spread into lazy inlets. All London past the Tower ran eagerly downhill to meet the river, scrambling through steep lanes to wharves and water stairs and spilling shops and houses over the Bridge with the tide roaring below. City and river were one now as London, curving down all unwalled at Thames side, gathered home another ship. But Crede felt still the lonely suspension of the traveler—no part of either shore. In returning as in leave-taking she had this moment of belonging nowhere.

Robin came to lean against the rail beside her. He had the *Katerine*'s manifest in his hand, the list of everything she carried which had been sealed in a copper tube at Antwerp and must be opened in the presence of a port officer here.

"We shall be cleared faster here if I take care of it for Master Blanket," he said. "Shall I take you home first?"

While away from the house in Bishopsgate Street Crede had believed that she could go back to it, in the prospect, so soon, of leaving for Bristol. But now she said, "Let me go to Alison's," and wondered that this happy solution had not come to her before. There was always room and a welcome in Alison's house, and it was Alison's lovely serenity she needed most of all.

"Do you want to go straight to Alison's now?"

"I can go myself. You must want to hurry things here and get home."

"I suppose so." He stood for a moment watching the water swirl alongside as they neared the wharf, then crossed the deck to join Master Blanket.

In front of Alison's door a litter waited with liveried bearers: Lady Featherstone's, Crede thought, and she did not want to break in upon that visit. She turned down the lane and let herself into the kitchen.

Alison was alone there, one of the Venice glasses in her hand. She set it down hastily, and then her arms were around Crede, her face turning pink with surprise and pleasure, her voice, with its quick lilt, crying, "Dearest, we hoped it might be this week! Are you just in? Where is Robin?"

"Robin is still at Thames side. Alison, could I stay with you here for a few days?"

"Of course, dear."

Alison glanced at her quickly. Then she smiled and kissed Crede again. She would ask no questions until Crede offered to confide in her. But when she did they would go to the root of things, and whatever muddle Crede had made would not shock her.

They were both swept almost from their feet now as a small gray tornado erupted from a basket in the corner and hurled itself upon Crede. "She has recognized your voice!" Alison said. "Maddie brought her here because she bothered Serena. Poor little thing!"

Crede gathered Fand into her arms and Fand, crying in her wordless but strangely human voice, burrowed into her shoulder, her body trembling convulsively. Very rarely did Fand forget her dignity. She was forgetting even the sharpness of her claws that clutched for reassurance, but Crede held her close, caring nothing for scratches, and if Fand was uncomfortably squeezed now she did not care either.

"I have a guest," said Alison, picking up the goblet again. "Crede, could you do an errand for me? Maddie went to the egg market, and if you can find her will you please hurry her back? The Lady Margaret wants to see her. The Lady Margaret comes sometimes—but I'll explain that later."

There was only one Margaret called The Lady, though it seemed incredible that the King's mother should be in Alison's little house and Alison speaking so casually of her. Certainly she ought not to be kept waiting. Detaching Fand from her shoulder and whispering that she would return, Crede closed the door upon Fand's frantic doubts and hurried off toward the Poultry.

She found Maddie there, doing her marketing with the leisurely enjoyment she always took in shopping. With a cry of delight Maddie dropped her new-bought eggs on their feet and hugged her.

"Oh Crede, I have been so lonesome for you! I thought you would never get back. How did you find me here? Where is Robin?"

"Maddie, you look wonderful!" Maddie, Alison, Fand, she loved them so—how could she have felt lonely on entering London?

"Look at our shoes, Maddie!" They both laughed and wiped egg off their feet on the grass of St. Milfred's Churchyard. "Robin is well. Alison sent me here, and we have to hurry back because the Lady Margaret wants to see you."

Maddie did not look at all astonished. "I can come back for more eggs," she said, giving her shoes a final scrub, and then she fell into step with Crede, keeping tight hold on her arm.

"The Lady Margaret has been wonderfully kind," she explained. "Dr. Linacre, who was Prince Arthur's tutor and knows her well, told her about Alison's Dame School, and she laughed at the name but said that it was a splendid idea and made him bring her to see it. Now she calls it her newest college. She is always endowing something at Cambridge and Oxford, you know. She said this must have an endowment too, and she was so generous that Alison can be sure of the means to keep on here and can get the things she needs for it. I can help a little too," Maddie said happily, "for when Robin arranged for me to have money of my own it was more than I need. The school has grown marvelously, Crede. Some days we have thirty."

"You and Alison are both working like slaves, I suppose!"

"I like it," Maddie said. "A good many of those girls come from ugly places, and I like helping them to make something pretty. Even Aunt Serena is in favor of it now because she thinks it puzzles Father if I am at home all the time. I sleep at the cottage generally, and Alison is glad to have me when Win is away so much."

"Win is away?"

"He is back and forth to Oxford, and soon he will be there all the time. Crede, there are so many things to tell you! He is to be given the next fellowship at All Souls College. It is a very learned college, for all of them are graduates of one of the others and there are only forty at any time, so it is a great honor. The Lady Margaret is arranging this too. Win is to take holy orders and be one of the priests who serve its chantry to pray for the souls of all those who lost their lives in the Hundred Years War—that is what the college was founded for."

"She wants to make a chantry priest of Win!" Crede cried in outrage. "Maddie, it can't be true! Win would be cutting himself off from everything—what has got into him?"

It seemed to her that something quite incomprehensible and calamitous had befallen Win—Win with his quick interest and pleasure in so many things, with his talents and the promise she had foreseen of his making brilliant use of them. The ferment of this pushing and worldly-minded age was part of her; she shared the impatience of bustling Bristol and London with intrusions of religious privilege in everyday affairs which expressed itself in distrust of monkish mysteries. When she thought of things of the mind she thought of her father's and of Cousin Allie's free speculations unhampered by taboos of the Church. Win was so like her father, his mind given the added benefit of Oxford and the New Learning. But was he really like her father? It occurred to her now that, while her father's detachment had accompanied an energetic interest in practical affairs, Win had to be drawn in through his affections. There was a devoted and romantic streak in Win, and if his devotion turned now to the Church—when so many attacked it but when his idol Dr. Erasmus saw it, for all his sharp criticisms, as still the greatest bond men had with Christ's Kingdom upon earth—mightn't he be happiest in a service which freed him from the distractions of daily living?

[263]

These questions had come unbidden, and she closed her mind against them. The Church was not what she wanted for Win. "Can none of you reason with him?" she cried.

"I think it is right for him," Maddie said slowly, "and so does Alison. Win loves learning for itself, not for what use he can make of it, but to be alone with it, undistracted by other things. He can add his own part to it. A life set apart from worldly events would not irk him as it did Dr. Erasmus, and he would use its quiet—like Roger Bacon, perhaps."

This from Maddie who had surely never troubled her head with such ideas before! Crede stared at her, forgetting to argue that Roger Bacon had not found much ease in the Church. As always, anything concerning Win brought a special radiance to Maddie; yet Maddie had changed, she saw now. Her face had a new thoughtfulness and had lost its childish roundness, though it was even more vividly lovely and as confiding and unhurt. Once Crede had feared that Maddie, who gave so unreservedly, was too vulnerable. She had felt herself much more than a year older and anxiously protective, but now it was she who felt uncertain, without some secret Maddie and Alison had found, although she had been given more scholarship and had learned to manage competently things beyond their experience.

Nevertheless, while she was reassured for Maddie and Maddie might content herself about Win, Crede was still far from feeling reconciled. "How far has this gone?" she demanded.

"The Lady Margaret has taken a great fancy to Win, but the question of holy orders is a very serious one and she wants him to be prepared. He is reading theology with Dr. Grocyn, and she has sent him on several errands about her benefactions to both universities—I think to make him known to her friends there. I have been doing all the talking, Crede, when you are the traveler! We are home before I have heard any of your news."

The litter still waited in front of the house, and Maddie would not let Crede slip around to the back but kept hold of her arm while she opened the door.

"Is it my little Madeline?"

The lady sitting in Alison's best chair by the window was so tiny that even Alison appeared large beside her, and Maddie, rising from a curtsy, seemed to be streaking upward like the magic bean.

The Lady Margaret looked quite old and frail, but the thin shoulders in the severe dark gray gown were held very straight, and Crede thought that she would need no jewels to distinguish her at the most brilliant court. There was something as uncommon in her as there had been in the slight, soberly-dressed figure and plain, sickly face of her son, surrounded by his glittering attendants on Cheapside. One had no difficulty in remembering that this little old lady had brought her son in her own right the Lancastrian claim to the throne, had done more than anyone else through long years of danger and discouragement to save his life and procure the crown for him, and was his most trusted adviser. Her manner as Crede was presented had the simplicity that needs to be nothing else.

Some good fairy at her birth had given her charm also. Under her strongly marked dark brows were the resolute eyes of the King's counselor, and the grave eyes of the scholarly religieuse who could instruct bishops in philosophy and was said to wear a hair shirt under her plain gown, but the curve of her lips was sweet and merry when she smiled. She told Crede that both of them must love the West Country and feel sometimes that London thought itself too great, adding with a twinkle that north of Severn they had thought Bristol overproud too. But she envied those who had lived among the stir of its westward ventures, she said, and she remembered graciously that Thorne and Canynges were names long associated with them. It was said of Tudors, Crede reflected, that they remembered common names better than some great ones, perhaps because it was the name of a Welsh commoner they had brought to the throne.

Then the Lady Margaret turned to Maddie. "Mistress Perry has been showing me the pieces of broidery anglaise your older girls are learning to work, and I think this lovely pattern of field flowers is your own design."

Maddie blushed scarlet.

"I see that it is. It is oddly conceived and very charming. I thought how well it would suit a country church for an altar cloth. Surely to work together for such a purpose would be as great a joy to these children as to daughters of gentlefolk who learn fine needlework in a nunnery school. If I sent cloth of silver, would you like to have those who do the best samplers work your design on it?"

"Oh—if we shouldn't be spoiling fine material!"

"I don't think you will spoil it, my dear. And I know where it can be used. Master Skelton who was once my grandson's tutor is vicar of a church in Northumberland, and I am gathering gifts for it. Could you extend the pattern for a longer stole?"

The work was spread out now, and three heads bent over it while the guest discussed stitches and patterns as seriously as Maddie and Alison. Crede, sitting a little apart, holding Fand who had found her again and meant to take no chance of losing her, thought that they seemed curiously alike. They were absorbed in this moment as perfectly as if it curved to contain them in a separate drop of time, taking it confidently and happily for its own value. Yet how unlike in all their circumstances—

the Lady Margaret whose will shaped great events, Alison who had been cruelly tossed about by fortune and had won only a small harborage to serve in, Maddie who asked so little for herself that it seemed she might always stand aside. Out of worlds so different how had they come together with understanding? Crede wondered.

There was a knock, rather timid and hesitating, but repeated twice at the door.

"It will be my poor Bella." The Lady Margaret laughed and got to her feet. "I leave her in the litter with a half-hour glass and the task she hates of knocking twice when I have overstayed my time anywhere."

She took her leave with a simple friendliness which did not exact formality, but now Crede saw her separately again. This was the great lady who was meddling in Win's life. Crede was annoyed with herself for having been charmed out of her hostility.

When the Lady Margaret had gone, Maddie picked up the silks and patterns and Alison set the table for supper. They must make it a party to honor Crede's return, she said, and while they were preparing it Thorne porters brought Crede's sea chest to the door.

Maddie looked puzzled.

"Crede is paying us a visit," Alison explained.

"Aunt Serena can't turn everything into make-believe!" Maddie said with surprising violence. "It is all right about me if it pleases Father, and I can still see him. But this is too much."

"Why Maddie, what is wrong?"

"Sometimes I think she wants to be the only one who does anything for Father. She puts a wall around him. Yet when she says something will upset him I am always afraid to risk it."

"Your aunt may be overcareful, Maddie," Alison interposed gently, "but she is very devoted."

"I think she might have let me talk about Crede and keep Father reminded of her while she was away! You know how easily he forgets, Crede, and now I suppose Aunt Serena has told you that it would confuse him if you were there!"

Maddie's distress touched Crede. She could see again how difficult Maddie's situation was for one so affectionate, yet she could not help feeling relieved that her own escape was made easier than she had expected. Sometime, somehow, she would manage to improve things for Maddie too.

"You mustn't worry about me, dear," she said. "I haven't even seen Dame Serena yet. I wanted a visit with you and Alison."

"And we want you here," said Alison warmly. "Supper is ready, and we have better than a minstrel to entertain us. Maddie, we'll be the first to hear all Crede's adventures."

[266]

Reassured that Crede had not been ill used, Maddie was ready to enjoy herself. They sat at table, with Fand curled in Crede's lap carrying on an odd duet of purrs and complaints, her small body quivering with her tangled emotions. She held Crede's hand clutched between her paws while Crede managed her food with the other and soothed Fand's feelings by bringing her name frequently into the conversation.

In reply to eager questions Crede gave Maddie and Alison as vivid a description of Antwerp as she could and a picture of Caspar which charmed them, but one adventure she left out.

When supper was over she opened her chest, for there were gifts in it, and she felt a child's eagerness to show what she had found for them. Fand immediately jumped into the chest, escaping from them all with one of Crede's best gloves which she naughtily pretended to mistake for a mouse; but it was a relief to find her in a mood for mischief again. They let her keep her trophy and returned to the exciting business of unpacking. Everything had to be admired . . . the carved box whose compartments held spices and condiments, some of which would be new even to Mona . . . the carefully rolled copy of a map of the world made by Juan de la Cosa who had sailed with Columbus. Cousin Allie would be delighted to find on this Bristol's discoveries marked with English flags down a long coast . . . the extravagant curiosity for Adam, a Nuremburg egg which marked the hours like the great clock in church towers though it was small enough to carry.

She brought Alison's present out a little anxiously, for the Venetian merchant's price was something she hoped Alison could not guess. It was a gown of Italian silk in the shade of lavender-blue which sometimes edges the horizon during St. Martin's summer, and it was finely worked with gold and silver threads and had a silver girdle. Crede explained that the Venetian had told her this gown was designed for a great lady who had turned to a religious vocation, relinquishing such adornments. When she held it up to Alison now, it was exactly right for her, as she had known it would be, and Alison exclaimed with pleasure, her cheeks turning pink as Crede and Maddie admired her.

"You chose something so beautiful for me!" she said, and Crede knew that it was all right, that Alison was not measuring the gift in silver marks but in the affection that had known so well what would suit her.

The gift for Maddie was quite different. Crede lifted out the plain wooden box she had bought from a Florentine, and Maddie's eyes grew round as she opened it. Bereft of speech she sat on the floor, surrounding herself with the pots of pigment it contained, and gloated.

They were in the midst of this when Adam came. It was Alison who opened the door and greeted him gaily.

"You deserted us for supper tonight," she said, to Crede's surprise. "You can't have known who else would be here—come inside!"

"I saw Robin at Thames Street."

His voice warned Crede that he had come straight here in anger. She had promised herself that she could have a reasonable talk with Adam and bring him round, but she knew well that when Adam's temper was roused it brooked no delay. He strode into Alison's parlor, apparently so much at home that the storm was going to break here and now, and Crede stepped forward to meet him in some trepidation.

"You know what I've got to say, Crede!"

Alison turned a startled face toward Crede, and Maddie, still surrounded by her paint pots, looked up in bewilderment. But sooner or later they must know that Anthony had the *Swallow* and it was better not to make a mystery now.

"Please don't go, Alison," she said. "What has Robin told you, Adam?"

"Robin told me that you thought best to dispose of the *Swallow* and buy this—tub. That is the story Harry Blanket and the crew had to take from him, too. Nat told me a different one, though he seems to have kept his own counsel with the rest."

"I have explained to Nat that I made the *Swallow* over to Anthony."

"That explains why he was clubbed and you were carried off, I suppose. Mother of God, only for Robin—how could you trust yourself with that young scoundrel? How can you shield him now? And what has got into Robin to abet it passes belief."

"Robin knows that I intended Anthony to have the *Swallow*, and what happened was—just a misunderstanding. I gave it to him freely, and I wrote Clem that it is entirely his."

"Philip's ship! Do you know how it will be used, or do you care nothing for your father's memory? By all the saints, Crede, I had rather you'd stolen from him while he lived."

"Adam!" Maddie was on her feet with a scattering of paint pots. She flung her arms around Crede and faced him in a fury no one could have thought her capable of. "Crede has never done anything dishonest in her life! And her father—don't you dare speak as if—don't you dare say such things!"

Maddie's championship waited on no explanations. Crede squeezed her arm gratefully, but it was toward Alison she turned. Adam had not hurt her so sharply as Maddie feared, for he had said nothing she had not thought of herself and she had expected him to say it. But she had told herself then, if I could talk to Alison, Alison might understand.

"I had to trust Anthony," she said. "I had to believe that when I showed him I do trust him he must remember how much Father hoped for him. Father did want to help him, Alison. Even after Tony ran away he tried to. I think Father would have risked something."

"I don't know all this story yet, Crede," Alison said slowly. "I can't half understand it. But I am as sure as Maddie is that you have done nothing deliberately wicked or forgetful of your father. I know that he was concerned for Cousin Sara's boy. He told me that he blamed himself for having somehow failed with him, and I think that he might understand whatever it is that you have tried to do now. Philip might have taken a risk too—you are very like him. I think you might remember that, Adam."

"I do," Adam said very quietly.

Crede, glancing toward him, surprised by the change in his voice, saw Adam for the first time with dismay in his face.

"I had no right to say what I did, Crede. Philip might find it harder to forgive me. I may still think this a foolish generosity, but I couldn't always understand things Philip was driven to do, and you earned a better right to speak for him. I'll help you with this—Oh, well, nothing more needs going over tonight."

He turned away suddenly and was out the door.

"Adam has his own kind of generosity," Alison said, "and no one's is finer. Crede, do you want to tell me what happened? But not now, dear, if you don't feel like it—you look very tired. Sit down here beside me. Adam's temper and Maddie's," she added with a quick smile for Maddie, making a place for her too on the settle, "have put us all in need of a breathing spell."

Yet Alison and Maddie must have been puzzled to make rhyme or reason of what they had heard, and they had heard enough of Nat's talebearing to disturb them. Even with Alison Crede had to pretend that Tony had been given the *Swallow* before her trip down-river. Though her brief account made her own adventure as accidental and unalarming as possible, Alison looked grave.

"Anthony is utterly wild," she said. "Crede, you must promise me never to take such a risk with him again. Don't look so frightened, Maddie— we have her safe home. And come to bed now, both of you. Do you want to make her bed, Maddie? You shall have Win's room, Crede, for Maddie shares mine."

She lit their candles, and when Maddie had gone upstairs she held Crede for a moment. "We can pray that what you have done for Anthony may touch some good in him, dear. Crede, I can guess the parts you won't tell against him, and I give thanks for Robin's good care of you. But I can guess other things too. Robin is so young," she said, and sighed. "Things he cares for deeply he can make no compromise with, and he has always been without fear for himself. Because of that he is the kind of idealist who can be hurt badly."

After Adam's outburst on the night of Crede's arrival he became his old self again, handling the *Katerine*'s business without further sign of resentment. Master Blanket would sail her home while Adam and Crede rode Grey Knight and Bess. But by disposing of her cargo first, Adam suggested, they could take on London goods for Bristol with a second profit. He needed the time, besides, to give Robin an account of his stewardship here and to work out an arrangement between them for other Canynges voyages this way or Thorne voyages westward. By exchanging such help both offices might extend their trade with advantage. This was the proposal he had brought with him to London, and he seemed increasingly taken with it.

Crede let him have his way. Only in Bristol, she felt with growing urgency, could she get her bearings; but with the promise of Bristol so near she spent this time with Maddie and Alison as a holiday from her own affairs. Their little household of three women arranged itself companionably. Adam brought Robin there with him often enough that Maddie found Crede's separation from Bishopsgate Street part of the same circumstance as her own—something which time must solve—and she and Alison spoke of Crede's Bristol journey as a short visit home.

Adam came to see them at least once a day. It seemed to have become a habit for him to drop in at suppertime, often bringing a present from the cookhouses. Sometimes, to Crede's astonishment, he came before the Dame School was out.

She could never have imagined Adam coming willingly into such a melée. He would sit down in a corner of Alison's crowded parlor among a litter of hornbooks and samplers, watching Maddie work out a needlework pattern with as much interest as if it were a problem in navigation. As he always had a pocketful of sweets to distribute at the end of the session, school was apt to be dismissed in some confusion.

Fortunately it had already been dismissed on the afternoon of Adam's arrival with Beaumains. The three instructresses were rather wearily restoring order after a large turnout when they glanced up to see Adam standing in the open doorway, looking a little unsure of his reception and holding one end of a leash. Beaumains was on the other end of it. After wrinkling his forehead and trying anxiously to look full grown and equal to any situation, he suddenly sat down on his haunches with an engaging smile and one ear cocked for the admiration his instinct told him would be forthcoming.

"Oh, you sweet, ugly darling!" Maddie said.

Beaumains, approving the tone of her sentiments, fell upon her with a flurry of ungainly legs and tail and a long, wet tongue.

"He likes you," Adam said unnecessarily, "and I'd feel a deal safer when we leave two women here alone if you will keep him. He comes of good mastiff stock from a kennel in Houndsditch, and when he is full grown very few on two legs or four would face him. But he will be quite gentle with anyone you approve. If you train him to go about with you, Maddie, I'd have an easier mind, for you do too much running back and forth alone between here and Bishopsgate Street."

"Indeed he shall be kept," Alison said. "He is just what Maddie needs, and I wonder sometimes, Adam, how you see the short, simple answer so quickly."

Maddie's remarks were still directed to Beaumains, who found them fascinating. When Alison extended a hand he recognized that it was well intentioned. Released from Adam's hold, he explored the room like a hurricane, gaining confidence and force.

A clumsier animal she had never seen, Crede thought on more than one occasion. He was a sad contrast to Fand's elegance, and before they could live under the same roof in peace Fand had to teach him several sharp lessons in deportment. He had come without a name, for Beaumains was Maddie's choice, out of Sir Thomas Malory's story, and it could only be hoped that he would turn out to be a "gentil parfit" knight. But his devotion to Maddie was from the first moment absolute; and as he grew almost visibly every day Alison said that Maddie could soon walk out of Christendom across the Turk's domain in perfect safety. The immediate problem was to teach Beaumains to cross London without creating an uproar. Adam vowed that before he left Beau should know the meaning of "to heel," and he began to call in at Cordwainer Street several times a day to help Maddie walk him.

On the day before the one which Crede had finally got him to set for their departure, it was her own manners he took in hand. When he arrived that morning he announced, "I have told Mistress Fenton we are coming to say good-by this afternoon."

"Don't you think, Adam, it would be better—"

"No, I don't," Adam said. "Dame Fenton may prefer not to disturb her brother, but if you and I are to face Mistress Mona you had best remember enough of her teaching to pay a call of common courtesy." Suddenly he put his arm around her. "If only Philip were here, instead of a clumsy ox like me!"

Robin opened the door and Dame Serena waited in the hall, as fine as an alderman in purple silk with a gold chain. Never before had Crede seen her dressed with such worldliness or looking so plump and content. The hall seemed different too. An embroidery frame near the window, ballad sheets on the table with a lute nearby, and flowers everywhere, gave it an air of intimate use which it had lacked before. While the furniture was the same, there was a shining look about it, as if it and its mistress were now on affectionate terms.

Dame Serena was very much its mistress as she seated them with ceremony and produced the hippocras and almond cakes kept for visitors. She even offered the politely-disinterested conversation reserved for such occasions. Robin and Adam did most of the talking.

"How soon are you coming to Bristol, Robin?" Adam said suddenly. "Perhaps you and I could take a turn about in the winter, when we are both less busy, if you would trust me again to manage here."

He had brought this out very casually, but Crede suspected that he had given it some thought, and she wished that he would let Robin make his own plans.

"We might arrange it in the slack season," Robin said vaguely. "Thank you, Adam. You know how well I can trust you with anything."

"I believe Adam must be losing his heart to London!" Crede said lightly, but to her surprise Adam flushed and seemed to find it necessary to justify himself.

"Anyone must be taken by it. I wager it will outstrip Antwerp some day, Robin. It has a security to grow in that can't be counted on across the Continent, where kings and nobles are still at the old feudal game of snatch and grab across their borders."

"Even there kings are getting strong enough now to set their houses in order," Robin said. "I suppose our new danger is that kingdoms grown more united can step harder on each other's toes. Sometimes I wonder whether nations may not be both too large and too small a grouping."

"Meantime, 'Let England keep the sea, environ,' as the old rhyme says." Adam smiled confidently. "We have a king at last who has the sense to bound our island with our ships and give us the best law and governance we have ever known."

"Some of it is lawless enough when he lets Empson and Dudley enforce it. This week our neighbor, old Master Pringle, was summoned on a trumped-up charge, and bought his freedom with a fat fine for cheating the King's beam, though I know that his accounts are kept as honestly as our own. Yet a jury of London citizens dared not stand up for him."

Adam frowned. "I was talking in the main, remembering worse days than you remember. There are wrongs, of course, yet sometimes it is no use charging against a stone wall. You are young and hotheaded, Robin, but I expect the jury saw it could do no good by making trouble."

" 'Howbeit they are good men, Moch herted like an hen,' " Robin said bitterly. "You don't see as much of it under your nose in Bristol. If you were here long, your stomach would turn too."

"It is foolish to brood over Master Pringle paying a fine he can well afford," Dame Serena said. "I have noticed you in poor spirits lately, Robin, and you might remember that your father likes cheerfulness, especially at meals, and that I try to make them an occasion. Fortunately he can enjoy Father Vincent's company at supper tonight, and their game is keeping him happy now."

She glanced toward the window, and Crede could see through it into the changed garden where space had been made for a bowling green. Master Thorne was clapping his hands at a good shot and running after it boyishly. Like Dame Serena he looked plump and pink and flourishing. Both of them seemed to have grown larger and sturdier, as if their bodies were defying age. Crede, thinking suddenly of Cousin Allie, who had to be reminded of food and sleep in the excitement of all that he must learn and do in his shortening time, wondered whether growing old might be a struggle between soul and body in which one or the other had to gain supremacy. In some old people the body had worn to an almost transparent garment, its demands lessening . . . Alison's spirit and the Lady Margaret's would outwear their frame.

When they had taken their leave, Crede found herself still in low spirits, although tomorrow was the day she had looked forward to. She and Maddie and Alison spent the evening pleasantly, knowing that it would take more than the miles between London and Bristol to separate them and making plans to meet again soon. But Crede's depression followed her to bed. She was too wakeful to hope for sleep and sat down by the window with Fand in her lap.

The house in Bishopsgate Street had always an unfortunate effect upon her, she thought resentfully. Yet it need no longer oppress her. It had found its own contentment, and within it Dame Serena and Master Thorne seemed happily enclosed. From the beginning of his hallucination they had been pleasanter to deal with than either had been before, discovering more grace in living, giving others more freedom.

Was truth only what served one best to live by? But this seemed to Crede more dreadful than all the sorrow and wickedness and failure she knew. Even some comforts of the Church had seemed to her too much what men desired or what would cunningly make them good, and she had feared them. If there was no truth, true in itself—if you could make it for comfort or convenience or even for better living, what meaning could there be in anything? Love, or hope, or honor, or duty, or courage, or compassion were only part of the illusion you had made, unless behind them there was truth toward whose worth in itself these human yearnings groped.

Father believed there was, she thought, and for the first time she could bear to examine the last words between them. He had set truth so high that even to comfort me he would not make more of it than the faint glimpse he thought that he had seen.

Men had died in torment, both for the Church and persecuted by it, because they would not change the vision of truth that had come to them. Some had mistaken their vision perhaps, or perhaps the part they saw did not agree with other parts because no one, yet, could fit them together. But unless there was some whole, whence came this impulse that set the mind to search for it and the spirit to yearn, counting easier pleasures and life itself well lost? Crede, who could not endure bear-baiting or even hawking and had a squeamish stomach for most popular sports, comforted herself now with the hideous suffering of martyrs.

After she had been sitting for a while in Win's austere little room with his books about her and his table furnished for the long labors of scholarship—which through the ages had linked men's minds and forged a chain of their most selfless thoughts—reassurance touched her more gently.

Fand stirred, finding the place she liked with her head tucked under Crede's arm where she could feel the movement of breathing. She reached her paw out to clasp a finger.

We are one in this riddle of breathing and feeling, that curiously sensitive paw seemed to say. A dumb creature's trust could offer this wordless bond of fellowship between all living things which speech blurred and overlaid. Crossing the barrier between them it seemed to reach past still more mysterious barriers, toward a design men had always longed to see beyond their own separateness. The words that drifted into Crede's mind now came from one of Mona's songs out of the far, pagan past of Ireland—"I am the wind that whispers on the sea . . . I am a billow of ocean . . . I am the venture upon the rock . . ."

Fand's paw clasped and unclasped with slower rhythm. Sometimes not even this warmth of touch was needed. Sometimes it was a field flower's tiny perfection of beauty, or the patient leafing of a storm-twisted tree that brought this fleeting intuition of harmony. While Fand's purring stumbled drowsily, Crede grew sleepy at last.

V

Knowest thou a holy saint that men call Truth?
Canst thou tell us the way where that saint dwelleth?

PIERS PLOWMAN

TWENTY-FOUR

Riding home, Crede had needed only to close her eyes for a moment to see everyone there exactly as she had left them. Yet she had been so far away, and the time from spring until autumn had seemed so long, that it appeared a special providence to find them really unaltered. Fand must have felt this too, for she could not rest in any one spot until she had reassured herself of every other. She pattered about the house, recapturing the scent and feeling of all her favorite objects before she settled down with a sigh of contentment between Cormac's paws.

How little they had changed! Will was his dear old cross-grained self and, although a wide smile sat oddly upon him for a whole day after Crede's return, he was not too much mellowed to grumble that Knight's coat looked ill-cared-for and that Bess had been poorly shod. Sadie had grown astonishingly, both up and across, but she was just as red and white and inarticulate and devoted to the society of coneys, while Kate gave Crede the kiss of those who have been children together, with gossip and secrets in her eye.

Cousin Allie, who had loyally turned his mind to the counting house, released it again for interesting new speculations to be shared with his pupil. His enthusiasms burned as brightly as ever; although none of his projects had stirred the world, it had never occurred to Crede to judge him by this. Even now, when she returned with eyes freshened by absence, she knew that there was no blight of failure upon him. The uses to which he gave his talents demanded no personal reward of success. That the mind should aspire to know was the sum of his philosophy, and the greatness of that tradition contented him. Without such as Cousin Allie, who sought understanding for no gain that could be measured, Crede reflected, we might believe that by making the world prosperous enough for all to enjoy it and dealing justly, we could satisfy all our hopes. But he needed Mona's firm hand upon the details of daily living, and it was a relief to find that he had settled comfortably into his room, surrounded by a litter of books and papers which defeated even Mona, and talked no more of returning to his cottage.

Nothing could ever change Mona. Crede thought with thankfulness that she could see no more difference after this separation than she had seen through all the years before. Mona's step was as firm and her hand as competently over them all and her orderly household, making home an enduring estate in which each one's place waited through any absence.

Because of Mona, Crede's mother had never been shut away from it—her daughter had felt that golden presence always. And because of Mona this was still Philip's house, something he had made and set his mark on. Yet there was nothing morbid in Mona; it was in the heart of the house that its builders lived, in that sense of a continuing purpose which was Mona's strength, while the house under her busy hands refreshed and renewed itself, and her care of the living fitted it to their needs.

Both she and Cousin Allie spoke often of Robin, making plans for his next trip to Bristol. But they knew how closely he was tied now. And so did the friends and neighbors who welcomed Crede home and saw nothing unusual in a wife who had inherited responsibilities of her own coming back to attend to them.

There was plenty for her to do. Nevertheless, when the first excitement of homecoming had worn off she knew that she had not found the resolution she had hoped would be waiting for her here. It had seemed happiness enough at first to find them all the same—like stepping back in time. And that is the trouble, she thought. They have all been going on in a way that is still right for them, but I am trying to step back. In Antwerp, her imagination had been caught again by the sweep of trade; now, although they were doing so well on England's swift-rising tide that even the loss of the *Swallow* would be made up in a very short time, she could not feel the zest of moving on toward any end. It had turned out not to be enough for Father, she thought—but she could not hunt new worlds.

She was being forced close again to things of her father's and they remained dumb and lifeless. In Mona's philosophy, Philip's big room, built for the master and mistress of the house, was not to be shut away, and Crede had found it rearranged for her use. Mona had quietly cut off her escape; her own little room had been given to Sadie, so that Clem and Kate could have all the space under the gables at the top of the house to make a home for their growing family. This seemed so fair and pleased Kate so much that, as always in Mona's arrangements, no sensible person could disturb them. Crede's books were on the shelf with her father's, her workbox and oddments stood on the table beside his hourglass and precious globe. If she avoided this room and the green parlor as she had thought at first she must do, she would fail them in a way that Mona understood better than she could. She must not shrink from this sharp pain; by accepting it she must reach the deeper peace and loyalty that Mona knew.

She worked beside Mona, admitted once more to the inner mysteries of a household with its orderly rhythm of events and its special occasions when Father Ambrose or other old family friends shared their table with Adam who was a regular supper guest; or when Stephen Chalkraft came to town. Though Mona did not favor Stephen, she liked to show him how well they did here and to get messages from Bessie and news of the astonishing achievements of young Stephen at one month of age.

Crede stepped back also into her old place in the counting room and her old partnership with Adam. As they went about the shop and warehouse they received a very satisfactory report of Clem's stewardship. Clem was no scholar, though he was struggling hard with his letters and figures at night, but the intricacies of trade seemed to come to him by instinct, and he got on well with the men, besides. Adam suggested that they let him gain further experience this winter, that with the season so far advanced they need not change masters again on the ships. While Clem liked sailing the *Brigid*, the prospect of several months at home with his little family pleased him very well, Crede thought, though he thanked her stiffly. They were not on the best of terms. Clem had carried out her instructions about the *Swallow*, but he had been outraged by the heavy charge put upon his profitable accounts, and it would take time for his resentment to wear off.

The matter of the *Swallow* had affected Kate quite differently. She was bubbling with confidences as soon as she could get Crede's ear alone. She had seen Anthony, and she had gone herself to watch the *Swallow* sail down Avon with Sebastien Cabot's expedition which meant to winter in Amerike and find the passage to Cathay and return loaded with treasure. Bristol had given them its usual send-off, and Crede was relieved to find that Quayside had thought it natural enough after her father's voyage for another Canynges ship to be risked in a westward venture. Kate could tell her nothing of the *Swallow*'s crossing from Antwerp except that they had stopped to take on some Cornishmen. Among them was a ship's boy named Davie who was Tony's devoted shadow and had thereby won Kate's approval. In her fancy it was Tony who led the expedition and would win most fame and fortune.

"If there is no gold and spice in Amerike and no way through, the *Swallow* will not waste time in the north," she said. "Anthony will dare anything, and an Englishman can outsail any Spaniard. Why should they have all the gold of the south?"

This sounded like a quotation, for Kate's imagination was unequal to such a flight. Tony had fulfilled the letter of her conditions, Crede thought, but she had not diverted him far from piracy. The principle of this did not disturb her since, like everyone else in Bristol, she thought that the pope had no right to set a barrier across half the western ocean for Spain's enrichment; but the rashness of the little *Swallow*'s challenge did. Tony would always tempt providence. She could never make him safe and content—nor Davie whom she had led to him by an odd chance. All she had been able to do was to pay a debt from childhood and close the book.

It was uncanny that Mona, who knew so little of the circumstances, should understand this. She made only one reference to the *Swallow*. "It was worth a ship," she said and with no effort to explain herself went on to talk of other things.

When Crede looked about for some new incentive now, it was an idea of Robin's that came to her. Adam had told her in London that Robin was planning to give Thorne workers a share of any increased profits they helped to make. Canynges men were well treated, but this scheme was something new. She might carry it even farther, perhaps, and let those who wanted to leave their reward in at a risk have a real share in the venture.

Adam, who was so level-headed, said, "The Thorne men have never had as much chance to prove themselves as ours, but what they are doing with the greater freedom Robin gives them makes me think that this last notion of his may pay for itself too, though most masters would call it crack-brained. Robin is apt to have ideas different from other men's, as Philip had."

That startled Crede. Yet when she thought about Robin's idea it reminded her of her father: in an age when everything was growing bigger, Philip had been concerned for the odds which the new power of capital set against small independent workers and farmers—and small ventures, such as his own had once been. He had gone hunting a world of fresh chances in Amerike.

If Philip had not dared that . . . if he had not thought of making a new England across the world . . . or if he had been only his daughter . . . he might have turned to a plan like Robin's.

She did not, however, follow it immediately and did not even discuss it with Adam, though usually she was impatient to begin anything she put her mind to. Her restlessness was too indefinite to find outlet with any certainty. As she tried to give it direction she kept hearing again things that Robin had said, things that at the time had seemed no more than an easy acceptance. When she set herself to work she often remembered some detail of their work here together.

In the counting room the three boys had at last decided to master their job. No one knew what had come over them. Whether Adam had finally overawed them, or Clem's rapid rise had been near enough to something they might emulate to stir their ambition, or time had imposed its drab change on them, they were getting through enough work these days to shame Crede.

This morning their pens were industriously scratching while Crede, who had before her a long list of Tim Arden's requirements for making the *Katerine* "shipshape and Bristol fashion" according to his exacting requirements, sat without making a mark, an unedifying picture of idleness.

I need something to freshen me, she thought, and responded to a suggestion from Cormac that a walk was what they both wanted. He had roused himself from a nap under the table to stand by the door with his ears cocked and his eyes so plainly inviting her to accompany him that he must have sensed her restlessness, for Cormac seldom proposed anything. He would follow Crede or Adam at a call, but he trusted neither of them now to stay with him and seemed afraid to attach himself to any particular person. Fand was his closest companion, and since Fand found many interests in mouse holes and domestic matters that bored him and was not afflicted with long legs that needed tiring, he often went for solitary rambles.

Crede was touched by his unexpected gesture of companionship. They would have a good long walk, she decided. She took her warm cloak and they headed north across the Frome to the downs at a pace of his setting.

The downs were bare and brown, and the north wind which blew across them had already a taste of December in it. After a while she tired of facing it and turned southwestward toward Brandon Hill. She had not come here since her return to Bristol and now, of old habit, found her step quickening. There was a light in the chapel, but she went on past it to the rock she and Anthony had called their castle and sat by their lookout, drawing her cloak around her and coaxing Cormac to move closer for warmth.

The sky with low scudding clouds was too gray for the view she loved —when sunlight gilded Bristol and found patches of gold on the downs and blue in the river and brightened a wide horizon. Today the view seemed narrow and unfriendly. This was not the world she used to come here to look upon, secure in itself and reaching out confidently. Those ridges on the downs held the bones of tribe after tribe that had come westering, had reached the farthest west any of them knew, and had never found the Blessed Isles. The troubles they had sought to escape had come with them or had overtaken them again, and it seemed to her now that it was such troubles and not some wide new promise that hid in this overcast skyline. It hung there like the fearsome curtain of the Turk over Europe, and under its low clouds there lurked all the things men looked away from for a moment when their eyes followed the sun's bright path westward: sorrows none could escape, misunderstandings that divided, and the loneliness of each one's perplexities.

It had added to her unease lately that Adam too seemed restless, for no reason that she could discover. He had come back by choice from his North Country valley, finding that he had outgrown it as she had outgrown her childish adventures with Anthony. She knew that what he had taken upon himself then as a trust from Philip he would never swerve from. Nor could he be longing to sail the *Brigid* again. Adam's interest in every part of the business had grown beyond one ship; he had told her since their return that he would like to take the partnership her father had offered him and put his own fortune into it. It had been easy enough to agree upon a partnership already existing except in name, but though they worked together companionably Crede knew Adam too well to miss noticing something unsettled in him.

She had felt it first in London when he had delayed their departure. If she had not packed them off, she had told him teasingly, he would have waited for days longer to train Maddie's dog.

How could I have been so blind? she thought suddenly. Adam had followed Maddie about as anxiously as Beau; he could scarcely think her safe in broad daylight on Chepe, though Maddie was far from fragile; he had more often than seemed reasonable chanced to be passing Cordwainer Street with time on his hands. Maddie who was usually so shy had bubbled into speech and laughter as naturally with Adam as with Alison and herself, happily sure of his interest in her pupils or paintings or whatever engaged her attention. Her childish worship of Win had never expected him to share such things.

What seemed plain enough now had escaped her notice, Crede supposed, because of all the years when the *Brigid* had been Adam's only love and the North Country held vaguely all his plans for settling down. Adam who had been her hero in childhood had seemed to her Philip's contemporary then as well as his friend, and nothing had made her pause since to revise that impression. Yet Adam must have been quite young when he came to Bristol. The years after had seemed long while she was growing up, but they had not been many and, though Adam might be counting them too anxiously now, they had done nothing shabby for him. It was someone so proved and generous that Maddie needed to put her first, Crede thought. She had been born too unselfish to deserve the trials of dealing with a younger man; for it was apparent that young men had little understanding and were driven by unpredictable motives. Maddie and Adam are just right for each other! she thought—but while they were discovering it she had made Adam, who was loyally trying

[282]

to take Philip's place, feel it his first duty to bring her home, letting him see how unsure and restless she was.

She would not be so wrapped up in herself any more. For a moment she thought happily of bringing Maddie here for a visit. But Maddie would not leave Alison and the school just when Alison was losing Win, and Crede realized that what she must do was to free Adam to go to London this winter. She must show interest in the plan he had been taken with there of sending some of their trade eastward. She must re-assure him that she could manage here with Clem while he looked into possibilities for expanding the new partnership in that direction. Clem was not Adam, however. She was shaken with loneliness as she thought of losing Adam.

Yet although it was a hard thing to face, here was one step she could see ahead of her. Was this all that choosing meant—could you never see the whole of your way? She patted Cormac in sudden fellowship with limitations of understanding which conceivably troubled him too, and Cormac licked her face politely but remained closed in his own medita-tions.

As she stood up, stiff and rather cold, the sun broke through briefly, and the wide view she loved came clear. Instead of going down the path she stood for a moment while sunlight touched the river, and over the downs and Bristol the clouds parted to show blue sky far above, shading to green at the horizon.

This was the picture of home she had carried everywhere with her. London towered confidently on its rising ground and its river flowed southeastward toward the ports of the known world. But Bristol was overshadowed by the hills and downs which channeled the Avon toward the Western Ocean. For ages Bristol's ships had sailed on the edge of the unknown—then venturing farther into it as Philip had done.

"We need not know the end to be content with the venture," Philip had said.

The words came as clearly to her ears as if he were speaking them now. He had said that, not when he was sailing to Amerike but when he was dying . . . when she would not listen. In all the months since, groping blindly to hold something of him, she had reached only grief and rebellion, but now he seemed to touch her and speak in his own voice.

Tears filled her eyes, and she stood scarcely breathing. There was only that instant touch. Yet, like the shaft of sunlight that had parted the clouds to show what they had only hidden, it gave Philip back to her. Though she could not prolong it or understand it, she knew that their closeness had been restored . . . that in some way what we love is not lost, what we give to a high venture does not fail. Without straining thought farther she closed her eyes and rested for a moment in peace beyond searching or limiting with words.

She opened them when Cormac started suddenly to his feet, and she saw Mona coming up the path.

"Will went to Quayside," Mona said, "but after he had gone I remembered seeing you set off with Cormac as if for a longer walk, and I thought that it was here you might be."

She had come out with a cloak thrown over her house dress and cap, and she was out of breath.

"Mona, what is wrong?"

"Now, I don't think for a moment it is anything to worry about," Mona began with that indirection that frightens worse, "and Win hopes—"

"Win! Oh, be quick, Mona, is it Alison?"

"Win just rode in, and of course it is some stupid mistake, but Robin is in gaol."

This was so far from the fear which had leaped to Crede's mind that for a moment she could not grasp it. How could Robin have done anything disorderly! Only—if Win had ridden here it was no light matter of a night in the Watch's compter.

"Mona, what did Win say—what happened? What have they done with Robin? Not—not that horrible Newgate—"

"They are keeping him in some place called the Fleet."

But that was the King's prison, not even London's!

"Don't look so, child. Win says he is all right. And they can't keep him long on such a silly charge," Mona said disdainfully. "'Contempt of the King's Court,' Win called it, and you know that Robin's manners are excellent. Besides, it can be settled with a fine, Win says."

Then why hadn't they settled it at once? What were they all thinking of in London? Crede was hurrying down the path now at a pace which soon left Mona behind. They must pay anything, of course. How could they have delayed even a day, with Robin in some horrible, damp, plague-infested cell?

A vision of the King's Prison of the Fleet rose before her with its stinking moat and slimy walls, and the thought of Robin within them, for even the time that it would take her to get to London and free him, since nobody else seemed to be doing it, was unbearable.

She ran across Frome Bridge, scarcely noticing that she and Cormac were pushing their way now through the busy center of Bristol. The world had turned upside down when Robin, whose ways had seemed to her so settled and conventional, could be in this plight. For the Fleet was a dreadful place, a place of fever and disease—she seemed to see

[284]

Robin in some noisome, crowded dungeon. Suddenly she saw him more clearly than she had ever seen him before.

For how long had she taken his help that had been ready whenever she needed it, his cheerfulness and kindness and courage, without giving anything in return? Now, because of her stupidity, she was miles away when he needed her.

She was home at last. As she stepped into the hall she saw Win sitting at the table, while Kate heaped food before him and Adam and Cousin Allie hovered uselessly about. They all looked up as the door opened and she said, "Mona told me."

"Crede, don't look so desperate!" Win smiled and came toward her. "Robin was quite cheerful when I left him."

"Win, if it is only a fine, why isn't it paid?"

"Because Robin won't let it be." Win's smile faded and without it he looked tired and anxious.

"Robin is a young hothead!" Adam said violently, awakening an echo of something Crede had given no thought to since. "Ramming his head against a stone wall," Adam growled.

He had called Robin hotheaded before—it was about Empson and Dudley!

"Win, is Empson or Dudley in this? Do they pretend Robin's accounts are wrong, and he won't bribe them?"

"It is not exactly that," Win said slowly.

He explained that Robin had been called for jury duty in the case of a neighbor. The jury had testified for the defendant, but when fines were clapped on them for "false witness" they had all weakened and paid—except Robin.

"He wants to be tried for it, and Thomas More wants to defend him— if they can get it brought to court," Win said.

What would such a trial mean? If Robin defied the King's agents and accused the King's Court, could even Thomas More persuade a jury to be braver than others had been? But Robin would not change what he thought was right or be frightened from it! Adam had realized sooner than she that there were things in which he was not easygoing. And in the heat of such a trial, what charges might not be brought against him? There were a dozen hanging matters in English law—how far from treason was a deliberate quarrel with the King's ministers?

"'Nor will we go against a man save by the judgment of his peers,'" Cousin Allie quoted thoughtfully. "Now, who are Robin's peers if he chooses to stand alone for what he thinks the muddle of our English law means? Don't answer at once," he added unnecessarily, "for I have studied both the laws of England and the Roman Law, which most other countries use, longer than any of you, and I know there is no easy answer.

[285]

Without question the Roman Law is neater and more logical, as if it had been made to stand forever, and it is easier to know each man's place under it. Yet there is justice which the heart knows the meaning of in the circumstances of each age, and because circumstances change we must buy it over and over again by such things as Robin is trying to do. They weave a bright, unbroken thread through the patchwork of our English law."

He put his hand on Crede's and said hopefully, "I think I ought to go to London, dear. I am older and remember things which this young lawyer may not, and perhaps I can help."

Crede squeezed his hand and in the midst of her anxiety wondered whether they could keep Cousin Allie from making some spectacular new discovery about law and justice which would land him too in trouble.

"I don't think it will come to trial," Win said. "I doubt whether even Thomas More—who is fearless enough to want such a case—can get it to court. We all know that the King winks at the methods Empson and Dudley use to raise revenue and the law gets short shrift. Why should they make a parade of it when they could keep Robin locked up forever for an unpaid fine? That is why I think he is wasting himself."

Wasting himself in that dreadful place where they could keep him until prison hardships or fever rid them of him! And it was whispered that they had shorter, more secret ways to deal with opposition.

"What can we do, Win? Did you come with some plan?"

"The best thing we can do is persuade Robin to be sensible. I managed to see him once and tried. But"—Win met her eyes with a measuring glance—"I thought you might do better."

"Of course Robin is sensible," Mona said stoutly. She had come in a little out of breath but was now ready to take matters into her own hands. "You had better ride back with Win tomorrow morning, Crede, if he is rested enough, and everything will soon be settled."

"Today," Crede said. "It is early yet. Could you, Win?"

"I'm not a bit tired." Win smiled at her, and she smiled back gratefully.

"And, Adam—" she could think of no support she needed more than Adam's sturdy common sense. "Will you come, Adam? Clem can manage again while we are gone, if Cousin Allie—" She turned toward Cousin Allie and slipped her hand in his again.

All of them were anxious to help, standing solidly behind her. Yet nothing, not even Win's swift journey here, had touched her so close as Cousin Allie's understanding of Robin and his proposal to put his frail old bones on an animal he had the liveliest misgivings of, to ride forth to battle. "Clem will need help here," she said, "could you—?"

"I suppose there is nothing I can help with in London," Cousin Allie said wistfully, "if there is not going to be a trial. Of course Clem and I will manage here, dear."

"You knew that you had no need to ask me, Crede." Adam was half-way to the door. "If we use post horses as Win did and change them often we can travel faster. I'll see what they have at the Green Lattice, and I'll have a word with Clem before we set out."

"None of you will set out from this house before you have eaten a good dinner," Mona said. She went instantly into action. "Hurry dinner along, Kate! I'll pack your bag, Crede. Go and put on your warmest clothes, now. And Win, you lie down and rest until we are ready."

Crede paused on her way to the stairs. "Win, what kind of place is he in?"

"Not so bad, dear. He has a cell alone in the upper part. Thomas managed that, and he has money to pay for decent food."

"Did he ask—does he know you came?"

"Why, we had only a moment together," Win said. "It was afterwards I decided to come."

Robin had not thought of sending word to her. She had been foolish to hope that he might have wanted her near when he was in trouble. Indeed, why should he have expected anything from her, and what likelihood was there that he would listen to her more than to Win?

But there was no time for regrets now. She must think only how she could manage to help him and how soon she could get to him.

TWENTY-FIVE

Crede stood at Alison's front window, watching anxiously downstreet for Master More. Although it was not quite time to expect him she had her cloak on so as not to delay a minute if, as she hoped, he brought permission for her to see Robin.

This was her second day in London. Alison had taken her in again, and Adam had returned to his lodgings near the river, appointing himself to watch over the Thorne interests on Thames Street. He had called Robin a young fool, and the kind of risk Robin was taking was something he could not understand since his own loyalties were personal ones. But anything that was Robin's would be touched over his dead body. Crede thought that if an agent of Empson or Dudley crossed the threshold Adam would be guilty of something more violent than contempt. She took great comfort in him, nevertheless, and things seemed brighter when he came to the house at short intervals; for no situation could be too discouraging with Adam roused to its defense. Things which went awry only made him angry and his anger was a formidable determination to get his strong, capable hands on them and set them right.

It was not easy to see what could be done to improve this situation, however, if Robin persisted in his present course. Master More had been encouraging him in it, still hoping to get a case to court which could be a public airing of abuses. To do him justice, he seemed to have no more concern for his own neck than for Robin's. He was putting himself forward fearlessly, with the same lightheartedness in his kind and thoughtful eyes which had charmed Crede at their first meeting—it had frightened her a little when she talked with him yesterday. It was said that he wore a hair shirt and had once lived for a year with the monks of the Charterhouse, that strictest of religious orders which even London's growing secularism held in affectionate respect. Although he had decided to use his talents in the world and used them so brilliantly, Crede distrusted his care of things in this life. Even Win thought that he was dangerously impractical.

Win had given Crede his room and was sleeping at the rectory of St. Lawrence Jewry, where the Lady Margaret had arranged for him to read theology with Dr. Grocyn. But he was in and out during the day, impatient for news or action and, while it still seemed to Crede that he was preparing to waste his own life, she had never felt closer to Win than in his anxiety for Robin.

She found it easier to share Win's restlessness than Alison's confidence that we must do what is right without worrying about the outcome. Although Crede knew that it would cost Alison less to take risks herself, and her love showed its concern in unobtrusive kindness, the ideal she held up was too high for comfort.

"The best that can befall any of us," Alison had said while she and Maddie had waited upon Crede with cordials and hot bricks at the end of her exhausting ride, "is to find something we would stake whatever we have on. Sometimes," she added thoughtfully, "I feared that Win might find no single-minded use for himself."

This was the nearest she had ever come to explaining her content with Win's choice or why. She could think it right for Win to give all his talents to the Church and for her father to have chosen a martyr's death against it. Her voice died away as if she had been thinking aloud, but she continued briskly with her remedies against her guest's possible chill.

Maddie clung to Crede and cried distractedly, "I tried to see the Lady Margaret, but she is with the King at Richmond and ill herself. And if I could reach her, what can I beg of her if Robin is defying the King's ministers? Oh, Crede, I am so thankful you are here! You always know what to do, and there must be some way we can help him. I don't care about anything except having him safe."

Neither did Crede.

Master More was coming down the street at last, and she flung open the door and ran out to meet him.

"We can go right away," he said cheerfully and was kind enough to turn about at once and keep up with her breathless haste.

"Have you seen Robin? Does he know we are coming?"

"He can have no idea of the surprise his good lawyer has for him, and I expect to profit by his astonishment and raise my fee." Thomas More's eyes twinkled. "I have a pass to visit Robin and another client this morning, and the simplest way of bringing you, I decided, was to have your name included." He did not say how he had managed this or what trouble it might have cost him.

As they neared St. Paul's they were caught in a crowd which appeared to be gathering for some spectacle. Crede, who had forgotten that she was back in the main stream of London's business and pleasures in which one family's troubles caused no ripple, found herself facing this bustle with unaccustomed timidity.

"The Flanders Embassy is riding through this morning," Master More explained, offering his arm. "They are home with the new treaty and a delegation from the Emperor to celebrate the betrothal of young Duke Charles to our little Lady Mary. King Henry means to leave his throne well secured—a daughter to Scotland and now one to the Empire. And the Spanish marriage is in the air again for Prince Henry. It is a pity we have nothing left for France. But I give the King credit that I think he means it all for peace."

They had to pause while a procession passed in the pomp and glitter with which Henry Tudor knew well how to celebrate his successes, though his own appearances in London were so unspectacular. Among the horsemen Crede recognized Lord Hertley. This must be the embassy he had been sent in advance of, she supposed, returning to such rewards that his thoughts would surely be far above Maddie.

As soon as they could move again, they went out Ludgate to the Fleet. Its dank and evil odor reached out to them, but they were hurried through a fetid lower corridor into an upper passage which was a little fresher and along which a number of doors stood close enough together that they must lead to separate cells. The turnkey unlocked one of these.

"Go in, my dear. I'll visit my other client first," Master More said.

Robin looked up as the door closed behind her upon a small bare room. He was sitting on a bench under its high window with a book in his hands which fell to the floor, and for the drawing of a breath he looked as if he had seen a ghost. Then he sprang to his feet and covered the distance between them.

"Crede, you came!"

His arms crushed her, until after a moment he held her away from him as if he needed to see her better. Crede, with tears smarting her eyes, thought that she was crying because prison had already sallowed his face a little and its lean bones showed even plainer.

"I was afraid that I had dreamed you," he said.

"And I—couldn't even hope that you would care whether I came."

"My darling!" He was kissing her wet cheeks, and she clung to him, crying unashamedly now. "I thought you must always have known that I love you! But I had promised myself—I'd taken advantage when you were so distracted—"

"How can you love such a fool, Robin? I didn't know anything about either of us. I kept looking back to—to things I know now were only—"

"Don't abuse my wife!" He lifted her lightly and, carrying her to the bench, sat holding her in his arms.

"I can't quite believe I'm not dreaming still," he said. "Crede, I've always known how much you had to give, and I couldn't bear to take anything on sufferance. It was nothing less than this I wanted for us both—to find it like this—and I had given up hoping."

It was not a place of hope or happiness. A close, chill dampness was shut inside the cell as if its air had been locked away for ages from sun and freedom. On the stained walls and the grimy bench and table, carvings of mottoes and devices—some cut so long ago that they were now illegible—spoke of a nameless succession of dreary, desperate days, all still locked here too. But neither of them noticed it.

"How did you get here?" Robin asked when finally it occurred to him to question anything. "I shouldn't have supposed news would travel so fast. You must have ridden at risk of your neck!"

"Win carried it straight. Adam and I rode back with him, and Master More brought me here." All this was past now and unimportant. "Robin, Master More will be here in a minute. If we offer your fine at once you might be freed today! We'll pay anything to hurry them."

She jumped up full of purpose and energy. Robin would not refuse her. And now that this horrible place had been recalled to her, she could not rest a moment when haste might mean that he could walk out of it with her this very day.

"Wait, dearest." Robin's voice had changed. "Crede, I hadn't minded this until now that it hurts you. But someone has to do what I am doing."

"Not you! Robin, I can't risk you for anything. I can't bear you to be in this place—I'm frightened."

"You can see that I have come to no harm," he said and smiled at her. "Overcaution has never been a fault of yours, my sweet."

"Don't put me off! Do you think I can't understand—"

"I think that you can understand very well," Robin said quietly. "You know as well as I do that if a jury can be frightened from what it believes is just, it makes a mock of what other men have struggled hard to win."

She was studying his face as anxiously as if she had never seen it before. She loved even more what she saw, though she feared it. What he was doing, prosaically, was a test of endurance Tony would have been unequal to. The gay recklessness which had made Tony seem romantic was something Robin amused himself with only in play acting, as if he did not associate it with his own character. He made nothing of things he did in his own person, doing them so matter-of-factly that even she had been deceived. Her father, Adam, Alison, had all read him better and had known how dangerously far courage that never sees itself dramatically can go.

"Robin," she said desperately, "don't you realize that you could be kept here, just for debt, in this plague hole until fever or—"

"I'm fairly tough, dear. And Tom More is a stout friend."

"Even if he could ever get this to court it might be worse for you. The others gave in—they are honest men but they know it is no use. Win and Adam know it is no use. Dearest, do you have to go against them all? What good can it do?"

"I don't know," Robin said slowly. "Crede, sometimes a choice is put to you that you know you can make only one way, even though you can see no farther."

She dared not let him touch something that might force her to stand with him. "I had not thought you set yourself so high above others," she said. "You have never talked about making the world over new, as Dr. Erasmus and the rest do, yet now you are trying to do alone what not one of them would risk."

"They would if they thought it a big enough thing, some plan for a new order," Robin said wryly. "I don't hope that I can change matters greatly, dear. I think that new worlds and new causes have to be made up of the same people and their small choices, and are better or worse according to them. That is why I think we have to make whatever choices come to us as honestly as we can."

"I only know that you want to waste yourself here," Crede cried in bitter disappointment and pulled free of his arms. Enclosed by them, she had believed for a few happy moments that nothing else could matter, and now she made the only appeal that was left. "I thought you loved me."

The color left Robin's face. "If you care anything about either of us, Crede, don't make a coward of me."

She could not do that. Even if she could have changed him, she would not. And she had been shamefully unfair.

She reached blindly for him and cried against his shoulder, "Oh Robin, forgive me! I'll help you all I can."

He held her gently until she could manage to look up and smile at him.

"We'll win something together, dear. Call Thomas now, and let me hear how matters stand."

After that there was only talk of the case. Master More had been waiting to come in and he and Robin discussed legal points and made plans hopefully. When it was time to go, Crede had only a moment while Robin held her close.

He whispered, "Don't be anxious, sweet. I'll not take the least risk I need not. I have too much to lose."

She managed to leave him as if they might meet again tomorrow, reassuring him that Adam was managing things on Thames Street, asking whether he had the books he wanted and money enough to buy whatever he needed. She returned to Maddie and Alison with Master More who gave them a cheerful account of Robin. She agreed when he explained that since passes were hard to get it was best to ask for one only when they had some special reason. She got through supper with Win and Maddie and Adam trying to hide how much they had hoped from her visit. The evening ended at last, but how many more would be like it after fruitless days?

Through the night, while the Watch passed and returned again, she tried to keep the confidence she had found for a moment to answer Robin's and felt only that she could not bear to be apart from him. Their closeness was so new a thing that she longed for the reassurance of his arms around her; when he had said that they would win together she had shared his confidence for a moment because she could see and touch him. But nothing had been left for her to do except to wait in this loneliness and try to have faith in events she could not see any hope in—try to stifle fears which had whispered to her down the corridors of that pestilent warren that troublemakers need not live too long there.

All through her life Crede had been able to bear anything better than the helpless misery of inaction, and her courage could only find itself when she could find something for it to attempt. There must be something she could still do, she thought over and over, and lay with her muscles tensed to be up and about it, while the Watch went on its round . . . "One o'clock and a frosty night" . . . "Two o'clock and all's well" . . . She had heard curfew from St. Martin's when London closed its gates and was shut in upon itself for the night, and she heard the first bell of the morning from St. Thomas of Acon when the gates opened for the business of another day.

As it rang she knew what she was going to do today. She had scarcely thought again of Maddie's reference to the Lady Margaret, for she could see no more help there than Maddie could. But now it occurred to her that there might be a way, between this trial Master More wanted and the submission Robin would not make, which he could still take honorably. No one could refuse a royal pardon if it was offered. And perhaps the King would give this small rebuke to his ministers in a case of no great moment, if the Lady Margaret asked it for love of Maddie. She was fond of Win and Alison too, but Maddie who was so young and appealing would not raise questions and would speak only to her heart. It might be better not to have some things explained too lucidly.

She must have closed her eyes upon this; and when she opened them it was broad daylight and Maddie was coming into the room.

"I've slept in," she cried and felt wide awake on the instant. "Maddie, I'll be dressed in a minute and we must go to Richmond."

"Crede, you have thought of some plan! I knew you would."

"Even if the Lady Margaret is ill she may see you, Maddie." Crede was pulling her clothes on. "Help me tie these points, dear. We can talk about what you ought to say on the way. And we shall have to see about horses—"

Maddie looked dazed but hopeful. "Adam could see about the horses," she suggested. "Maybe he would ride with us.— Crede, how do you get into a palace?"

With Adam beside you it seemed possible to ride more confidently toward palace guards, or dragons or Turks, and apparently Maddie was discovering this. They would look better attended in his company too.

"We'll go to Thames Street first and ask him," Crede agreed.

She told Alison only that they were going to Thames Street and might persuade Adam to go riding, for somehow she did not want to explain her purpose. And Alison who pitied her restlessness made no objection except to say that some bread and brawn must be downed first.

The girls slipped away without Beau, for even Maddie felt that he would be no help. In the street outside she said, "Should we have a letter to leave? If we can't get in, I mean?"

"You do have splendid ideas, Maddie!" Crede was thinking quickly. "A letter might help us to get in. Maddie, Dr. Linacre is known at court, and if he would write a note—could you try to see him? You know him better than I do. And I'll get Adam to arrange about the horses."

They separated, and Crede hurried toward Thames Street, passing the Lady Margaret's town house of Coldharbor on the way. Its great gate, which led through an arch under the steeple of All Hallows' the Less, was standing open, and smoke was coming from all the chimneys. It seemed to her that more than the servants must be using it. While she hesitated in the lane that led to the gate, a tall man with an air of authority and the gray habit of a Franciscan passed her to enter it.

"Father!" Crede ran forward upon impulse.

"*Pax vobiscum,* my daughter."

"Father, have you news of the Lady Margaret? Forgive me—but I heard that she was ill."

Very keen brown eyes studied Crede's anxious face; his smile was gentler than his haughty bearing. "Good news then, my child. The illness was not serious."

"She is here?"

"She moved from Richmond where there is too great a stir on account of the Flanders lords."

"I have need to see the Lady Margaret, Father."

The smile faded. "The Lady Margaret would spend herself for every need, but she is not well enough yet to hold audience."

"You will see her, Father?"

"I cannot take a message." He turned to go.

He had entrance here while others would be refused, and it seemed to Crede that chance had put a thread into her hand which she must not lose. She must at least find out how soon they could hope to be admitted. "Father, if I wait here for your return, will you tell me how she does?"

The penetrating eyes studied her again. "It will do no harm, my child, for you to wait in the hall out of this wind."

Before she could reconsider her impulse she was inside, the emptiness of the great hall proclaiming that its mistress was not yet openly in residence. While the servant who had admitted them waited to conduct him farther, the Franciscan pointed out a seat by the fire and said with kindness in his voice, "Sit there and warm yourself. You look white and chilled."

He seemed quite at home here and had been admitted with the respect due a person of some importance. King Henry favored the Franciscans, Crede knew, and perhaps the Lady Margaret did too. At the foot of the stairs he turned back and said, "Remember, my daughter, to pray for help in this trouble that I can see in your face. But if there is any sin of yours in it you must go to confession and pray first to be delivered from that, and there must be no hardness in your heart for anyone."

"Father, do you love Empson and Dudley?" Her protest had been impulsive, but surely he would not love them either. The Church did not love their reaping ahead of tithes and their nibbling at the rights of Church courts and sanctuaries.

He had turned to go, but he paused and looked at her sharply. "What is this?"

"It—it is just that Madeline Thorne whom the Lady Margaret has been kind to hopes to see her as soon as may be."

"You shall tell me more of this later. Be sure to wait," he said and hurried away.

What had possessed her! First she had given this stranger a hint of her errand and then in sudden confusion had blurted out their own name.

She had felt some strength and kindness in him when she needed them badly, had been seized by an instinctive trust and an impulse to hold fast whatever it was that fate seemed to be offering from the instant she had noticed that open gate. But it was her own impatience for action which had led her on, the urgency to be doing something. She might have done harm to her own careful design, she thought miserably. For it was a delicate matter to keep Robin's case separate from dangerous undercurrents and a tangle of intrigue, in which the Church too was concerned. She should have trusted no one.

She would have liked to escape now, but she had said too much and had to stay to mend it if she could. In a confusion of anxious plans and misgivings she waited, staring into the fire without noticing anything about her or the passing of time.

She was startled by the friar's return. He was standing beside her before she was aware of it.

"The Lady Margaret wishes to see you, my child."

Crede caught her breath sharply.

"Sit still a moment," he said. "I found the Lady Margaret much better. When the matter in which she had sent for me was settled I mentioned the name you had given and her interest was so warm that I told her what I knew of your errand. It suits me very well to help errands of that kind, so you need not thank me."

Crede was not at all sure that she wanted to thank him. She was not ready for this, and Maddie could have done much better. She had only wanted some assurance that Maddie would be admitted.

"The servant is waiting," said the Franciscan. He put his hand on hers for a moment, "Don't hope too much, my child. The Lady Margaret has the King's ear, but in the case of certain names we have mentioned it is a deaf one."

Crede managed a word of thanks and followed the servant who led her upstairs and through a long gallery. A door off it was opened by a young lady in waiting, while an older woman sat inside it at an embroidery frame. Across the room a day bed was drawn close to the fire, and among its cushions the Lady Margaret, in a loose velvet gown lined with fur, looked smaller than ever. But her voice was strong and quick as she cried, "Come here, child." The lady in waiting stepped back, and Crede crossed the long room alone.

The Lady Margaret's eyes turned to her with surprise in them—had she thought that Maddie herself waited below? Crede's confusion increased. She made an awkward curtsy and stood tongue-tied.

The Lady's remarkable memory served her. "It is the little sister, Mistress Thorne? Tell me quickly, what trouble is my Madeline in?"

"It is her brother—my husband's trouble concerns us all, Your Grace, and Maddie has wished to see you. I didn't expect—"

"Don't beat about the bush, child."

Crede told her story as briefly as she could, praying her own Saint Brigid's help to put it so that Robin's stand against an unfair trial could be kept clear of higher and more dangerous matters. He had said himself that he was only doing the small, immediate thing which seemed right to him.

"Your Robin has a stiff neck," the Lady Margaret said at the end of it. But her firm mouth curved slightly. "It is not a fault I may condemn. Sit on that stool, child. I have questions to ask."

Crede sat down in trepidation, beseeching Saint Brigid again to guide her wits. In sudden emergencies Mona's teachings prevailed over speculations set loose by Cousin Allie's.

"Whose plan was it to come to me?"

"Only mine and Maddie's, Your Grace," Crede said hastily. "Robin would not dream—"

"I thought not. What does he hope to accomplish?"

"Robin said," Crede answered slowly and prayerfully, "that we have to concern ourselves with the small choices which come to us and that sometimes there is only one way we can choose honestly."

"Not trusting our own judgment rashly but with the help of our spiritual confessors," said the Lady Margaret who was notably orthodox. A smile touched her lips again. "I don't doubt that he would have it. I have been talking with Friar Anselm."

"He knows nothing of this case," Crede cried in alarm. It was enough that Robin should be risking himself for the law without setting up for the Church too! "Your Grace, no one has put Robin forward in this. He was called in a neighbor's trial, and it is a small matter of his own fine now—"

"But he sees a little farther into it, I think, than that. How far?"

"In the matter of a jury's verdict he could not—he thought that he must stand by the law—"

"Is it in such danger in the King's Court that he must stand against the King's ministers?"

This was the issue she had feared that Master More would stir up—and this was the King's mother! Oh gracious Mary, pray for us, I should not have come here, Crede thought, fighting panic.

"Not against them," she said faintly. "Only for something that—that they may sometimes forget our King has such care for—"

"I think myself," the Lady Margaret said in a surprisingly friendly voice, "that certain ministers may sometimes overlook wrongs which the King would right if he could know every case. And," she added after a pause and as if speaking to herself, "to mend one small matter easily will not prove it."

She seemed to have forgotten Crede for a moment, and then the bright, dark eyes returned to her.

"I could, of my favor, ask that someone who has won my interest in a small case be set free."

Crede's heart leaped.

"But I doubt whether your husband is thinking so much of that as of other such cases. My child, do you want me to stop what he thinks it is right to do?"

Crede had told herself that she was not doing that. But now she could see, too well for comfort, what the Lady Margaret meant. Because they had her favor Robin might be set free without paying the fine which others had paid, but he would think that no more honest. She had only made herself believe that such special treatment could alter what he had thought he must stand against. When she had promised to help him she had been thinking only of having him free and safe.

"I was wrong to come," she said and got to her feet blindly.

The Lady Margaret put out her hand, not to be kissed but to hold Crede's in a firm clasp.

"We never know when we may be touched close," she said softly, "or what instruments God may choose. He does not always choose what we think of consequence." She seemed to have forgotten Crede again, but then the strangely youthful eyes looked for a moment straight into hers. "I won't keep you, my dear. You may go now. But never lose heart when you have been worth showing a hard way that is right. It is not the risks we have taken that we regret but those we feared to take."

Crede had never any clear recollection of how she got out of the room and the house. She had gone through swift changes of anxiety and sudden hope, and then had faced this hard resolution which she had seemed to take in spite of herself. When she was outside the gate she felt that she must have a moment's quiet somewhere before she met anyone, and she turned into All Hallows' Church.

It was between the hours of terce and sext, and the small, rather dark nave was empty. There were no prayers in its winter chill and dampness except her own, and no forms she had been taught seemed to fit them. Doubt pressed closer.

For what hope of setting things right in this world must we put our own dearest hopes in hazard? Yet, here upon earth, something spurred men to risk known things for the sake of those which a conviction they could not silence called more just and true, and closer to a pattern that they dimly saw.

Perhaps we had been placed here not only to fit our souls for heaven, but to help complete the pattern, she thought. Perhaps the two worlds had been bound closer than we knew, with the choice of which we would live in always before us. We could not foresee how such choices would come to us and, because of this, we could not plan a whole life for ourselves as she had once thought—or choose for those we loved.

Could it be that God needed us to help with His purpose, even His purpose for eternity . . . needed our small choices toward such things as truth and justice and love and constancy, because these had not been established in some safe, far haven beyond the struggle of our straining toward them . . . must still be won? In straining toward them we could feel the strength of God reaching out to uphold us, the love of God that cares for us and for the sparrow.

Philip had called the venture good enough. Crede felt his nearness again, answering with her, by some instinct in them both, to a yearning of pagan ancestors who had been buried, sword in hand, to fight beside their god. Somehow this ancient heresy wove itself into the peace and promise of the Church while she prayed—as, perhaps, many gropings, but dimly understood, could find their place in a promise that the One who gave it had called a house of many mansions. Her anxious care for Robin was enfolded by it.

A candle was burning by one of the stations, and she lit another from it, remembering that Philip had done this once beside her in St. Mary's, saying, "Watch the flame ascend, and be content. Do not always pray for the descent of blessings."

Then she went to Thames Street to find Maddie and Adam waiting anxiously. Maddie was in the little office behind the counting room in a state of complete distraction, while Adam paced like a bear in a cage. At sight of Crede his anxiety exploded in wrath.

"Where in heaven's name have you been, Crede? Maddie has you dead and buried, and I have been sent every place she could think of. Did you have to frighten her like this?"

"Never mind, so long as you are all right, darling," Maddie said, clutching her. "I was a goose to worry, but such dreadful things seem happening

[298]

to us. What kept you? We have to change our plan anyhow, for Dr. Linacre says that the Lady Margaret—"

"I know," Crede said slowly. "I saw her house open—and I went in."

Maddie's eyes opened wide with astonishment, but then they brightened with her confidence that Crede could manage affairs whose complexity baffled her. "Crede, did you see her?"

"She is quite of Robin's mind, Maddie dear. She made me understand that we must not interfere with him."

She would tell Maddie the details later, but she was not able to make a long story of it now.

"Stuff and nonsense!" Adam said angrily. "But we don't need her help." He put his arms round the girls. "Stop worrying, both of you. I hear the talk along Thames Street, and Robin has plenty of good friends. He can't be shut away and forgotten, and to touch him would stir up a hornets' nest of grievances simmering here. Very few, king or common, have ever roused London without ruing the day."

Adam, who had pointed out the folly of running one's head against a stone wall, would be the first in any assault, where those he loved were concerned, Crede thought. As usual she found comfort in him, and Maddie looked less forlorn when he announced that he would walk home with them and stay for dinner.

TWENTY-SIX

Alison asked no questions about their morning outing. While Crede and Maddie made a poor pretense of eating dinner, she talked about her pupils.

A persistent aversion to hornbooks was still her chief problem, she explained. It was hard to say what was so offensive about hornbooks; indeed, their shape pleasantly suggested a popular game. Across the face of a flat wooden bat was printed the alphabet, or crisscross row which began and ended with a cross, and under this were the numbers from one to ten and the Lord's Prayer, the whole protected by a thin film of horn. According to pedagogic theory, memorization of the alphabet led to a perception of its use in the prayer and by divine guidance to reading and writing. But whenever the hornbooks were brought out, half the class remembered duties of extreme urgency at home. It would help greatly, Alison said, if Crede could arouse new interest in this part of the curriculum.

When she was asked to struggle with the Dame School just after her exhausting interview with the Lady Margaret, Crede thought this was the last straw—all the worse because she could not refuse Alison who so rarely asked anything. But it helped to fill that afternoon, and it was something to help fill the days that followed.

They were long and dull. The anxiety she had felt while she was riding as fast as she could to London, while she was waiting to see Robin, while she was planning an appeal to the Lady Margaret, had been easier to bear, she thought now, than anxiety which could only wait on things beyond her help. Master More saw Robin occasionally and carried messages. He was working diligently and cheerfully in their behalf, but in these gray days Crede could see no hope of change except for the worse.

Why was it that she could not hold the moment she had touched in All Hallows? It was depressing to find that one could rise to noble thoughts and a hard resolution without the effect on one's character which might have been hoped for. Crede's temper was becoming a trial to herself and others, and one particular outburst was enough to shock anyone.

One afternoon from the best of motives she had offered to go with Maddie to Bishopsgate Street; she wanted to come closer to Robin's home and Robin's people. The door was opened by Susan, who immediately threw her arms round Crede and sniffled against her shoulder.

"Oh, my dearie, it's put me all of a tremble to see you. There's news?"

"Nothing different," Crede answered, patting Susan's plump shoulder with real affection while Beau, whose manners were not yet what Adam had promised, burst past them and careered joyously down the hall.

"But you'll be setting things right, I know." Susan looked up trustfully. "Mark my words, I said to Dick and Polly, the young mistress will find a way out of this now she is back. We're that worried, though, and you can't speak a word about it here."

"Maddie, can't you control that brute? Your father is having his afternoon sleep." Dame Serena appeared from the passage. "Susan, stop making a fool of yourself and go back to the kitchen, I don't trust Polly to dress a peacock properly—leave it for me to gild the feathers."

"Peacock indeed," Susan sniffed but disappeared muttering, and Dame Serena came forward.

"You must try to be quieter and not disturb my brother. Sit down, Crede. I am glad to see you looking so well."

Crede sat down gingerly while Maddie managed to subdue Beau and held him beside her.

Dame Serena wiped the flour daintily from her fingers. "Master Pringle is coming for supper and a game of chess with your father, Maddie, and I want him to enjoy it. I think you had better not stay to see him this afternoon. I warned you last time that you must come looking more cheerful."

"I do try," Maddie began, looking still less gay, "and I am always careful not to upset Father."

Dame Serena had turned her attention to Crede. "Naturally I am worried too, but my brother's happiness comes first. I have more responsibilities than Maddie and Alison Perry who can spend their time weeping over this folly of Robin's—finding something romantic in it, I daresay, when he is simply conceited and heartless. Who he thinks would be looking after his father's business now if Master Bell had not so kindly come, I don't know. Since you have taken a fancy to return, Crede, I hope you can talk some sense into him."

Crede found herself on her feet without choosing the words which came coldly, while anger, past the heat of temper, drained the blood from her cheeks.

"You are too small and mean to know the least thing about Robin," she said. "And you didn't care about your brother until you could own him body and soul. What you love is this chance you have always wanted to be God Almighty somewhere."

She was out on the street before she had time to be ashamed of herself. Who was she to pass judgment on Dame Serena and set herself up for Robin, when even yet she could not stop wishing that Maddie had been the one to see the Lady Margaret and had touched only her sympathy?

But she did not turn back. What she had said was past forgiveness. And she felt instinctively that her distresses and Dame Serena's fulfillment could find no meeting ground. In a minute Maddie caught up with her.

"I don't blame you, darling," Maddie said. "She hardly lets me see Father lately, though I wouldn't do anything to harm him. I was ready to lose my temper too."

But Maddie would not have attacked anyone with such venom. Crede, whose temper had never before swept her so helplessly beyond control, was feeling the reaction now. She had been making poor Dame Serena a whipping boy for things which had much better have concerned her own conscience.

Just keeping busy was the safest thing, and she threw herself into Alison's school, thankful to have something to do. Having set her mind diligently upon the subject of hornbooks, she conceived some ideas regarding them which were of doubtful propriety but were beginning to get results: Tabitha Marshall could recite the whole of her crisscross row, while Sally Clark soon learned the letters of her own name. Maddie and Alison, amazed and delighted by such triumphs, now entrusted the whole of this period to Crede.

This afternoon they had gone to visit a neighbor who was ill, leaving Alison's pretty room littered with samplers from the previous lesson and

[301]

Crede facing twenty-odd pairs of bright eyes fixed upon her above horn-books—their antagonism to these suspended by a growing conviction that she was quite irresponsible and that something was in prospect which might be worth waiting for.

"I know a new game," Crede said shamelessly.

It was by such immoral approaches to learning that she had fastened her hold upon them, depriving these poor innocents of the stern discipline of mind and body which was considered the most salutary part of education.

"It goes to the tune of, 'Kit has lost her key'—you may sing that first."

They had lusty voices, and this was an opening so much to their liking that it seemed for a while that the lesson might get no further. A moment's quiet was induced by surprise, however, when Crede announced that she now had to name them. Amidst delighted giggles each was named for a letter and they sang these in tune. Beau, who had been left behind by Maddie as unskilled in comforting the sick, was needed for Z —he barked his part enthusiastically.

"Now," Crede said, knowing that she was about to bring worse upon herself, "you march around the room singing, until each one can find her right place at the front, in a line like the crisscross row."

She would stand them together to make words later, she thought. But it was doubtful whether much could be hoped for beyond the present pandemonium, since most of them had short memories for the order of the crisscross row and a delight in matching nonsense syllables to a lively tune. They pranced up and down the room with Beau at their heels in a state of liberation from which only Adam could have recalled him.

No sound could have prevailed over their efforts, but something drew Crede's eyes from the bedlam around her. Robin stood in the doorway!

She stumbled over Beau and two hornbooks and crossed the room trailing samplers in her path. "Robin, did you escape?"

She could think of no other possibility of sudden release, and it flashed wildly through her mind that jailbreaking, which was certainly a form of contempt, might not be against his principles—why hadn't they thought of this sooner! She dragged him inside and bolted the door. Whatever they must do now, they were together. In this thought there was such confidence that, standing beside him, she knew nothing would ever be too hard if they shared it.

Robin's eyes danced. "I must away to the Greenwood, Mistress. Wilt come? Crede, I believe you would!"

Suddenly aware of a rapt audience, he pulled out his purse. "Children, would you like to have a holiday, right away, and a penny for sweets?"

They made a rush for their wraps without bothering to look toward Crede for confirmation. For they were well schooled in ballads and knew that she must be off at once on a fleet steed without giving them another thought.

"Didn't you hear some bells?" Robin asked. "But I don't wonder you didn't. Your teaching methods rouse a good deal of enthusiasm, my love. They rang the bells and opened the gates and said that King Henry of his good grace had pardoned all save robbers and murderers and paid the fines of debtors and asked our prayers for his better health."

"You have won, Robin! The King himself admits these wrongs!"

"I can only have been one of many prodding him, dear. But I think you know that is the way I like things best. There is more to raise the heart in it. I could wish they had inquired into the rights of cases—however, a number of unfortunates, and some rogues, are out of gaol. Though I haven't heard that Empson and Dudley are inside, this may be enough to give them a fright. King Henry is a dying man, I think, and it seems likely that the Lady Margaret is working on his conscience—smoothing his way toward heaven as she smoothed it toward everything else."

This might be the Lady Margaret's doing, Crede thought gratefully, but she could spare her only a passing thought. "You are free and safe, Robin—I can't care about anything else yet."

Robin closed the door behind the last child and put his arms around her. "I was going straight home to boil myself clean and burn these clothes, but then I had just to look at you for a minute. I'm not fit to be touching you, dear—I'll be right back. Tell Alison I hope to be asked for supper."

"Oh, not yet!" Crede held fast to him. "I don't care if we have to burn my clothes too." At any minute Maddie and Alison would be returning, Win and Adam would have heard the news, and they would all come to rejoice together. But this first moment was hers and Robin's.

She pulled him toward the fire and, sweeping a scholastic litter from the fender seat, settled herself beside him. They would sit here beside Alison's hearth as if it were their own and share this first lovely certainty of all it promised.

"Gaolbirds must fascinate you," Robin said. "I have so often been clean and tidy and wanted to hold you like this. My darling, I suppose I shall never know what you see in me—the only time I ever managed to hold your attention before I became disreputable was in borrowed rags with a mop of unkempt black hair stuck on."

"I have seen it tidier," Crede laughed, "but you can't suppose it's quite black—what was that you said?"

"I thought you had guessed long ago. That day at Thames side when you saw the *Pelican* and were so put out—"

"Robin, you weren't that outlandish seaman! Play acting! And Win tried to warn me against you." She was shaken helplessly by laughter. "You did fascinate me."

"A pity I lost the knack of it so soon. Crede, I was thoroughly ashamed of that silly boy's trick afterwards. I had been Herod in a play and had the wig, and the sudden chance to see more of you outside a conference of parents—I had fallen so hard in love, of course—"

"Robin Thorne, if you make such lame excuses for what you do it's a blessing Master More did not get your case to court! You had never seen me before."

"But I had, dear—by the Watch's lantern in Philip's Field. I heard your name then and saw the slip of a girl who had stayed beside me when she was so frightened, wanting to help because she had called for help, and keeping her wits bravely about her."

Crede was back in Philip's Field again, her mind whirling. Robin had been that swordsman in green! Had some intuition stirred faintly when the fight on the *Swallow*'s deck had seemed to blend for a moment in that earlier struggle? Now she felt, also, a suspicion she might never know the truth of—and did not want to know—let that other cloaked figure remain a chance ruffian.

"I had never thought of you as—such a habitual roisterer," she said unsteadily. "Oh, Robin, you have had to rescue me twice. Why didn't you tell me?"

"Pop out of the trees while you were convincing the Watch no one was about?"

"Not then, of course. Some other time."

"It wanted this kind of sharing, dear—to laugh together at the pickle it put me in. I had gone walking after a quarrel with Father for trying to drag me to you, and suddenly I was only afraid that he would spoil my chances. You were so set against me. I had to come posting back, as soon as I could risk trying to mend matters, but, dearest, I had never wanted to be crammed down your throat. And then I thought that after all I had been." He laughed softly and held her closer. "When I was trying all ways to recommend myself, I couldn't guess that going to gaol would help!"

Crede, leaning comfortably against his shoulder, could smile even at that. "I was miserable without you before then, darling. I didn't know what was wrong with me in Bristol when I had wanted so badly to go home."

"But Bristol is home, isn't it? And you love it there. Would you like us to go back together for a while this winter, if Adam will stay on here?"

Happiness that could so suddenly brim over was swifter than words, and for a moment it caught only images like dancing reflections on a sunny pool . . . things she loved at home that now she would share with

Robin . . . Mona's face when they returned together to the place she kept for them.

As if he could answer her thoughts, Robin said, "I'd like to bring our happiness there first. I'm greedy for everything we have ever missed together, dear—even that kiss I'd have liked to snatch in Philip's Field."

"With Timothy Polkhorn to hold a lantern for you? What a romance!"

"We could go west soon and spend some time there, if Adam is willing."

"Adam will be willing." It would be hard to drag Adam away from London now, with Maddie turning to him so happily. Trouble had hurried forward more things than Robin knew, Crede thought, and she laughed, thinking of the surprise it would be to him. But he would be pleased too. He knew Adam's worth.

"Is it Adam or your husband you find amusing, Mistress?"

"You shan't be told. I want to see how clever you are."

"Sheer waste of time, dear, when we may have only fifty years or so for better things."

"Let us start home tomorrow if we can," Crede said, "riding together again— Robin, let us go round the long way again! The weather isn't too bad yet. And let us stop at the Star again. We were almost their first guests, I think, and I have always hoped that they were succeeding." She had never forgotten that eager welcome in the bright new rooms and something confident built into them which she had felt so lost from then.

TWENTY-SEVEN

Between the joyous pealing of London's bells they heard the drums and the whifflers.

"They are coming," Maddie cried, her fingers tightening in Crede's.

Crede's other hand held Robin's, and Adam's arm was around Maddie, his bride of a week, as they leaned from the window together. It was the same window from which they had overlooked the Marching Watch last summer, for Master More had brought his friends again to his cousin's house in Cornhill which was so conveniently on the route of most great processions across London.

It was Saturday, the Eve of St. John, when days are longest and brightest and all the gardens sweet with June flowers. Every house front was decked with garlands or roses, and all over London people were singing Master Skelton's new song, "The rose both white and red, in one rose now doth grow." For today the young King Henry the Eighth, heir of the Red and the White Rose, would ride across London on his way from the Tower to Westminster to receive the crown of St. Edward. Tomorrow Archbishop Wareham, that high-minded advocate of the New Learning, would give his blessing with a full heart to a prince of so much promise, and the blessing of all England would go with it.

Prince Henry's father, who had loved learning too but had found little leisure for it, had fought and intrigued, until his body was broken and his spirit hardened, to set the bankrupt throne of England above quarrelsome feudal families, to win a new respect for it abroad, and to help middling folk make the country peaceful and prosperous at home. He had won. And two months ago he had died, worn out at fifty-two, asking that his funeral should be "without damnable pomp and ridiculous superfluities." It had been held with the magnificence which London and Prince Harry preferred, and now all that he had won would be his son's beginning.

His son, who had inherited the safest royal crown and richest royal purse in Christendom, with a network of profitable alliances, could afford to be more generous and heal the scars of the struggle. He had been taught by scholars of the New Learning, and these were his friends who would have the place of honor around his throne to bring in the new age of peace and justice and plenty and reason. Men of science like Dr. Linacre, and men like Thomas More, learned in the law with a passion for justice, had great hopes of him. Reforming churchmen like Dean Colet and Archbishop Wareham believed that a prince once intended for holy orders would help defend the Church Universal (which long ago had received the first vision of a brotherhood of all mankind) while a rebirth within it purified and strengthened the faith.

It was not only the hopes of Englishmen that were fixed on this young king. Humanists and men of learning—Dr. Erasmus chief among them —were turning from the old rivalries of Europe to this fortunate island of new beginnings. An island, once at the far edge of the known world, whose bowmen had terrorized the continent in the bad old days, might become the cradle of the free commonwealth of Erasmus' dream. This would spread until it united men of good will everywhere above the quarrels of nations; it would have a strength of freedom within it greater than the total power of the Turk.

Everyone was saying that this new century, not yet ten years old, was marked already as the age of enlightenment, when the world's discords would be resolved as foretold in the quaint old composition called the *Little Book of English Polity:*

> *And then should every land one with another*
> *Entercommon as brother with his brother*
> *And live together werreless in unitie*
> *Without rancour in very charitie.*

[306]

It was curious that something so like the hope of this modern generation should have been written long ago, when the policy of England
concerned itself with the Hundred Years' War, and the new discoveries
and the New Learning had not yet stirred the world.

They could hear bursts of music more clearly now, though the procession had not come in sight.

Master John Rastell crossed from the other window to say, smiling at
Maddie's excitement, "They are not nearly here yet. They must come at
a snail's pace to divert everyone and reward the preparations made along
every foot of the way."

From these windows were hung the best tapestries any of them owned,
as from houses all along the route, those of Goldsmith's Row in Chepe
displaying cloth of gold and rare Spanish carpets. Here in Cornhill, the
Church, which looked forward to a reign that would set right certain
regrettable misunderstandings of the privileges of Church courts and
sanctuaries, had prepared a special pageant to honor the occasion. The
street below was lined with young girls in snowy white, holding palm-
leaves moulded of white wax. They were kept in decorous formation by
priests who wore their richest robes and carried censers to bless the royal
progress.

The Lady Margaret would not ride with the royal party. The son
whom she had counseled throughout his life and sustained in his death
now rested in the chapel he had built in Westminster Abbey, and it
would soon receive her too. For two months she had been the regent
appointed by his will and the Council of England, until Prince Henry
came of age, and now she was contentedly nearing her end though she
would not spoil the coronation festivities by dying too soon if she could
help it.

"Have you heard from Bristol," Master Rastell said, "that Sebastien
Cabot's expedition is back from Amerike?"

Crede forgot to watch Cornhill and turned toward him quickly. "Have
they gained anything? Have you news of a ship called the *Swallow?*"

Robin's hand in hers did not stiffen but pressed closer in understanding.

"I hear they found no gold in Amerike and no other profit in it, though
Cabot still claims there is a northwest passage to Cathay. But he means
to take service with Spain, I understand, since King Henry has not his
father's interest in western voyages. 'Western wind, when wilt thou
blow?'" Rastell hummed softly. "It is one of the young King's songs—
written, I misdoubt, only for a wench's ear, for the rest is amorous. Yet
the first line sings to me. I mean to move him, if I can find influence, toward a venture from London, and I care more for what Amerike may

hold for us than for a passage through it. Yet I fear that the King's heart is set upon being first in Europe."

Master Rastell who had seemed lost for a moment in thoughts of his own recalled himself suddenly. "I beg your pardon, Mistress Thorne! I had no news of any ship called the *Swallow*. But one ship, my Bristol letter said, left the others and turned south to poach in Spain's preserves."

It would be the *Swallow,* Crede knew in her heart. She knew also that this might be the last word she would ever hear of Tony. Something bright and daring in him, which she and Philip had both loved, had seemed better always than the uses he could find for it, and she prayed still that it might not be squandered in shabby purposes.

The burst of music had been swallowed again in the din of the streets, without coming nearer. And Crede had lost a little of the day's high expectation. She held Robin's hand tighter and whispered, "Do you think this will be the new Golden Age?"

"I suppose it will be a mixture, like any other, of what we all make it. But it is ours to share, sweetheart, and that seems good enough."

His arm slipped around her; whatever it was, they were beginning it together. And they were going home to Bristol after this London visit made for Maddie's wedding. They had spent the winter there and it had been arranged that the Thorne and Canynges enterprises should be joined as Master Thorne and Philip had once hoped, with a partnership for Adam who would manage the London office. He was as much at home there now as Robin was, and there was nothing else that Robin could do for his father except to make the visits "from Oxford" which pleased Master Thorne and were as much interference as Dame Serena welcomed.

Returning to Bristol had been Robin's own choice. He had first fallen in love with the Cotswold country, he said, when he lived at the Oxford end of it and Bristol was home to Thornes as well as to Canynges. So Robin, who had grown so close to Philip, would keep his hand with Crede's upon what Philip had worked for; and if they could carry out Robin's plan of letting their men earn a share of the profits, finding in this small way close to their hands some part of the fairer chances men hoped for in new worlds, this too would have pleased her father, Crede thought.

In the house that Philip had built for happiness, the child they were expecting would be born—with Mona's arms ready to hold it and Cousin Allie waiting to train its mind. It would be hers and Robin's, but it would belong also to all the Thornes and Canynges who had helped to build Bristol and its restless ships—to forgotten ancestors who had followed the path of a westering sun there, to Philip who had seen its promise in Amerike, and to Crede of Ireland whose people had ventured

first of all into the Sea of Darkness to hunt for the Fortunate Isles. The
hopes and hungers of so many strains must be born within it—what simple answer could there be for any of us? And the dearest things in life
were things that not even Dr. Erasmus' Commonwealth or Master More's
Utopia could ensure. Against such hazards do we live and love, each one
of us, that of all illusions upon this earth security must be the vainest.
The least afraid must be those who found a cause greater than themselves
or changing things to serve, as Cousin Allie served knowledge. Yet sometimes you could find love brave enough to endure the chances that made
it vulnerable, to trust that it must reach beyond them.

Crede looked across to the other window where Alison stood with Win
beside her. Alison could seize the joy of any moment. Win was established now at Oxford but he had come with many others from there to
see the crowning of the young King in whom the universities also had
set their hopes of soaring beyond past limitations of knowledge and defi-
ciencies of budget. Alison would have him at home for several days, and
she glowed with happiness which completed itself in each occasion and
would not fade. When Win returned to Oxford she would have Maddie
and Adam near her. For Maddie still wanted to help with the Dame
School, and Adam had discovered that it was possible to buy the house
next door. Besides being so close to Alison, it was, by a magnificent stroke
of fortune, in so tumble-down a condition that Maddie could have the
joy of making it over in her own way. It was a tribute to the splendor
of this occasion that she had appeared for the first time since her wedding
day without a smudge of paint on her beautiful nose.

London would always have a share of her heart, Crede thought as her
glance met Alison's and returned to dwell fondly upon Maddie and
Adam. Maddie squeezed the hand she still held and sighed contentedly.

"How lucky we four are, Crede! No one in London today can be
happier. And when you and Robin come again, Adam and I will have
our own house settled and ready for you."

"You know very well we shall always get smudged with wet paint in
it," Crede teased. "Poor Adam!"

They laughed and glanced with a satisfaction they shared toward
Adam and Robin who had drawn close together in conversation. The
trust and liking between them was one of the fortunate circumstances
Crede and Maddie rejoiced in. The happy mixture of their affairs must
justify, they were resolved, frequent visiting back and forth.

Thomas More ran up the stairs and found a place beside Master Rastell
at their window. "Here they come!" he cried.

The musicians . . . the knights . . . the dignitaries of Church and
state and London . . . the yeomen of the guard. The young King, two
days past his eighteenth birthday, rode among his nobles, larger than

most men and glowing with health and high spirits, with a girl's pink-and-white skin, the red-gold Tudor hair, and the shrewd gray Tudor eyes. His eyes were lifted for a moment toward the crowded upper windows and Crede, with a sudden recollection of his father's wasted figure and white face outside a goldsmith's shop in Chepe, thought them too small and sharp. The old King's had been finer.

"Young Harry can get on as well as any 'prentice boy with London crowds," Master Rastell chuckled. "See how he smiles and checks rein and gives back as good as he gets."

The new queen, who rode in an open litter hung with cloth of silver and drawn by two white horses, did not exchange pleasantries in this free way with the crowd that pressed against it.

"Spanish court etiquette is stiffer," Master Rastell said. "Yet those who know Queen Catherine say that she would distress herself more for a beggar in trouble than the King would."

Catherine's gown was of white embroidered satin, and her beautiful auburn hair, confined only by a jewelled circlet, reached below her waist. It was the dress of a maiden bride and she wore it in defiance of Archbishop Wareham. With Pope Julius' sanction the royal marriage so long discussed had taken place last week, though quietly, without the Primate of England attending the ceremony, and now the ladies of the court jolted over the cobbles in whirlicotes behind Queen Catherine's litter to grace her triumph, while the street crowds hummed one of King Henry's own songs:

> As the holly groweth green and never chaungeth hue
> So am I, ever hath been, unto my lady trew.

The minstrels drowned them out . . . the clatter of horsemen . . . the cheering.

"Pray this may be what we all hope for," Master More said. "Lord Mountjoy, Erasmus' old pupil who first brought him to England, showed me the letter he has written to invite him back from abroad, 'What may you not expect from a prince whose godlike character you know so well? The heavens laugh, the earth exults in this new auspicious star.' Yet I think we can expect too much of a leader and ask too little of ourselves," he added thoughtfully. "Surely, though, no one has ever been given a better chance to stand for bright new hopes. 'Now or never,' Erasmus wrote lately, 'may spirit renew the world.'"

The procession wound on through the street with more cloth of gold and jewels and more cheering crowds than even London had got together before, and Crede leaned far out the window to scatter red and white roses.

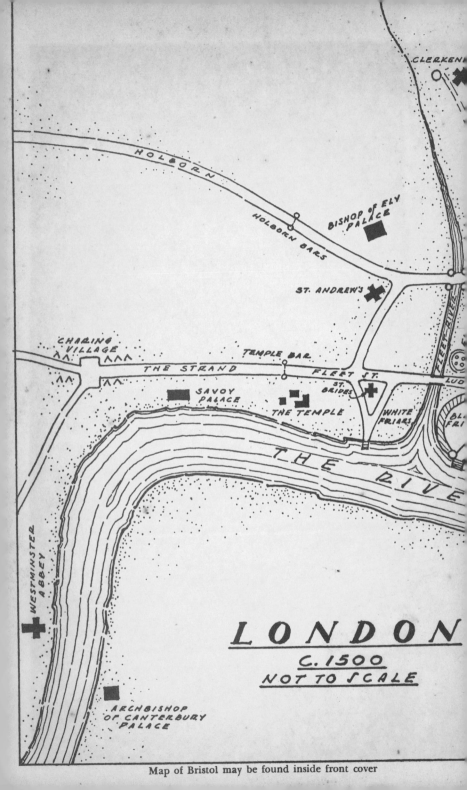

LONDON

C. 1500

NOT TO SCALE

Map of Bristol may be found inside front cover